WUR

This worm loo

It looked—

Alive . . .

And he thought . . .

Everything dies when it's brought to the surface.

Everything.

But this piece of the worm wasn't dead. The way it shimmered, rippling, moving in the pincer grip of the manipulator's claw. No, not dead at all.

"Don't," Simonsen started to say. "Don't touch that."

But Reilly's hand had already grabbed the worm, trying to circle its thick body. He was grinning at his prize . . . not seeing it move, not caring—

"Don't!" Simonsen yelled again.

But it was, of course, too late . . .

ALSO BY MATTHEW J. COSTELLO:

MIDSUMMER

"PERFECTLY PACED HORROR . . . FULL-SPEED AHEAD!"
—Rick Hautala

"*MIDSUMMER* IS ONE HELL OF A BOOK!"
—Joseph A. Citro

"UNEXPECTED TURNS AND TWISTS . . . UNPREDICTABLE . . . MEMORABLE."
—*Science Fiction Chronicle*

BENEATH STILL WATERS

"TERRIFYINGLY EFFECTIVE . . . SUBLIMELY CREEPY."
—Edward Bryant, *Locus*

"WE'LL BE SEEING A LOT MORE OF MATTHEW J. COSTELLO!"
—*Blood Review*

Books by Matthew J. Costello

BENEATH STILL WATERS
MIDSUMMER
WURM

WURM

MATTHEW J. COSTELLO

DEDICATED TO NORA COSTELLO . . .
ANOTHER GIRL WHO KNOWS HER MIND.

WURM

A Diamond Book / published by arrangement with
the author

PRINTING HISTORY
Diamond edition / April 1991

ISBN: 1-55773-488-7

Diamond Books are published by The Berkley Publishing Group,
200 Madison Avenue, New York, New York 10016.
The name "DIAMOND" and its logo
are trademarks belonging to Charter Communications, Inc.

PRINTED IN THE UNITED STATES OF AMERICA

10 9 8 7 6 5 4 3 2 1

# Acknowledgments

For technical information on the creatures of the deep-ocean hydrothermal vents, the submersible Alvin, and the ROV Jason II, thanks to Paul Sampson of the National Geographic Society and Robert Brown of the Public Information Office of the Woods Hole Oceanographic Institute. Marie Tharp and Bruce Heezen's map of the ocean floor was inspiring and invaluable. And thanks also to Rick Miller of The New York Aquarium for information on the discovery of *Bythnomus giganteous*, and its subsequent death.

WURM

Prologue

"BINGO!" Jane North said, her hands hovering over the camera controls.

John Simonsen stood behind her, watching the two monitors, each with the same fuzzy color picture of the ocean floor.

The ship rolled a bit, still caught in the aftermath of the summer's first tropical storm, Zelda.

Simonsen braced himself against the cabin wall. "Bring her to a stop, Tom," he told the captain, pressing the button down on the radio.

"Shit. It's gone," North said, turning to Simonsen. She was frustrated. Pissed off. She had picked up something in her screen, and now there was nothing but the beginning of a steep underwater ridge. Some broken rock and the ever-present tiny bits of debris.

Simonsen stepped closer to her.

"It's okay, Jane. Just rewind the tape. We should be able to hold our position here."

"That's a laugh." It was Reilly, the cocky young biologist and general pain-in-the-ass. "We might as well be using inflatable boats, Dr. John. This goddam barge has all the handling of a washtub."

One of the monitor screens showed the current view from the Prom II underwater sled. There was only the one camera, compared to the two cameras on Argo, a Class-A sled now working the East Pacific Rise. But with one camera, Simonsen knew, there was a lot that could be missed, a hell of a lot. With just one, straight down view, there was about 270 degrees of ocean floor that could be missed.

In fact, if North found something, it would be amazing. Simonsen had pitched this project to Woods Hole and the NSF knowing it was underfinanced, and underequipped.

But it was this or nothing. Better a shitty shot at a major

discovery than sitting in an office reading other people's monographs.

Because this was where the action was, the brave new world of the hydrothermal vents. A couple of miles down sat gigantic stone towers, the black smokers, spewing forth smudgy gases, heating the water up to 500 degrees Fahrenheit. But it wasn't the geological stuff that had everyone freaking out.

No.

It was the animals. Over 300 new species, with the number climbing every month. Unbelievable . . . 300 *new species*, living in the most stressful habitat imaginable . . . no light, incredible pressure, surrounded by toxic water.

It was like discovering a new planet. And Simonsen had to be there.

"Ready," Jane North said to him.

Reilly lit up a cigarette.

"Hey!" North screamed, turning in her seat. "Will you put that goddam thing out? How the hell are we supposed to breathe?"

Simonsen turned to Reilly, but already the biologist had thrown down the butt on the floor, rolling his eyes. The door opened.

"Got something, kiddies?"

It was Allan Beck, the team geologist and good friend to the oil industry. He made no secret that his interest in the *Achilles* expedition was strictly commercial. Everyone knew that the vents promised an incredible bonanza of ore and petroleum possibilities. Except nobody had the foggiest ideas how to get them up to the surface. "Where there's a will there's a way" was Beck's position.

"I have the tape ready to roll," North said.

She looked back at Simonsen and he nodded, signaling her to run the playback.

Now the left screen replayed images from a few minutes ago. The digital VCR was delivering pictures at one-fourth the normal speed, while an elapsed time counter at the bottom of the screen told the time of the "event."

"Looks pretty normal so far," Beck said, taking a few steps closer to the screen.

"Just wait," North said.

Then there was something there.

"Hold it!" Simonsen said, pushing back his glasses that were always slipping down his nose. He was sweating even though the ship pumped cool air into the windowless room.

The image froze.

The sled had been hovering over the ridge, a volcanic scarp that meandered away from the major vents in the Gulf of Mexico. It looked like a dry riverbed. Dry, and totally devoid of life.

But at the upper right corner of the screen, Simonsen saw a fluffy white patch.

A bacteria mat . . .

"How far away is it?" he asked North.

She pushed her long brown hair back and checked the navigational computer. The data logger on Prom II fed information directly to her computer. She could match every frame on the tape with a pinpoint location on the bottom of the sea.

"We've drifted about half a mile away," she said.

"How about a few more frames, Janie," Reilly said, draping an unwelcome hand on her shoulder.

It was the smallest team that Simonsen ever worked with, but, damn, they were easily the most irritating. The crew of the *Achilles*, including the Woods Hole interns, all got along fine. But the scientists had developed an immediate loathing for one another.

He had to take who he could, however.

"Go ahead," he said. "See how much more of it we can see."

A few more frames crawled by, each shot lingering on the screen before being replaced by another, almost identical shot.

Simonsen watched a bit more of the fuzzy white patch come onto the screen. Then he saw the dark shadow of the crack leading away, off to the right.

Another frame, and it was all gone, replaced with yet another shot of the empty barren scarp.

"Well done," he said at last, quietly to North. She was a dead-serious, no-nonsense scientist, and damned good at what she did. Simonsen was attracted to her, probably all the men on board were. But she kept up a professional, icy wall that clearly discouraged any such musings.

Good thing too. That kind of problem he didn't need.

"So what now, John?" Beck said.

But Reilly was already at the door.

"Why it's show time, boys and girl," Reilly said. "Time for Lil Shit to do his stuff."

Reilly walked out, laughing.

The ship bobbled, and Simonsen stumbled against Reilly, who was working on the ROV, the remote-operated vehicle. Though Simonsen wasn't prone to seasickness, the constantly churning waters of the Gulf were starting to get to him. He skipped breakfast, and he wasn't too sure that last night's dinner had completed its safe passage.

Two of the interns, barely paid grad students who treated their presence on the expedition as if they'd won the lottery, were under the ROV checking that all the cables were in place.

Simonsen looked at the whitecaps and said, "I don't know, Ed. It's a bit rough out there."

Reilly was attaching specimen vials, the small plastic cylinders that the remote-operated vehicle used to scoop up samples.

"Hey, John, down below it's as gentle as a lake. So we bounce around a bit up here, what's the big problem?"

"The problem is that I'm responsible for Lil—for the ROV."

"Look, once it's away the only problem *you* have is staying on your feet. The ROV will be fine."

"And if the swells start up again?"

"We'll pull it the hell out. Besides, the storm is over. If anything, the sea's going to get calmer."

Simonsen nodded.

Then why am I so worried? he wondered.

Because the ROV cost half a million? Not as expensive as Jason, the ROV that explored the *Titanic*. No, it wasn't even a distant relative. Jason carried seven thrusters, three cameras, its own data logger and navigational computer. But the S-202, "Lil Shit," had only three thrusters—really cutting down its maneuverability. And only one video camera, with an effective pan and tilt range of 180 degrees. The manipulator arm was sufficient, almost identical to Jason's, but the ROV had no side scan sonar—which could be a problem in tight spots.

But it still was an expensive toy—his responsibility—and he didn't like Reilly acting so damn cavalier about it.

"Hey, John," Reilly said to him. "Don't worry. We're fine . . . *no problemo*."

The interns scuttled out from under the ROV and Simonsen stepped back and watched them attach the *Achilles*'s winch hook to Lil Shit's lifting bail.

The captain came out of the bridge and called down. "Ready?"

It's my decision, Simonsen thought, as the ship rolled back and forth. My goddam decision. My goddam ass.

"Ready?" the captain called down again.

Simonsen nodded.

The winch groaned, a painful shriek as the diesel engine took up the slack in the cable, struggling to hoist Lil Shit's squat 3000 pounds into the air.

The umbilical cable, consisting of the video and computer lines, as well as the tether, dangled behind it. Prom II, the imaging sled, was still dripping wet, sitting on a nearby pallet, its work done.

The cable tugged and Lil Shit was in the air, looking too heavy for the winch. The engine groaned in a different way, and then the ROV swooped out, over the rolling waters of the unquiet Gulf.

The captain lowered it. The lifting bail sprang open. The ROV splashed leadenly into the water.

It was dead weight now, and after a moment's hesitation, it quickly vanished under the surface.

Nobody was talking.

The room was crowded, not with just the scientists, but the interns, squeezed into every corner.

"Cameras okay," Jane North announced. "Navigational data good."

"The arm?" Simonsen asked. If the ROV's arm didn't work, there was no point in sending the vehicle down. And according to the Woods Hole tech boys, Lil Shit had a history of going gimpy.

"I'll test it when we're down. I don't want to put too much stress on it while it's diving."

Simonsen knew what she meant. The ROV was careening straight down, dropping thousands of meters in minutes. An aquatic free-fall that would be stopped only when sonar reported the bottom rushing up.

Then everyone had to hope that the thrusters worked.

Simonsen's stomach gave a little kick. He felt a funny pulling in his bowels, a tightening. Hit middle age, and the damn human machinery starts to fail.

Shit, he thought. Not now.

The find, the white bacteria mat—if that's what it was—lay at 3200 meters. When the monitor showed 2800 meters, North hit the thrusters. The readout slowed.

"Three thousand," the ROV operator said.

"Three thousand fifty."

Then, after a pause, "Thirty-one hundred."

Simonsen looked over her shoulder at the green screen, watching the depth indicator slow down. 3120. 3130. 3140.

"I'm going to hold it at 3150. To start with, at least," North said.

"Good idea."

"Everyone bring their binoculars?" Reilly joked. The interns, all fans of the bearded biologist, laughed.

Simonsen cleared his throat, about to explain his caution . . . his timidity.

But the hell with it, he thought. He was tired of fighting Reilly's sarcasm, his easy popularity.

The monitor screens went pitch-black, but then North turned on the 2000-watt high-intensity lights and everyone got a clear look at the Gulf floor.

"How far away are we?" Simonsen asked her.

"Not far." The thrusters made a tiny whirring sound heard through speakers in the control room, letting the operator know that the ROV was moving under its own power.

"Take us away, Janie," Reilly said.

Beck came close to Simonsen and whispered in his ear. "Can't you get that asshole to shut up?"

Simonsen shrugged.

He just hoped everyone would settle down once the ROV started working.

"Here we go," North said.

At first, it was more of the same boring scene. The silty sand of the sea bottom, dotted by the occasional erratic rock or boulder. But then the ROV picked up the main rift, the cleft in the sea floor.

"Should be just ahead . . ." she said quietly.

"There you are, babe!" Reilly announced as the white fluffy mat came onto the screen. Everyone clapped, and grinned. A few of the interns whistled.

Simonsen cleared his throat, feeling a need to restore order, some semblance of scientific atmosphere.

But he also smiled. Because this discovery proved that his ideas were at least half-right.

Despite what everyone believed . . .

The oceanographic community—the Office of Naval Research, The Scripps Institute, and all of Woods Hole—were beside themselves with the discoveries at the hydrothermal vents. And nobody seemed dismayed that there were more questions being raised than answers.

Lots of questions . . .

For example, there was the mystery of the twelve-foot worms found near the vents. They were white animals, topped by a bloodred feathery plume. They were exciting, strange, and there were dead specimens in every marine biology lab in the country.

Yet nobody had a clue how they lived.

There was no light down there, and no free-floating biotic

material. They existed outside the normal chain of photosynthesizers. It was a new niche. An alien niche.

They were chemosynthesizers, able to create food from the poisonous hydrogen sulfide that gushed out of the hot vents. And why were they red? That was even more peculiar. They used hemoglobin to ferry oxygen through the system.

Just like people.

Pretty strange stuff . . .

And there were other problems . . .

The worms had no mouth. No gullet. No digestive organs at all. Instead, the worms, *Riftia pogonophosa Jones*, played host to a chain of parasitic, toxin-eating bacteria, bacteria that lived inside the worms and somehow produced sulfites and free carbon. The parasites enabled the worms to grow to gigantic size in a deadly environment.

Nobody knew how it worked. Who called the shots? The bacteria or the worm? Who was landlord and who was tenant? And how the hell did the *Riftia* worms reproduce—if they reproduced? How did they move to different vent openings—if they moved?

There were more than enough mysteries to fuel research for the next century.

Which was how Simonsen got his research grant.

It was a simple idea, *too simple* most of his compatriots felt.

But it seemed obvious to him.

There had to be a web of underground channels that were used by the sponges, the crabs, the *Riftia* worms, by the whole community of chemosynthesizers.

A hidden planet.

The smokers, the towering vents that everyone was exploring, were only pricks in the sea floor's crust. A more wide-ranging search would reveal the real extent of the new discovery.

At least, that's what Simonsen proposed.

And, he thought, maybe he'd find another 300 species living in even more bizarre ways.

The geobiologists had their doubts. But if the vent system was only the gateway to a subterranean warren, it would have gigundo implications for the commercial ore interests. Money reared its head. The vents could be a bonanza for the mineral resources of the world.

If Simonsen was right, they had only begun to imagine the true size of the treasure trove.

"Well done, Doc," Reilly said, clapping Simonsen on the back.

Reilly sounded almost genuine.

Almost.

Simonsen smiled, watching the screen. Here it was, a fluffy white bacteria mat well away from any large vent. As the ROV sailed over the furrow, Simonsen guessed that there had to be hot springs under the crust, leaking superheated water and chemicals.

"Crabs," North announced, pointing at the screen. And there was more applause as a few large albino crabs, eyeless monsters, scuttled away nervously at the approach of the ROV. The trench deepened, and there were giant clams, all tinged with the weird crimson color typical of so many vent creatures.

"Maybe there's just a vent ahead," Beck said.

"Possibly," Simonsen muttered. "But I doubt it . . ."

If there was, his theory was blown away. This would simply be a new smoker, another interesting discovery off the Florida Escarpment, but nothing more.

"But there's no Jones yet," Reilly said, calling the rift worms by their nickname. Jones . . . like the Worms, new, undesirable neighbors.

The white bacteria mat gave way to a brilliant orange colony that took its color from the zinc and copper in the water.

Another good sign, Simonsen thought.

The ship rocked.

"Oh, shit," one of the interns said, sloshing her coffee onto the floor. Again, the *Achilles* rolled to the left. There was enough slack in the ROV's tether that it probably felt nothing down below.

But it was getting mighty bumpy in the control room.

Simonsen picked up the radio speaker. "Tom," he said. "Are we okay . . . should we bring up—"

The captain's voice cracked over the cheap speakers in the room.

"No, Dr. Simonsen. It's getting a tad rough out there, but mostly we're just hitting the swells at a bad angle."

"Okay," Simonsen said.

He put the speaker down. The ship had to follow the ROV . . . the captain had a constant display of the course. And they weren't moving more than a few knots an hour. But if the *Achilles* was at a bad angle, there was nothing he could do about it.

He tasted something burning, something acid at the back of his throat.

It was close in here, filled with the scientists and the interns.

The air was damp with sweat. A few of them could have done with a shower.

He took a big breath through his mouth.

He looked at the monitors.

As a whole field of rift worms filled the screen, looking like alien wheat, ripe for harvesting.

It was a dense field, the ruby-red color of the worms waving, rippling, brilliant in the glare of the ROV's light.

"Hello, Jones," Reilly said.

Without waiting for an order from Simonsen, North stopped the ROV, letting it hover above the field. And then, very gently, she started to bring Lil Shit farther down . . .

"Did someone fart?"

Again Reilly made the interns laugh.

But Simonsen knew the biologist was feeling the tension, just like him. Feeling it, and trying to dissipate it.

After all, if this find panned out, all their careers would be made. No question about it . . .

Everyone's eyes were glued to the monitors, their link to the underwater vehicle miles below them.

Simonsen took a step closer to Jane North, wanting to be close to it all. He patted her shoulder.

And the field of *Riftia* disappeared.

"What the—" he started to say.

"Good-bye, Jones," Reilly said.

"Well look at that," Beck said appreciatively.

The ridge—just a narrow cleft in the sea floor—suddenly widened, turning into a basin. The water was shimmering, the usual tip-off to vent activity.

But there was nothing. No vent. No worms. Nothing.

"What's the temperature?" Beck called out from the back of the room.

"Three-fifty, and rising," Simonsen said.

Reilly came closer, suddenly serious now.

"What happened to the tube worms?" he asked. "One minute they're there, and the next—"

"Hold it," North said. "Getting something strange from sonar."

There was nothing on the screen except the ever-widening basin, the bottom falling deeper, the walls receding. "I'm going to let the ROV drop a bit," she announced.

She looked up to Simonsen for his agreement. "Go on," he said.

Then he saw what sonar had picked up. This little crack in the floor had opened up into an enormous, deep fissure. Not especially wide, but incredibly deep.

Simonsen looked at the computer readout. The numbers spun around like the cherries and grapes on a slot machine.

"God," he said, watching the digital depth indicator spinning out of control. "How deep is it?"

Beck was at his side now, his small yellow note pad out, quickly copying down the information just as fast as the computer spit it out. Simonsen turned to him. Beck was the expert, their underwater rock man.

Maybe *he'd* have some fucking idea what they were looking at.

"What's going on here, Alan?" he asked.

The interns were quiet, stock-still, obviously aware that an important find was being made.

"I don't know . . . The temperature's too high for a dormant fault, and it's too damn low for an active vent."

"And there's no smokers," Reilly said, referring to the typical chimney formation that capped the hydrothermal vents.

"In other words," Simonsen said, "you don't know what the hell it is?"

Beck smiled. "Right, Chief."

"Can I take the Lil Shit down some more, John?"

He turned back to North, to the screen.

It might be better to pull the ROV out, he thought . . . send the sled back down. If anything happened to Prom II, it was a fraction of the cost. Get some more sonar readings, let it glide over the fissure, check the pictures some more. A little caution . . .

Just wait a bit.

But Reilly was at his elbow.

Like he's reading my mind, Simonsen thought.

"Hey, come on, Simonsen," Reilly said. "We're here—let's take the robot down into it, for Christ's sake. For all we know it's just an old vent that just went quiet. I say let's get a look at it while we can."

"How come there's no fauna?" Simonsen asked. There was nothing there. None of the typical bacteria mats. No brittle stars, no eyeless crabs. No worms. "What the hell happened to everything?" he asked.

"Maybe it's too hot," Reilly said. "Or not enough hydrogen sulfide."

"It's almost four hundred degrees," North said.

"I don't know what's going on . . ." Reilly said.

Simonsen licked his lips.

"Take a water sample," he said.

North pressed a button and the ROV stopped moving while it filled one of the plastic specimen tubes attached to its side.

"All done," she said.

Simonsen nodded. "Okay. Let's take it down. But slowly. I don't want it to get hung up down there."

And everyone crowded around Jane North, and the odd images on the monitors . . .

At first there was nothing unusual. The high-intensity lights of the ROV illuminated the sheer, smooth walls of the cleft. But the blackness below it, blackness that should have ended in a rocky lava bed, just never appeared. As the cleft narrowed to an irregular, jagged bumpiness, their sonar became useless.

"Temperature?" Beck asked again.

"Getting cooler," Simonsen said, looking down. The water around the ROV was cooling fast. "Take another sample," he said.

And everyone took a breath, in the damp, stuffy room, while Lil Shit's vacuum pumps sucked in another two ounces of water.

"Okay," North said, flicking back her now-limp, stringy hair. The ROV started down again . . .

Then the floor moved under their feet.

The *Achilles* made a sudden tremendous lurch to the left.

Simonsen grabbed at Jane North's chair, but he was too late, slipping to the floor.

Beck fell into Reilly.

"Didn't know you cared," Reilly cracked. The ship jostled them back the other way.

"What the hell—" Simonsen said, trying to get back on his feet.

The radio crackled. "Sorry, Doc. But things are acting up out here again. You may want to—"

"Jesus H. Christ!"

It was Reilly, scrambling to his feet, bringing his face right up to the monitors. "What the hell are those things?"

Simonsen, his left knee hurting from his landing, stood up and looked at the screens.

The walls of the cleft had changed. They were no longer smooth. Now they were pitted with holes, big, black holes. They looked about the size of bowling balls, they looked like—

"Right there!" Reilly said. "Unbelievable . . . Will you look at *that* . . ."

Something emerged from one of the holes, something big, like the *Riftia*, but thicker, coiling as it came out. As if it sensed the intrusion of Lil Shit.

A worm.

"Is it a *Riftia*?" Beck asked Reilly.

Simonsen watched the screen, fascinated, as the wormlike thing pulled back into its burrow, and another emerged from a different hole. It might have looked curious if it had anything resembling a face, eyes—

Which it didn't.

It had a mouth, though. At least, it had something like a mouth.

"No way it's a *Riftia*," Reilly said. "It has no plume at the top, nothing to capture the bacteria with. And look at the way it moves. The damn things seem mobile."

Jane North stopped the ROV, then used the thrusters to turn it. Now the camera was facing the burrows along one wall. Facing them, as more and more of these worms popped out.

"Can you get one?" Reilly said, leaning close to North. "Huh, Janie? Can you just grab one of those suckers?"

Simonsen said, "I don't think that's a good idea, Ed. Let's just—"

"Can you do it?" Reilly asked North again, insistent.

"I can try," she said, looking over her shoulder at Simonsen. "I mean, if the arm can snag one—"

"Look," Beck said.

Now all the holes were filled with the worms, curious, poking out of their holes. They were large, twice as thick as a *Riftia*. And whatever the hole near one end was, it sure as hell looked like a mouth.

"Incredible," Beck said.

Reilly grabbed Simonsen. "We've got to get one, John. Now."

The radio crackled just as the ship lurched again.

"Doc, you'd better get off the bottom. There's going to be a lot of pull on your cables."

Simonsen licked his lips. A new geological formation. A major new species. Things were looking good. But if he lost the ROV it would ruin everything. Woods Hole didn't look kindly on those who lost its toys.

"Okay," he said abruptly, "let's—"

"Get one!" Reilly hissed in his ear. "Damn, let's bring one up."

Simonsen looked around, as if it was someone else's decision.

Jane North turned and looked at him. "I think I can grab one, John. Get it into the compartment."

It would be dead by the time they had it up, he knew. Everything they brought up from the deep ocean always was. The strange animals were adapted to life under phenomenal pressure. Brought topside, their cells popped like overfilled helium balloons.

He watched the worms, twitching and writhing around in their holes.

"Okay," he said. "Try to get one. But one shot. That's it. And then I want the ROV the hell out of there."

Reilly patted his back. "Atta boy," he said. "Now we get to make history."

Simonsen nervously watched North.

She inched the ROV closer to one of the holes. Lil Shit had only a fraction of the maneuverability of Jason II. But North played the three thrusters off against one another. And the ROV nudged so gently close to burrows.

Reilly stood next to him. Simonsen saw that his face was flush with excitement, knowing this find will make his reputation, no doubt about it.

"I'm moving the manipulator arm," North said.

At first, they didn't see the arm on the screen, but then it crawled from the bottom of the screen, its twin mechanical fingers wide open, a hungry mouth.

And Reilly muttered something.

"Wurm," he said quietly.

The arm inched toward one hole, and the fat worm that waited there.

"What's that?" Simonsen said.

"Wurm. An Old World myth. Something from an undergrad Lit class . . . from Goethe's *Dr. Faustus* . . . 'to die, to meet the cursed wurm.' "

"Easy," Beck cautioned North as the arm closed on a worm. "Don't spook it. Don't—"

But when Simonsen turned, he saw that she had moved quickly. Perhaps she thought she'd lose it to the darkness of its hole. Or maybe she just wanted it over so she could bring the ROV up and get the hell off her chair.

But the arm suddenly jutted forward, grabbed at the worm—

Missing it.

"Shit," she said.

But then the worm was out again.

"Get it!" Reilly screamed. "He's right there! Get the fucker."

And this time the claws of the manipulator closed around the fat body of the worm, just below what might be a mouth.

The hungry wurm, Simonsen thought. Watching the mouth open. It filled the monitor now, twisting, turning. No teeth in the mouth. Nothing to cut, or rip or—

"Shit," North said. "Something's—" She fiddled with the ROV's controls.

"What's the problem?" Simonsen asked. "What's wrong?"

Her voice was high, frantic. Everyone was watching the monitor, watching the bizarre worm twist around the arm. It was at least two meters long, and it still wasn't completely out of its burrow.

"Goddam it!" she yelled. "Something's smashed the electronic thermometer." Then a soft pinging sound began.

And on the monitor, the ROV rocked to the left.

Simonsen watched Jane North look up, her face bathed in the glow of the green monitor and the glare of the video screens. "Something's wrong."

Then the monitors flashed, and went to snow.

"Shit," Simonsen said. "Get the hell out of there."

"I'm trying," she said. "But the thrusters aren't working right. Damn! There goes sonar. Now I don't know where the hell we are." She turned, and looked at Reilly. "I've got to let the specimen go. I mean, if I still have control. I've got to pull back the arm, and I don't have any time to try and get some of the worm into the specimen compartment—"

"Just do it!" Simonsen yelled. "We can always go back."

And he prayed. Please God, don't let me lose their fucking ROV. Don't let me screw up.

North hit some buttons, and leaned back in her chair.

"There," she said with a chilling finality. "That's it. Ballast is away and the syntactic flotation on—if it's working. That's all I can do. The arm should be back, tight against the body of Lil Shit, and it should be pulling straight out of gorge." She turned and looked right at Simonsen, almost apologetic, he thought.

The ship rocked continuously now, and a few of the bilious interns had ducked away to toss their cookies in private.

"Let's go outside," Simonsen said.

And then, he added quietly, "And see just how big a screw-up this has been . . ."

* * *

It was raining, a warm, soothing tropical rain.

But the steady downpour made it difficult for Simonsen to see anything, the sheets of water running off his glasses.

I need goddam windshield wipers, he thought.

Jane North stood next to him. She felt bad, he guessed. It wasn't her fault. But if the ROV didn't pop to the surface, she'd blame herself.

"Where do you guess she'll surface?" he asked.

Normally she'd sit at the console and guide Lil Shit right next to the ship. But blind, with no navigational data, it didn't matter. Either the ballast was released . . . or not.

"I don't know. Not too far away from the ship. She was about at the end of her tether."

He nodded. The captain was on the deck ready to help get the submersible on board just as soon as it surfaced.

They waited.

And Simonsen had just about lost hope when the bright red dome of the ROV broke the rough surface.

Everyone clapped and whistled. The captain wasted no time getting the *Achilles* alongside.

And Simonsen looked over at the ROV, just the upper few inches of its domelike body bobbing on top of the water. The surface was all scratched, like it had been scraped with a knife, or a razor, over and over, a mazelike pattern.

The captain lowered the hook of the winch.

The hook slid past the lifting bail. Once, then again. But then the ROV was finally snared and Simonsen gave the captain the signal to haul away.

The churning sea splashed against the ship, against Lil Shit. Everyone was soaked.

But they all wanted to see what had happened to the submersible.

It popped out of the water. Streams of water rolled away from it.

"Holy shit," Reilly said.

The arm was still extended. Extended, and twisted at a sick angle. It was broken.

But that's not what Reilly was excited about.

There was a big chunk of the worm still held tightly to the manipulator arms.

"We've got a piece of it!" Reilly yelled over the wind and the rain. Simonsen watched him hurry to a sullen Jane North and give her a hug. "Way to go, doll, even if you did fuck up Lil Shit."

The ROV dangled in the air, still swinging over the water. Then the captain swung it over onto the main deck, beside Prom II.

Simonsen kept looking at the chunk of worm.

Well, that's good, he thought, glad to have a piece of it.

But there was something about it that bothered him.

He watched Lil Shit come to a gentle landing on a wooden pallet.

Reilly hurried to the front of the ROV.

There was something wrong . . .

Reilly knelt down, next to the broken manipulator, a big grin plastered on his soaking face.

Simonsen took a step close to him.

And then he remembered.

He had seen *Riftia* worms brought to the surface before. And he remembered how they looked all squashed, exploded by the change in pressure. Every cell of their bodies dead.

But this worm looked different.

It looked—

Alive . . .

The smell, the rotten egg smell, was strong, even while the wind blew the warm rain into their faces. It was the stench of sulfur. Powerful but familiar . . . expected.

But this was too strong. *He could taste it!*

"Ed, don't you think you'd better get some gloves, a specimen bag, some—"

And he thought . . .

Everything dies when it's brought to the surface.

Everything.

Simonsen took another step. "Ed . . ."

But this piece of the worm wasn't dead. No, he could see that. The way it shimmered, rippling, moving in the pincer grip of the manipulator's claw. No, not dead at all.

"Don't," he started to say. "Don't touch that."

But Reilly's hand had already grabbed the worm, trying to circle its thick body. He was grinning at his prize, holding it up like a suburbanite gone fishing . . . not seeing it move, not caring—

"Don't!" Simonsen yelled again.

But it was, of course, too late . . .

ONE

CONEY

Chapter One

"YO, Doc! How's it hanging?"

Michael Cross made a small grin, an obligatory acknowledgment of the fist-up greeting of the proprietor of Grandma's Attic.

How's *what* hanging? Michael felt like asking as he jogged by the garage-cum-storefront that seemed to deal mostly in nearly new bicycles (just ripped off!) and repossessed fiberboard furniture.

There was a row of these depressing "antique" stores leading the way into the wonderland, the tingling grandeur that was Coney Island, circa 1991.

He came to the corner. The sign said "Don't Walk," but with a runner's peripheral vision, Michael saw that the nearest car was somewhere down near the crumbling Belt Parkway. He ran right into the street.

The street was layered with wrappers and garbage, like the underbelly of his desk back in grade school—the way it grew all pock-marked with the stalagmites and stalactites of chewing gum. Hey, he thought, as he did nearly every time he made his lunchtime jogging loop through Coney Island. Is this much decay legal? How can one place be so forgotten?

And Michael would remember the vivid black and white photographs of Coney Island from the turn of the century, and Weegee's post-war photography, capturing the last innocent decade, the last clean decade before Coney, and a good portion of the rest of the country began a seemingly irreversible plummet.

His Nikes smacked down into an isolated pond collected at one curb. The street was so twisted and bent that there was little chance for rain, or piss, or whatever to find its way to the sewer. Who the hell is in charge of repairing them? And how much are they making?

And why doesn't somebody fry their ass?

Then he was up onto the sidewalk, dodging the people who couldn't stomach the beach anymore. (It's clean, the Health Department said. Only a few needles this year, over at Manhattan Beach. Miles away. Miles. Everything's just hunky dory here.)

That was good enough for most people. But the more fastidious Coney Island habitués, the older people who walled themselves inside their apartments in Brighton Beach, knew better. This isn't the way a beach is supposed to look. The old ones remembered clean sand, clean water.

Amazing . . .

He heard the calliope. So incongruous, with the smell of french fries and the stale salty air, the jumble of languages and accents that were part of this new New York.

A calliope!

Louder now as he neared the shedlike building that housed the carousel.

At least this made Michael smile. These were his friends, these wild-eyed horses prancing and rearing, with their brightly tinted nostrils flaring, as if they were startled to be trapped on the platter, going round and round to the crazy thumping music.

And every day he saw the same man at the controls, the same face every day—a novelty along the Coney Island strip. It wasn't a particularly warm face. Even as the kids squealed, grabbing at the rings he disinterestedly fed to them, the man was completely deadpan. Sullen.

What's his story? Michael wondered. Is this one of the job opportunities open to ex-cons fresh out of Sing Sing? Hey, Leftie, we've got you a gig. Yeah, out on Coney . . .

And though the carousel operator had been watching Michael jog by since last summer, then winter, and now summer again, he never looked up. He just rang the great bell, signaling that the frozen race was once again about to begin. Same clanging bell, whether there was one shivering kid on the ride in the middle of a frosty January or if it was crowded with souped-up teenagers, flying on whatever was the drug of choice of the moment.

Michael reached another corner. A few cars were turning onto Surf Avenue, so he jogged in place, ignoring the wisecracks and glances of the dudes standing near Elsa's Fudge, the sweet smell mixing dizzily with the foul fumes of fat old cars from the early seventies.

Once across, he ran past a souvenir shop, and then McCann's Bar, already two deep with desperate characters putting away enough bats and balls to blot out the glaring Coney sun.

Then Michael cut across Surf Avenue, dodging the cruising cars, over to Nathan's Famous.

Ah, Nathan's . . . Here at least was one Coney Island landmark that, like the Parachute Jump just down the street, still stood tall. Nathan's still served incredibly tasty fries, great chunky things gouged out of potatoes, and a hot dog that said, yes, some things *don't* change. Many a night Michael locked up, and walked down past the blaring ghetto blasters, past the stumbling crowd whose fun-loving appearance was completely deceiving, to enjoy a genuine Nathan's Famous "with the woiks."

But now all he wanted was to get back, have a shower, and get back to—

Another sound roared from ahead of him.

It was music. At least, it was labeled music. Horrible screeching, the scratching of a needle skating across a record, then a mindless, percussive roar while someone rapped about "gettin' it on."

The music bellowed out of JJs Bump-o-Rama. The outside of JJs was limned with glitter and flashing bubble-gum lights that looked like they were lifted from squad cars. Once in a while, the sound from inside the massive bumper car hall screamed out into the street.

And he remembered the first time he saw JJs. And why it gave him a sick, icy feeling every time he looked at it.

He had Jo with him. She was all wide-eyed, as only a kid can be. Looking at the rides, and the cotton candy, and only seeing the fun.

They had just fished a royal lunch at Nathan's, and were walking back.

They passed JJs, and Michael was lost, thinking about the marriage that had just bit the dust—a casualty of modern science, his ex-wife Caryn said. And he was lost in his thoughts, a not-uncommon state. Science dealt with manageable things, quantifiable. Relationships threw all that shit right out the window.

He walked on. Not noticing that Jo had lingered, snared by the thumping beat of the Bump-o-Rama. She had stopped, near the entrance.

And when Michael finally snapped out of his reverie, turning, ready to say something, she was gone.

He imagined that the street people were looking at him then, with their strange, alien faces—we're not in Kansas anymore, Toto. Certainly not on the Berkeley campus. Looking at him, laughing, grinning . . . lose something, mister? Kind of a bad place to lose something . . . or someone.

But the faces looked away, as if embarrassed by the look of panic, the terrible sick look of fear that bloomed on Michael's face. He didn't wait a second before screaming . . . "Jo! Jo!" as he ran back.

Thinking in those milliseconds that she could be anywhere. Snatched up, hauled away, just like that. *Anywhere*. The people who did those things, they were pros, they knew what they were doing. Sure. Didn't take too long. Like professional safe-crackers, blink your eyes and your kid could be gone.

Poof.

"Jo!" he screamed.

She didn't answer.

Some crazy wailing, a James Brownish call of the wild screamed from the Bump-o-Rama.

He looked in there. A spinning mirror ball sent glittering specks of white careening across the metal floor, across the iridescent bodies of the cars, and up the wall, onto the wire mesh that innocently hid the thousands of volts needed for the bumper cars.

It was dark. Black shapes in the cars, more shapes waiting in the discolike darkness.

Until something, a strand of her hair, a bit of a ribbon that held her ponytail, caught one of those glittering specks.

And he ran over to her, standing there, entranced by the music, the lights, the noises, the fun, oblivious to the hulking shapes Michael was convinced had their eyes on her.

He grabbed her, pulled her out.

Roughly at first, but then he just gave her a hug, so damn relieved to have her back. We don't always get second chances. It's not in the rules, Mikey boy . . .

Jo wanted to go back, to ride JJs's finest.

Michael said something about some other day.

And the name of that day? Michael said to himself—

Is Never.

He reached down and felt his pulse for fifteen seconds. Then he multiplied that by four: 120.

Not a bad run. Keep the ticker pumping that blood on through.

He was almost at the Cyclone, one of the world's great roller coasters. It's probably another death trap, he thought, looking at the splintery paint, the mesh of girders, the high-pitched shriek of the coaster as it took a corner and dropped into space.

But it was a benevolent death trap. Honest in its intention to scare the hell out of you by risking your life. Michael had taken Jo on it once. And he might do it again. It was like flying. The kind of risk that you tried to parcel out.

He cut through an opening in the parking lot, only a few cars dotting the mostly empty space. The hot summer sun always did that . . . the sun, and the influx of fun-loving degenerates.

He sprinted up to the entrance, to the side staff door, hoping he remembered his key. He felt in the tiny pouch pocket inside his running shorts. He stopped in front of the door, fishing out the key, looking at the door, and the sign beside it.

Staff Entrance, The New York Aquarium. Dr. Michael Cross, Director.

And with one final breath, he opened the door.

His hair was still wet from a quickie shower when he left his office and walked across the S-shaped open area to the penguin bays.

And he felt oddly reassured to see his daughter crouched upon the spattered rocks—penguins can be the messiest animals—flipping herring to the noisy antarctic fowl.

Jo was making sure everyone was fed . . . not just the loudest, most obnoxious ones. She scolded the bigger, more pushy birds greedy for another fish.

She didn't notice him until he was standing by the railing, beside two moms with a bunch of kids all so excited to see a kid—one of their own—feeding the funny-looking birds.

He watched her for a minute. Quietly.

Thinking.

There was a lot of her mother in her. The hair, certainly. A brilliant blond, glowing yellow. And her eyes, a gray-blue that didn't seem to brook any deceit.

Was it too much to ask? he thought. To have a marriage that worked? To go against the odds, and keep the whole thing together? How hard could that be?

Too hard. For Caryn, certainly. After one warning too many, one more night trying to nail down some research money before middle age claimed him. Or planning to spend a weekend together until she flew away to cover some cheese-ball politician trying to create news on a slow Saturday.

Then she accused him of cheating.

Not true, he said.

Not true, he lied.

But how could you call it cheating? An overeager grad-school assistant. She did everything but pull down his fly. He was only human.

Then, the minute he denied her accusation, he saw something in her eyes.

You too, he wanted to say. *You too* . . . Angry at her, knowing that she had done it too.

But he understood its inevitability. Sure, their relationship had nose-dived into a business relationship, a corporate planning session. Who'll take Jo to ballet? Who will be here this weekend? Who will be home for dinner?

And does anyone give a shit about anyone else anymore?

And only when it was all over, nice and friendly, so different from their many friends who fought over every inch of communal property, did he realize what happened. Their divorce was civil, intelligent. "Humane," he smiled to her, even as he signed almost complete control of his daughter to his wife, now a cold-eyed stranger.

Only when it was all over, and he was truly alone, living a few blocks away from the Aquarium in a one-bedroom apartment, did he think that yes, he probably still loved her.

It was just too late.

Cue twanging guitars and Waylon Jennings.

Jo looked up, flashing a wonderful smile.

"Dad! You're back. How was your run?"

The attendant moms and children looked over at him.

"Hot and sweaty, pumpkin. You taking care of everybody here?"

One of the small brown and white penguins, a first-year bird, came up to Jo and nipped her elbow.

"Looks like you missed one."

He watched her shoo the bird away. Then she dug out a silvery herring and flipped it to the penguin. She laughed, standing up, and picked up the pail of fish. Some of the penguins waddled after her, eager for a try at seconds.

Michael went to the gate and opened it for her.

No scars to look at her, he thought. She's acting so grown-up, so mature. Lots of her friends had divorced parents, she said. *Lots*. No big deal.

He ran his hand through her hair.

"Having fun?" he asked.

She nodded. "It's great, Dad. Super. Just that—"

"Just what?"

She turned to him, squinting in the sun. He heard the tumbling sound of waves crashing, just past the east wall of the Aquarium.

"What about the sharks? I'd love to feed them."

He laughed, as she returned to her favorite topic of late.

"Sorry, Jo. That's still out of the question." He started walking back to the main building. "Penguins are noisy and obnoxious. But the sharks, well, they're something else."

Jo ran in front of him, walking backward, making her plea.

"But I've watched Annie and Steven feed them. I could do it, you know *that*."

"Sure. And I know what your mom would say if she called and I told her that you had joined the Aquarium in a permanent way." He stopped, his face earnest now. She really thought she could do it. Really wanted to.

"Try me in a few summers, Jo. I'm not going anywhere—not for a while. And the shark tank will still be here. Now," he said, smiling again, "I believe you have customers waiting at the Petting Pond?"

She threw her hands up in the air, not mad, but putting on a fetching show of exasperation. "Right, sea turtles and hermit crabs. Boy," she said, rolling her eyes, "I'd better be careful feeding *those* monsters."

He laughed again, watching her walk away.

One weekend a month. A few midweek visits. And two weeks at summer.

That was the extent of his relationship with his daughter.

He kicked open the door to the main exhibit hall, startling an elderly couple about to come out.

He walked right past them.

Thinking of Jo, and Caryn, his life. Thinking . . . Did I blow it or what?

Chapter Two

JO reached into the shallow pool, watching the hermit crabs hurry around, so timid and nervous. She picked up a sea star and held it out for a chubby curly-headed kid sitting on his mom's lap. The little runt grabbed at it as if he wanted to jump into the pond.

"See, Steven," the mom cooed as Jo held up the golden sea star, "touch the starfish."

Groan. It's not a fish, lady, Jo wanted to say. Do you see any fins, any gills?

Duh.

But the kid, all drooling and wearing a goofy grin, batted the animal away, sending it flying roughly into the pond.

"Oh, did it scare you?" the mother asked. And then little Steven nearly made a flying escape from his mommy's chunky arms, into the warm, foot-high water of the Petting Pond.

Unfortunately his mom caught him.

Jo didn't like this. Not at all.

Everything else—feeding the penguins, testing the water in the tropical tanks, even slicing a bucket of fish for the killer whale and its baby—that was fun. But sitting here in the hot afternoon sun and showing shellfish to toddlers, well that was something she could do without.

The woman and her brat finally left, and there were just two other kids—looking like they also were in sixth or seventh grade, like her—at the pond. They kneeled at the other end of the bench that surrounded the pond. They were having a great time lifting up the rocks, startling the tiny flounder that liked to hide in the shadows.

Then she watched them drop the rock roughly, as if they wanted to squish the fish.

"Please be careful," she said.

But the kids just grinned at her, as if to say "Who are you?"

One of the kids picked up a too-heavy rock and it slipped from his grip, splashing noisily into the water.

"Oh, shit," he said, obviously sending the rock down on some poor animals. The kids ran away then, spinning around, poking each other, doing all that goofy stuff that boys liked to do.

And she was alone by the pond.

The sun glimmered off the now-still water.

So peaceful . . .

She heard the waves crashing in the distance. Sounding inviting, even if she'd never swum there. You'd have to be positively mental to swim anywhere near New York. No . . . at least back at her mother's co-op there was a health club, and a big pool with clean blue water. And not too many kids. It was mostly—what did her mom call them?

Yuppies.

Sounded like a new breakfast cereal.

Try some Yuppies in the morning! The only way to start your day!

She took a breath, then blew a stray strand of her hair off her forehead.

The pond water, despite a pair of bubblers in the center of the tank, smelled. A dry, salty smell. The way her body smelled, walking back from the beach in Provincetown—P-Town, her dad called it.

Last summer . . .

A family vacation. Everyone together, just having fun. It was great, the fudge, the ice cream, swimming together, and she couldn't help notice how her mom and dad got along so well. No real arguments, and lots of hugs, and, at night—when they thought she was asleep . . .

She felt herself redden at the memory, or was she just getting hot, ready to faint right into the pool?

She understood divorce. She read all the books, the Judy Blume stuff, and other stories about kids with parents that split. It happens. It's not the end of the world. No big deal at all.

She let her hand drop into the water.

But it didn't feel cool. A large hermit crab scuttled out from a rock thinking that something good to eat had just dropped near his home. The crab raised up his big pincer and squeezed her finger.

"Ouch . . ." she said, surprised by the crab's grip. She looked at her finger. For a little critter he had made a good-sized indentation in her skin. She rubbed it, watching the skin rise, the bump fade.

The dry, salty smell made her thirsty, made her want to go inside.

She turned around. And she saw the entrance to the smallest of the three aquarium buildings. It housed just one tank, but a big one. Filled with giant turtles, and rays that seemed to fly through the water, and crusty, bumpy puffer fish that looked like rocks, and—the big attraction—sharks.

She looked at the entrance.

Some people missed the building, caught up with the whales and the tropical fish in the main building, or the penguins outside, or the dolphin show that all her dad's staff was sick of running.

Everybody loved to see the dolphins nose a volleyball into the air and then beg for a fish. They called it training but it was just stupid pet tricks . . . .

She stood up, tasting the sweat running off her upper lip, the seat of her khaki shorts sticking to her bottom. She wrinkled her nose, all itchy from tiny drops of sweat.

And she looked at the building behind her.

She knew the combination to that lock too, leading to the back of the tanks, to the rooms where they fed the fish.

Her fingers played with her shirt buttons.

And, with one quick look at the deserted Petting Pond, she walked away, into the building.

"Give me a break," he said to himself, looking at the register tape from his desktop calculator. As director, Michael had to file budget estimates and expenditures four damn times a year. And given his lack of interest in such matters—tallying what he'd spent and what he would spend—usually turned into a nightmare.

Everything else went to hell while he played accountant.

How come I never saw any of this shit on *Wild Kingdom* or *Jacques Cousteau*? he wondered. Can't picture old Jacques hunched over an adding machine figuring out how he was going to pay for the *Calypso*'s next jaunt to the South Pacific.

The knock at his door was a welcome interruption.

"Come in," he said.

"Dr. Cross, Wally looks in trouble," Martin said.

Michael nodded. Martin Langelaan, one of his two research assistants, was a bearded, new-age scientist. He wasn't afraid of his odd theories that ignored every previous supposition.

Even if there was nothing to support them.

And Martin had no interest in land-based research. His current position, he assured Michael with no attempt at masking his dismay, was strictly "temporary." Soon as he got a good opportunity for some field-based research, hopefully working the deep Pacific hydrothermal vents—the oceanographer's Disneyland—he was out of here.

Michael punched in one last number, and then let the machine add up his numbers. Then he stood up.

Grabbing his microcassette.

"What seems wrong . . . more twitching?"

They walked out the door together, past the inflatable dolphins of the souvenir stand, toward the cramped lab behind the main pool.

"Worse. It's been moving violently, snapping its tail back and forth, rubbing its plates together, then stopping . . . like it was waiting for the next attack."

Michael nodded.

Trouble with Wally wasn't unexpected. Not at all. In fact, since Wally and his brethren had been found—forty-six of them, 1500 feet deep in the Gulf of Mexico, 150 miles west of Tortuga—all of them had died.

Except for this one.

And Michael took no small satisfaction in that. It proved his ideas were right, that there was something to his concerns—

He opened the door to the lab and saw that Wally was in deep distress.

He hurried to the tank, and turned on his recorder.

"July fifth, 1990, 1:35 P.M.," he said, speaking into the recorder. "*Bythnomus giganteous*, labeled 'Wally,' is writhing at the bottom of the tank, its plates rubbing together." He clicked the recorder off.

It was dying. No doubt about it.

For a while, they had the animal on display. It was a big attraction.

But people found it disturbing. The visitors from the city thought it looked like an enormous, nasty-looking cockroach. But the suburbanites rightly saw what it was. It looked like an isopod, a pill bug, a sow bug, one of the countless names for the armored little insects that gathered under the tops of sand boxes or under a lawn chair, liking the damp, the darkness.

Except that *Bythnomus*—Wally—was gigantic, nearly half a meter in length, larger than a lobster. And it was pure white, an eerie opaque albino creature. Its eyes were not real eyes at all . . . just odd light-sensing organs.

After all, it came from a place where color was superfluous.

There was no light. It was dark all the time, dark, cold, and under tremendous pressure.

And how did Wally and the other creatures survive such conditions? After a year of study, no one had a clue. Most of the specimens, including the juveniles hatched from the collected eggs, died.

Just as Michael argued they would.

Look, he had said, meeting with the consortium of labs and aquaria that were cooperating in a study of the incredible find. They weren't eating *anything* we were throwing at them. Not the squid, not the fish, and yet they were obviously meat eaters. Voracious ones, to look at their mandibles and jagged claws. They're adapted to incredible pressure, near freezing water temperature, and an absence of anything to feed on.

At least as far as we can tell, Michael said.

But it was no good. All the big oceanographic institutes rushed to study and test the animal and, denied their normal deadly conditions, they died.

Except for Wally.

Michael kept it in a pressurized tank. While the animals survived coming to the surface, he guessed they'd prefer their normal high pressure. Then he kept the tank dark much of the time, eventually removing the creature from display.

A sign informed disappointed visitors that the gigantic deep-sea isopod was being protected.

He experimented with food, finding that Wally ignored all fish and meat, but attacked mussels, and then deep-sea clams . . .

Not for their meat, but for their shells.

Very peculiar . . .

He watched the animal crack the shell, desperately grinding the calcite material with its mandibles.

But even that wasn't enough.

Wally started fading. Then, a horrible wrenching began. At first it was just in the morning. But then, it happened all the time . . .

Wally flipped in the water, smashing against the tank. Martin jerked back from the sudden movement.

Michael clicked on the recorder.

"Specimen shows increasing evidence of internal dysfunction. Spasms are almost constant now. There may be some danger to the walls of the tank . . ."

Martin Langelaan looked at him wide-eyed when he said that. "You don't really think—"

Michael clicked off the recorder.

"You know how much it weighs. And their shell is harder than any chitinous material we've ever seen." Michael raised his hand and touched the side of the oversized, pressurized tank. "A few more wild flips like that, and it might give way—"

The lab door opened. Michael turned and saw Steven Borg and then Alice Bowen walk in. Their concern was the day-to-day running of the Aquarium, but, like a lot of people, they were interested in Wally.

The isopod flipped again, less violently.

Michael leaned closer to the tank.

He clicked on the Olympus. "I see a small tear, a rip of some kind, just starting between the"—he counted the back plates of the animal—"between the eighth and ninth plates. Two of the seven pairs of legs are twitching, but the somites appear useless, dragging from the body. Perhaps—"

He clicked off the recorder. And turned to Alice. "You left Jo at the Pond?" he asked.

She smiled, shook her head. "No . . . I mean I just passed there, and it was deserted. I assumed she had come over here, come to see—"

Michael nodded.

She's not there. And she's not here. Where could she be?

Lots of places, he thought.

Lots.

He remembered a fight he had with Caryn . . . about Jo. She's so strong-willed, his wife had said. You've got to do something, as if he had made her that way. So strong-willed and stubborn. She does exactly what she wants to do.

He handed the recorder to Martin. "Note everything it does," he said, and he hurried out of the lab.

Paul Barron stared right back at the bitch, sitting at her desk, so goddam smug he would have liked nothing more than to stand up, grab her by her hair, and—

But no, he must calm himself. He didn't want to appear—what? Didn't want to appear nervous . . . or upset?

Desperate.

No, this wasn't like the old days, back when he had his own Center—*his own Center!*—in Aspen. Things were different then, he had money, and people to service his every wish, his every whim. He had power, real power, and influence. Things were just starting for him.

Then something happened. Maybe it was the drugs, or the

women . . . and the men. Maybe he forgot who he was—hah, hah—really working for. Maybe he forgot who really called the shots.

Maybe he stopped believing.

And he lost it all.

The glittering patrons with their jets and their fat endowments. The people who called him late at night, asking for Paul Barron's advice, for Paul Barron's prayers.

Hoping that Paul Barron would intercede.

Intercede with *them*.

The ones he was close to.

Except that he'd lost his way. Woke up one morning to feel that they were gone, the contact, *their presence*, had just disappeared.

He had been abandoned. Left behind.

And nothing he did. The ceremonies, the gestures, the frantic digging through the books he kept inside his safe, books he had stopped believing in, none of it did anything.

He was alone.

Just another person.

Another bug.

Another morsel of food on this planet of herd beasts.

And he cried, scared, losing everyone, losing everything.

Now the secretary looked at him, as if she could see the crazy swirl of thoughts in his head.

Don't worry, he grinned back at her. I'll remember you, baby. I've got a list of nice things I could do to you. Just wait. Just—

She shook her head, then looked down at the papers on her desk.

Then her phone buzzed.

She picked it up.

Turned to him.

"Mr. Cowell will see you now, Mr. Barron."

And he walked into the office, past the secretary.

Cowell was at his desk. No smile on his face. But looking as successful as ever. And again Barron had to wonder . . . why was it just me? Why did I have to pay? What did I do to make it go wrong?

Cowell didn't ask him to sit down.

"Real estate must be booming," Barron said, nodding and grinning at the plush office.

Cowell nodded back. "Yes, Denver is having a miniboom, Paul. Nothing much. Just new industry, the new airport—the usual."

Cowell looked at his watch, pointedly.

Bastard, Barron thought. I remember you on your knees, *on your fucking knees*, babbling out their names, swearing obedience, complete obedience. And now you treat me like—

"What can I do for you, Paul? I've got a full schedule." Cowell shuffled a paper on his desk. "Very full."

"Sure. I understand, Thomas—"

He saw Cowell wince, as if offended by using his first name.

A bit too intimate, for you, eh, Cowell? All that's behind you. Probably you put it down to some passing fascination with a cult. That's all it was, right?

Wrong.

He took a step toward Cowell's desk.

Barron cleared his throat.

"I could use a loan." He raised a hand. "Not a lot. Just enough to help me move to someplace else, some other city." He grinned at Cowell. "New opportunities . . ."

Cowell already had his desk drawer open, and quickly tossed an envelope toward Barron.

"There. Should be enough to see you . . . settled elsewhere."

Barron reached out, thinking.

You can't buy me out of your life.

Because I remember.

I remember!

He picked up the envelope.

"Thank you, Thomas. It's just a loan. And if ever I can help you, in the future, with—"

Cowell stood up, his face still set, so damn smug, almost disgusted.

"As I said, I have meetings . . . so if you'll excuse me . . ."

Cowell walked to the door, and opened it.

And Barron nodded.

And he walked out slowly, enjoying giving Cowell the creeps.

Yeah, things have certain taken a down turn for me, he thought. But the situation can change. Yeah, going to New York was a good idea, a righteous fucking good idea.

Things were happening.

He felt their direction, their control.

He walked past Barron, out of the office.

The door closed behind him. Too loudly.

The secretary didn't look up.

No matter. So I lost my house, my beautiful house in the

mountains, and all my people, my wealthy, obedient people. It's all gone.

But things change.

All the time. *They change!*

He grinned.

The situation is fucking fluid . . .

Chapter Three

JO knew the combination to the electric lock on this door, like she knew the combinations to all the doors in the Aquarium. At first her father had tried to keep some of them secret. There are places here I don't want you exploring, he had told her.

But it wasn't long before he was asking her to run and get specimen containers from the freshwater lab, or some pails of chum—gloopy fish heads and spiky tails—to throw to the seals who barked so greedily every time they saw her.

One by one, her dad told her the combinations. Until she knew them all, memorized them. Easy as pie . . .

And he didn't mind, she guessed. She was a hard worker, as good as any of the adults, better than Steven—that's for sure.

She was *responsible*.

Except now—she thought, standing by the door that led to the back of the giant shark tank—I'm about to blow it. God, maybe he'll go and change all the locks. Maybe he'll stick me in the gift shop selling inflatable porpoises!

And there aren't even any real porpoises in the Aquarium.

She pressed the last number of the small keypad and the door popped open. It was hot, a dry, salty heat. Her upper lip balanced a thin line of sweat.

I could just shut the door, she thought. Pull it slammed and go someplace else, someplace cool, air-conditioned, like the tropical fish building. It's nice and dark and cool there. Cool, and safe.

But no. She gave her head a shake, as if shaking away her fear. I can do this. And once I do it, Dad will think it's fine. Well, maybe he'll be a *little* ticked off, but he'll cool down.

She pulled the door open quickly, hurried in, and slammed it shut behind her.

There was always the chance that there was someone else in

here, Alice or Steven, someone to see her and wonder just what in the world she was doing.

But Jo stood there a few seconds, her heart beating so strongly it was as if she heard it thumping near her ears. The droplets of sweat above her lip and on her brow turned cool, clammy, in the darkness.

She heard noises.

The steady, low rumble of the tank's filters. Just like a kid's aquarium, her father had explained. Same thing . . . only ten thousand times bigger. There was the sound of bubbles, great popping balloons of air near the top of the tank.

And then something else. A sudden splash. The sharp, cutting sound of something breaking the water quickly, then diving deeper.

Jo took a breath. There were smells. Dried fish—this morning's breakfast. The stale, salty air. She licked her lips.

The door was right behind her, she thought. I could just turn around and leave.

But as soon as she had that thought she became more determined to do this. She walked into the darkness, to the back wall of the tank, all black, with dots of water on it. She put her hand to the wall, touching it. On the other side was the tank—only one side was glass. She let her hand trail along the wall as she walked to the—

Ladder.

There it was, a sliding ladder, on wheels. Jo had seen the routine dozens of times. Watching the sharks feed was something she didn't like to miss.

First you get a bucket of fish, whole sea bass was the sharks' absolute fave. Then you climb up the ladder to where the tank was open. If you were on the other side of the tank, you could look and see the sharks' meal come plopping in from the opening.

The only thing is—Steven told her once, when she stood at the foot of the ladder and watched him—you have to get the fish in there quickly without just dumping the whole bucket in.

"Make a big splash"—he laughed—"and it gets them kinda excited. Trick is," he said as he started scooping up the fish and shoveling them into the tank, "you gotta slip them in nice and smoothly . . . but fast."

He looked down on her then, his face in the shadows.

"Cause, believe me, you don't want them getting excited."

She had nodded then, remembering it all. She could picture what might happen. It was weird enough watching them feed normally. Their big mouths would open—do they really need all those teeth? And then the sharks would tear at the fish, as though to merely eat wasn't enough. No, they had to snap at the bass, pulling at them, cutting them into two bigger-than-bite-size pieces.

Then they quickly gobbled the pieces down while still moving, still circling, their dull eyes looking left and right, daring some other shark to stick its snout in the way.

She grabbed the ladder and gave it a small shake. It rolled smoothly a few inches.

She looked around.

There, behind her, next to a large aluminum sink, was an oversized bucket. She walked over to it, grabbed the handle, and then walked over to a squat freezer, down toward the other end of the shark tank.

Maybe it's locked, she thought.

(And there was part of her then that hoped it was locked. An easy way out, she could tell herself. I tried but, well, the *stupid* freezer was locked.)

Only it wasn't.

It popped open with an eager sound and—almost disappointed—Jo began pulling out the foot-and-a-half-long frozen fish. They looked like chunks of silvery wood with dull faces. But the eyes, the fish eyes, were so expressionless. As if they could say, "We don't mind being frozen . . . we don't mind being eaten by the sharks."

She filled the bucket with the stiff fish, wedging them in, trying to get more than the three that easily fit. She knew that Steven usually brought up about five or six. She took two out and tried again. And this time, with a bit of force, some pushing and squeezing, she got five fish into the bucket.

She picked up the shark's lunch pail.

It was heavy. The thin metal handle dug into the palm of her hand. She took a few steps, and switched hands.

It's not going to be too easy getting this up the ladder, she thought.

She heard a noise. Outside, near the door. She froze, the dead weight of the pail pulling down, digging into her hand.

Someone was by the door.

A voice. Someone laughing. But then the sounds were gone.

Just kids, she thought. Goofing around.

She blew a puff of air at some strands of her hair that tickled her forehead. Now she had both hands holding the pail.

Jo looked at the ladder.

Figuring out a plan.

Take a few steps, she thought. Then rest the pail on one of the steps. Then a few more steps. Until I get to the top.

Yeah. I can do it, she thought. No problem.

She stepped onto the ladder and swung the pail onto the second step. But the sudden movement made the ladder glide a few inches to the side.

"Damn," she said aloud.

Her voice sounded small surrounded by all the other noise.

She brought the pail up another step. Then her feet. One hand held the ladder. Her other hand hoisted the pail up, step after step, following her feet.

When she rested—about halfway up—she looked down at the pail, now catching the full milky glow of one of the ceiling lights. One of the fish heads looked up at her.

She looked away.

Then she took a big breath, and started up again. Another step, and then—with a grunting effort—she pulled the pail up. And each time she let it clang down harder on the step.

It seemed to take forever.

But then she was there.

At the top of the tank.

At first, all she saw was the mirrorlike surface of the water. So clean and clear . . .

Then—and her breath caught when she did this—she climbed up another step, her hands now grabbing at the small platform at the top of the tank, a metal lip that ran around the top.

And she saw shapes swimming below her, just a few feet away.

"God," she whispered.

They looked only a few feet away, the pair of tiger sharks, and then a hammerhead, and a bunch of harmless dogfish. But that was the water . . . magnifying everything. They were probably nearer the bottom.

But Jo didn't waste any time watching them.

There's work to be done, she thought. And she didn't want to have someone come in before she even started.

That, she thought grimly, would be that.

She knew the rest of the procedure. Get the pail up to the metal lip.

Easier said than done.

Then crawl up a bit more, so I can lean on the lip and get a good look at the tank. Then get the fish in, quickly.

She reached down for the pail. There was no ladder handle to grab with her other hand. Her fingers scratched at the lip, trying to get some support. But there was nothing to hold on to. So she simply tilted her body closer to the lip, leaning in toward the open tank.

That should give me some balance, she thought.

And, grunting, she hoisted the pail and started to swing it up . . .

There's nothing to worry about, Michael told himself. Jo was always wandering off, finding hidden corners of the Aquarium. She probably was over by the dolphin pool . . . or by the seals.

Except he didn't check either of those places.

Somehow, he *knew* where'd she be.

She was stubborn. She did what she wanted to do. She was smart and pigheaded.

Just like her mother.

And now he was running.

While all sorts of grisly pictures danced in his head.

I'm too lenient with her, he thought. Too damn lenient. I shouldn't have given her the run of the place. She's just a kid. And kids do dopey things. Dangerous things, like—

People were watching him run. Turning from the animals to look at this crazy man dash past them.

Please, he thought. Let me be wrong.

He saw the shark building—for some reason all by itself, at the back of the grounds.

It looked almost disreputable.

Needs a paint job, he thought. Maybe some cute picture of sharks, done in the style of Charley Tuna.

"Hello," a leering shark in a fedora might say. "Missing any kids?"

"Shit," he said.

He thought of running into the exhibit entrance. If she was there—doing what he thought she was doing—he'd be able to look up and see her.

But then what? Bang on the glass. Motion to her to get down, get away. Before something happens.

He shook his head.

And instead he ran right up to the locked door. He punched in the combination once, messing up the last digit.

"Damn it," he said. And he did it again, forcing himself to go slower.

And the door popped open.

* * *

Bang!

Jo smacked the pail down on the metal lip hard. The sound echoed in the room, and bounced off the water. The enormous sea turtle—one of the few animals that can safely hang out with the sharks—was gliding below her. Around and around the animals swam, a living merry-go-round.

She crawled up a bit more.

Moving onto the metal lip.

Did she feel it sag a bit when she put her weight on it?

No, she thought. That was pretty unlikely. Steven and Annie are always climbing onto it. They even walk around the lip, checking the tank and the filter.

It scared Jo to *watch* that. What if they fell in?

So she was sure it could hold her weight.

Except . . . except . . .

She had both feet on the top rung of the ladder. If she was going to get the frozen fish into the water she'd have to—yes, she knew what she'd have to do.

She'd have to slide her fanny up just a *bit* more.

Her feet would have to kinda dangle in the air behind her.

She rubbed her brow with her forearm, trying to wipe the sweat away.

Well, she thought, if that's what I got to do . . . *that's what I got to do.*

She scrunched up a bit.

One foot left the top step. Then—no stopping now, girl—the other foot. She sat there, perched.

She grabbed two of the frozen fish. Except now they had started to thaw a bit, growing slimy in her hand . . . slippery.

I'm a two-fisted shark feeder, she thought, holding the bass near their tails so they wouldn't slip away.

She looked down.

The hammerhead—the biggest shark in the tank—was just below.

"Lunchtime," she said.

And she slid the fish into the water.

("You can't throw them," Steven had said. "No splashing. Just glide them in . . . nice . . . and smooth.")

She didn't watch the fish slide down. She didn't see whether they bounced off the steel-gray skin of the circling shark.

She grabbed two more fish, sticky . . . slippery.

She swung them around.

(Wanting to hurry now.)

Out of the corner of her eye she saw some movement below her. The big shapes were speeding up.

And this time she didn't exactly slip the fish into the water.

No. That would have meant getting too close to the water, and the sharks.

This time, she let them drop. And they plopped into the water.

And as Jo turned she saw one of the tigers, its spooky eyes locked on the silvery fish. She watched a moment. The shark seemed so close . . . too close.

The shark chomped at the fish, its dozens of razor teeth neatly cutting it in two. The other tiger was right beside it, fighting for the other piece. A big tail fin broke the water, spraying her. She saw something moving over near the other side of the tank.

Jo was scared.

She backed off the lip a bit.

One foot—

(She pictured her foot, the sneaker, in her mind. White with electric pink ribbons. L.A. Gear . . .)

She searched for the ladder.

Oh, God, where is it, she thought. She slid back, away from the water a bit more.

She saw the pail, with one fish sticking out.

Her toe touched the top step. She took a breath.

And—a last-minute thought—she reached out and grabbed the last fish.

Finish the stupid job, she scolded herself. You wanted to to it, *so do it*.

And she brought her arm back, ready to swing over the tank.

I don't care if they do go crazy fighting over it, if they—

The door opened.

She turned to see who was coming in.

And in turning her foot pushed against the ladder, just a bit. But it slid away, just a few inches . . . moving away from her foot.

The fish, the scales cold and sticky, slid from her hand.

And then—as she tried to get her balance back . . . to hold on to the fish—

('Cause I don't want it plopping into the water here, right here, right near me . . .)

She tilted back, toward the tank.

Oh, God.

Her father screamed her name.

"Jo! Get—"

But she was trying to catch herself—still trying to hold on to the fish—can't let it go. Not here. Not so close—

Her hand reached out to slam down against the lip.

A last chance to stop her weird tilting backward.

She didn't hear her own crying.

Her hand reached out.

And touched *water* . . . .

Chapter Four

JO'S hand touched water and then she cried out, tilting backward, back into the tank.

Funny, she thought. It all seemed to take so long, everything was moving in slow motion. The water felt warm, inviting. Her leg kicked against the side of the tank. She heard someone screaming and—her elbow in the water—it was odd realizing that . . .

That's me. That's me screaming.

Please, she thought. Don't let this happen.

And something grabbed her.

Michael saw his daughter, his bright, stubborn daughter, perched on top of the tank, falling back, rolling into the tank.

He heard the ladder roll away.

As if it knew . . .

You won't be needing this anymore.

Jo screamed.

A primal sound. "Mo-m-eee! Mo-"

Michael didn't believe in God. "No empirical evidence," he used to joke to Caryn, who had a strong Calvinist streak running through her genes.

No fucking evidence of any kind. All we got here is a planet, with a lot of pain. An old altar boy, he didn't believe in anything now.

But now, as he ran to the tank, the words inside his head, a mental stream of babble, came so easily.

Please God, don't let this happen, don't let this—

(Over and over and over, keeping those other images away, the sleepy-eyed sharks, prehistoric eating machines, ripping up his daughter. Maybe there were people watching outside. Maybe they'd get to see the whole thing.)

With one hand he stopped the errant ladder, and thrust a foot on the bottom step.

He screamed her name. "Jo!"

And he leapt up, not caring what happened, just putting as much effort as he could into his leap, up, until his outstretched hand touched her sneaker, her ankle, and closed.

Fast. Holding her tight, as he tumbled down, back, off the ladder, his fingers slipping a bit, and then—oh, God, yes—pulling her down, on top of him.

He heard Jo squeal as she flew through the air.

A small spray of water sprinkled his forehead.

It made him think of church, and the priest, covered in thick incense and robes, dipping a metal prong in holy water. The priest waved it over the worshipers, blessing them.

Spraying them with magic water.

Michael crashed onto the cement floor. The air was punched out of his chest. And before he could take another breath, Jo landed on him, crushing his midsection, slamming against his groin.

Her wet arm flopped against his face.

She was crying, sobbing terribly. Her arms reached up to the air, searching for comfort.

Michael was still trying to breathe. A burning pain filled his back.

Slowly he became aware that Jo needed him.

He brought his arms—slightly pinned by her body—around, encircling her. He whispered into her ear.

"It's okay, baby. It's okay. You're fine."

But already he felt angry. How could she do this . . . how could she do such a stupid thing?

He couldn't say anything now.

All he could do was hold her tight, and whisper, over and over into her ears . . .

"Everything's fine, baby. Everything's okay . . ."

While above them, Michael heard the sound of splashing, movement . . .

Disappointment.

By the time Michael led Jo back to the main building she had gone quiet. He still held her close. There would be time to ream her out later. For now, he thought, she needs a father.

Or a mother.

Never was too good at this nurturing thing. Probably part of the problem. What was it Caryn said? I'm too preoccupied with myself to give a damn about anyone else.

"What you don't know about love could fill a library," she said.

He accepted that. So what? A minor character defect. Everything else, though, is in tiptop shape. Yes, sir.

Jo leaned into him, shivering, even though it had to be over 90 degrees. And it was so humid that the air tasted foul. He gave her a reassuring squeeze.

"Daddy, I," she started to say. But he shushed her, the way he remembered doing when she was a toddler and she scraped her knee.

"It's okay, honey . . ."

They were at the main building. And Michael looked up.

Martin was there, at the door, and behind him, in the shadows of the exhibit hall, Alice and Steven looked uncomfortable. At first, Michael thought that they were waiting to see what might have happened to Jo.

"She's okay," he said as he reached them. "She just—"

But he saw their faces. It wasn't Jo they were concerned about. Bad news was written all over them.

"What is it?" he said, stopping.

Martin cleared his throat. "Wally's gone, Michael."

Michael nodded. I should have been there, he thought. Another reason to be mad at Jo. Damn.

"He died five minutes ago."

Michael let his hand slip from Jo's shoulder.

"Okay . . . all right . . . let's take a look at it."

"Is this the bus to Chicago?"

The Greyhound driver, crisp and fresh in his gray paramilitary uniform, looked up. "Yes, it is, sir. If you have any bags just—"

Paul Barron smiled. "No, I don't," he said flatly. "No bags."

Later, there would be time for clothes and things. At least, he thought there would be. Now, he could only follow the commands he heard—felt—through his body. It grew clearer every minute. New York, that's where they want me.

The driver turned away and went back to loading bags into the underbelly of the bus.

And Barron walked past him and on, up into the double-decker bus. It was cool—almost cold—as he went inside. The glare from outside had turned gray, muted by the heavily tinted windows. About half the seats were taken. Some people were chatting. A few turned and looked up at him as he navigated the narrow aisle.

Why a bus? he wondered. Why not fly?

But he knew that it *had* to be like this. There *was* a reason.

I've never taken such a long bus trip, he thought. Not across the country to Chicago, and then another bus to New York.

He looked around for an empty seat, away from any other passengers.

Not that I'm questioning anything. No. Not at all. I'm ready to do whatever has to be done.

Anything.

He sat down.

His heart started beating fast.

He licked his full lips, so dry, he wished he had brought something to drink, something—

Faster still.

His body began to tingle.

He felt warm all over, pleasant. Protected.

And then, just as quickly, cold, frigid. He whimpered.

They were here with him again.

Checking in.

All right, he thought. I'm ready. I'm listening.

Teasingly, a jolt of pleasure—remember pleasure? he thought . . . it had been so long—traveled up from his feet, through his legs, lingering in his groin. He moaned, a small mewling sound lost in the rumble of the bus's idling engine and the grunting of the heavy-duty air conditioner.

Then it moved upward. A different sensation, past sensual pleasure now, calming his heart. His mind was suddenly clear. Cool, as through his open brain was surrounded by a wonderfully icy breeze, taking away all the confusion. Anything is possible, he knew. Anything at all.

The seats, the people, the bus, it all began to disappear. He caught a ghostly image of the driver taking his seat, smiling back at his passengers, shutting the door.

All melting, fading, disappearing.

There was the slightest sensation of movement before that too was gone.

And he waited.

They had much to tell him, to explain.

And now he had nothing but time, to sit here, his eyes closed, and *listen* . . .

"Turkey?"

Michael peeled back the foil wrap of the TV dinner.

"I don't like turkey," Jo said, sitting at the table as if she were a prisoner of war.

Michael took the seat facing her. From the kitchen window he had a view of the Coney Island El, an elevated part of the mammoth New York Transit System that forever seemed on the verge of collapse. And on real clear nights, he could catch a tiny patch of blue. The Atlantic, off nearby Sheepshead Bay.

But now, he sat down and looked at his pouting daughter.

"Well, look, it's turkey or it's turkey. I had no time to shop and turkey's the only thing in the freezer."

She looked away from the steaming foil platter of food that, Michael had to admit, looked completely unappetizing.

"In Mom's building they have a D'Agostino's right there."

"Yeah, I know. And a health club, and racquetball, and a minimall, and glass elevators. But this isn't your mom's place."

Jo looked back at him and with devastating accuracy gave him a look that said, "Tell me something I don't know."

"And I don't care if you want to spend the next week sulking. You did a stupid, dangerous thing today, Jo. You could have been killed. If I hadn't—"

"I want to go home."

The word—"home"—hit Michael like a hammer.

Neither of them touched their meals.

Michael waited. Afraid of what he'd say. Too hurt, for the moment, to say anything.

And then . . .

"You can't go home. Your mother is in Italy."

He noticed a bit of puffiness near Jo's eyes. So damn stubborn.

But when she breaks, it's like a wall crumbling.

"Well, I don't want to stay here."

Michael uncovered the potatoes, a mottled, unappealing-looking side dish. He jabbed his fork into the tiny pasty pie filled with a cherry goop.

"You'll stay here, and you'll stay with me. Wherever I am, that's where you'll be." He skewered a sliver of leathery turkey. "Because you've shown me that I can't trust you."

Now it came. She pushed her chair back sharply, away from the table. She nearly sent it flying, tipping backward. When she blew, she blew. Her anger, her violence, could scare him sometimes.

"And I'll hate every minute of it!" She shouted it. The eyes reddened. Tears—instantaneous, flowing—seemed to gush out of her eyes. "I hate your stupid Aquarium."

"Jo," he said, wishing now he had done something different,

something to avoid this. She was lost to him now. For hours . . . maybe days.

Maybe . . .

He reached out, across the table, trying to pull her back.

But her red blotchy face looked at his hand in horror. "No. I just want to leave!" she cried out.

But he saw something else in her eyes.

A sadness at what she was saying, even as the hurtful words gushed out. And a plea for help, for love.

"Jo," he whispered. She had always been this way. But now, after the divorce, it was much worse.

"Jo," he said again, louder, over her crying.

But she shook her head, and ran away, back to the small guest room, "her room," as he called it, keeping it stocked with her dolls and extra clothes. An illusion of constancy in a kid's world wrecked by two adults who couldn't get their act together.

He stood up, hesitating, thinking he should go after her.

He heard the door to her room slam.

And then Michael sat down again.

The fucking Italian phones, Caryn thought.

"Signore?" she said, hoping to get the operator back on the line. She should have been able to dial the number direct. This was 1991, after all. God, it's the end of the millennium. And you can't place a direct call from a hotel room in Italy to Brooklyn?

Jesus . . .

There was a crackling of static, and a few queer beeps, and then the long-distance operator was back on the line.

"*Grazie*," Caryn said sweetly. She was tired. She had spent the day trying to schedule an interview with the new Italian premier, a jovial-looking Socialist named Itto Ungaro. His press secretary kept reassuring her that "Signore Ungaro will be delighted to do the interview."

And meanwhile, she was eating up her expense budget cooling her heels in the hotel.

The operator came back on the line. With unseemly excitement, he announced that sì, the connection had been made. She waited—more transatlantic clicks and beeps—before hearing the faint sound of a good old American phone ringing.

After three rings, Michael answered. "Hello," she heard him say, sounding almost sleepy. What time was it there?

"Hello, Michael, it's Caryn."

There was a pause. She looked at her watch. It was midnight here . . . seven o'clock there. "How's Italy?" he asked.

"Italy's fine. How's Johanna?"

Another pause, and she squinted, feeling a bit afraid.

"Jo . . . is fine. Sulking a bit, the usual. But otherwise, she's in tiptop shape."

Caryn sighed. "You know how she gets, Michael. You know—"

"Yeah," he cut her off. "I know all that shit. Don't read me a list of suggestions from Psych 101. She's high-strung . . . gifted . . . And—"

She waited, waiting for his harangue to stop. Some things don't change, she thought.

And . . . and she nearly became shark food today, he wanted to say. We almost lost her today, Caryn.

But that would be cruel, Michael thought. Not that he was beyond that. He could imagine her playing around with his visitation privileges. No, sir, on a good day I can be as mean and nasty as the best of them. But Caryn already doubted my inestimable fathering skills enough.

"Can I speak with her?" Caryn said.

"Sure," Michael said.

Sure. There was a part of him that wanted to go on talking with Caryn. God, it would be nice to have *someone* to tell things to, to say, hey, Wally died. The last living *giganteous,* and I'm going to find out why. And you, what did you do today?

Someone to talk to.

They had done that once. Before they started screwing around. They had had it.

Hadn't they?

"I'll get her," he said.

He put the phone down and went back to Jo's room.

He knocked gently and opened the door. Her room was dark and he barely made her out in the bed, in the twisted sheets. Had she fallen asleep, or was she curled up, crying into her mattress?

"Jo," he said quietly.

"What?" she answered, not turning around.

"Mama. On the phone from Italia."

She turned around. Eager. Happy.

Go ahead, kid. Give me another kick.

She hurried past him.

And he wondered what she was going to tell Caryn. There's

nothing like an I-almost-fell-in-the-shark-tank story to get Mom hurrying home.

He stood by the doorway and listened.

"Hi, Mom." A pause. "I'm fine. Real good." Another pause. "Nothing special. Mom, I feed the penguins—every day!—and—"

Michael scratched his chin. Jo and her mother were close. Could she keep a secret from her?

"And I practically run the Petting Pool."

He walked into the kitchen, passing near the phone.

"How's Italy?" she asked brightly. "Uh-huh. Great."

Michael dared running his hand through Jo's hair, all stringy and gnarled from rolling around in the bed. She looked up at him, still smiling.

"No, Mom. I'm having a great time . . . great."

You're a crazy kid, Michael thought, smiling.

Crazy.

Just like your mother . . .

Chapter Five

BY morning, Michael felt that Jo was out of her funk. They didn't talk about what had happened—it just sort of hung over them, unspoken. And as he drove with her over to the Aquarium, down a crowded Ocean Parkway lined with narrow brick two-family homes, then on to Surf Avenue, he told her some things that needed to be done at the Aquarium that day.

"I'd like you to hose down the penguins' rookery," he said, turning right on Surf. Someone was sleeping on the corner of the avenue, a blackish-brown lump sprawled out. A great welcoming sign for Coney Island.

He felt Jo staring at him.

"I thought that I—"

He kept looking ahead. "What happened yesterday is over, Jo. You've learned your lesson and I screamed too much. You're a big help." He looked at her. "Really, you are. Promise me no more shark feeding and you can still have the run of the place."

She grinned.

The best thing he'd seen in days.

"Really?"

"Really."

The broad avenue was deserted. It was a bit too early for the more bizarre denizens to be out and about. There were always a few hours of peace and quiet before the looniness kicked in. He turned into the parking lot. There were two cars there already. Martin was always the first to get to the lab, and Annie was probably giving everybody breakfast.

"Dad," Jo said quietly, serious again. "That stuff I said last night. You know, about you and Mom. Well, I didn't really mean it. I just get mad. Lose my temper."

Michael stopped the car and put on the parking brake.

"I know, pumpkin. It's a family trait."

She nodded, happy again, and followed him up to the blue and white building.

"There," Martin said. He had the giant isopod spread out on a table, lying on its back. Martin held open a small chitinous plate on the animal's underside. "We could never pull these plates back when it was alive and kicking. You can get a real good look now. What do you make of them, Michael?"

Michael leaned closer to the table.

The smell from the albino crustacean made Michael's light breakfast of oat bran and OJ rumble ominously in his stomach. But more than any biliousness, Michael felt disappointed. He had kept Wally alive longer than anyone, longer than Woods Hole, or Scripps, or even IFREMER, the Institut Français de Recherches Pour l'Exploitation des Mers.

He brought his finger near the plate Martin had pulled back. And underneath the plate there were these graying-green things, feathery things. They looked similar to brachia, the comblike gills, found in a lobster. But, he thought, leaning closer, there was no way they could serve the same purpose. No, if anything, they looked more like the tendrils of filter feeders . . . like barnacles . . . or shrimp.

"Very strange."

"Yes," Martin said. "And watch this." He took a metal probe and touched the clump of fibers.

They moved.

Startled, Michael actually took a step backward.

"Whoa. What just happened there?" The fibers seemed to press against the probe, surrounding it.

Martin laughed. "That's the incredible thing, Mike. It's been dead for over twelve hours and there's still some sign of life."

Michael shook his head. "I don't know. It could just be some kind of primitive nerve response, something like rigor mortis. Maybe some of the isopod's fluids are moving around, settling."

Martin touched the fibers again. And this time Michael had no doubt that it was movement, independent movement. The fibers reacted to each small touch of the probe . . . surrounding it.

As if they were examining it.

"Très bizarre." Michael rubbed his chin. "No one's written about this. I don't see how the hell they could have missed it."

Michael looked up to Martin. He was clever, a creative marine biologist. The small Aquarium lab was just a brief stop for Martin, Michael knew.

Martin rubbed his beard.

"The others had all been dead for too long. Half of the *giganteous* died in shipment, most of the others died quickly, killed by low pressure, overoxygenated water . . ."

Michael was half listening. "Give me the probe," he said. Martin handed him the nasty-looking instrument. "Keep the flap pulled open." He brought the probe near to the tip of one of the tendrils. And then he gave it just the faintest touch.

The tendril moved. God, Michael thought. It seemed to seek contact with the probe. "Damn," he said. He pulled the probe away. The tendril wavered a bit—searching—and then went still.

"It's like part of it is still alive," Martin said.

But Michael shook his head.

"No. Not quite." He kept on touching the tendrils. Some of the tendrils moved more quickly than others. He guessed that they were all dying.

"They're not part of the isopod, Martin. Not really. Take a look."

Martin made a nervous laugh, then smiled. "What do you mean?"

Michael rubbed his eyes. He'd want to get a bright light on the area, maybe an overhead magnifying glass. The patch was tiny. It hurt to keep squinting to look at it.

"My guess is that it's a parasitic colony of some kind, a colony of creatures that developed a symbiotic relationship with the isopod. I'd bet that all the deep-sea isopods have these fibers."

Martin bent down for a closer look, almost getting his nose real close to the greenish patch. "Yes . . . you might be right. But then what do they do . . . what's the parasites' purpose . . . and how do they live?"

Now Michael laughed. "Beats the hell out of me."

A small Adelie—a one-year bird—waddled over to Jo and tried to grab the fish right out of her hand.

She held it tight and the bird grunted and squawked, tugging at the fish.

"Oh, you're hungry, huh," she laughed. "Well, go ahead then," she giggled. And the penguin waddled quickly away, carrying its prize to a small cave in the rookery.

I love this, she thought. She shook her head, thinking . . . I can't believe I said those terrible things last night. What if I never came here again? In fact, I'd like to spend more time here, maybe the whole summer.

The morning sun just broke the top of the penguins' rocky mound. It felt hot already, even with a steady breeze blowing off the water. Too bad the water's so yucky that I can't go swimming, she thought. Well, at least I can get wet over at the dolphin pool. They splash around so much, *everyone* gets wet.

"Looks like they're getting to know you . . ."

Jo turned around and saw Annie standing near the gate.

"That one is," Jo said, pointing at the small penguin still chewing on its fish.

"Penguins are fussy birds. They don't accept strangers too easily. You must be a natural."

Jo smiled, pleased at the compliment. When she first met Annie, she felt an instantaneous dislike. Annie was pretty, with long brown curly hair and a body that her Barbie would have envied.

It took Jo a while to figure out why she had that feeling.

But when she saw Annie and her father together it all became clear.

Jo thought that Annie and her father were lovers or something. And she didn't like *that* at all.

Except she soon flashed on the fact that Annie and Steven were—as they say in seventh grade—an "item."

And then she relaxed. Annie was fun. She always showed Jo how to feed the different animals. She treated Jo like a person, not a kid.

Annie was okay.

Even if she did like Steven.

"Well, carry on. The big boys over there want some fish too . . . even if they won't fight you for it."

Annie turned to go away.

"Hey, Annie," Jo said suddenly. The woman stopped.

"Yes?"

Jo paused a moment.

(I like it here, she thought . . . and I want them to like me.)

"You heard what happened yesterday . . . at the shark—"

"Oh, that," Annie said. "Yes . . ." Then the woman's voice went all low and serious. "You gave us all a big scare, Jo."

"I know. I just wanted to tell you that—well, I won't do anything like that again. I mean, I'll do the stuff you've shown me . . . but nothing else . . . not unless I ask first."

Annie smiled at her, bright, brilliant. "Great. Then how about when you've finished here you meet me at the old Aquacade and you can help me feed Moe and Larry."

"The dolphins! Really?"

"Why not?" Annie grinned. "See you over there . . ."

Jo watched her walk away, wearing clunky greenish-brown hip boots.

And when Jo turned around the penguins were stealing all the fish from her bucket.

The bus became more crowded.

And Barron opened his eyes.

It stopped. He heard the driver call out a name over the loudspeakers.

Omaha, the driver said.

Not Chicago, Barron thought, about to close his eyes, go back to listening. Chicago is still far away . . .

(There will be time to think about this later, he thought. To marvel at all this. *So much* that he never understood, even when he served them before, when he helped his followers contact them. It was all so . . .)

He shut his eyes, but the people, noisy, so preoccupied with their things, their bags, their children, their conversations, filled the bus. Someone had a noisy radio.

The bus kept filling.

Barron heard the driver tell the boy—no, a man dressed in tight black pants and a tank top—to lower his radio. Barron read the words on the shirt.

LL Cool J. The tank top had a swirling picture of another black man dressed almost the same way, shooting out a fist . . . punching at the air. Rap on, he said.

The man kept the radio on, but lower now. He prowled down the aisle, looking for a seat. There were more people behind him. He looked over to Barron.

"Yo, man. That seat em-tee?"

Barron looked at the seat, then back at the man. His sound machine, his black box, dangled from one hand.

There's nothing in my mind now, Barron thought. For a second he was scared. They've left me again. They're gone. Not again, he thought. They can't leave me again. No way. No—

"Yo, can you hear? Is that—oh, fuck it!"

The black man crawled spiderlike over Barron.

"Shee-it. Stupid damn . . ." Out of the corner of his eye, Barron saw the man touch a large black knob on top of the box.

The noise, this music, became louder. It was aimed right at

Barron. Thumping and banging. Barron tried to block out the sound, the words. But it was right there, right in front of him.

Then Barron heard a loud whoosh. The doors to the bus closed, sealing in all these people, all this *noise* . . .

And it pulled away.

Barron closed his eyes, waiting, listening . . . but nothing came.

Martin had cut one of the tendrils and put it on a slide. "See," he said to Michael. "There's definitely capillary action."

Michael adjusted the Bausch and Lomb Stereo Microscope and a bright 3-D image filled the eyepiece.

"Yep. Sure is," Michael said. The tendril now looked like a gigantic pipe, like the transatlantic cable, gutted out. Layers of scales lined the outside of the tube, some kind of microscopic armor. And at the top of the opening in the tendril he saw tiny hairs. They were blurry, a bit out of focus. Using the fine focus adjustment, Michael moved the lens a few micrometers.

The hairs ended in small hooks.

"That's incredible," he whispered.

"What?" said Martin, close to his elbow.

"Take a look. At the top. It's like Velcro, you know . . . those small hooks." He gave the microscope over to the young researcher. "Curiouser and curiouser . . ."

"I think," Martin said, "that we'd better get some other people to take a look at these. Could be important . . . could be big."

Yes, it could be.

"A National Geographic Special . . ." Michael joked. "The hidden world of the deep-sea isopod."

"No, I'm serious, Mike. No one has ever—"

The intercom bleeped, loud, amplified, designed to be heard whether he was in the john or working in the lab.

"Real life calls," he said. He walked over to his office.

"Yes."

A call, the latina at the switchboard told him. From Woods Hole.

Ian Cameron. The director. Fund-raiser par excellence, the PR expert who put oceanography on the front pages of the country's newspapers.

The man who was responsible for Michael Cross puttering around in the cramped lab of the New York Aquarium instead of—damn—instead of heading up generously funded research for the Oceanographic Institute.

Dr. Ian Cameron.

Michael picked up the phone.

"Ian . . . how the hell are you?"

It just didn't stop!

This sound, this stupid thumping, even louder as this kid tapped the top of his box, letting his gold ring hit the handle.

"I'm a gonna tell you sumpin' . . . and dis is a fac . . . people will kick you down . . . and step on your back . . . step on your back . . . step on your back!"

Barron looked around for some other seat, but the bus was filled. And he was trapped with this sound and this man.

The man looked at him. A thin black mustache outlined his mouth. He mouthed the words, and banged out the rhythm.

Barron could smell him, the sweat and something sweeter, cloying from his hair. His elbow occupied the whole armrest, jutting onto Barron's side.

Barron waited, blank, lost. Waited for them to come back.

And then they were there.

With him. Inside him.

He smiled. But then he felt his insides twist. He felt the coils of his intestines turn, slowly, tighter.

"Oh . . . no . . ." Barron moaned.

Then he felt his bowels release, sliding over each other, the coils returning to normal.

The sensation moved up.

Then there was pressure on his lungs. They were closing, squeezed. Barron gulped at the air.

"Hey, chill down, man," the man next to him said. Barron turned to him. Barron's eyes were all filmy, all wet from the pain. And there was still more pain. Until Barron was gagging, trying to force some air into his compressed lungs.

"You gonna fokin' barf on me, man?" The man slid away. "You betta not barf on me!"

Then it was gone. And Barron just breathed. In and out, each breath more wonderful than the last. Enough, he begged. That's e—

He felt something around his skull, around his head. Tickling him, just a faint sensation, under his skull. Near my brain.

(Never felt anything there before, he thought.)

It felt like something pressing into the wrinkles of his brain, a finger pushing into the doughy thing. Barron yelped, a loud "ow" that had people looking over at him.

"Are you all right?" a woman said in a loud, clear voice, leaning across the aisle.

He nodded.

(I can't tell them, he thought. No, I can't—another finger pushing into yet another fold in his brain—tell them that this is just—a—demonstration . . .)

"Man, what are you sick, or crazy, or—"

He gagged from the pain, from those invisible fingers worming their way down, pushing the brain material away. He could see it somehow, could see the invisible fingers . . . nails . . . claws . . . probing him.

Just a demonstration.

He gagged again. His stomach heaved. He spit up something onto his lap.

Then it ended.

He almost felt his brain bouncing back.

Good as new.

The bus sound was still there. And the thumping.

And he knew.

(Yes, that was the point of the whole thing.)

He knew he didn't have to put up with it. Not at all.

"Turn that off," he said, touching the man's box.

"Fuck you!" The man's sunglasses slid down his broad, sweat-covered nose. The man touched the knob and made the assault louder.

I don't have to hear this, Barron thought, a small smile appearing on his sweaty face. Not at all.

I only ask once, Barron thought.

That's my new rule.

And what shall it be, he wondered. The lungs, the gut, or—

No. The brain. It would be poetic justice.

Barron looked at him, eager now to practice what he had learned.

He looked at the man's skull, and thought about it.

(That's all. That's all he had to do. *Just think about it* . . . !)

It's my fingers this time. Digging into his brain.

He saw the man's face grimace. He shook his head, as if bothered by a mosquito or a bee. The dark sunglasses went flying onto the floor.

"What the fuck—"

More. Barron reached down and—all in his mind—he gave the lumpy brain, this worthless brain, a nice big squeeze, like sponge.

The man screamed.

Half the bus turned around.

The box clattered to the floor.

"I'm going to shut this 'music' off," Barron said, explaining, grinning now, so happy.

(I've got power again, he thought. *Real power*.)

He reached down and flipped a switch and there was no music.

The same woman who had tried to help him now stood up in the aisle, leaning over Barron.

"Is *he* okay . . . what's wrong with the man?"

And Barron let go.

Here's your brain back, meat head, he thought. Do you get the connection now? I say something . . . and you do it. You got it?

The man rubbed his head. He was crying, a babylike whimpering.

"Oh," Paul Barron said, turning to this nice lady, this nice busybody, and said, "Oh, he'll be fine . . . now."

And the bus rumbled east.

Chapter Six

IT was incredible.

Not just because Cameron had the balls to call him.

The bastard never did have any class.

And if it was my ass hanging five yards out, I'd probably call my worst enemy for help.

Which is pretty much what Cameron had done.

No, what was really incredible was what Cameron told him.

He put down the phone.

"Bad news?" Martin asked him, his owllike face all pinched with concern.

"No . . . well, sort of. Something has come up at Woods Hole . . . something they'd like me to come up and see."

Martin smiled. "Great. Maybe they'd like to make peace."

Michael made a small grin back. He had asked only two questions.

Where is it now, where is the *Achilles*?

And . . . when do you want me there?

Tell no one, Cameron said. And Michael agreed . . . at least until he had a chance to go there and see for himself.

God, what could have happened?

Cameron told Michael that he'd give him a complete briefing when he showed up. But what Cameron did say—and the way his deep, normally steady voice shook when he spoke—told Michael that the director didn't know a hell of a lot about what had happened.

I knew it, Michael thought. I fucking *told* them that something like this could happen.

It had to happen sooner or later.

The Research Vehicle *Achilles* was found dead in the water. It didn't answer radio signals, it didn't respond to computer inquiries, and the fax line was silent. It just sat there, in the Gulf, absolutely dead.

It was only luck, Cameron explained, that the local Coast Guard based in Louisiana hadn't boarded the ship. That was, of course, SOP. Except there was a special directive for the *Achilles*. If ever anything happened to that ship, Woods Hole was to be notified prontissimo.

That was my plan, Michael thought, listening. They used my fucking plan, procedures that most of his overeager peers described as "radical" and "alarmist."

Michael felt Martin watching him, studying him, The guy's brilliant, Michael thought. His sizable brain is working overtime to figure out just what the hell is going on here.

He promised Cameron to keep his mouth shut.

"I've got to leave for Woods Hole . . ." Michael said.

Martin grinned, responding as if it were good news. "When?"

"Now . . . I mean, I have to speak to Jo."

Jo. What am I going to do about her? I can't bring her there. That would just be too crazy.

Then, he had another idea.

"Maybe you could bring along our slide, the parasite we found on Wally," Martin said, interrupting his thoughts. "They'd probably have some ideas—"

Michael shook his head.

Then, realizing how distracted, how lost in the ether, he must seem, he put a hand on Martin's shoulders. "No . . . not this time. But put all this stuff on ice, go on looking at it, type up our observations. When I come back, I'll see that we get it the attention it deserves."

Martin nodded, without, Michael noted, a great deal of confidence. He knows I'm on the outside track of the research world. His future, wherever it may be, isn't here.

Not with me.

Except—funny thing—he thought . . . if what happened on the *Achilles* is what I think happened, well it could mean a rather dramatic reversal of my profession career.

And the careers of everyone else in the field.

"I've got to find Jo," he said, leaving through the back door of the lab.

He hurried outside, the sound of the visitors mixing with the not-so-romantic screeching of dozens of gulls eager to snatch food away from the penguins, and the dolphins, and the sloppy hordes that littered the boardwalk with bits of burger and fries dolloped in red goo.

And he hoped—despite everything—that he was wrong.

Moe, the larger of the two bottle-nosed dolphins, popped up right near the small dock. He squeaked for his food while treading water. His mouth wore a goofy grin.

Jo smiled back at him. "Do you think they ever laugh or anything like that?"

Annie shook her head. Then, staring right at the dolphin's big eyes, she pointed to a hoop and made a clicking noise with her mouth.

"How do you do that!" Jo laughed.

"Practice," Annie said. She made the sound again, and with a big sweeping gesture, she again pointed to the hoop.

Now the dolphin dove under the water.

"You know he'll do it?"

"He knows he won't get his fish unless he does."

"Pretty smart," Jo said.

"And pretty stubborn. They learn fast, but they like to do what *they* want."

Larry, the other dolphin, was just swimming around at the back of the pool.

Jo kept her eyes on the shimmering blue water near the red and yellow hoop suspended over the far end of the pool.

Then, like a rocket, Moe shot out of the water. Its sleek gray back glistened in the sunlight. For a second Jo thought that there was no way the dolphin would have enough speed to get up and through the hoop. It was too high, she thought. But Moe just kept arching upward before flipping around. It went flying through the hoop and landed with a great splash on the other side.

Jo clapped her hands.

"Neat!"

"Now watch this," Annie said.

Moe popped up right next to the training deck.

"You've got to make eye contact. You want the dolphin to know that *you're* rewarding it . . . it's not just fish food flying out of the sky. And I make the sound again . . . like this."

Again Annie made the clicking noise, a lip-smacking sound that seemed more appropriate for getting an old horse to pull a buckboard. She tossed the fish into the air and Moe neatly caught it and vanished under the water.

Then Larry popped up next to the deck.

Jo said, "He knows it's his turn, doesn't he?"

Annie crouched down, close to the smaller dolphin. She patted his bottle-shaped nose, and Larry squeaked even more. "Sure he does. And he's hungry. They'll get more fish at the twelve o'clock show. But they need their early A.M. refresher. Keeps all the patterns fresh . . ." She turned to Jo. "Want to try it?"

Jo screwed up her face, not at all sure she could get the big fish—no, mammal, she corrected herself—to do anything.

"All right," she said quietly.

Annie gestured to her face. Then she whispered, "Click. Go ahead, try to make the sound."

Jo tried to make the sound, but all that came out was a goofy pop that made her laugh.

"No," she giggled, "I can't . . ."

She looked at Larry. He tilted his head—still smiling—waiting and wondering.

"Like this," Annie said. "With your tongue. Against the roof of your mouth."

Annie made the sound quietly, and Jo shrugged and tried again. And this time something like a click escaped.

"I did it!" she said.

"Now point." And Jo made a large gesture, pointing at the hoop.

"Keep clicking . . ." Annie said.

Jo giggled some more. "I don't think he—"

But then Larry disappeared.

He disappeared, she thought. And I made him do it. It was amazing. It was like some magical power, to make such a big animal do something.

And she waited, half expecting that he'd just swim around a bit and then pop up near the deck, begging for a fish.

But there, near the hoop, she saw his dome-head break the water. He screeched loudly, excitedly, as he hurled himself out of the water.

Jo clapped her hands together.

But then there was something wrong.

The air, laced with a cool breeze, went still. She smelled the chlorine, the bucket of fish at her feet. The dry splintery wood.

And Larry seemed to get distracted, his body arced out of the pool, twisted and then—

Annie got to her feet.

"What's—" Jo started to say.

And she watched Larry's tapered body collapse onto the hoop.

Smashing into the circus-colored metal circle. He jerked it down, off its rack, into the water.

Jo heard him cry out. A different sound now. Pained.

"What happened?" Jo said when he disappeared.

Annie shook her head.

"I don't know. Sometimes they miss . . . or they just dive under the hoop. But he just froze, as if—"

The breeze started again, blowing Jo's hair off her sweaty forehead.

"Don't worry about it, sprout, we'll give it another go."

And just then Larry popped up by the deck, still looking happy and excited.

"Okay?" Annie said.

Jo nodded. She started to point at the hoop when she heard her father call her name.

The Chicago bus terminal was filled with all kinds of unpleasant smells.

Barron looked at LL Cool J, sitting quietly beside him.

He was going to just leave him there, to the rest of his noisy, stupid life. But then Barron had another thought. "Jay," as he called him, was big, strong, mean-looking.

Why not start building my flock with him? Barron thought. I have enough money for his bus ticket to New York.

Why the hell not?

And so, he told Jay to follow him, behind him, as he made his way to the crowded Greyhound ticket booths. He noticed people looking at him, staring at this white man—short, a bit pudgy, Barron admitted—being followed by the lanky bad-ass dude.

Sans box.

Right on, bro, Barron grinned.

There was a wait to get to the front of the line.

"Two tickets for New York on the next bus," Barron said when his turn finally came. "For me and my friend."

The ticket agent arched his eyebrows at his companion, at Jay.

"Forty-eight dollars fifty, each," the man said, passing the two tickets to Barron. "It leaves in one hour."

Barron smiled. And asked, "And what time does it get to New York?"

The man looked at a schedule to his side.

"Eight A.M., tomorrow morning."

Barron thought about that for a second, his face confused,

thinking. Is that enough time? He chewed at his lip. An old shaving nick opened. He tasted a tiny drop of blood.

Enough . . . time . . .

It would have to be.

He laughed to himself.

Because they won't wait.

Oh, no.

"Excuse me, sir?" the agent said, hearing Barron laugh.

But Barron shook his head, took the tickets, and walked away.

"There's nothing I can do about it, Jo." Michael had walked with her out to the main courtyard of the Aquarium. Brightly colored bricks led to the different buildings and open-air exhibits. A trash can with a walrus's hungry face stood right next to them.

He looked at her, her face all scrunched up in the bright sun. "Why can't I go?" she whined.

He shook his head, hoping that she'd see his resolve. Annie stood to the side, looking uncomfortable. "I should get back to the pool."

"No," he said gently, but strongly. "Please stay a second." He turned back to Jo and put his hands on her shoulders. "I can't bring you, Jo. I'll be busy. There's been some kind of . . . accident. I can't have you up there, I can't be worrying about you."

She shook his hands off her shoulders and then she grabbed one of his hands with her two, squeezing hard, pleading. "Please, Dad. I've never even seen an Institute."

He grinned. "It isn't that exciting."

"Please!"

He shook his head with what he hoped was unshakable finality.

"So who will stay with me?" she said sullenly.

Michael looked up to Annie. "I was hoping . . . Annie, do you think you could stay in my apartment, with Jo. Just one night . . . maybe two?"

Annie came over and draped an arm around Jo. "Sure. We'll have a ball, huh, sprout? I'll teach you all my dolphin tricks. And wait until you taste my lasagna."

"Thanks," Michael said to her. "If her mother was here, I'd—"

"Don't worry about it. We'll be fine."

Jo wasn't quite ready to give up. "I still want to come."

He ruffled her hair.

"I know you do. Now get back to work. I'll come over and give you a kiss before I leave."

He turned and jogged back to his office.

* * *

Michael tried to reach Caryn, to tell her. He knew how she liked to be informed. Making up for lost mothering time, he always threw in her face.

It took forever to get a connection to Italy, to Caryn's hotel. Michael's pidgin Italian was answered by the hotel's operator launching a barrage that left him whimpering, "Lento . . ."

The operator spoke more slowly.

Michael thought she said something about the Signora Cross not being here now.

But that wasn't what she said at all . . .

Chapter Seven

FUCK him, Caryn thought.

There was a limit to how much she'd let herself get jerked around no matter how important the goddam interview.

And just how important was this?

Prime Minister Ungaro would probably say the same conciliatory crap he'd already said, about building bridges between East and West, and rebuilding Italian trade, while saying absolutely *nada* to irritate the crazies who actually ran the country.

The unions—a new strike every week! And the professional terrorists. The capos and godfathers who dipped their beaks in every honey pot from sunny Capri to Milano.

Besides—she thought at lunch, always eating at the hotel, always waiting for a call from Ungaro's PR *comandante*—I've got enough background, person-on-the-strada reaction to the new government, to write the piece. Toss in a bit of commentary from some U.S. political mavens, and a short history of Itto Ungaro's wondrous rise, and voilà! A piece *The Atlantic Monthly* should be more than happy with.

In fact, she grinned, dipping some stale bread into her blackish coffee, it gave the article a whole different slant. Who is this fabled leader, this new-age generalissimo, that he won't sit down and be grilled by the American press? Doesn't he have the cojones to answer questions about his reputed dalliance with the Red Guard?

She let the bread suck up some of the too-sweet coffee. It kills the taste a bit, she thought. And then—

I don't like being so far away from Jo.

Even if she is with her father.

Maybe . . .

Maybe *because* she's with her father. What if something

happened? What if the absentminded ichthyologist, the oceanographer manqué, let something happen to her?

I want to be there.

With Michael, it was all too possible.

Attentiveness to people's needs—physical, emotional, whatever—just wasn't one of Michael Cross's strong points.

She spied a waiter—they're always so clever at staying hidden—clearing a distant table.

"Signore!" she called, embarrassingly loud. She didn't want to give him the option of pretending he didn't hear. Diners have been known to die and melt into the floor waiting for service in Italia.

He looked up. And—his mistake—he looked over in her direction.

Rather than yell again, Caryn mimed writing out a check. He grinned, his mouthful of teeth the only bright thing in the old hotel's dingy, shadowy dining room.

Yes, she thought. Enough waiting.

She stood up.

Wondering what was the earliest flight to New York she could catch . . .

Michael played with the radio dial, looking for some station that played some music he recognized.

A trip to Cape Cod can be a painful thing, he thought. You have to fight the trucks of the New England Thruway. These monsters, gleaming, with an obscene number of wheels, armored with embossed mud flaps, were the thundering malevolent dragons of the road.

He just loved the way they would roar right up to the back of your car, their grills looking like hungry teeth.

It put a nice pit in one's stomach.

The drivers—tired, juiced up on bennies and who-knew-what—were, according to jukebox legend, the modern cowboys of the road. But Michael saw them more as blacktop outlaws . . . crazy, bronco-busting bullies who'd just as soon chew up a family of four in a Ford Escort than be late hauling their load of Cheez-Doodles to Boston.

The truckers made it clear that it was *their* road.

And occasionally, when some eighteen-wheeler jackknifed and stopped traffic dead for miles in both directions, the other trucks passed solemnly, as if shuffling past the funeral bier of a fallen comrade.

It was a shitty way to travel, Michael thought.

And then there was his car.

His Subaru wagon—three years old and already showing signs of early senility—

Why won't that parking brake light ever go off?

—was an underpowered mouse dodging some big, nasty cats.

And God! The air conditioner was on the fritz too, so that he had to have the window down. He heard the trucks, passing him, blowing their horns, flashing their lights. Honking new-age dinosaurs, screaming, "Get the fuck out of my way!"

Or I'll eat you alive.

It would be a grim couple of hours until he reached Providence, and the route east, to the Cape.

And yet all the noise, the smell of carbon monoxide, the hulking trucks, couldn't stop him from thinking about where he was headed . . . and what it all might mean.

"What are you doing?" Jo said, sliding on top of Annie's desk, crowded with papers, books, and now a brown bag.

"Eating lunch," she laughed. Annie unwrapped her sandwich and held it toward Jo. "Tuna on rye. Want some?"

Jo shook her head. She had the run of the cafeteria, and a chili dog and greasy fries were more of her taste. She watched Annie take a big bite.

"Gonna sit there and watch me eat?" Annie said between chews.

"No . . ." Jo said, slipping off the desk. Her father had only been gone an hour and already she was feeling kind of peculiar. She liked Annie well enough. That wasn't a problem . . .

But she did feel a bit abandoned.

On her own.

(And there was part of her that found that exciting. Not that she'd even go near the shark tank again. No way.)

"You okay?" Annie asked.

"Sure," Jo said, walking around the office. She pretended to stare at a big colorful whale chart, glancing at the names: humpback, blue whale, killer whale . . .

She turned back to Annie.

"What are you going to do later . . . after you eat, I mean?"

Annie gestured at her desk. "I've got some paperwork to do. Food to be ordered, and paid for. That's one of my responsibilities. Why?"

"I don't know. I thought maybe I could help you, with some of the other animals."

"Of course you can." She patted her desk. "After I finish all this junk."

Jo nodded.

And she had a thought then.

I could go anywhere.

I'm sort of on my own.

She thought of the rides, and the games, and—God—the fudge, right outside the Aquarium, right here in Coney Island. And she had a couple of weeks allowance back at the apartment.

Maybe . . .

Maybe nobody would even know that she was gone.

"What are you thinking about?" Annie said. "Miss your dad already?"

Jo nodded.

She came to another chart. Mammals of the Atlantic. And she saw a picture of the bottle-nosed dolphin. She brought her fingers up to it, touched it. And she remembered what had happened just before her father had shown up.

"Annie," she said, turning back to her, "what do you think happened to Larry?"

Annie shrugged. "I don't know. They miss sometimes . . . get distracted."

But Jo shook her head.

"It wasn't like that," she said. "He was up, nearly through the hoop, and then—"

Annie wiped her mouth. "Yeah, I know what you mean. He just froze . . . went rigid."

Jo nodded.

"Well, maybe we'll see how he does at the show. But now," she said, crumpling up her bag, "I've got to get some of this work done." She stood up and came over to Jo. "Can you find something to do?"

Jo nodded. And left Annie's office.

Just before Providence, Michael stopped for gas. And he cast a thoughtful glance at the Big Boy's. What is it, he wondered, about thruway driving that makes the thought of a thick shake and a greasy burger irresistible?

But he didn't want to waste any more time. He stuck another piece of sugarless gum in his mouth (tasting so sweet you knew it had to be bad for you) and contented himself with taking care of his car's needs.

Then, back on the highway, it was only a few minutes until he left the highway and begin the trek east, to Falmouth.

Now traveling became slow. He was freed of the multiwheeled behemoths, but there were lights, traffic circles, two-lane bridges. Over to Fall River, then to New Bedford, where the first telltale signs of the land of the *turista* began to rear their head. The first Taffy Palace. Bait stores. Fast-food eateries standing cheek to jowl, seductive sirens of indigestion. Hey, sailor, want some heartburn?

He passed Basket World, an establishment where wicker had run mad. And the farther he traveled along Route 195 to Falmouth—all but impassable on weekends—the more he remembered.

About his days on the Cape.

At Woods Hole.

He had left Berkeley's Marine Biology Department, where he ran three sections of undergraduates through their hoops, to go to the Scripps Oceanographic Institute. That was five years working on microorganisms that nobody had seen or classified before. He wrote a series of monographs—well received by the oceanographic community, and a feature in the UK's *Science,* the one magazine, bar none, that every natural scientist wanted to be published in.

Things were looking good. And when the deep-sea vents were discovered, and the bizarre creatures found there, he knew that's where his future lay.

Or so he thought.

(He was at a traffic circle. The New England Creamery, an ice-cream parlor of the highest order, looking neat and properly New Englandish, was to his left. Temptation begone, he thought. And once again he went on.)

He applied to Woods Hole for a staff research position, working on the ecosystem of the hydrothermal vents. And he got the job.

Though ecosystem proved to be the wrong word.

How could you call it an ecosystem?

When you have animals living in a completely toxic, alien terrain?

When they live in bizarre parasitic relationships that defy explanation? Who's the parasite, everyone wanted to know, looking at the exploded bodies of the *Riftia* worms. Who the hell calls the shots?

And how do they reproduce . . . or move . . . or—

And that's when he got his idea.

They were about two years into the project—

(Route 195 suddenly hooked into 495, and suddenly there was much more traffic, the Boston crowd, the stream of people heading to the claw-shaped vacationland called the Cape. Provincetown had lost some of its allure in the plague years of the eighties. But the Cape was still considered a primo place to frolic. Michael always thought that the water was too damn cold.)

It was just an idea he had, but the more he thought about it—and there were nights that he couldn't sleep, couldn't fucking sleep thinking about it—he felt, *he knew,* he was right.

Woods Hole had just scratched the surface of the deep-sea animals, the chemosynthesizers that weren't tied into the photosynthetic food chain. Every expedition went deeper, farther, finding dozens of new creatures. Weird crabs, enormous albino anemones, and everywhere worms.

He wrote up a report.

The hydrothermal vents represent another planet, he said, in language that even the laymen on the Woods Hole board would understand. As new life forms are discovered that becomes clear and obvious. It's a toxic world, an alien world.

And yet—

And yet we keep bringing the creatures topside—albeit dead—with no regard for any precautions whatsoever.

The potential for danger was immense.

Just as you'd quarantine any life form found in space, to study it extensively in isolation, so all creatures from the vents should be treated the same way. All this collecting mayhem, this dragging the worms up, laying them out on the deck for photographs as though reeled in by big-time game fishermen, is foolish.

Perhaps, deadly.

Who knows, Michael argued, picturing the possibilities, who knows what impact the strange bacteria living inside the rift creatures could have on our fragile ecology. We already know they live in colonies, taking over the host creature, producing food from the sulfuric hydrides, a goddam poison.

What else could be hidden down there?

(He was at the bridge to Falmouth, the sun still high in the sky, but he began catching the evening rush hour, businessmen hoping to hurry home, start up the old Evinrude, and go trolling for blues. Cars inched forward, and traffic crawled. After he was across the bridge, he saw the sign for Route 28. He made the sharp right, down to the heel of the claw-finger. Woods Hole was about forty-five minutes away.)

And what else don't we know about these animals? he asked. Until we know, there should be strict quarantine procedures imposed on all future expeditions.

There were meetings. Lots of them. With the Woods Hole director, Cameron, and the research staff. Cameron was immediately hostile to Michael's warnings. It didn't read well in the newsletter. When nothing happened, Michael asked to meet with the board, going over the head of his boss. He knew that he was committing professional suicide.

He brought slides, showing that the bacteria were *still alive* inside the dead creatures. The hosts had been killed by the incredible change in pressure.

But the bacteria lived.

And no, he said, in answer to some old woman with thick glasses. No, nothing dangerous, nothing opportunistic, has shown up yet.

But if it did, it would be too late already, it would—

Then his time was up. There was business to be discussed. You understand, the board president said. Fund-raising. Very important. They had to talk about the TV Special about Woods Hole, about the China Sea discoveries . . .

Important things.

Michael gathered his papers together, turned off the slide projector.

He walked out.

But he didn't go home.

He went to his girlfriend's apartment.

(For one of the last times. Caryn had already figured things out. Perhaps, she had already retaliated. Sometimes Jo was alone with the nanny—a nice woman, no spring chicken, who was born on Martha's Vineyard. While both of us were screwing around. Nice . . .)

The next day, hung over and feeling like shit, Michael was called into the director's office. Cameron had a serious expression on his tanned face. His balding skull reflected the glare of the fluorescent light.

There were to be some staffing changes, Cameron said solemnly. The Institute was moving in different directions, expanding its education department, getting more involved with educational TV . . . more field research, less lab work.

There would have to be some changes, he smiled.

I'm afraid—

But he didn't have to say any more.

"I understand," Michael said tiredly, feeling almost foolish, the boy who cried wolf.

How unscientific.

"I am sorry," the director said. "Of course, you'll get the finest references (a bit of a threat there), and a month's severance. And in the future"—he grinned—"well, who knows? Perhaps we'll see you back here."

And as Michael hooked his way southeast now, past North and West Falmouth, with their understated motels (VACANCY! HBO! AC!), and gabled inns with sun-bleached signs, he thought . . .

I'm finally coming back.

Because Ian Cameron, the schmuck who fired me, the successful director of the Institute, is absolutely scared shitless . . .

Chapter Eight

ANNIE locked the staff door to the Aquarium.

"How does the guard get out?" Jo asked, standing at her elbow.

The blue and white building was bathed in a golden light, not as hot as before, cooled by the breezes blowing off the ocean.

Annie laughed. "He's got a special key, sprout."

Jo nodded, and looked around. Behind her she saw a subway screech to a stop at the elevated station. Green, crimson, and blackish-yellow letters, smudged and ugly, filled the cars. People pressed into the cars, loaded down with ice chests, and straw bags, and—everywhere—big radios.

The Aquarium parking lot was nearly empty. The lot attendant had gone for the day.

Then Jo saw some people, standing off to the side, near the fence, in the shadow of a sickly looking elm tree.

Jo looked at them for a minute, thinking they'd look away, maybe they'd hurry to catch the train, or they'd pile in their car.

But they stood there. Three people. Men, wearing dark clothes, laughing in the shadows. One of them passed a bag around. They drank from it. She heard them talking loudly, laughing, pointing at them

"There," Annie said. "Everyone's locked up for the night. Let's—"

Jo felt Annie catch herself, seeing them too.

"C'mon, sprout," she said now, quietly, "let's get some lasagna stuff."

She started off toward her car, a small gray Toyota.

Which, Jo knew, was right over there, right next to the fence, and the tree, and the men, laughing, looking—

Jo didn't move. "Maybe we should wait. Until they go, I mean. Maybe—"

The subway pulled away.

The Cyclone roller coaster went clickety-clacking up the great hill, struggling to pull its line of cars up, up, until it just let them go, slowly gliding around the track, slowly, until—

Annie stopped, looked at Jo.

The sun was behind her. Jo couldn't see her face, couldn't see whether she was worried. "It's okay. We'll just go, get in the car. Not to worry, Jo."

But Jo heard it in her voice. The way it caught, trying to sound unconcerned . . .

Brave.

Jo nodded.

And went beside Annie. And they walked over to the car.

(All the time the voices grew louder, the laughing coming right at them, the words—Spanish words—strange and dangerous.)

"We'll get some lasagna and cheese and sauce, and let's not forget the bread. Does your dad have—"

Then, when they were only steps away from the car, one of the men took a step away from the group, closer to the gray car. He let his hand touch the hood of Annie's Toyota.

One of his friends said something to him in Spanish.

The man touching the car laughed. He took a swig from a bottle in the brown bag.

Jo reached out and grabbed Annie's hand. She never felt this scared in New York at her mother's apartment. Never. There were doormen there. And special doors that opened when you walked up to them. And cameras.

Annie gave her hand a squeeze.

The man took some more steps, his hand sliding along the hood, closer now to the door.

"Hey," the man said. "Where are you two nice ladies going?"

"Don't say anything . . ." Annie whispered.

Jo saw her digging her keys out of her jeans.

The man was right by the driver's door. "My friends were thinking, y'know, that—"

He started laughing, doubling over. Some of the stuff in his bottle tipped out, onto the ground. He screamed out, laughing.

Annie fit the key into the lock. Jo looked around. There should be a policeman here, she thought. She looked all around. But the beach had emptied and now Surf Avenue was filled with the great gunning sound of cars roaring up the block, loud, crazed sounds from big rust-eaten cars that hung low to the ground.

Annie missed getting the key in.

The man's hand fondled the mirror.

"How about you and your little friend coming to party—" More laughter.

(And one of the other men now started to come close to the car. And then the third.)

Annie got the key in.

The button popped up.

Jo looked at Annie. She was staring right at the man.

"Hey, c'mon. Whad'ya say?"

He turned to his friends, right there behind him. More Spanish.

Annie grabbed the handle and quickly jerked the door open.

"Get in!" she hissed to Jo.

Jo was frozen for a second. Watching it, like it was some terrible movie.

The roller coaster rumbled down the hill, loud, covering all the sounds, all the screaming.

Any sound that anyone would make.

Jo crawled into the car.

She turned to look over her shoulder.

The man had grabbed Annie's wrist. And another hand was at Annie's shoulder. Then lower, to her front. Touching her breast through her khaki shirt. He turned to his friends, saying something, laughing.

Please, Jo thought, get in now. Hurry. Before it's too late . . .

And then, when he turned, Annie pulled away, jumped in and slammed the door behind her.

"Hey," Jo heard the man say, his face irritated, his eyes crisscrossed with a web of red veins. "Hey, bitch—"

Annie popped down the lock.

She put the key in the car. One of the men came around to Jo's door.

"Is it locked?" Annie hissed to Jo. She started the car and fiddled with the gears.

Jo spun around. She saw a hand reaching for her doorknob.

"Hey!" the man called, banging on the car.

Jo pushed the button down. The car's engine started.

They were banging on the hood, louder, hitting it with the bottom of their bottles, laughing, then angry.

"Hold on," Annie said.

And she made the car back up, violently, like a rocket shooting backward.

The men stood there for a moment. Behind them, Jo saw the roller coaster beginning another climb.

Annie put the car into forward and peeled out—just like in the cop shows, Jo thought—to the exit. Jo looked over her shoulder, expecting to see the crazy men chasing her, running after them.

But they just stood there, laughing, watching them leave.

And Jo took a breath.

"Sorry about that . . ." Annie said. "It's a creepy neighborhood when it gets near night. The crazies come out."

Jo nodded, still feeling her heart thumping away inside her.

But by the next day, she would have forgotten the men, their crazy laughter, and—as she always did—her terrible fear.

The best flight—the *only* flight with seats—was the transatlantic equivalent of a red eye. Even though it was near midnight, the Rome airport was alive, with everything from sleek-looking men in sunglasses rakishly smoking cigarettes, to oversized women surrounded by blackish-tan children scurrying around like gnats.

Security was excessive, fascistic. Everywhere there were crisp *polizia* armed with machine guns, and hungry-looking German shepherds, and metal detectors that seemed to beep every time someone walked through them.

And Caryn was glad of it.

As she checked her TWA flight, she had to ignore the clumsy advances of men who—unlikely as it might seem—thought she'd drop her plans and run off for a quick fuck, Italiano style. She was tall, in good shape, and, fatal lure for the Italianos, she had blond hair. She was every swarthy gigolo's dream.

But her plane wasn't delayed. It boarded quickly and she settled into her seat on the DC-10—not her favorite aircraft, with its famed cargo door that tended to implode. She grabbed a pillow and a blanket from the luggage rack and then—when a stew came by—she asked not to be disturbed.

Not for the complimentary cocktail.

Not for the dinner.

And certainly not for earphones for today's movie, a limp-sounding comedy about babies and marriage, with a gaggle of ex-TV stars.

All I want to do is sleep.

Caryn let herself nod off as the plane rumbled down the runway.

The first thing Michael wondered, as he passed Little Harbor and drove straight toward the setting sun and the Woods Hole campus, was where the hell is the ship?

Where is the *Achilles*?

Out in Little Harbor and out beyond the Woods Hole complex, in the bay itself, there were boats everywhere. Small fishing boats, day sailors, and sleek yachts. It was a clear, gusty day, with a brilliant sunset and strong winds.

A summer sailor's dream.

But where was the research ship?

He passed one parking lot for visitors—there'd be spaces closer to Cameron's office in Bigelow Lab. He took a quick look at Crowell House, then Challenger House, buildings that brought memories of exciting summers when Woods Hole was the place to be and he was part of it.

He passed Iselin Lab. Some young men and women were outside, talking, enjoying the sunset. They could be back from the China Sea expedition, he thought. Even Michael watched that one on PBS—live broadcasts from the deepest recorded depths of the ocean. Incredible scenes—courtesy of the ROV Jason—of the greatest abyssal canyon in the world. Enough geological information to fuel ten, twenty years of research for hordes of scientists.

Michael looked ahead.

And he saw how incredibly tight he was holding the steering wheel.

Dreams die hard, he thought.

He saw Bigelow Lab.

Looking more like a Harvard dorm in Cambridge. There were plenty of spaces in front of the building.

And with no great enthusiasm, Michael got out of the car and ran up the stone steps to meet Cameron.

"Mike! How the hell are you? It's been a while."

Michael nodded. Despite requests to the contrary, Cameron always persisted in calling him Mike. *Big Mike,* he'd joke. *Our A#1 microorg man. Big Mike with a big future.*

Until I opened my big mouth, he thought.

Cameron looked good, nice and tan—not too much, just a burnished healthy glow. His sparse gray hair was combed neatly away from his mostly bald head—a sore point with vain Cameron. Outdoors, Cameron always wore a hat that was labeled "WHOI Director."

Cameron didn't get up.

"I'm fine, Ian. Couldn't be better."

"Business booming at the old Aquarium?"

Michael nodded. He couldn't stomach much of this old-buddy stuff.

"Can we cut the bullshit, Ian. You sounded scared shitless on the phone, now you're acting as if I were just in the neighborhood and decided to drop in."

He saw Cameron's face fall. The smile, the warmth, disappeared, to be replaced by an expression that gave Michael a clue as to what was really going on.

He's still scared. And he's worried about what I might be able to do to him. He's making nice with the ex-employee . . . before charges are filed, before the investigation and the hearings.

"Still the same Mike, eh?"

"I'm here. So now . . . where the hell is your ship . . . and what happened to it?"

Cameron cleared his throat. He looked over his shoulder. Half the sun had vanished, shimmering, into Vineyard Sound. It was brilliant orange, beautiful beyond words. But when Cameron's face turned back, he looked pale, drained.

"Sit down, Mike. I'll tell you everything we know. And what I think we have to do . . ."

And like Tonto, looking at the Lone Ranger surrounded by marauding Indians, Michael wanted to say . . . "We"? What do you mean "we," kimosabe?

But he just sat down quietly on the hardwood chair.

And watched the sun disappear.

As he listened to Cameron's story . . .

Chapter Nine

HE watched Cameron rub his chin, fidget, all the time fighting the obvious conclusions.

You screwed up, Michael wanted to say. Because you didn't listen to me.

Asshole.

Michael knew that's why he was here. And he knew where this was all heading.

But for now, he just listened . . .

"Simonsen's initial radio reports—I've had them transcribed," the director said, sliding a manila folder over to Michael—"only mention the damaged ROV. I was—well, you know me—I was pretty pissed off about the damaged ROV."

Michael nodded. Money was Cameron's *numero uno* concern. That, and his own personal celebrity.

"I was glad they grabbed a sample of a new worm, this animal they found living in burrows. It wasn't a total loss. But then—the next day—"

Michael flipped open the folder and rifled through the reports. Each one was dated, and labeled . . .

Field Expedition. R/V Achilles. Dr. John Simonsen, Project Director.

As he listened to Cameron, he went through the pages. He came to a report, smaller than the others. There was one paragraph. It said that two of the crew—interns—had vanished.

"Gone . . ." Cameron said, echoing Michael's openmouthed stare. "I got that fax late in the day—I wasn't in the office."

Another screw-up, Michael thought. Where were the procedures, the fucking emergency procedures? Michael wanted to scream.

"Next morning I radioed back for more information." Cameron made a hollow laugh. "You know interns. Boys fucking girls, boys fucking boys. Hell, they could have fallen asleep in the hold."

Michael flipped to the next page.

Two sentences. And the heading. Different this time. It was sent by a Dr. J. North.

"The ROV operator," Cameron said. "A woman."

Michael read the document. One sentence about more people missing . . . Simonsen, others. And a strange sickness. People just keeling over. An SOS was being sent to the Louisiana Coast Guard, the Navy.

"I got that one quickly . . ." Cameron said. "And I acted on it." Michael looked for another sheet, but that was it. The end. "I was here when it came in . . . and I, er, remembered what you had said."

Damn straight you did, Michael thought.

"Of course, I tried to contact the ship personally. But there was no answer. I used the Oceanographic Division of the Office of Naval Research to countermand the normal SOS."

"Good thinking," Michael said.

"It's all part of your procedures . . . but I guess you know that. The ship was dead in the water, but the ONR were able to stop anyone from boarding her . . . which is, of course, what would have happened. I worked with an Admiral Torrance, he's a—"

"I know him," Michael said. Torrance was a crusty, no-nonsense career Navy man who ran the Navy's Research Office.

"We arranged to have the ship towed here . . . to be anchored out there, in the Sound." Cameron pointed. "Well away from the coast, but close enough so that we can go on board—in protective gear, of course—and study it." Cameron's face seemed to crinkle in disgust. "Find out what the hell happened out there."

"Nice story. So why am I here?"

Now Cameron snapped at Michael. "Don't be cute, Cross. You *damn* well know why you're here." Michael watched the lanky director stand up. "And it's not because there's any love lost between you and me." The director looked right at him, his eyes glowing. "It's your fucking scenario, isn't it? It's what you were always bellyaching about, your 'new planet' theory."

Cameron looked at him, hateful. "The whole nightmare . . . It was *your* baby. And as soon as I notified the Board, they *insisted* on having you in on the investigation. Outside of you, the ONR, and the Marine Environment Department of the Coast Guard, there is a complete security lid on the whole 'event.'"

"And what if I say no? What if I say go solve your own problems?"

Cameron licked his lips. "I don't know. I guess there are other—"

"Forget it," Michael interrupted. Just curious, shithead. It was great to watch Cameron squirm. "Are there videos, computer logs—?"

Cameron nodded. "Yes. Everything." He paused, uncomfortably. "It's all still on the ship though. The *Achilles* wasn't equipped with a satellite linkup."

Michael shook his head. Another one of his recommendations ignored.

"And when does the ship get here?"

"It's being towed up . . . by a Navy destroyer. Very fast." Cameron looked at his watch. "It should anchor in Vineyard Sound sometime around four . . . maybe five . . . this morning."

"And when do you want to go on board?"

Cameron looked sick, sheepish.

Scared.

"Dawn," he said, almost whispering . . .

For a second his brain was clear.

After so much whispering and pictures and promises in his mind, the silence, the blankness, disturbed Paul Barron. He shifted in his seat.

There was a pause.

And he looked at the man next to him.

He *smelled* the man next to him. The pungent smell of stale sweat. Beyond healthy, and well into a foul ripeness.

Barron could taste it. And something else. Lanolin? Baby oil? Something on the skin, something sweet.

He looked at this man he now called Jay.

He sat *so peacefully* now. See, Barron thought. You don't need all that crazy music, not at all. You're just fine, sitting there. Nice and quiet. Peaceful. Just like—and Barron turned around to see whether the old lady was still behind him.

She was.

Yes, you're sitting just as nicely as that sweet old lady back there.

Barron looked past Jay, out the window. It was black outside. He could be under the sea, for all the blackness. Occasionally there were lights from a car or truck coming from the other direction. Or they'd be passed. Other than that, it was dark . . . and quiet.

He looked up at Jay's face. And he saw something. A glob of drool had gathered in the corner of his mouth. It made him look even more idiotic.

Do I have to tell you everything? Barron wondered.

Lick, stupid, he thought.

Lick yourself clean . . .

Then, like the tongue of an anteater, but slower, lumbering, Jay's tongue snaked out of his mouth—

(Is he hungry? Barron wondered. Does he need to piss? And do I give a shit?)

The tongue snaked out and dabbed at the drool, sucking it back into his mouth.

Barron watched, fascinated. Jay was like a great robot, no, an android . . . almost human.

Jay's tongue went back into its mouth cave, snaillike, and then came out, clear and clean, ready to wipe his mouth.

I've got to tell you everything, *everything* . . .

Barron made a small private laugh.

The bus hit a bump, and it jostled Barron. He felt tired then, as if maybe he'd like to close his eyes . . . sleep.

He scrunched his head against the back of his chair.

He closed his eyes.

But then—like a TV signal coming back after the storm—they were there. *They were with him again.*

And inside his mind, he listened, and watched, so attentively.

Because he knew—so obvious—it wouldn't be a good idea to get them mad.

That would be a very bad idea.

Jo pulled the sheet tight to her neck. She could still taste Annie's lasagna on her lips.

They had fun making the dinner, talking about the Aquarium, talking about Steven . . . her boyfriend . . . and the boys Jo knew in school . . . the ones she liked, and the ones she couldn't stand.

They ate the dinner late, and after they cleaned up, Annie was yawning, ready to fall asleep even before Jo. It wasn't hot, so Jo had her bedroom windows open.

After she shut the bedside lamp off, she heard the distant sounds of Coney Island, faint rattles from Astroland, the Cyclone coaster . . . the sound of cars, screeching away, voices . . .

the subway—another kind of roller coaster—barreling right past their apartment.

She thought of the next day. The money she had stuffed in her backpack.

And what she was going to do with it.

It would be fun, she thought.

And she fell asleep.

She was at the Dolphin Pool.

She saw it so clearly, even though she knew it was just a dream. Everything was so bright, so sparkling. The water shimmered, magical and deep. The people in the stands looked so colorful, dressed in crazy summer outfits. They were all smiling. They all had sunglasses on.

"Go on, Jo," Annie said.

And Jo looked around. She was alone on the training dock. All by herself.

"Go on," Annie said again, gently.

I'm doing the show, Jo thought. All by myself. She smiled at the thought.

Knowing, all the time, it's just a dream.

She saw her father looking at her, so proud. And there, next to him, Mom. They were together, side by side, as if they never had—

Just a dream, she reminded herself, turning back to the glistening pool.

And there, in front of her, were waiting the two dolphins. Big Moe, and the smaller, younger Larry. She made the clicking sound.

(—and in the distance a car without a muffler roared past the apartment building. She turned in the bed, twisting the sheets.)

She took a ball and threw it into the center of the pool. It landed perfectly, right in the center, bobbing up and down, its red and green stripes so wonderful and bright. Moe popped up right under it. Then the audience applauded. And Moe tossed the ball deftly back to her, spraying her with water.

And she caught it.

"Great, Jo," her father said.

"Wonderful, Jo," her mom whispered.

"Atta girl, sprout," Annie cheered.

But then Annie took a step close to her, away from the stands, her parents, out to the dock, at her elbow.

"Now do the hoop trick. Go on. Make Larry do the hoop."

Jo was still smiling, but when she looked out in the pool, there was no Larry. And the water had lost its luster. It had turned dark, murky. Overhead, a big gray cloud covered the sun. She looked over her shoulder.

The people didn't look so happy anymore. Even their clothes looked different.

Her mother and father weren't side by side anymore.

"Go on, Jo. *Do the routine*," Annie said.

(And she knew that something had happened, that her dream had changed. It was different now . . . it was, yes, a nightmare. I should end this now. Think about something else.)

But there were noises from the crowd. An angry stirring. They started yelling things at her. Her father wore a scowl on his face.

"Do it," Annie ordered.

Jo turned to the water. She made the clicking sounds with her mouth, sounding so dry, and hollow. And Larry popped up. Jo pointed to the hoop.

It grew darker.

Almost like night.

A breeze, cool, than cooler, blew in from the ocean, swirling her hair in front of her face. She clicked and pointed.

And Larry dove under the water.

He disappeared.

Everyone waited.

Watching the hoop, watching over there. It was darker still. Colder.

Jo licked her lips.

When the dolphin flew up in front of her—right next to her!—a great gray blur, rising out of the water right beside her.

She screamed, backed away. And still Larry was climbing up, the water sliding off his body, his marble eyes locked on her. She was shivering, cold, and now wet from the spray.

And Larry turned, twisting in the air awkwardly, like he did before. He fell at her feet, landing with a terrible thud that tipped the dock. She tumbled forward, onto the dolphin, onto his fat, slimy body. Her hands slid into the water.

(No sharks in the pool, she told herself. She looked up quickly, looking at the water. Worried. In a dream, anything is possible.)

Anything.

She started to pull back from the edge of the water, over the dolphin.

She looked to the left, at the dolphin's head.

One big marble eye watched Jo. He looked pained, angry. She froze for a second, looking at the intelligent eye.

Then the body of the dolphin began to ripple under her. It was a tiny, tickling sensation. Then stronger, a great ripple, rumbling beneath her. She tried to push away from the animal, but her hands kept slipping on his slimy skin.

(I don't want to see this, I don't want to see this, I don't want to—)

She pushed against the gray-white belly. And just then the filmy skin started to peel away, like shiny wrapping paper.

The dolphin screamed out, a horrid, ear-piercing sound unlike anything she'd ever heard.

Now the skin started to bubble and pop. The crowd groaned behind her.

"Daddy!" she screamed. "Mom!"

The dolphin's eye rolled in his head, rolled in agony.

As the body split open.

And all these things, these tiny, twisty things, started to bubble out, onto the deck, onto her hands, touching her bare legs.

She screamed.

She heard herself moan. And take a gulp of air.

Outside, someone pressed down on their car horn and held it forever.

She waited, covered in sweat. Annie must have heard me, she thought. She'll come in here. Ask me what happened. What's wrong.

She waited.

But the apartment was quiet. The small digital clock on the desk read 12:30. Then, 12:31.

I must have only been asleep for a while, she thought.

And now I'll have to go back to sleep.

She shook her head.

But not right away.

She turned on the lamp near her bed and picked up the book she had let slip to the floor.

And she hoped a couple of chapters of the latest Babysitter's Club adventure would chase the stupid nightmare away.

Just a stupid old nightmare, she thought.

Trying to convince herself.

At Kennedy Airport, TWA had its own terminal and its own customs.

That's why I fly them, Caryn thought.

But even TWA's speedy customs were dragging. Drugs and terrorism had neatly tied up international air travel.

Just ahead of her, a young mother and father were trying to cope with three sleepy, growly children, leaning into them, begging to be picked up when their parents were already overloaded with bags.

Three kids, Caryn thought. It looked overwhelming . . . debilitating.

There was a time she wanted lots of kids. She and Michael would fill some seaside mansion with a bunch of kids. He'd work at an ocean lab while she wrote. An absolutely perfect au pair—not too pretty, hah-hah—would cook the meals, do the shopping, and pick up after all the kids.

In the afternoon she'd stop working and take a walk with the kids, holding their hands on the beach.

Life was going to be perfect, wonderful.

Amazing, she thought, how we buy into illusions.

The mother in front of her—mid-twenties, going on fifty—finally relented and picked up the littlest, a runny-nosed, bleary-eyed two-year-old who held a bit of yellow cloth up to his cheek.

"There, there," the mother whispered, as if she had the patience of the universe. "That's better, isn't it?"

Such patience . . . Caryn marveled. Maybe that was my downfall.

She looked at her watch. It was after one A.M. New York time.

I won't get to my apartment until three . . . if I'm lucky.

I'll get some sleep . . . and go see Jo tomorrow. Let her know I'm back.

Just to check, she thought.

A surprise visit.

And it wouldn't hurt to see Michael again, she thought.

To talk with him.

The customs line inched forward . . .

The room Cameron assigned him in Challenger House was spartan, just a bed, a small desk, a three-drawer dresser and mirror. The room was heavy with the smell of cheap pine and stagnant air.

Michael lay on the bed, with the windows now open, letting the breeze blow through the small room, cleansing it.

It had been in a room like this that he first cheated on Caryn.

The smell, the look, the exciting tawdriness of it all so fresh in his mind, in his senses, as if it had happened yesterday.

The lights were off now. He wanted to sleep. Get plenty of rest for tomorrow.

The girl had been a bright lab assistant. Pretty enough, he supposed. Slender. All of twenty-four.

He didn't think much about it, or her, for that matter. He just let it happen. And again, the next time. No big deal, he thought.

Until, somehow, it was all over. A marriage down the tubes.

He turned on his side. And he could see the harbor, the Eel Pond, and the tiny lights of the ships on the water. Somewhere a buoy bell rang as it rocked drunkenly back and forth.

He squeezed his eyes shut.

Sleep, he told himself. He took some measured breaths. Sleep . . .

He opened his eyes. If I stay like this, he thought, I'll see the *Achilles* being towed into place.

What will it be like on board? he wondered. What the hell will we find?

And as soon as he thought of that, he wished he hadn't. He wished he had just kept that question out of his mind. Because then it was like opening some overstuffed closet. All these crazy ideas and pictures tumbled out.

Would the ship be littered with dead bodies? Would there be signs of a fight . . . maybe the crew went crazy with some deep-sea St. Vitus Dance?

And—if there was no one on deck—where would they find the crew? How far into the ship would they have to go?

And—God!—what would they look like?

The buoy bell rocked dully, somewhere out there, as if calling out to something else, another buoy, a lost ship, lost memories.

And Michael lay there in the darkness and listened . . .

TWO

STOWAWAY

Chapter Ten

HE woke up.

A muted light reflected into the room.

Michael thought he heard the ship. The sound of it being slowly pulled through the water, creating sluggish waves that noisily rocked the moored fishing boats. He thought he heard a great chain, now taut, now loose, jingling-jangling as the naval destroyer gingerly pulled the *Achilles* into the bay.

He sat up, sweaty, his ears straining to hear those sounds again.

But all he heard was a faint tapping at his door.

"Mike . . ." the voice said.

"Yeah . . ." Michael said, digging up an awake voice from somewhere. "Come in."

He rubbed his eyes and looked out the window. The bay was quiet, flat and still save for a small lobster boat, and then an early-morning fishing boat chugging out to the Atlantic.

There was no *Achilles*. No destroyer.

Ian Cameron opened the door.

"Morning. I let you sleep a bit."

Michael sat up, yawned. And he wished Cameron was holding a hot cup of coffee in his hand. Michael saw light out the window. He said: "What happened?"

"They hit some rough weather off Cape May. Summer storms. Made it a bit hard to tow the research ship."

And Michael imagined the *Achilles* rolling in rough water, shrouded in fog, covered by great foamy breakers. He imagined the ship tipping over, sinking.

Dumping whatever was on board right into the water.

"There's coffee over at the lab. Rolls . . . Danish. The Coast Guard people are here. The rest of the team. It's still going to be a while. But whenever you want to walk over, we'll go through the routine . . ."

Michael nodded.

The sun was up. But still it was goddam early. The air—so dry and hot last night—was now damp, cool. He rubbed at the gooseflesh on his bare arms.

Cameron made a little saluting gesture from his WHOI cap, and then left him to get dressed.

Cameron performed the introductions in his easy, affable manner, as though everyone was there for a fund-raising soiree. Michael shook his head at Cameron's *savoir rien*.

(It was rumored that Cameron had negotiated a bottle of Bordeaux from the *Titanic*, some algae-covered relic that he planned on drinking on the hundredth anniversary of the ship's sinking. "Here, have a sip," Michael could imagine him saying to the Institute's big supporters . . . here, it's even chilled.)

"Michael Cross," Cameron said, gesturing to him. Apparently three men were set to go out with them. Two were Coast Guard, dressed in crisp white summer uniforms.

Cameron introduced them, though one of them was known to Michael.

Colonel Alan Barsky was the operating head of the U.S. Coast Guard's Marine Environment and Systems Office. His department was in charge of tracking down and containing over 400 toxic spills and dumps in the nation's waterways and oceans.

He was a short, squat man. He looked appropriately amphibian with his closely cropped brush-cut of the frequent diver. Barsky, Michael knew, pioneered toxic diving techniques and the underwater detective work that put the poison dumpers in jail.

He smiled—none too warmly, Michael thought—and stuck out his hand.

A junior Coast Guard officer stood next to him.

"Lieutenant Dailey is a very experienced diver," Barsky said. "Our best man on toxic dives."

Why all the divers? Michael wondered. Does Cameron know something that he didn't tell me?

As if reading his mind, Cameron explained: "Mike . . . The Coast Guard has pioneered toxic materials' work—both in the water and on the shore. We'll be using their expertise . . . and their suits."

Michael nodded. He saw a fifth person lurking in the back. Where Barsky had a severe brush-cut, this man had a fine coating of peach fuzz on his head, Marine style.

Only he wasn't a Marine.

"And this is Captain Lake. USN, SEALS."

Michael nodded with genuine respect. SEALs were—if you believed the media hype—the crazies of the military. Their military code—covering actions on sea, air, and land—hearkened back to the good old days of the Roman Legions. They were their own special club, clannish, secretive, and absolutely deadly. Forget the few good men of the Marines and the jaunty Green Berets.

The SEALs were the real McCoy.

Captain Lake—J. Lake, it said on his name badge—merely nodded.

Michael felt guilty already. It was like being in an Alistair MacLean novel. Which one of us is the Russian triple agent?

He noticed that Captain Lake had two weapons in front of him . . . a short, snub-nosed type of machine gun that Michael thought he once saw in a movie. It blew holes the size of dinner plates in doors, people, cars. Whatever.

The other was a more normal-looking weapon. Some kind of automatic rifle.

Cameron cleared his throat, aware that Michael was studying the SEAL and his toys. "Captain Lake will provide security for our investigation."

I bet he will, Michael thought. I think I'll hire him for my next cocktail party. He should be able to handle my rowdies. Excuse me, sir, no more drinks or I'll cut your throat.

"Okay then, let's get started." Cameron looked at his watch. "The ship will be here by nine . . . nine-thirty. Gives us some time for a briefing. First," he said, grabbing a chart mounted on cardboard, "why don't we take a look at the ship."

He put the chart on the table. And everyone—even the somber Captain Lake—came close to get a good look at a schematic of the R/V *Achilles* . . .

"You okay?" Annie asked as the staff door opened.

Jo nodded. She was thinking about the money in her pocket and what she was going to do later. It was going to be fun. Her father always kept her close at hand, and he *never* wanted to go down Surf Avenue, down to all the neat places.

Only when he jogged there. Alone.

Not to get fudge, or play the video games, or the bumper cars in Astroland.

She followed Annie inside.

It was going to be neat, Jo thought.

"So what are you going to do?" Annie said, glancing at her, but then quickly looking down at some papers on her cluttered desk.

"Oh, I don't know. Feed the penguins . . . check the Petting Pool . . . come bother you . . ."

She saw that Annie was only half listening.

"Sounds good, sprout." Then she looked up. "So, I'll see you later . . ."

Jo smiled.

She turned to go outside but stopped to get a bucket of herring. Then she walked out to the open-air exhibits. Already some moms and their little kids were running around, dashing excitedly from one place to another. The women looked exhausted . . . overwhelmed, chasing after their kids.

Jo opened the gate to the penguins. They started squawking at her, hungry, knowing that she was bringing food.

And she thought about later, when Coney Island, all the fun things, started to wake up. She smiled, excited about all the neat things she was going to do . . .

"Get up, Jay," Barron said. He was standing in the aisle, while Jay still sat in his seat, zombielike, looking forward.

As if he were on a fucking bus trip to Alpha Centauri.

"Get up, Jay!" Barron said louder.

And Barron felt a hand grab his wrist. A small hand, gnarled, bony. But strong . . . .

The old woman leaned into him and whispered, a loud hiss that was horribly irritating.

"I think it's wonderful," she said, "just wonderful the way you take care of the poor boy . . ."

Barron turned to look at the woman. She was shaking her head, looking at Jay.

What the hell is she talking about? he wondered.

Oh, he thought, flashing on an answer, smiling now.

She thinks he's *retarded*. A big retarded black man. And me—I'm so patient, taking care of him.

"Yes," Barron said, barely suppressing a laugh. "It is wonderful, isn't it?"

Together they watched Jay get up.

He stood up straight, awkwardly, bumping his head into the low luggage compartment above the seats.

"Oops." Barron laughed, turning to the lady.

"Shouldn't you—" she started to say.

Then Jay turned, as if he didn't fit in the seat, as if it were some kind of puzzle, how the hell was he going to get out.

The bus was emptying. There was just Barron, Jay, and this old lady, who watched, the aisle blocked by Barron.

Jay pulled himself out.

Barron watched the old lady staring at him.

Jay had great bug eyes. Empty, blind.

Soulless.

The woman recoiled a bit.

Barron took a step to the front, making room for Jay to get into the aisle.

(He *is* a big one, Barron thought. Real big. Nice strong body. Why, in the good old days I wouldn't have minded—)

The woman looked up at the strangely moving black man. Now her face—so pleasant, so full of the warmth of humanity—was pinched with concern.

Barron turned around and saw the driver step off the bus, hurrying to get everyone's luggage out.

Barron turned to Jay.

"Say good-bye to the nice lady, Jay," Barron said.

The woman shook her head, a small shake.

That's not necessary, it said. No need—

Jay turned to the woman. Opened his mouth.

Wide. Bits of dried spit, all gummy, stuck to his lips. A gluey net covered his mouth. His tongue moved around in his mouth.

"Ha-a-a-lllll, g-g-g-g . . ." he sputtered. His head rolled back and forth on his shoulders. More sounds, guttural nonsense. "Ba-ba-ba—he-he—nnnnnnnn, mmmmm-ga-ga-ga!" He was screaming now. Loud.

The woman was crying as Jay, a crazy windup man, just kept on trying to talk.

Barron enjoyed watching it.

Look at him try to talk, ladies and gents. The amazing zombie boy. Just one thin dime gets you inside the tent.

But please be careful! Watch the spittle flying from his mouth. The management assumes no responsibility for any damage to clothes—

Or sanity.

Barron laughed out loud.

The old woman, the stupid busybody with her old fart heart on her sleeve, was crying. Scared. Terrified.

Barron kept laughing.

"That's just how he says good-bye," Barron said heartily. "We don't got the speaking thing down just yet. Not a pretty sight . . . not a pretty sight at all . . ."

And then he led Jay away.

(He just told him to follow, just thought it, of course. There was no *real* need to talk.)

And Jay shambled behind him.

I'm glad I brought him along, Barron thought. It's not like it was in the old days, when I had hundreds of followers.

But—he thought, hearing the woman crying—it was fun.

And better days were ahead!

After what seemed like a much-too-cursory study of the *Achilles*'s innards, Cameron turned the floor over to Barsky.

The Coast Guard officer opened a heavy canvas duffel bag and pulled out a white suit complete with fetching hood and visor.

"This suit is made of one hundred percent vulcanized rubber, the same material we use on our dry suits in aquatic toxic situations."

Michael looked over at Lake, their resident SEAL. He had one eye on Barsky's demo, while he kept looking out the window.

"It carries the least number of microorganisms back into the disinfectant area. While nylon and all synthetics pick up bacterial contamination quite easily and hold on to it days after being disinfected—suits made of EPDM—vulcanized rubber, like these—are easily and completely disinfected."

Michael nodded. The man sounded so cocksure. When do I tell him that we don't know what kind of contamination—if any—is on the ship?

"Once on the ship, we'll go on tanks." Barsky turned the suit around. "The tanks on the back have enough air for one hour, and we'll bring spares with us. If it proves we don't need them, we can switch to external air. But that—of course—will be your decision, gentlemen," he said, looking at Cameron and Michael.

"The most important thing is that all the connecting patches and seals are completely closed. The hood piece"—he demonstrated by pulling a zipper around the neck of the hood while Lt. Dailey held the suit up—"has twin seals." He opened up the second zipper, and the hood—with a Plexiglas visor—tilted forward. "As do the hands. Under no circumstances should you open a seal until the disinfectant procedures have been completed. A compact microphone/speaker system will let us communicate."

Cameron slid off the desk. He spoke directly to Michael. "We have five suits, one for each of us. After we finish on the *Achilles*"—he looked around now to the others—"no matter what we find, we will disinfect ourselves on the launch. Col. Barsky will handle that."

"Nothing to it," Barsky said. "A betadine scrub, followed by a rinse, can neutralize chemical hazards and all dangerous biological agents."

Michael cleared his throat . . . "All *known* biological agents, Colonel."

"Well, I'm sure," Cameron started to say uneasily, "that anything we find will—"

Michael stood up.

"I don't know what the director has told you guys, but there's the possibility that what's on that ship is from the hydrothermal vents."

The SEAL looked over, his interest piqued.

"And if that's true you can throw out anything you've experienced before. Anything. It's a goddam new planet down there. Terra incognita." Michael reached out and touched the suit Dailey was still holding up. "Very nice suits. But have they ever been on Mars?"

Cameron laughed uneasily. "Good point, Mike. Still if we're careful everything—"

Captain Lake moved away, over to the window.

Michael watched him.

It was like being in a room with a caged lion. He moved slowly, each step precise, ominous. The SEAL looked out the window.

Then he turned to the group.

"The ship's here," he said laconically.

Then Michael watched Lake reach down and pick up his two fucking guns, as if this were a shootout at the O.K. Corral.

And he wondered . . .

What the hell am I doing here?

Chapter Eleven

MICHAEL looked straight ahead. He grabbed the sides of the rocking boat. The water was getting choppy.

Cameron stood up at the front of the flat-bottomed launch, a modern-day Ahab. Chaotic cross currents fought each other, slapping together. The tiny foamy dots seen from the dock transformed into nasty whitecaps way out past Little Harbor.

Cameron turned back to them.

"We'd better suit up," he said.

Michael stood up uneasily, feeling his last donut sloshing around somewhere in his gut, mixing with oversweet coffee and grapefruit juice.

The *Achilles* bobbed in front of them, an unsteady image from the point of view of the bouncing launch. The destroyer *Teddy Roosevelt* had pulled away from the research ship. The big Navy ship had looked crisp and professional from the shore, but now Michael could see that it was old, the gray paint dull, chipped. A tired ship—left over from what war? he wondered.

Reduced to towing.

Michael dug out his heavy white suit and started slipping it on. He got the feet backward at first. He was still fiddling with the arms when Barsky hurried over, all suited up in white.

"Need some help?" he said, his voice crackling through a small internal speaker.

Michael smiled. The Coast Guard diver looked like one of Woody Allen's spermatozoa about to make the big jump into the vaginal void.

"Sure," Michael said.

Then, with practiced hands, Barsky had Michael suited up, pulling the hood down tight, sealing the zippers. Michael breathed the air inside the suit, stale, unhealthy. Barsky fiddled at the back at the tank, and fresh air whooshed in. The Plexiglas visor began to fog up.

Barsky tapped the faceplate.

He said something to Michael. But Michael couldn't hear him.

Then Barsky turned a switch on the side of Michael's hood.

Two small speakers inside the hood came on.

"—will clear up when the suit warms up."

Michael nodded, understanding that the fog in front of him would disappear.

The boat made a sudden lurch to the left and the prow took a big gulp of the still-cold water.

"What about radios?" Michael said.

He found that he was standing stiffly, as if he were trapped in a giant plaster body cast.

Cameron answered him.

Michael was surprised Cameron didn't have his spiffy director's cap perched on his hood.

"We're not going to split up." Michael heard Cameron's voice clearly amplified inside his hood. A bit too clearly, he thought. Is there any volume control on this thing? "We'll stick together. But we will bring two-way radios . . . just in case." Cameron pointed to a small box that obviously contained the walkie-talkies.

Good, Michael thought. It always knocked him out how—in the movies—people always split up. Okay, you go in the dark basement, while I go all by my lonesome to the attic . . . Now, doesn't that sound like a good idea?

He was glad to see that life wasn't going to imitate art.

Dailey—the young lieutenant—was slowing the launch.

The *Achilles* was ahead, so still in the choppy water. Unconcerned by the small swells and troughs that had the launch bobbing around.

They came closer, and the sun was blotted out by the ship.

The side of the research vehicle was black. Dailey started bringing the launch to the back. Michael saw that there was a loading bay near the waterline. The *Achilles* was equipped to hoist a submersible out of the water.

Once they were there, they'd be able to get a rope ladder up to the railing.

Michael watched the ship. So absolutely still.

Dead.

Nobody said anything.

And then—he didn't know why—he turned around and looked

back, past the Nobsko Lighthouse, toward Little Harbor and Woods Hole.

There's something very wrong here, he thought. And what happens when we find out what it is?

She heard sounds coming from outside.

Somewhere beyond the wire fence that sealed off the Aquarium from the rest of Coney Island.

Jo stood there—just outside the main building, a dark cavern filled with the bright tropical fish glowing in the darkness. She held the door open and listened.

It was quiet in the building. There were only a few people, their noses pressed against the tanks. Tapping to get the fish's attention. Why do they always do that? she wondered.

Jo took a breath. She heard sounds.

Clickety-clack. And voices, faint, as if lost, miles away, lost in their fun. And other sounds. A ping from a shooting gallery as a BB smashed into a tin can, making a mechanical squirrel rear up and open its eyes.

She imagined it.

Annie was still in her office doing paperwork. Stephen was cleaning some of the small tanks. And Martin—

He was always bent over his microscope until someone yelled lunch.

Now was the time, she thought.

She wouldn't even be missed for an hour or so.

And Jo shut the door and casually walked past the cafeteria, the outdoor tables with their bright blue umbrellas, then out the turnstile, to the parking lot.

She smiled to herself.

This is fun, she thought.

As she walked, she didn't look back. Someone might stop her. Call her name. And as she got farther and farther away from the building, she started smiling.

As all the attractions of Coney Island awaited her!

Caryn Cross woke up when her phone rang.

"Shit." She moaned into her pillow. Then, "Fuck."

She hated herself for forgetting to turn the damned electronic ringer off.

Bleep. Bleep, it kept shrieking. Then the answering machine kicked in. She waited. When her message was over, she heard the caller.

"Hi, Caryn, It's Tom. Just in New York for some meetings. Thought I'd check in. I'm staying in the Hilton till Friday. Give me a call if you're around."

The machine clicked off, as if gobbling the message.

Tom. One of her post-divorce zipless fucks.

Though she knew that *experience* was less in favor these days. She was careful.

Now, she had a headache. She looked at the answering machine, its red light blinking urgently. Though the curtains in the bedroom were pulled tight, thin cracks of light sliced into the room, blinding and glaring in the gloom.

She pulled a pillow over her head.

But she heard another ringing, inside her head this time.

"Goddam," she moaned. And she knew she wouldn't be able to get back to sleep. She needed an aspirin.

Caryn took the pillow off her head and opened her nightstand drawer. It took two hands to get the child-proof cap off the ibuprofen. The smooth-coated pill didn't taste bitter . . . or effective like aspirin.

What the hell time is it? she wondered.

She looked at the clock radio and its greenish dial: 10:15.

Why did I come back early? she wondered.

Right. *Jo*. I didn't like being away. I was . . . worried.

Or maybe just got tired of waiting for Ungoro.

10:16.

A shower, she thought. Hot coffee. A toasted English muffin. Blueberry preserves.

She rubbed her eyes, hating the phone, hating Tom who wouldn't just disappear, hating the knife-thin slit of light in the room.

I'm up.

I'll go see Jo, she thought.

And with the legs of a drunken sailor, Caryn got out of bed.

"Jesus! Can't you keep it steadier than that, for Christ's sake!"

Cameron's hysterical voice screamed at Dailey. His voice had a weird cartoon quality when heard through the speakers. Shrill and powerless. Twice Dailey had brought the launch flush against the back of the ship, and twice Cameron had missed hooking on the rope ladder, nearly tumbling into the water.

Finally, in a move long overdue, Col. Barsky took the ladder from Cameron and—on Lt. Dailey's next approach, he easily hooked the ladder to the railing. Lake threw Barsky a rope from the front to moor the launch.

And, without waiting, Barsky climbed on board the *Achilles*.

Michael saw Lake grab his weapons and sling them over his shoulder. Can he fire them with these ungainly gloves? Michael wondered. He looked at his own chunky hands.

Dailey killed the engine.

"Go ahead, sir," he said to Michael, gesturing at the ladder.

Michael smiled—an invisible grimace under his hood.

He said: "Thanks."

And he climbed on board.

They were at the rear of the ship. Above them was the gigantic U-shaped hoist that could handle everything from the three-man deep-sea sub, Alvin, to an assortment of ROVs.

The first thing Michael saw when he got on the deck was that the winch hook wasn't empty.

The *Achille*'s ROV, a smaller, less expensive version of Jason, was sitting on the deck, the lifting bail still attached to the hook.

He heard a step behind him.

It was Dailey, now clambering over the rail. He had the two-way radio with him. With Barsky's help, he pulled up a heavy bag filled with spare air tanks.

Michael turned and walked over to the ROV.

Cameron was reaching out to touch an enormous hole on the underside of the ROV. It looked like a gigantic blister that had popped open . . . right near the name of the ROV, in bright orange balloon letters. Lil Shit.

"I don't think you should touch that, Ian. Not until we look around a bit . . ." Michael said.

"Huh?" Cameron said, his hand at the hole already, his fingers touching the puckered, twisted metal.

Michael looked at Lake and Barsky. They both were looking around the deck as if they expected a horde of terrorists to come swarming up from below deck.

Cameron pulled his hand back.

"What the hell did that?" the director asked.

Michael came closer.

His lens was still fogging up a bit. And Michael wondered whether he should be breathing through his nose. Or was he just sweating too much? The suit was hot, uncomfortable.

Michael shook his head. "I don't know. It looks like something exploded inside, like—"

"Something went into it," Lake said.

"Yeah," Michael said, seeing no need to question the SEAL's opinion. "Well, then that's really strange. What did it do? Get hooked up on some coral, or rock or—"

Michael looked around. Barsky had walked away from the group.

Toward the middle of the ship.

"What the hell is that?" Barsky said, pointing.

And Michael looked away from the ROV to see what Barsky was staring at.

First stop was the carousel.

Not that it was such a great ride or anything. But the music was loud and crazy, the mechanical drums and organ thumped out spastic circus music.

And there were the rings to catch.

She bought a ticket from the ride operator. He didn't smile. His face looked permanently sad. Then she picked a wild-eyed horse, the paint fresh, smooth to the touch.

"Easy, boy," she said, patting his flaming nostrils.

She tied the worn leather belt around herself. What's this supposed to do if I slide off? she wondered. Strangle me?

She looked around, eager for the ride to begin.

There were a few other people on. A fat black woman had a tiny, round-faced kid, almost a baby, perched on a horse. She was holding him in place. And there were two teenagers, a boy and a girl riding together, laughing, goofing on the whole experience.

Jo snapped the reins.

The ticket seller now walked over to a great bell. He rang it twice, its clang louder than the thumping calliope.

And the carousel started turning. And her horse began its gentle rising and falling, round and round, faster and faster.

The wind blew her hair back.

Every time she circled past the opening of the carousel's shed, she smelled Coney Island. The hot streets and fresh corn with butter. Sweet smells—cotton candy and fudge. Smoke and exhaust from the old cars that cruised Surf Avenue.

This, she thought, was great.

But then, she looked around.

Where were the rings? The man is supposed to go up to his platform near the back of the carousel and feed the hard metal rings into a holder.

She looked around.

Where was he?

Then she saw him.

On the carousel.

Walking around, with incredible grace. As if he knew just how you walk on a moving carousel. He didn't waver at all as he moved from the mother and her baby . . . to the teenagers . . . and then over to her.

"Ticket," he said.

She handed him her ticket, smiling, happy.

But he took it. Ripped it.

And she felt scared of this man, this thin, drawn man who controlled the painted wild horses.

She felt him looking back at her.

She went flush, and looked away.

And—after a pause that made her heart thump, like the drum in the calliope—the man slid away.

The ride wasn't as much fun then.

She had felt him look . . . had *felt* his thoughts.

The carousel seemed to go faster.

Then she looked up. The man was on the platform. He dug into a wicker basket—like the type they have in church—and pulled out a handful of rings.

She flew past him.

The next time around she saw him feeding the rings into a long arm. The arm looked like something she saw at Mystic Village, like some torture device used to punish people hundreds of years ago.

It was a strange thing.

She went flying past again before the rings had rolled down to the end.

She came around.

Up and down, her horse, never tiring, nice and steady.

She reached out to grab at a ring.

He watched her, leaning against the wall. The master of the horses, the master of the rings.

Her hand slapped against the arm. Her finger hooked a ring.

She got three more tries, and she hooked two more.

The last ring was golden, a scratched brass ring that barely glowed in the shed.

A free ride, a sign said above the man, a free ride for the golden ring!

Finally all the rings were gone, the two teenagers each dangling whole fingerfuls. The man leaned out, holding the basket.

Jo passed him and tossed her rings, jangling, into the basket.

Just like church.

He smiled at her.

She saw brown teeth. It was an ugly smile.

The song the calliope was pounding—she thought of the words.

"I'm looking over—boomph, boomph—a four-leaf clover—boomph, boomph—that I overlooked before."

The man put down his basket and hurried into the center of the carousel, to the controls. Her horse started slowing, the race was over.

And Jo reached for the belt buckle, loosening it even before the ride stopped.

Knowing that she didn't want her prize, didn't want her free ride.

Michael thought that Barsky had seen someone . . . or something.

"What is it?" he said.

"Up there . . . a door moved . . . it just closed. I saw it."

"What is it?" Cameron said, coming over to him.

"A door, moving," Michael repeated. "What's up there?"

Cameron had the schematic of the ship in his hand, folded in fours. He opened it up. "That's the main lab. The pilothouse is just in front of it."

The door flapped open again. And then, maybe caught by the wind, or maybe the gentle roll of the ship, the door banged shut. Open, shut, open, shut. It was damn eerie, Michael thought.

They all stood there, waiting.

As if we expect someone to come out.

He felt better when Lake came and stood by them.

"Let's go look," Cameron said without any great enthusiasm.

Michael waited, and let Cameron and Lake take the lead.

Chapter Twelve

"NADA," Michael said as their five bulky white suits filled the lab.

The equipment—the computers and monitors—were all dead. The *Achilles* had lost power, its batteries drained dry.

But Michael saw that everything had been left on.

In medias res . . .

There was no sign of any struggle.

There were some half-filled coffee cups, capped with white scum. And the chairs were all in order, poised at the computer tables. Some paper . . . notebooks on the tables.

"Is this where the radio reports came from?" Michael asked, tapping a shoulder, thinking it was Cameron. But Barsky turned around.

Cameron answered him from across the room.

"This is where they communicated with the ROVs . . . and Woods Hole."

"Doesn't seem to be anything wrong here . . ." Michael said quietly, his voice sounding weird, echoing inside the hood. "Where the hell is everybody?"

Cameron was fiddling with the machines. "Everything was left on. No power left, but they're all still on. Computers, data loggers, video relays, the whole lab. God, this is weird."

"It's like that yacht."

It was Barsky, speaking quietly.

"What yacht?" Cameron said, still fiddling with all the buttons.

"The one that went into the Bermuda Triangle . . . and they found no one on board, nothing, except—"

"Christ!" Cameron literally leapt away from the table.

Michael looked at him.

Cameron's fingers were covered in a dark red goo . . . dripping onto the floor.

And then Michael looked at the table.

A small, sticky puddle sat on top of the table. It was red, covered with filmy crust. Michael took a breath.

"Jeezus, I moved a pad, and that was there."

"Wash your glove down in water," Barsky said. "Right away. We'll disinfect it back at the launch."

Cameron nodded. He moved to a sink at the back of the lab. Michael heard the water sputter. Cameron wasn't enjoying this. No way. He'd much prefer a cocktail reception somewhere. Shmoozing with the fat cats.

But he had to be here. It was his ass on the line. The ship, the damaged ROV, and the crew!

All of it, his baby.

Lake moved closer to the puddle. Looked down at it.

The door opened.

Everyone turned and looked.

Then it slapped shut.

"Well," Lake said, filling the void of command. "There's nothing here . . . except for this blood. Let's get on with it."

And he walked out of the lab.

"I'd like a piece of the vanilla fudge . . . without nuts, please," Jo said.

The woman's big fleshy arms wiggled as she cut a piece of the creamy tan candy and slid it off the tray.

Nuts, Jo thought . . . Nuts would definitely spoil the fudge, as Rain Man would say.

Definitely.

Jo smiled at the lady as she finished wrapping the piece of fudge and put it on the shiny metal countertop. Two young men behind her were mixing new batches of fudge, pouring the thick, gloopy mess into molds.

The woman took her money but didn't smile back.

It was strange, Jo thought. Why sell something as wonderful as fudge and not enjoy it?

But the woman had small beetle eyes that looked as if they hadn't had a laugh in a long time.

No matter.

Jo took the fudge, and continued walking, unwrapping the wax paper, biting down. It was like chewing on rubber cement. But then—a wonderful moment—the fudge began to melt in her mouth, all creamy and sweet.

Half the piece, she promised herself. Half the piece for now, and I'll save the other half for later.

Don't want to pig out on the stuff.

She came to a corner and looked around . . .

Coney Island was alive. Most of the stalls were open. A combination clam bar/fresh corn place was right next to her, the little necks and cherry stones waiting patiently on melting ice. The picture of the corn in the sign (Coney Island Corn!) looked much brighter and fresher than the pale steamed corn sitting behind the counter.

She was across from the beach side of the street.

Across the street from JJs Bump-o-Rama. She remembered when her father came and pulled her out of there. The music was loud, even from all the way over here. It was some awful rap stuff. There were lots of people hanging outside of JJs.

None of them were children. No kids. There was something wrong with that.

She kept walking.

Chewing at her fudge. Crossing the halfway mark and taking another illegal bite.

Then, with a resolve that made her proud, she rolled up what was left and put it in her pocket.

Nathan's was across the street. Maybe she'd have a hot dog later, she thought. Sometimes her dad stopped on the way home and they bought two frankfurters for dinner, washed down with a bag of Wise Ridged Potato Chips.

Mom would freak.

Mom believed, her father laughed, in nutrition.

She looked ahead. Astroland, the only real amusement park in Coney, was just down the next block, and Jo decided to cross Surf Avenue.

She had to dodge the cars and buses, all of them spewing great clouds of smoke. She ran across.

Halfway across the street, the fudge fell out of her pocket. Onto the black cracked asphalt.

She had to take a few more steps, then stop, turn, and head back.

She saw the light at the corner turn green.

She ran to the fudge.

Great, she thought. Though the wax-paper wrapper had opened, tumbling from her pocket, it had landed paper side down. The fudge was safe. She scooped it up.

While a line of cars was heading toward her.

They'd stop, wouldn't they? she wondered.

Good question, she thought.

And she dashed to the sidewalk.

Touching down on the concrete as if she were running to first base after hitting one of her usual dribble hits to left field.

She loved baseball. She was a natural pitcher, her father said. A female Orel Hersheiser.

But her bat always seemed to have a hole in it . . .

She kept walking down the block.

Past a shooting gallery . . . with its mechanical squirrels and a honky-tonk piano player. Past a wheel of chance. (A game of skill! Stop the wheel by pressing the button!) There were cigarettes to be won, and black Metallica T-shirts with weird iridescent colors. Mirrored clocks with the names of beer on them.

She walked idly.

And she felt people watching her.

She had felt them watching her when she ran breathlessly onto the sidewalk. As though what she did was strange enough to catch everyone's attention.

She felt eyes on her. They felt hungry.

And—for the first time—she thought of turning around and—

Crossing the street . . .

Going back to the safety of the Aquarium.

She walked a bit faster when she came to one of the wide alleyways that led past a strip of more attractions . . . a leather shop . . . Madame Lena's, a fortune teller . . . and people, standing around . . . men . . . boys . . . looking up as she passed.

She thought of going back.

When she came to the arcade.

It had an old-fashioned sign on it, outlined in flashing bulbs that seemed to send the light traveling around the word, leaping over the dead bulbs.

"Fascination" was the word. Then smaller words, without lights. Skee-Ball . . . Po-Kee-No . . .

She looked inside.

It was filled with video games. All the new ones, she saw. And some of her favorites. Outrunner. Mega Man. And then her #1 favorite.

All the sounds blended together, crazy, exploding, hissing, and beeping.

She walked inside.

* * *

They were in New York.

And nobody took any notice of them, Barron was glad to see. Back in Aspen every yuppie shopkeeper would have stuck their coked-up nose out their door to look.

But in New York? In the Big Apple?

You'd have to have three heads to make anyone look twice.

Barron smiled at this. Three heads . . . it can be arranged . . .

He walked from the new bus terminal at 42nd Street down to 23rd Street, with Jay following, passing streets clogged by trucks, and people hurrying to work—

(Like rats, with their beady eyes, just thinking about one thing . . . gettowork—gotta gettowork.)

That's about to change, thought Barron.

New priorities are coming.

They came to the building. It was just like he imagined it. Yes, he said, checking the number. This was the right one. An ornate gold-plated arch was at the entrance, suspended over two revolving doors. Barron walked in, going right to the directory.

Just to check, he told himself.

And there it was. Small white plastic letters against a black background. Twelfth floor.

Unicorn Studios.

Jay stood right behind him, looking up dully, purposefully at the board. An elevator opened. The operator—a thin, emaciated man, sunken, cancerous, dressed in a dusky maroon uniform—looked out.

"Going up?" he said.

Barron turned to Jay. Then he walked into the elevator, with Jay following a few paces behind.

Jay didn't turn around and face the door.

He stood there looking at the back of the elevator.

Like some human parcel.

"Twelve, please," Barron said. And he watched the man's gnarled, tobacco-stained hands throw the gate shut and move a lever.

Jay mumbled something then—as the elevator glided upward.

The operator looked at him.

Barron smiled.

It was nothing, he knew. Just Jay's animal response to the sudden movement.

Like the moaning sound a sick old cat might make . . . when you're taking it to be gassed.

* * *

The pilothouse was empty. All engines had been stopped, Michael noticed. The *Achilles* had obviously stopped moving before everyone "disappeared."

Cameron led them out to the bridge, also deserted, then back, into the small chart room behind the pilothouse.

Michael looked at his watch. They had been on the tanks for about thirty minutes. They had another thirty minutes, and then they'd have to use the replacement tanks.

And when they were empty they'd have to leave.

He saw Cameron look at his watch. Then Cameron led everyone back to the radio shack. The radio was on. No power, but it was on. There was a pad there. Messages, scrawled.

Cameron picked it up.

"What's it say?" Michael asked.

Cameron pulled the pad away. "Nothing," he lied. "I don't know . . ."

Michael took a step toward the director. Though Cameron at a good six feet three towered over Michael, he was not one for physical confrontation.

"Come on, Ian. Let me see it."

"I—I don't know what it is," he stammered. "Maybe nothing. But it might be classified. I'll have to wait—"

It was odd talking to a pair of eyes and a bobbing white hood.

"Fine. Then I'm getting off this ship. You can solve your own fucking mess yourself."

Michael was ready to make good on his bluff. He turned, and started up the steps back to the chart room.

"I don't think that's a good idea," Lake said.

Cameron grabbed Michael's shoulder, stopping him.

"Okay. Take a look. Doesn't mean anything to me. I just don't want any stories getting out. Not until I know what really happened."

Michael reached out his gloved hand and took the pad.

There were notes, written in an almost undecipherable scrawl. Michael held it up to his visor. They were nothing for a second, just sweeping lines of gibberish.

Then he made out words. Names.

People.

Simonsen. Reilly. Beck. More names. About a dozen. Then a few names with question marks.

The words at the bottom of the page didn't mean anything to Michael.

He felt Lake looking over his shoulder, their hoods butting together.

"What's S. Store . . . and Rope Locker?" Lake asked.

"Good reading," Michael said. He couldn't make out the words, surrounded by heavy circles.

Cameron cleared his throat.

"Science store . . . it's the room where they store all their science equipment . . . and the rope locker is the room where the ship's extra lines are kept."

Michael nodded. "Well, it seems like someone here was concerned about something in those rooms . . . huh, what do you think?"

Cameron nodded. "Maybe."

"Ten minutes," Barsky said. "Ten minutes of air."

"Well, where are they, these rooms?" the SEAL demanded.

Cameron opened the map, taking a step closer to the small porthole. A pale, washed-out light fell onto the drawing of the ship.

"Here's the rope locker," he said, pointing at a room near the bottom of the ship, forward, just above the two lead ballast rooms. "And here," he said, moving his finger almost to the other end of the ship, under the large space labeled "submersible hangar," "is the science storeroom."

Cameron looked up at everyone.

Dailey shifted, two canisters of air rattling heavily on his back. Four minutes left. And Michael knew what Cameron was going to say.

Damn, he knew what Cameron was going to say!

Chapter Thirteen

"WE have to split up."

"I knew it," Michael groaned.

"We don't have enough time . . . I'll go to the science storeroom . . . and Mike, you hit the rope locker. And we can check everything between, meeting somewhere"—Cameron pointed at the cutaway view of the ship—"here, near the boiler room."

Of course, Michael knew, it then became a question of who got to take Captain Lake and his armory.

(What am I worried about? The ship's deserted. If there was anyone alive we would have heard them . . . seen them. There's no one home, Jake. Then what the hell am I so scared of?)

Michael looked at the map, irritated with himself for getting so damn jittery.

"You take Captain Lake," Michael said, surprising himself. "You have farther to go . . . and if there's any stowaway terrorists, you're more likely to run into them."

Cameron nodded agreement without delay.

What a guy!

"Th-then, Barsky, you go with Mike."

"And take this," Lake said, unslinging the semiautomatic rifle and handing it to Michael.

"I've never fired a gun," Michael said. "Wouldn't know—"

"I have," Barsky said, taking the rifle and slipping it onto his shoulder. "Better switch tanks now," Barsky said. "And after thirty minutes, everyone should start heading back to the launch."

Dailey handed everyone a tank out of his duffel bag.

And when they were hooked up, Cameron said, "Let's go."

"Would you take a seat," the secretary said.

Where do they get them from? Barron wondered. These

women, these bitch gatekeepers who humiliate you with the press of an intercom button.

Barron nodded.

We'll sit and make nice for a bit.

Rest our dogs.

Sit down, Jay, he thought.

After a moment's delay, Jay plopped down heavily on the earth-colored couch, his lanky body sinking back into the cushions.

Boy, is he ripe. So am I, figured Barron. We both could do with a shower. Maybe a little fun in the tub.

When we're done here, that's exactly what we'll do.

Barron looked up at Jay's face. His stupid mouth was hanging wide open.

Close the mouth, Jay . . . Barron thought.

And he did. Slowly. Like some ancient vault slowly sliding shut.

Barron looked at the glass case that lined the wall leading to the big empty receptionist's desk.

There were books. *The Power of Crystals. The Coming Revelation. The New Age Handbook. Messages from Beyond. Aliens Among Us. Ramfar Speaks.* The covers were all dreamy pastels, swirls of blue light, muted color that spoke of the peace and tranquillity that awaited followers of the new-age shamans.

Another case was filled with crystals, also sold by Unicorn Productions. Barron had caught the new-age hucksters selling the trinkets on one of his boring jaunts up and down the cable freeway. Just $19.95 can bring you a whole set of powerful crystals that can change you life today! Lose weight. Get a job! Be happy!

The secretary, so severe in her summer suit and brilliant white blouse, looked over at him.

"I'm afraid that Gene's schedule is filled for today. Gene suggests—"

It's amazing, he thought. The way she used his name just now—Gene! As if the spiritual bunco artist-millionaire was actually accessible, actually a friend.

I know that fucking scam.

Barron shook his head. He caught the secretary looking nervously at Jay.

An imposing presence, eh? Barron thought.

But just you wait . . .

He took a step toward the secretary.

"Tell Gene that we—me and Jay—will see him now . . . tell him."

"No," she said, stern now. "I'm afraid that he's in the middle of a Deprival Campaign. He can't be disturbed. Now if you—"

How much pain? Barron thought. Not too much. Just enough to get her attention. Then, a glimpse of something else. Something warm, something beautiful—

Like the covers of those books. Pretty, placid.

She winced. Blinked her eyes.

He knew she was beginning to feel a slight migrainish feeling.

"He's too—" she tried to continue.

Then, Barron—so pleased to have his powers back, after so many years—gave her a bit more, digging deeper into her little regimented brain.

She whimpered.

And Jay grunted, stirring on the couch.

Easy, boy, Barron thought. Uh-oh. Maybe the old boy's hungry? He grinned.

"Uhh," the secretary moaned. The phone buzzed. She ignored it. And then, when Barron saw tears building in her eyes, little glistening pools—so sweet!—he stopped the pain. He walked in front of her. And he took her chin.

I wonder if she's a believer, he thought.

Or just an employee?

No matter. She'll be a believer after today.

He took her chin in his hands, the way he used to touch people and cure them.

Binding them to him.

He raised her face so that it tilted up to him, looking at him. "Please," he said, his fingers rubbing the smooth skin of her cheek, the top of her neck, "tell Gene that I'm coming."

Then he let her feel it. The warmth, seeming to come from his fingers, covering her face. She went flush. The pain vanished. Had it ever been real? And then he knew she felt a tremendous beauty, a wonder at this man, this *healer*.

She made another sound, a moan.

A groan of pleasure this time.

I could push it, Barron thought. Give her more. Let her orgasm, right here! Wouldn't that be sweet? And again and again, over and over, mixing in a tremendous feeling of sublime beauty with something so base, so physical.

But when her mouth opened and she moaned again, kissing his fingertips, he knew that it was enough.

Mustn't get carried away, he thought.

I must remember why I'm here.

He pulled his hand away and he felt her sadness . . . her loss.

"Tell him," he said.

She picked up the phone.

"I'm sending someone to see Gene," she said. "Someone important."

She pressed a buzzer and held it.

Ah, Barron thought, the gatekeeper has opened the way to the sanctuary.

He went over and opened the unlocked door.

And he waited for Jay to follow.

Jo stood in front of a game called Golden Axe.

She had played it before. It was a role-playing game of dragons and brave warriors.

You picked your warrior, and she always picked a woman with a giant sword and not much clothes.

The best thing about the game was that it gave you a password when you finished your adventuring, and your quarters, for the day. And you could go to any Golden Axe machine anywhere in the world and use that password to pick up the game just where you left off.

She had a pocket filled with quarters now, and she put one in the machine. Then there were some quick scenes of fighting, a castle, flames, a robot voice said "Golden Ace." Then a sound, a bloodthirsty yell.

Followed by the drug message.

"Winners Don't Use Drugs," the screen flashed.

The password screen appeared and she used the joystick to select her six letters, which she had memorized.

And then she concentrated on slashing and jumping, finally getting to the third level of the castle for the first time.

She talked to herself as she played. Feeding in more quarters when her character finally took on one rat bite too many.

She was down to her last quarter. Of course, she could go get some more change if she wanted to. She still had a few dollars left.

She put the quarter in.

And she saw someone watching her.

Someone was in the back of the arcade. It was dark back there.

A black knight jabbed her character. One life down.

I'm not paying attention, she thought.

She took a quick glance, back into the gloom, back where there was a whole wall of kung-fu games, each one grunting and groaning as the cartoony fighters hit each other.

There was no one there.

She blew at her forehead, blowing some hair away.

Her character sliced the Black Knight in two. And she moved deeper into the castle.

Until—

She knew he was there again.

Behind her.

Looking at her.

She was aware of her body. Her legs, her shorts, her bottom. And someone watching her.

A toadlike creature jumped on her fighter. One life left.

She looked quickly to her side.

But she didn't see anyone.

A wall slid open in the game. A skeleton warrior. Piece of cake, she thought. Hit them once and they fall apart.

She looked to her right.

And she saw someone standing there.

Dark, tan skin, He wore a mesh tank top. His hair, his eyes, were dark. He was grinning at her.

No, not grinning.

It was something different.

He looked like he might have been one of the men from yesterday.

She froze at the joystick.

He smacked his lips together. Or something. He made a wet, popping sound.

Her warrior was jabbed by the skeleton. She fell to the ground. There was a little pool of blood on the dungeon floor.

"Game over," flashed on the screen, over and over. Then her code word.

Another smacking sound. Then a laugh.

She backed away from the game, her eyes fixed on the screen, the nonsense letters of the password.

CXLPHY.

As if it meant something.

She turned to her right, to the sidewalk only steps away.

She started walking out.

Wondering . . . is he still looking at me? Will he follow me?

But when she reached the sidewalk, nearly bumping into an old man who was walking along, gumming the air, muttering to himself, she quickly spun around to see if the man—the kid—was following.

But he wasn't.

She stood there. Waiting for him to appear somewhere else.

As if she were in one of her games.

Only I don't have a sword.

But he didn't appear. And now, she thought glumly, I don't even have my new password!

Barsky had the walkie-talkie, and Michael took the lead going into the bowels of the ship.

The first thing he realized was that they should have brought more powerful lights. The ship had no power. All the cage-enclosed bulbs were dark. And though there was some light from small portholes, the corridors were black. And the small lamps they carried were inadequate, the light gobbled up by the dull blackness.

Then there was getting down . . .

Metal stairs, and narrow corridors . . . stooping to open doors, flashing the light in, sticking his head in, and then grunting to Barsky—

"Nothing."

Empty.

They passed a room with some beds, a desk. The Science Officers' Quarters, Michael thought. He made the light cut a sweeping arc through the wood-paneled room. A shirt draped off a wooden chair. A book lay open, upside down, on the bed.

He couldn't smell anything.

They were sealed in.

The walkie-talkie squawked awake. Cameron spoke, too loudly, blurring his voice with static and hiss.

"Everything okay?"

"Yes, sir," Barsky said. "We're in the"—Michael nodded. pretty sure of their location—"Science Officers' Quarters. There's nothing here."

"Ask where *they* are," Michael said.

Michael waited for Cameron's answer.

There was static. They lost the first few words. "—the main lab. Microscopes are . . . they must have been . . ." More static, more garbled words.

Michael shook his head and took the walkie-talkie from Barsky.

"Ian, don't hold it up to your face—" Asshole, he wanted to say. "And speak in a normal tone."

Maybe it was fear making Cameron speak so loudly, so shrilly.

Michael clicked off. He handed the small handset back to Barsky. Cameron came back on, quieter, his voice clear.

"We're going on. The science storeroom is just past the battery locker. I'll see if we can't get some emergency power . . ." He paused a second. "Over."

"Over," Barsky answered.

Michael said, "Come on. We're wasting air."

The next room, just a few feet away, was Simonsen's quarters. As project director, he got his own private digs.

Michael looked inside. It was a cramped room, and messy, as if someone had trouble finding two socks to match. And decided to rampage through the drawers. Michael aimed the flashlight around. There were shirts on the floor . . . underwear . . . papers.

"What the fuck happened here?" Barsky said.

Michael shook his head. "Looks like someone was looking for something . . . bad."

Barsky took a step into the room, pushing aside the chair.

And—through the speakers in the hood—Michael heard something.

From behind them.

Farther below.

A metallic sound. Something moving, grinding.

Barsky turned and looked at Michael.

All Michael could see were the other man's eyes. Questioning.

Don't look at me, man. I don't have any answers.

"Just the ship moving . . ." Michael said, half believing it.

He turned to go, aiming the light out into the narrow passageway.

(And is it my imagination, he thought, or is the light a little less white? A bit more yellow?)

But—thinking that by saying it he would make it real—he didn't mention it to Barsky.

Barsky was in the front now.

"There should be a stairway ahead," Michael said.

And that would lead to the crew's quarters, the place where all the randy interns did their fucking. And then another stairway, down to the forward ballast, an air lock, the dry stores, and the rope locker.

Barsky waited for Michael to pass him, to get in front.

They both heard the creaking sound again.
And they both ignored it.
Then Michael got in front.
After all, *he had the light*.

Chapter Fourteen

ONCE Jo was outside—in the heat—she knew she had just gotten scared for no reason.

Lots of kids watch other kids play video games. It's no big deal.

And maybe, she thought, yeah, maybe she shouldn't be so bent out of shape if someone—a man—wanted to look at her.

It's no big deal, she repeated to herself, closing the matter.

She felt the lump of fudge in her pocket and decided to break her pledge. She dug it out, unwrapped it—the waxy paper sticking to the now-soft fudge. It was too soft to break off a chunk. So she brought it up to her mouth and bit down, pulling a stringy gob up and away.

There, that was better.

She reached the corner.

Astroland was ahead.

Her father once told her that Coney Island used to have some great rides, more than just the Cyclone, and Astroland. There was a place called Steeplechase, a place where a dopey-looking clown sprayed girls with air hoses sending their summer skirts flying up. And there was a great horse ride, the steeplechase ride, where you could ride a great carousel horse that really sped around a great track, all around the outside of the park.

Her father even showed her the symbol of the park, a man with a weird grimace, his face locked in a skeleton smile.

He looked more evil than fun . . .

But Steeplechase was gone.

All that was left, standing just there, behind Astroland, was the Parachute Jump.

No parachutes, no customers, a landmark. Rusting away right next to the splintery boardwalk.

The light changed, and she crossed the street.

She walked into Astroland. The first part, right near the entrance, was kiddy rides. She looked at the silly rides—

(Remembering rides like these. Her mother and father watching her, getting it all down on video tape. Hi, Momee! Hi, Dadeee! Waving, smiling, happy. Ringing the bell on the metal boats that went around and around. Bouncing up and down on the tiny helicopters.)

She looked at the rides. Not too many little kids in them. And then she looked at the operators.

They were thin, hungry-looking teenagers. Their hair was long, dirty. One of them looked back at her, and she turned away.

She kept walking.

There were ice-cream wrappers on the ground. And bits of cigarettes.

The rides changed, grew more exciting, the deeper she walked into Astroland.

She saw the Round-Up, a spinning hoop of metal. When it goes fast enough, the floor drops out and there you are, pinned to the wall of the hoop, spinning.

Maybe I'll go on that, she thought.

That might be fun.

She passed a ticket stand. She bought enough for a couple of rides. Then she kept on walking.

The Buccaneer was in front of her.

The ride looked like a long metal telephone pole. At one end there was a pirate ship, at the other a weight. She had seen the ride before, swinging back and forth, higher and higher until the ship went completely upside down.

Yeah, she thought. I'll do that.

She ran to the ride, getting on just before the opening was barred with a chain. The operator ripped her ticket and she found a seat by herself, near the back of the ship.

It started swaying, back and forth higher and higher. Her hair flew behind her.

Then she saw the beach, not too crowded today. Of course, nobody wanted to swim there anymore. You sit in the sand, get some sun. But swimming . . .

No way. Not unless you like needles. And–God!—used condoms.

(Once, when they took a walk on the beach—right into one—her father tried to explain what it was. It's okay, Dad, she had said. They told us all about them in school. It's okay, *honest*.

Oh . . . he said. And they walked on, stepping around the slimy, jellyfishlike thing.)

Then higher, and she saw the base of the Parachute Jump, all overgrown with reedy grasses, yellowed now by the hot sun. It must have been great, she thought. To go up that gigantic tower in a parachute and then—*whoosh*—to fall through the air.

And never having seen it work, she missed it.

She looked to her right.

The fun stuff ended on just the next block. There was a yellow brick hotel. And a small supermarket with glittery letters that fluttered in the wind.

Higher and higher.

Until she was looking straight down, squealing, laughing.

Someone behind was crying, scared.

It was a neat ride.

Up. And down. And up again, until the pirate ship went nearly to the top, nearly over.

Looking at the ground, at the people looking up at them, some of them probably wondering whether they could handle the ride.

Looking down . . .

She saw the man.

From the arcade. With the mesh tank top.

The pirate ship flew down again.

And her smile was gone.

The light was definitely fading. Michael banged it once, hoping to snap the heavy nine-volt battery out of its doldrums.

"We don't have much more time anyway," Barsky said behind him. "We don't have a lot of air."

Michael nodded, not sure whether the Coast Guard officer could see him.

He hurried past the crew's quarters, a messy warren of bunks and twisted sheets, and a clothesline dangling semiwashed underwear, now crinkly dry.

He had trouble finding the other stairway.

"There's a door there," Barsky said, coming beside him. And Barsky pointed to the oval outline of a hatchlike door at the back of the crew's sleeping quarters.

"That's it," Michael said.

He went to the door. The latch didn't budge when he tried to twist it open.

"The other way," Barsky said, gently nudging him aside.

Sure, Michael thought. Now the latch moved.

When the door opened, there was an even more profound blackness ahead. No portholes, no tiny circle of light.

There was just their weakening lantern.

"God, I'd hate to get stuck down there."

"Don't worry," Barsky said, patting him with his gloved hand. "The rope locker has to be just down the stairs, and then to the right. Not too far . . ."

Michael nodded. I'm losing it, he thought. A fuckin' crisis of the nerves. Forget musty old houses.

This was the goddam scariest place he'd ever been.

And he wanted out.

Fast.

"Want me to lead?" Barsky asked, gently, Michael thought. He's trying not to rub my face in it.

All the more reason Michael had to say, "No, Colonel."

Michael started down the stairway. With his clunky boots. These steps felt narrower. He bumped his head against the ceiling on the way down. His right headphone picked up some static then.

The light was worth shit.

"Fuck," Michael said. "Maybe we should bag it. Go get some proper lights."

"I should have brought our underwater tungsten lamps," Barsky said, annoyed. "Those monsters would make it like daytime in here."

Michael tried to go down a step that wasn't there.

He stopped, hearing Barsky's clunky steps behind him.

But he was listening for something else. That sound.

Whatever it was.

"Just ahead," Barsky prompted.

"Yeah . . ." Michael said.

He barely fit in the passageway. The walls touched each of his bulgy arms, pushing against him. He passed a small room with just a refrigerator inside. A heavy lock hung from its latch.

"I guess we could look in there later . . . if nothing shows up," Michael said.

He turned a corner.

There was some graffiti on the wall. A woman with unnaturally large breasts.

He took a few more steps.

And he saw another hatch.

"There it is," Barsky said from behind him.

This time Michael opened the hatch himself, twisting the latch correctly.

It popped open noisily,

Something ahead of them made a creaking sound.

Michael pushed open the door.

It swung slowly open.

Okay, he thought. We've seen it. We can go now.

Let's sink this stupid ship and be done with it.

"Go ahead, Mike," Barsky said.

And Michael walked in.

Funny, he thought. I'm wearing this suit that covers me from head to toe and I feel like I'm walking into a swamp naked.

He took a step.

He had the lamp pointing straight down.

(Why hadn't they heard from Cameron? he wondered then. And maybe they should stop—right here—and call him.)

He saw the floor, a patterned, metal grid with diamond-shaped bumps on it.

Another step.

Part of a rope coil. He moved the light to the left. Another rope coil, thick rope, as thick as his forearm.

Nothing here, he thought, taking a breath inside his hood. Nothing but rope in de old rope locker.

He wished he had more of a view. There was just a narrow band of the visor.

"Look around a bit . . ." Barsky prompted.

Michael raised the lamp.

He saw more rope.

And then.

(The lamp stopped moving for a second while he looked at something, taking it in . . . wondering . . . now what the hell is that? Just what do you suppose that could be?)

It wasn't rope. It looked like a gnarled root of a tree—no, more like a bit of twisted rawhide that his dog would chew and chew until one day it was as thin as paper. He moved the light.

Up now, quickly, hoping he was wrong, and then—

Not believing what he was seeing.

Barsky spoke first. "Jesus . . . what the hell—"

They were bodies. *They used to be bodies*. They were stacked together like rashers of bacon, piled together, flopping over each other, in a big pile. Like a scene from a World War II documentary, a scene from the terrible camps, Germany's contribution to the definition of the word "evil." The bodies. Gaunt. Emaciated.

Except, yeah—this was worse.

They were like that rawhide . . . just like that dog chew . . . sucked dry.

Barsky pushed his way into the room.

"Oh, fuck," he said.

They were dried. Crispy. Michael was damn sure they'd be crispy if he touched them. They had been—

Yes. Drained.

There was nothing left.

Except leather skin, and bones, some cracked open.

To get at the marrow, he guessed. Nice . . .

Barsky went close to the pile.

Michael stood there. The lamp seemed to go even paler. Its yellow light was so weak it gave the bodies a dark, burnished look.

Barsky stood right next to them.

"A-Alan . . . I—"

"Look at that," Barsky said, pointing to the top of the pile, where a few of the bodies lay, exposed.

What? Michael wondered. What the hell are you talking about. Look at what? All the fucking dead people. What the hell are you pointing at?

Then he saw it.

Three people were sprawled on top, bent back, like discarded dolls.

And their stomachs were split open, peeled back.

Inside there was nothing. Just a big opening, with dry skin and cracked bones. Their spines were split in pieces.

"Something blew a hole in them . . ." Michael said, trying to sound cool. I'm in control now. Everything's okay. Everything's—

Barsky shook his head. "No. Look again."

Michael let the light fall right on the center of the pile.

A bad thing that. He and Barsky stood in complete darkness.

"Something—" Barsky stopped. Then, "Look there. Something blew out of them."

The light shook. Michael forced his hand to hold it steady. He was freezing inside his suit. Why am I so cold? Why . . .

Blew out of them . . . he thought, looking at the bodies, knowing that Barsky was right.

There was silence for a few seconds.

A bizarre memorial.

And then—

A sound that made them both yelp, jumping back.

The walkie-talkie.

And Cameron.

Again speaking too loudly, spitting into his receiver, garbling his words, his message.

"Great news!" he yelled. Though it sounded like "Ate Ooze . . ."

Barsky picked up their walkie-talkie and spoke into it. "We hear you . . . what is it . . ."

Michael looked at his watch. They had to get going. Get out of here.

Thinking. No disease did this. No fucking deep-sea microbe did *this*.

"We've got a survivor!" Cameron yelled, the words clipped, sputtering on the walkie-talkie.

"A survivor!"

—

Chapter Fifteen

DR. Gene Fasolt stared at the camera. He knew that part of his grizzly gray—but very well-clipped—beard was off the screen.

That didn't matter.

It was the *eyes* that were important.

He pulled the cigar out of his mouth. A small puff of smoke escaped his lips. The cigar was thick, blackish-brown and gummy at the tip.

When he started his TV ministry, he never smoked on camera. But then he felt it would make him more real, more human to the people watching.

A good thing in the post-PTL days.

His glasses—real, not a prop—slid down his nose. He looked over the rim of the glasses, right at the camera.

I can see you, his eyes said.

"I'm still waiting," he said, before putting the cigar back in. There was no impatience, no sense of disapproval in his tone. Simply stating a fact.

His technique was simpler, more refined than scolding and guilt trips. He denied them his presence. They saw him, watched him.

But Gene just sat in front of the camera, and watched back.

They—the audience—would have to *win* back his presence . . . his persona.

And he was tired.

It was the second day. He had taken a few naps, using the film breaks to quickly lie down and get his brain waves into alpha. But his bones were starting to ache. He was sitting there, thinking about the next break.

The film segments were even worse. Some Windham Hill music overlaid endless film of the city—the streets, the buildings, and—at other times—the suburbs. No theme, no meaning, nothing documentary about it, just pictures of the city.

Vapid. Soulless.

The audience thought that Gene waited there.

His face was always there, in the same position, when the ten minutes of inane film ended.

"Number five," he barked through clenched teeth. "Where is number five?"

He kept his eyes squinted. Not too much, less is more, in a Deprival Campaign. Make each person think that they are the one, that they are the "number five" that he is waiting for.

Yes, you out there. You're the one I'm talking about. You're number five!

The phones were constantly busy, constantly raking in donations from followers who thought that yes, I'm number five. I'm one of the ten who've been waiting for a message. Who's ready to help Dr. Gene and his Church in a special way.

"Where are you?" he said, pulling his cigar out again. "We're waiting."

This campaign was going even better than the winter one.

He had long since stopped wondering what kind of perverse mechanism kept people watching his head—on the screen—barking at them, while an 800 number scrawled along the bottom of the screen.

Waiting for Godot.

Something to happen in their lives.

He made an O, and blew the smoke out. "I know you're there," he said. "We can't get movin' again until you call."

Then nothing, silence. He looked to the side, disinterested, bored.

Gene saw his director giving him the one-minute signal.

One minute and then there'd be the mindless film. Wet city streets. Midtown traffic. No horns, no brakes squealing, just soothing guitar music . . . chimes.

And I'll get some goddam rest, he thought.

He looked back at the screen.

Number five—the halfway person would magically appear after film break.

Then he'd start looking for six, seven, and all the rest.

Some people pledged money over and over, thinking that if they weren't one number, then maybe, yes, they were the other.

Gene didn't disabuse them of that notion.

It was the chosen people shtick, he knew. Updated to the age of crystals and channeling.

He looked at the camera . . . sucked on the cigar.

And the red light on the camera went out.

"Great, Gene," the director said as if he had just wrapped an episode of *Masterpiece Theater*.

Everyone called him "Gene."

It was a rule.

Gene got out of his chair.

And he heard noise from the back of the studio.

Gene didn't like noise. But when he was this tired, this fucking beat, he hated it.

"You can't go out there," he heard someone say, one of the production girls.

Gene looked over at his bodyguard.

Walter. Always by his side.

Walter had to be even more tired than he was, standing there, in the shadows. For what? Almost two days now.

Walter moved up.

Gene walked closer to the director. One of the young girls, a cute thing he favored with an encouraging smile from time to time, handed him a glass of Evian. Ice-cold.

He took a slug.

"You can't—" he heard the woman say.

But then, there they were. Two men. A sorry-looking pair. They looked dirty. He wanted them gone.

Gene wasn't worried.

Walter was beside him.

The men came out into the light, stepping over the cables. The director, a young string bean with the fanny of a thirteen-year-old ballerina, went in front of them.

"Just where do you think you're—" he whined petulantly.

Gene stood his ground, sucking his cigar. With Walter next to him, he was mostly interested—kind of intrigued—in what was going to happen. He certainly wasn't scared.

There was a short man. Dressed in a shabby, rumpled suit.

A nothing, Gene decided.

And a tall black man, in a black tank top. A piece of silver—or some silvery metal—dangled from an ear. His shirt had ugly iridescent colors.

The black man was a pretty big fellow.

Gene felt Walter tense next to him.

They pushed past the director. Walter took a step forward.

Kong kill . . . Gene thought.

Old Walter's biceps were as big as most men's thighs.

But Gene grabbed him on the arm.

"Just wait a second," Gene said quietly, through his clenched teeth.

The short dumpy man came up to Gene. The black man stayed in the back, his mouth open. His eyes were covered by sunglasses. But he appeared to be looking straight ahead at absolutely nothing.

"Gene," the man in the rumpled suit said, sticking his hand out. "I'm Paul Barron."

Gene nodded. The name rang a bell of some kind—

(How the fuck did they get past the receptionist? Why didn't she call security?)

Paul Barron. He had heard it before . . . somewhere. He wasn't too sure where.

"I'm afraid, friend, that you'll have to leave. I'm in the middle of a Deprivation Campaign and—"

Barron shook his head.

"No. Not anymore, Gene. I—"

This Paul Barron smiled, a sick, craven grimace. Gene touched Walter's arm, freeing him to toss these two bozos off the bus, as Barron said: "I have a better idea for you . . ."

Martin hadn't moved from his stool in—

He looked up at the clock.

Two hours.

Positively unhealthy.

His fanny was permanently taking on the oval shape of the stool.

And I'd like another cup of coffee, Martin thought. Some java to keep the blood cells alive.

But he didn't want to stop looking through the dissecting microscope.

The fucking thing—this parasite thing they found attached to the posterior of the *Bythnomus giganteous*—was still alive. Barely alive, barely moving. But God, it should have been dead yesterday.

Every minute might be its last.

And now—damn—he knew what it was. He surfaced for a second. Rubbed his eyes, pushing his black-rimmed glasses off his head, then back down.

No, he thought, looking at the crystal-clear 3-D image. I don't *really* know what it is. Not at all.

But—

He brought the fine-tipped probe into his field of vision. The needle-sharp tip looked blundering, gigantic, wavering around drunkenly as he tried to aim it, looking at it through the eyepiece.

I know what it's like. Now.

He couldn't wait to tell Michael.

And more. I want to ask Michael what in the world it was doing attached to the deep-sea isopod.

He studied the top of the probe.

Only a few of the parasite's tendrils, the thin filament hairs, were still febrile, reddish, still moving, still responding to his touch.

There were only minutes left.

He had tried cutting a small sample away from the dead *Bythnomus*. He put it in a salt tank. But it was dead by the time he had the material cut. It wasn't able to live with its host dead so long. At least, he didn't think so.

There was one thing he wanted to see again. God, he wished he could set the micro-VCR adaptor up. Get some tape on the thing.

But there wasn't time.

He wanted to see the way the tendril moved to the probe. Seemed to surround it . . . feeling it.

As if looking for something.

He touched a tendril.

It moved, sluggishly now, almost disinterested.

The tip of the filament opened. It looked like some kind of mouth organ. But that didn't make sense. Not if it was a parasite, not if it fed off the isopod.

The filament curled next to the metal.

The door to the lab opened.

Martin didn't look up.

"Martin," someone said. A woman. Not Annie.

"Martin," she repeated.

"Yes," he grunted. The tiny mouth, more like a sucker, he thought. I've got to sketch this stuff, while it's still fresh in my mind.

"Martin!"

"I'm working," he said, to whomever it might be. "I can't—"

He heard the woman walk over, tap his shoulder.

"Where is Jo?" the woman said. "Where is my daughter?"

Paddy Sullivan, oldest of the four Sullivan brothers, the grumpy one, the sourpuss, his mom always said, sat down on the bench. It was a used-to-be green. And he thought . . . When was the last fucking time someone painted the damn thing?

It was missing two wood slats.

Doesn't anyone in the city give a damn?

So Paddy's ass slid into the gap, pinched and uncomfortable.

He thought about getting up. Finding a better bench.

If there was a better bench on the boardwalk.

But he knew what would happen then. He'd get up and walk.

(How fast, Paddy? How fucking fast . . .)

Right over to McCann's on Surf.

Where they knew him real well.

Where the bartender nodded, then turned away. As if he hoped Paddy, some human fly, would find some other piece of shit to land on.

And Paddy would smile, wobble the stool a bit closer to the bar, lay down his buck-fifty.

"The usual, Jack," he'd say. "Bat and a ball."

Then it would be homerun time, out of the park for another day, knocking them back, hoping to hell to keep those home fires burning.

He used to be a cop.

Then he used to be a fireman.

He used to do things. Good things. He had friends. Wife. Kids. Family.

He used to like sports. Boxing. He went to the second Clay-Liston fight.

He used to like to fish. Goin' for the blues off Montauk.

He used to like women.

And clams at the raw bar at Lundy's in Sheepshead Bay—

(Is that gone? he wondered. When was the last time he was there? Is Lundy's gone too?)

He used to have all that.

But now, there was just this.

Here. Surrounded by shit. Waiting for the disability check.

A bad back, too many bodies carried out of too many burning tenements.

Made in the shade. A fuckin' regular check. Never have to work again.

Why, I can spend my whole day, putting down those bats and balls.

He licked his lips.

He tried to ignore the shaking of his hand.

Sometimes, sitting here, hearing the waves flopping down lazily on the shore, the gulls screaming, fighting over pizza crust and sun-dried fries, he could—yeah, just a bit—put it off.

Not forever.

No, he was no fool. It was—

Fuckin' inevitable.

Absolutely fucking necessary.

But there could be a few moments of clarity. When he could pretend that some other shit mattered. The morning sun. The people on the beach. The boardwalk, rotting away.

Just a bit.

Before he stood up, so damned hot for that first chug—straight back—of Seagram's followed by a down-the-hatch chaser of ice-cold beer.

He rubbed at his nose.

It was itchy.

His hand stopped in midair, all shaky, movin' all over the fuckin' place.

The beach, the water, saved him a bit . . . just the tiniest bit.

On those mornings when the larder was empty, when he didn't leave anything in his home stash from the night before.

He could sit here . . . and make that hungry thing wait.

It was something at least, he thought.

Something . . .

I'll go back, Jo thought.

This wasn't any fun. This was being dumb, acting so scared.

(I saw the guy, she told herself. Looking up at me, *waiting* for me.)

But, getting off the ride, she saw nobody. Sure there were people around. Funny, no kids. They all looked too old to be here. As if they were here for something else.

"Winners Don't Do Drugs," the video game flashed.

Here, it looked like that's all these people did. But then again . . . they didn't look like winners.

The rides were just something to watch.

The man—was it the same man?—wasn't there.

She got off, thinking. There's somebody here like me. No young girl with fudge in her pocket.

She thought of going back the way she came, out to Surf Avenue, past the Arcade, and Nathan's, and JJs . . .

Then she looked up.

The boardwalk was only half a block away. Past a deserted lot.

Then she could run along the boardwalk. It went right to the Aquarium.

That was the thing to do, she thought.

And she started walking, out the exit that led to the side street, past a group of kids coming in. One of them held a big box, and it boomed a song in Spanish.

She chewed her lip, leaving Astroland.

The pirate ship had new people screaming. But she didn't look back at them.

She just thought . . . *I don't belong here*.

Chapter Sixteen

MICHAEL hurried, realizing that he was sucking hard at the compressed air, not knowing whether the protective suits were even needed.

He thought of the twisted, dry bodies. No virus did that.

Not even close.

Something sucked the bodies dry and then punched a hole in their gut . . .

From the inside.

He was about to climb up the ladder near the Scientists' Quarters when he had an idea.

"Let's cut down this way," he said, turning back to Barsky, spraying him with the yellow light. Barsky's white suit looked jaundiced . . . diseased.

Barsky held out his gloved hands, asking what the hell for.

"The ship's infirmary is down here," Michael said. "I want to see if . . . anything was left . . . anything to explain . . ." Michael looked at the chart of the ship. "There's another ladder straight up to the main deck from there."

Barsky nodded—none too happily, Michael guessed—and Michael jogged clumsily down the corridor. His bulky suit rubbed against the walls.

The light bobbed in front of him.

He heard his own panting, labored, struggling. And Barsky, clip-clopping behind him.

Then he saw the door to the hospital.

Wide open.

He ran in. And stopped there, gasping at the air, droplets of sweat making his eyebrows itch. He aimed the light around the room.

There was nothing there. No sign of any problem, any crazed, hurried activity. It looked nice and peaceful.

Barsky touched his shoulder, and Michael jumped.

"What did you expect to see?" Barsky asked.

Michael shook his head.

I'm not surprised, he thought. There's nothing here, no sign of sick people and overtaxed resources. The hospital looked like it hadn't been used in months.

Whatever happened on the ship happened fast.

"Hey, we've got to go," Barsky said, tapping him again.

And Michael trotted through the room, to the stairs leading up. He could see light from above. A pale glow, and as he reached one landing, he saw a piece of the sky.

Then, as he kept climbing, almost at the main deck, he heard voices, laughing.

And when he got outside, he saw Cameron talking with someone. Lake stood behind them, and Dailey.

They all had their hoods off.

"Mike!" Cameron said, seeing him pop to the surface, a white gopher.

Michael moved aside to give Barsky room to get out.

There was a man next to Cameron. They both had smiles on. Like this was a college reunion. Just another Woods Hole party.

"Why is your hood off?" Michael said to Cameron.

But he was looking at the man. Dressed in neat khaki shirt and pants. The crisp, clean shirt had rectangular fold marks. And the pants had a razor-sharp crease. As if—

"Mike, it's okay. Don't you know who this is?" Cameron draped his arm around the man.

Michael shook his head.

And he saw—to the side—Barsky unzipping his hood.

"I wouldn't—" Michael muttered.

Cameron shook his head. "This is Ed Reilly, the *Achilles*'s biologist." Reilly grinned. "He says there's no biological contaminants, he says—"

What, asshole? Michael wanted to yell. What did Reilly say about not answering the radio. And what the hell did he say happened to the rest of the fucking ship?

"Ask him what happened," Michael said.

And he took a step back, away from Cameron, away from the others.

In the distance, off in the direction of Martha's Vineyard, a bit of color caught his eye. An orange and yellow sail. He felt the quiet hiss of his air tank stop.

"Ask him about the bodies . . ." Michael said.

"All in good time, Mike. Now, we have to get him back, put him up in the medical building for a few days." He turned to Reilly. "Not a real quarantine, Ed. But just a few days of observation. Try to figure out why you lived and—"

The change was subtle.

At the word "quarantine."

Michael saw it and then he saw that Lake noticed it too. The SEAL moved closer to Cameron.

Reilly shifted on his feet. His face looked pained. It was something that Cameron had just said. About the medical building . . .

"Ask him about the rope locker . . ." Michael said. "Ask him about the fucking rope locker . . ."

Caryn found Annie in her office, hunched over papers, chewing an apple, her legs crossed underneath her.

"Do you know where the fuck my daughter is?" Caryn said. Martin had already explained her ex's trip to the Cape, leaving Annie in charge.

Annie Bowen—not one of Caryn's favorite people—untangled herself and stood up. Caryn knew that the girl admired Michael and Caryn was assigned the role of the bad wife. She thought that he and Annie had been lovers . . .

"What do you mean, Mrs. Cross? She's here . . . out there—"

Caryn saw Annie looking over her shoulder as Martin came into the office.

Martin shook his head.

"She's not in any of the buildings . . . she's not somewhere *out there* . . ." Caryn watched Annie lick her lips. And any hope she had that the young woman would know where Jo was disappeared.

"We'll find her . . ." Annie said. "She's around. Don't worry. We'll find her."

She was so young. Assured.

Stupid.

It was then that the obvious occurred to Caryn. Michael was gone. And what was it that Jo complained about all the time . . . whenever she spent time with her father?

Every time, the same complaint.

Coney Island was just outside, she whined. So close . . . With rides and candy, fun and games.

Forbidden fruit.

And then Caryn knew where her daughter was.

She turned and ran out of the cramped office.

This might not have been a good idea, Jo thought.

On the other side of the street there were faded storefronts, old games, and an abandoned cotton candy place with a peeling, washed-out sign.

And right beside her, surrounded by a chain-link fence, an empty lot behind Astroland. Left over from some other amusement park. Maybe from the days of Steeplechase. The yellow stalks of grass grew through every crack in the ground, separated by chunks of tar and piles of sand.

It was deserted down here.

The boardwalk wasn't far ahead. The sidewalk led to stairs leading up, above the dark tunnel that ran under the boardwalk.

And who goes under there? she wondered. Do people sleep under there? Hiding from the sun, the light? Do they look up at the day people, through the cracks, the people on top of the boardwalk?

She thought of a story, about billy goats . . . and trolls.

But she saw no one.

Maybe this wasn't such a good idea.

"Duuuuh," she said quietly. No, it's a stupid idea.

Stupid, stupid, stupid!

She turned around, thinking that she'd go back, back toward Astroland, and Surf Avenue. Back to where—God!!—there were people at least.

And she saw him.

Walking toward her.

Slowly.

The sun made him a blackish blur.

"No," she said. Her voice small, swallowed by the hot air.

She stepped back.

To the side was the empty lot, dotted with beer cans and waxy bags that fluttered around. And sparkling bits of glass. Old bottles . . . maybe vials of crack . . .

Like they showed her at school.

This is crack, the health teacher, the football coach, said. Now, kids, call the police if you see any vials like this . . .

She stepped back again.

And bumped into something.

Jo fell, groaning, her hands flying out to break her fall.

But always looking down the block, back at the blackish blur walking toward her. Her bottom cracked against the sidewalk, and her elbows slammed into the cement.

And her bare legs fell across something—

(She risked looking away from the blur. As if to look away would make him appear—*like that*—right next to her.)

She looked at the bulky thing she had tripped over, not really thinking about what it might be. Her legs were splayed over it.

It seemed to be a cloth bag. No, not a bag. But something round, stuffed.

She leaned up, pushing at the ground with her hands, her elbows throbbing, scraped, bleeding.

She looked at it.

It had legs. And there, pressed against the fence, a snout. One lip curled back by the metal. All dry. And things moving in the mouth, over the fangs.

And—

She was trying to talk. To say something.

Her legs were on top of it.

Her hand moved.

And her fingers touched a paw. All hard. Rigid.

She screamed.

Kicking back, scrambling away.

The dead dog was frozen into its position. And her kicks made its sticklike legs kick back at her bare legs, scratching them.

She yelled at it.

As if her screaming, her crying, would make it stay there, stay on the ground.

It's going to get up, she thought. It's going to get up and come after me.

Her knuckles dug into the speckled concrete of the sidewalk.

I've got to get up, she said.

Now. Get up, and turn and—

But—just like she knew—she had taken her eyes off the man.

And he was there.

Just a shadow.

Standing next to the dog.

"Aw, wha' happ'n to the liddle puppy?"

She heard him laugh. Another sound. Like the screaming of gulls. But louder.

It's me, she thought. I'm making that sound.

The man crouched low to the dog. "Poor puppy."

She reached out to the fence. Grabbed the metal.

The man picked up the dog by its blackish-brown tail. He lifted it up, slowly. It came up frozen, like something her mom would take out of the freezer.

She smelled it then. The dry rotten fur. A sick smell that made her gag.

And underneath, on the other side of the dog, the flat side, she saw these . . . things. Little squirming things that danced around the inside of the dog's body. Some dropping off as the man—giggling, laughing so loud—kept lifting it higher into the air.

What is he going to . . . she wondered.

She squirmed back a few more feet.

He held the dog up.

A prize.

Then he let it swing back and forth, while all sorts of white wormy things sprinkled off it, toward her bare legs.

"Don' worry. I'll take care of dis puppy." He came closer. "And I'll take care of you . . ."

And then he flung it over the fence, into the weeds, the sand, the broken glass. A speck of something landed on her face. It moved. She screamed. The hot air swallowed the sound.

He stood over her.

"It's cool . . ." he laughed . . . then he sang . . ."under the boardwalk . . ." another step . . . "boardwalk . . ."

She sprang up now, turning, trying to run past him, back to people.

But he snagged her hair and snapped her back, still singing . . . "Boardwalk . . . boardwalk . . ."

His hand covered her mouth. She tasted the metal of his rings. The sweat. He put her into a head lock, and walked her to the streaked shadows under the boardwalk.

His other hand squeezed her. Around her stomach. Feeling her. Then his hand moved higher.

Paddy Sullivan stood up. It was time to move on. Hit the trail. Yes, sir. Enough procrastinating, for Christ's sake.

Let's start the day's festivities.

When he heard the sound. A strange whimpering noise.

Coming from one of the side streets.

Normally, he minded his own business. If someone wanted to blow their brains out with crack, that was none of his goddam business. We all pick our poison. And if the paranoia boo-joos got someone, then that was their fuckin' breaks.

I got my own problems, he thought.

But this was a curious sound.

And though it had been centuries ago that he had been a cop, he walked off the boardwalk, down to that street, following the sound. Breaking his code.

A simple rule.

Not to get involved with someone else's shit.

No matter what.

He saw the girl. She looked young. She wore nice clothes, white shorts, a pink and white top. The man was dragging her toward the tunnel.

Lots of strange shit went on in the tunnel.

At night, some freaks liked to just walk on top, and peer down through the cracks in the boards and catch all the sick action going on down below.

Lots of real unsafe sex.

And crack parties all the time.

The girl kicked at the man.

What is she doing here, Paddy wondered, walking down the steps. Maybe they're together. Fighting over who gets that last toke. But no . . . she looked too nice . . . too young.

He held the handrail. The shakes had started. He knew they would. He waited too damn long. He could almost enjoy the rattling, now that he was—yes, sir—on his way. McCann's was only two blocks away.

He licked his lips, feeling how goddam unsteady he was.

He heard the girl whelp.

I should do something.

They were across the street.

And only a few feet from the boardwalk. From the tunnel.

He pulled up his sagging pants. Am I shrinking? he wondered, every morning when he tightened his belt to keep his baggy trousers up. I'm fuckin' wasting away. I'm fuckin' dying. And I don't give a shit.

His heart was thumping away . . .

Just thinking about doing something. He was scared. It had been so long since he had to do anything, anything except walk down his stairs, to get to McCann's, to go buy a bottle, to cash his disability check.

"Hey," he said. "What are you doing there?"

Paddy heard how thin his voice sounded.

Thin, and desperate.

The kid ignored him. Maybe didn't even hear him.

He was almost there.

And Paddy could imagine what the kid would do to the girl. A nice girl like that. She was a kid. A baby.

I've got a daughter, Paddy thought.

Somewhere.

He walked across the street. His feet seemed clumsy, ready to trip over themselves. He called again. "Hey, you . . . stop!"

The kid looked up. Unafraid.

"Fuck you!" he screamed.

Paddy grabbed at his pants. The kid sneered at him.

Maybe I can't do this, he thought. Maybe I should just—

The girl looked at him.

He saw just one eye. A pretty eggshell blue. But wild, wide open.

And Paddy hurried to her as best he could.

The punk saw him coming and tossed the girl away. He greeted Paddy with a too-quick chop to his stomach.

"Aw!" Paddy groaned. Then, still trying to get some air, he felt the kid kick his balls.

The kid laughed as Paddy doubled up, ready to go to his knees.

Can't do that, he thought. This animal would just keep kicking and punching and kicking—

He looked up. The kid was close. A pencil-thin mustache on his upper lip. Long, straight black hair. *But close.*

Paddy thought . . . Can I still throw a punch? Jesus.

And while still bent over, Paddy brought his meaty fist up, right into the punk's midsection, and then he brought his other fist around and caught his kidney with another blow.

Now the kid was bug-eyed.

Now he looked scared.

Paddy stood up.

The girl should run away, he thought.

"Go. Get the hell away," he snapped at her. But she stood there, watching.

He half expected the kid to have a knife, or a gun. Something that could really hurt him. But he came at Paddy with his bare fists, angry.

Careless.

Paddy smacked the kid's face, a loud thwack that snapped the kid's head back.

Some things you don't forget, Paddy guessed.

The kid stopped. He blinked. Wondering whether to try for it again.

"Come on, you little fuck," Paddy sneered. "Come here and let me break your fucking head open."

The kid hesitated.

And then a bit of a grin sneaked onto the kid's face.

"We'll get your ass later, you dumb old fuck . . ."

And then the kid tore away, down the block, into Astroland.

Paddy turned, smiling, proud of himself. Not bad, he thought. After all these—

Then he saw the girl, her hair all stringy, strands stuck to her face, wet from the tears. She was crying, leaning against the wire fence.

Paddy walked over to her.

He touched her shoulder tentatively. "Come on, miss. Want me to walk you home . . . ?"

And the girl looked up at him, all blotchy eyes and tear-streaked cheeks.

She nodded.

Chapter Seventeen

WALTER didn't move.

Built like a tank, and he just . . . *stood there*.

Gene looked at him, rubbed his beard. His program staff were running around, oblivious to anything wrong. They knew better than to bother Gene.

They'd just look over and think—

What was there to be worried about?

Walter was with him. The human tank.

But Walter stood stock-still. And Gene thought about yelling for help.

He looked up at the tall, dull-eyed black man, looking like a lumbering zombie from an old Val Lewton movie. And the man next to him, smiling at him, as if he was selling religious pamphlets door to door.

"Walter," Gene said again, louder.

The short man shook his head.

"Five minutes. That's all Jay and I require, Gene, five little minutes of your time. And I promise that you won't be disappointed . . . not at all."

Gene licked his lips.

I could walk away. I could scream, he thought. Yell for help. There were security guards . . . over there, by the side doors. And lots of production people, and—

He felt the man touch his shoulder. Patting him.

Turning him around back toward his office.

"All set, Gene," someone called to him from the side.

And he let himself be led away, pulled by the man.

"I go on the air in—"

The man laughed. "I know. Don't worry, Gene. You'll have plenty of time."

And he wondered why—funny thing—nobody seemed to think it odd to see him walking off the set, with these two strange men.

"If anything's happened to Jo," Caryn said, walking out the main gate, past hot parents and tired, sweaty kids, "I swear to God, I'll—"

She pushed through the turnstile. Annie, Martin, and now Steven followed her.

She kept talking.

It kept the images away.

Fuzzy pictures of children, beautiful children, dressed in new clothes from J. C. Penney's, with bright sneakers and colorful clips in their hair.

She knew what these people—these monsters—did to children.

She did a story once.

On parents in the Big Apple.

And the creatures that waited for them to slip up, to get careless . . . to forget.

Look at a picture, she thought. A crisp Kodacolor picture of your smiling ballerina, your star gymnast, your ace goalie.

Then cut off the head.

Take their clothes off.

And dump them somewhere dark . . .

Let the animals—the vermin—get at them.

Now look at them.

Look at them . . .

She moaned. To the wind. To the stale Coney Island air.

When she nearly walked into her daughter.

"Mom," Jo said.

Caryn looked up.

"Jo," she said. Then louder, screaming gleefully. "Jo!"

She kissed her daughter, pressed her lips against her cheek. She tasted the salt.

Then Caryn pushed her away, holding her shoulders as if they were in pincers. Jo's face was lined with wet blotches. Her hair was stringy, pasted to her face.

"Jo," she whispered, the word lost to the screams echoing from the Cyclone. "What happened?"

"I . . . a man chased me . . . he grabbed me—"

Caryn looked over her daughter's shoulder. There was a man there. A bum. Baggy pants. A threadbare yellow shirt. A crazy patchwork of veins crisscrossed his nose, his cheeks.

Caryn stared at the man.

He seemed to back away.

Jo looked up at her . . . saw where she was looking.

"This man," she said, turning, "saved me."

The man nodded. But Caryn kept looking at him, not believing that this disheveled wreck could have anything to do with her daughter, her beautiful daughter.

But Jo squeezed her hand.

"He saved me, Mom . . ."

Michael bumped into the railing.

His fingers went to his hood. He was out of air. And he had no choice but to take the hood off.

No danger there, he realized. There's no bacteria . . . no weird virus here.

He saw Reilly's face go pale, all sick.

Then he spoke.

"I'm okay," Reilly said, looking at Cameron. "I don't need any quarantine."

"Sure," Cameron said, still oblivious to the fact that there was something wrong here.

(But Michael now saw Lake back away . . . watching everything.)

Reilly shook his head. "I'm fine. I just—"

Michael pulled his hood off. He took a big breath and shouted at Reilly. "What about the rope locker? What the hell happened there?"

Reilly's face looked all confused.

"Mike," Cameron said, annoyed. "What's all this shit about the rope locker?"

Michael saw Barsky distance himself from Cameron and the survivor. He had seen the bodies and now he was catching on to the fact that there was something wrong with Reilly.

"They're all in the rope locker, Cameron. All the bodies . . . stacked four feet high, drained, dry, their skin thin as tissue paper."

Reilly looked like he was going to belch.

Michael glanced down to the water. The launch bobbed behind the research ship. And the only way to get to it was past Reilly.

"He told me . . ." Cameron said. "Everyone got sick . . . food poisoning . . . or something. The radio went dead and—"

But even Cameron isn't that big an idiot, Michael saw. At first he must have been happy to see someone alive. But now he was belatedly flashing on the fact that there was something peculiar about Reilly . . . about his story.

Cameron moved a step away from Reilly.

"Drained?" Cameron said quietly.

Another step.

Not in time. Not nearly far enough.

Reilly's eyes went wide, suddenly alert with a speed and purpose that made Michael stumble backward.

I don't want to end up like them, Michael thought. He remembered their faces, their lips pulled back from dry gums. Chunky woodlike tongues hanging out of their mouths. The face muscles tight, locked in a permanent scream.

"Watch—"

He started to yell.

Lake brought his gun up.

Reilly turned to Cameron.

His face was grim, determined. Then his crisp khaki shirt began to glisten in the sun as a sopping red stain spread, bloomed on his chest.

Cameron tried to step away.

But Reilly reached out—so fast—and grabbed Cameron's wrist.

Then the blooming red stain suddenly opened, like a hot chestnut popping open. There was the sound of tearing skin being stretched open and apart. Tiny showers of red began squirting on the deck.

"Oh, Christ!" Cameron said.

He tried to wrangle himself away from Reilly's grip. But he only succeeded in pulling Reilly along with him.

Now the shirt buttons popped open.

Lake took a step closer to them.

"No," Michael yelled.

Don't get close to it, he thought.

Don't . . .

Lake stopped.

The SEAL pulled back the latch on his rifle.

He brought the gun up.

Just as Reilly's shirt ripped open. His chest was wide open, glistening red, and white, and then—

Michael saw it. A chunky tube thing. It lashed out, like a garden hose gone amuck.

Cameron was screaming, crying, begging for help.

Reilly's face gave no sign of being in distress. His eyes watched Cameron writhing, grabbing at the railing.

Michael watched Lake pull the trigger. It seemed to take forever.

The gun's blasts momentarily covered Cameron's screaming.

Reilly's head was blown away.

Bits of skull and brain showered onto the deck.

But still the thing inside Reilly, the tube, snaked out, streaked with globby red. An eel . . . a snake . . . a worm . . . It moved too fast, whipping around.

And Reilly still held tight to Cameron.

The worm—eyeless, seemingly without a head—landed on Cameron's leg. And stuck there. Michael heard violent sucking sounds.

Lake fired again, the powerful gun sounding like a cannon.

This time he aimed at the thing inside Reilly.

The shot blew right into Reilly's midsection.

The headless body flew backward, sliding on the bloody deck, sitting down. Chunks of the worm thing flew into the air.

Don't let any of it land on me, Michael prayed. 'Cause he knew . . .

Knew.

That wouldn't be a good thing.

Cameron was screaming, clutching the rail like a baby who didn't want to leave a toystore, yelling and screaming.

But the worm was off his leg.

Leaving a saucer-sized hole just below Cameron's hips.

Lake fired again.

But this time Reilly's body—sitting on the deck, surrounded by bits of bone, and worm, and blood—flopped around.

Like a flounder about to be pounded on the head.

The snapping noise it made on the deck was terrible, a horrible pounding as if it were knocking on the door to hell.

Let me out.

For the first time, Michael thought—

What the fuck is this?

But then he was too caught up in watching the thing.

What was left of the tube slithered out of Reilly. It slid onto the deck, wriggling as if it were on a griddle. One end was smooth, tapered to an edge like an ivory letter opener.

The other was ragged, cut off by Lake's blast.

Michael hoped that the SEAL would hit it again. Real fast.

But his next shot caught Reilly's abandoned body, sliding it down the deck like a platter in a shuffleboard game.

"Get the fucking thing!" Michael screamed.

Knowing—even then—what it all really meant.

What was *really* happening.

And just how goddam important the next few seconds would be. "Get the—"

Lake fired.

But the thing slid straight toward the rail. As if it sensed the water ahead. Like a cat, scratching at the door on a miserably cold winter's night.

It moved awkwardly, flailing around. But it had tremendous strength, as it flipped to the edge of the deck, to the railing, and then—

As they all watched—

It went over the side.

Into the glistening blue water of the Atlantic Ocean.

Cameron stood still . . . whimpering.

Michael took charge.

"We've got to gather this stuff," he said, pointing to the chunks of the worm on the deck. "As much as we can."

"And the body?" Barsky asked, pointing to Reilly's body, still sitting up, near the bow of the ship.

"Yeah . . . Christ, we can get that too. But later. We need the video tapes . . . and the disks from the data logger."

Then he turned to Cameron.

Saw him standing by the railing. No longer all crouched up, grimacing, in agony.

He stood up straight.

"Ian . . ." Michael said, coming close to him. "How's your leg?"

And Cameron smiled.

As if nothing had happened.

(Michael felt gooseflesh rise on his arms.)

Cameron smiled.

As if they had all just spent a day sailing the Vineyard Sound in a catamaran with orange and yellow sails.

"Fine," he said, shrugging. He brushed at the wound, as if it were merely an annoyance, like a fly. "Sucker nipped, that's all. No big deal." He nodded. "I'll dress it when we get back."

Michael nodded.

He saw Dailey, the young Coast Guard lieutenant, wobbling near the rail, looking as if he was going to upchuck over the side.

"You okay?" Michael started to say.

Then the young lieutenant did just as Michael expected. And

while Dailey hacked away, Lake came over to Michael. "What the hell was that thing? What kind of animal was it?" Lake asked.

Michael shook his head. He'd take some pieces back to his lab. Back to Brooklyn.

He looked down at the water.

It was out there now.

Shit, it was fucking out there!

He looked up again.

Cameron was walking back to the launch.

There were specimen bags there, sterile containers, a first-aid kit.

And—as Cameron walked away—Michael watched his leg, the one with the wound. He watched how well it moved, how naturally. As if it hadn't been chewed up by a tapeworm from hell.

He watched Cameron climb down the steps to the sub hangar, then down to the submersible winch, past the damaged ROV, past Lil Shit.

As if there were nothing wrong with him . . . nothing at all.

"Go ahead, Mr. Barron," Gene said nervously. "You've got your five minutes."

Barron smiled. He looked at Jay.

Then back at Gene.

(I bet I can guess what you're into, Barron thought. The good things, the prizes. Beautiful women. A nice mansion in the Hamptons. Maybe a bit of nose candy, now and then. Just a snort or two. All part of the rewards . . .)

"Jay, here, has a message, Gene. He speaks for them, Gene. He's their *voice*."

Gene shook his head. "What do you mean . . . 'he speaks for them'? Who are 'they'?"

Barron made a small laugh. "Why, I'm surprised at you. Aren't *you* one of their intermediaries, one of their earthly representatives? For the true spirits." Barron stood up. "You claim they speak through you, don't you? People pay for your messages. You sell them the toys, the crystals, the books. You're in contact with them, aren't you?"

There was a knock on the office door. A voice. "All set, Gene."

Barron stood up. He walked to the door. And locked it. Just in case.

He looked down at Jay. He looked at his eyes, hidden behind his bad-ass shades. His mouth hung open, all dull and drooly.

"Well, yes, I've had some contacts—" Gene started to lie.

"Oh, yes, Ramfar, Seth, Laen, Elak . . . yes. I've heard of them. You channel their voices, don't you? Their desires . . . their wants. And for a donation, you can even arrange personal visitations. It's wonderful. Inspirational."

Gene stood up. "Yes . . . I'd better go, I don't see—"

Barron put up a hand.

Jay stirred in his seat.

"They need you, Gene," Barron said. "They need your show, your new-age network. You see, a very special time is coming—"

He walked over to Jay and took his shades off.

He fought to keep the grin off his face.

"And Jay here is the real thing. The real McCoy. And he has a message for all your viewers . . . all your followers. And you, you're very lucky. Because you get to see it first."

Barron tossed Jay's shades onto the desk and he walked—not too fast—toward Gene.

"Wh-what?" Gene said.

Barron looked back at Jay.

Of course, I'll have to watch it too, he thought.

Though I'd rather not.

And Jay opened his mouth. He tilted his head. His eyes, just half closed a moment ago, now opened wide.

Jay looked up at Barron, then turned to Gene.

"I have to get—" Gene said.

Barron came closer to him.

To cover his mouth.

When the screaming started.

It would take only minutes. And Gene would know his new role.

For as long as they wanted him to have it.

And like me—Barron thought—he'll do it. Because anything—anything—is better than becoming one of the others.

He saw Gene looking at Jay. Jay's face suddenly looked alert. His skin looked tight, glistening under the fluorescent lights.

And Jay spoke.

"Gene . . ." he said, a voice that was an ageless hollow. It filled the room with blackness. Pain. And in Jay's eyes, there was something cold.

Poor bastard, Barron thought, looking at Gene.

Poor fucking bastard.

Barron quickly slipped his hand over Gene's mouth.

The screams were muffled against his chunky palm.

And Barron had to arch his body away . . . as Gene let go, pissing on the ground.

Poor fucking bastard.

And Barron tried not to look.

I don't want to see this . . . I don't have to see this.

But he looked.

And even he whimpered.

THREE

REVELATIONS

Chapter Eighteen

MICHAEL shut the car radio off and once again tried to get the air conditioner to do more than wheeze out some weird-smelling air.

But the compressor, or whatever made the air cold, just gave out a bunch of pained clicks and whirring noises, and Michael was forced to open the windows.

It was past eight, the sun was nearly down. And still the temperature was over 90 degrees.

At least he beat the city after the commuters had finished tying up the New England Thruway.

He hit a bump.

And he turned around and looked at the back seat.

The vials bounced and jiggled, but they rolled together on the seat with a muted sound. There were three of them, wrapped in a Styrofoam matting.

Cameron would freak if he knew he had them.

When Michael asked to take the samples, just as soon as they got back to the Woods Hole dock, Cameron had turned around, a nasty sneer on his face. "It's Woods Hole material," he snapped. "And it stays here. You're welcome to help, Cross. But nothing goes to New York. Got that? Nothing."

Right, thought Michael. That was perfectly clear.

But fuck him. He invited me up to help. And there's no way I'm not going to attempt to find out what happened to the poor bastards on the *Achilles*. Did they all get those tube worms inside them? Did it kill them, like it killed Reilly?

Where did the worm come from? A bad batch of canned chow mein? Shoppers, avoid batch twenty-three . . .

And what happened to the worms? Are they down in the rope locker, buried under the crispy-thin bodies?

(And would I ever go in there to take another look? Not a chance . . .)

The worm would probably die in the ocean. But he might find out what happened before Cameron's people. It might free up some grant money.

Michael didn't have any problem getting chunks of the dead worm out of the lab. His key still worked in the lab door, and the security guards all knew him.

Hiya, Dr. Cross.

That was easy.

But duping the video tape had been another story altogether.

Cameron took that, and the disks from the data logger, directly to his office. Michael imagined a paranoid Cameron locking them up in some vault, just behind his teak-framed degree from Yale.

The *Achilles* was a Coast Guard matter now. Cameron would have to file a report on what might have happened . . . after he studied the tape, the disks, the samples. But he left quickly, mumbling something about going to his doctor.

Reasonable enough. Considering the thing nearly chewed a hole through his leg.

(And why the fuck didn't it bother him?)

A meeting—about the *Achilles*, the dead crew, everything—was set up for the next morning. A press conference was scheduled for that afternoon. Until then, no one was to say anything. And when Cameron left, his office was locked.

But that didn't turn out to be such a big problem.

The cleaning lady showed up at five o'clock. Michael had to wait for her, killing time in the lab. She opened Cameron's office. Then all he had to do was go in there, saying he had left something just that afternoon, and—ah, here it is—

Cameron had left the tape right on his desk. The computer disks, though, were nowhere in sight. Michael thought of opening the desk drawer, but he didn't want to get the old woman suspicious. Let's do this clean, he thought.

He used the main lab's high-speed VCR to make a copy of the tape. Then he brought the original back to Cameron's office just as the cleaning woman was finishing up.

Now, moving quickly on the New England Thruway, he was hours away from getting some ideas what happened to the *Achilles*. He was glad to be driving back to Brooklyn. This might be important.

He thought of Jo. She'd be in his apartment, sleeping. He'd have to watch the tape with headphones on. No sleep tonight. That was okay. His adrenaline was up.

He thought of the bodies in the rope locker, and then Reilly and the thing he had inside his body.

What the hell was it? How did it live?

And only one idea suggested itself.

Parasite.

But that was impossible. It was too damn big. Three, maybe four feet long . . . and Reilly didn't know it was inside his body?

He had to know.

And he thought of Cameron, walking away from the attack like he had just been bitten by a mosquito. No big deal, gang.

There's something screwy there.

And despite the terrible, suffocating heat, Michael shivered.

Yeah, he thought. I've got to get a handle on this, he thought. And I've got to do it fast . . .

Cameron went to bed early.

The bedroom was barely lit by the pale summer twilight. His wife had been worried. She wondered what was wrong. He mentioned a bite. Nothing important. Nothing to be worried about.

He said everyone had been dead on the *Achilles*. He didn't know what happened.

And he lay there, no pajama shirt on, but with the pants covering his leg, covering the wound that he had bandaged himself.

He tried to understand what he was feeling.

He tried real hard.

He felt good. Very relaxed, calm. There was no concern about the *Achilles* or Reilly. The meetings tomorrow. The press conference. That would all sort itself out. Or not. It didn't matter.

Before he came to the bed, he thought he felt hungry. But when he bit into an apple it tasted bitter, waxy. Then he had opened a blueberry yogurt, stirring the mashed fruit up from the bottom. But just bringing the fruit close to his lips made him gag.

But he felt healthy. Real good, as a matter of fact. As if he should go out and run, do a nice three- or four-mile jog. Maybe some racket ball at the club. Maybe jump his wife's scrawny bones when she came in.

And that's when the odd twinge, the odd hunger he felt, seemed to slowly come into focus.

Instinctively he let his hand trail down his side, past his hip, to the bandage.

He wanted to take it off.

To look at it.

See how bad it is.

Maybe I should have gone to the doctor, like I said, to the hospital.

But no. He knew that that was something he didn't want to do. It was an uncomfortable feeling, like knowing you were supposed to go to the dentist.

Only a thousand times worse.

No, he wouldn't go to a doctor.

Besides, he told himself.

(*Lied to himself.*)

It's nothing.

He touched the bandage.

The phone rang, startling him. His hand quickly snapped away from his bandage.

It rang again. He waited for his wife to get it. He heard her voice from the living room. Then her steps, as she walked into the bedroom, darker now, as the twilight gave way to a hot, sticky night.

"Someone named Colonel Barsky, Ian. He said he was with you today, on the ship."

His wife was a tall shadow, outlined by yellowish light from the living room.

He felt his pulse quicken as he looked at her.

"Should I tell him you'll speak to him tomorrow—"

He was tempted to say yes. Tell him tomorrow. Then, come here.

Next to me.

But then something worried him.

"No," he said. "I'll talk to him."

Cameron turned and picked up the phone.

"Yes."

Barsky's voice sounded strained, distant. Like he was calling from a pay phone.

"I spoke to my base commander, Dr. Cameron. They'd like us to have another look at the ship, perhaps—"

His wife was watching him. She was wearing a thin summer nightgown. He was aware of her legs moving as she shifted her weight, listening.

"No. I don't want anyone on the ship. Not until we—"

She moved closer. Sat on the bed.

He smelled her hair. A bit of perfume, faint from the morning. Her skin.

"—know some more. Absolutely not."

Barsky said nothing for a moment. Then Cameron heard him sigh. "I'm afraid that the ship is under Coast Guard jurisdiction, sir. There's nothing you can do about it." Barsky waited. Then when Cameron didn't say anything, he said, "We're also going to dive tomorrow . . . in the Sound. See if we can—"

Cameron sat up. He squeezed the phone, yelled into it. He felt his wife touch his shoulder.

"Didn't you hear me, Colonel. I said no one does anything—"

"It's out of your hands, sir. I've already got approval for a dry suit dive with toxic gear. First thing tomorrow. It's out of your hands."

Barsky waited. And Cameron looked into the blackness and then, slowly, turning, looked at his wife. She was lying beside him. Stroking his bare shoulder.

Right, he thought. There's nothing I can do.

It doesn't matter, he knew then.

Not really.

Cameron heard Barsky's voice, still faint, mouselike, as he began to slide the phone back to its cradle.

"Of course, we'll share anything we find with—"

Cameron clattered the phone onto the receiver.

"What was it?" his wife whispered, her fingers still touching his bare shoulder. Her eyes caught some of the half-light then. Tiny little sparkling droplets.

What's her name? Cameron wondered. What's this woman's name?

His heartbeat seemed so loud it was thundering inside his chest. He felt a warmth far below.

Like getting an erection.

Only there was no warmth coming from his penis. It was lower still—

"You should rest," she said. "You've had a harrowing day."

He nodded.

He turned to his side, facing her. He felt her body shift on the bed, as if in answer.

These moves, this dance, was familiar to him. This slow edging closer together.

It brought her close.

He reached up. Touched her hair, stroked her cheek.

Eileen. That was her name.

It doesn't matter.

She wiggled even closer.

(And now, the warmth began to spread, filled him. He mumbled a sound, a moan. Her pelvis pushed against him.)

"Oh," she said, her voice coming from nowhere, from everywhere. Her hand reached down, burrowing under the sheets, and touched him, touched his flaccid penis. "I thought that you'd be ready."

She must feel the heat, he thought, the tremendous searing warmth.

But no. She just pulled at him.

"Maybe," she said, leaning up a bit, "it needs a little help."

And he felt the bed move as she slid down, lower, lower, until her head was right near his belly. Her fingers hooked under his pajama bottoms. She pulled at the elastic, easing it down.

And he arched up, letting her slide them down, slowly, over his hips, and down his legs.

Her fingers brushed against the bandage.

He licked his lips.

The need was clear now. Like nothing had ever been clear before. Not food, not sex. This was what life was about. This moment of tremendous need and filling it.

She tossed away the pajamas.

And lay her head on his thigh.

Just inches away. Her hair fell across his groin.

She brought her lips close to his skin.

(He could almost smile. How deceiving things appear. It's not what she thinks, not at all. There's something far more wonderful going on here.)

Her tongue lashed at him.

She said something again, something light and funny. Something about sleeping dogs. Because nothing was happening.

He didn't hear her at all.

He just heard the sound of the tape peeling off his leg, the bandage being pushed off his leg. He felt it pull at his hairs.

All by itself.

Because something was pushing at the bandage, pushing it up, away.

Pushing from inside.

He wanted to reach down and touch it, to feel it. It was small now.

Now . . .

But he was too crazed to move, to do anything, but just wait.

He heard a rip.

She heard it too.

She moved her head away. Just a bit.

"What's that?" she said.

She looked over. Down to his leg.

She screamed.

For just a moment he couldn't see what happened. He just heard the odd gurgles coming from her mouth . . . or was it her throat? Bubbling . . . popping sounds . . .

Then the only thing he heard was his own gasps, as wave after wave of pleasure, ecstasy, rippled through him.

And he knew what he lived for.

Chapter Nineteen

BARRON watched a cute young thing come up to Gene and dab at his brow with a pad. The brilliant white light gave a wonderful sheen to his beard.

Why, I'd trust him too, Barron thought. Just look at those blue eyes! Yes, on a big color set, Dr. Gene Fasolt was a most-impressive religious huckster.

Of course, it took poor Gene some time to recover from his new message, his calling. Gene had to regain his composure. And he needed a clean pair of pants. Soiled himself, he did. His TV crew just had to run more footage of Manhattan, the cold, cruel travelogue of desperate city streets.

Hopelessness is the problem. And Dr. Gene has the answer.

That was the message.

Now, Gene looked almost all right. His lower lip still trembled a bit. And he seemed to be looking away, somewhere out there, beyond the cameras and the lights.

Looking for a way out.

Despite air ducts pumping in refrigerated air, the studio was hot. There was a smell of electricity and hot lights.

A clean-cut young man stood near a camera, checking his watch, listening to a voice over his headphones.

Gene was about to go live.

And then Barron saw the new-age charlatan look across the studio. To another battery of cameras.

They were all aimed at Jay, who sat slumped over in his chair as if he was just about to nod off.

Barron heard the people buzzing about, wondering what Gene had planned. What was up? And who is this black guy? they whispered. What's he doing? Why are we putting *him* on?

Barron heard them. Just wait, he thought. A little patience, that's all. He looked at Gene, then back to the young director.

The director put up two fists. Then he said, "Now—"

And he opened his fists, showing ten fingers. Then nine. Eight.

Gene looked away, as if he wanted to dash out.

But that was impossible. Barron was sure he knew that.

Five. Four. Three.

Now, the director made a big gesture for—

Two. And a one . . .

And he pointed his finger at Gene.

Barron took a step closer. He could see the red light blink on.

"You're out there," Gene said. "I know you're out there. Waiting for—" Gene hesitated. Looked to the side. Barron heard more buzzes from the back. He heard them whispering, "What's wrong? What's wrong with Gene?"

But then Gene looked back at the red-dot eye of the camera. He cleared his throat. And again . . .

"You're out there. Number five. Number six. All of you. Everyone waiting for a voice, a message . . . an answer." He licked his lips. "Someone to help you out of"—his voice raised, an old horse pulling familiar traces—"the stupid mess you made of your lives."

Another whisper. Right near Barron's elbow. "Where's his cigar? Why doesn't he have his cigar?"

Barron was tempted to turn around. And tell them—don't worry. Gene just decided to quit smoking.

For health reasons.

Gene shifted in his seat.

"But I'll tell you what we're not going to do here anymore. We're not going to be running this campaign anymore. We can't wait. Not anymore . . ."

Barron heard Gene lower his voice, as if he lost his thread.

Come on, Barron thought. Get on with it.

(Because maybe they'll let me go. Maybe they'll cut me loose to get some good food. Or check on some of the action in the city. Take a look at the almond-eyed boy-girls who prowl the city when the worker drones flee to suburbia.)

"Now I have something for all of you. I—I—"

Shit, Barron thought. Hold it together. Don't fall apart on the camera. Not now, asshole. He saw a tiny wet drop in one eye. The poor bastard's remembering . . . remembering what he saw, what it felt like . . . what it could feel like again.

"There's a new spirit," he went on. "A spirit that wants to talk . . . to *all* of you. A spirit that wants to invite you to leave your old ways, your old broken-down life that doesn't work anymore. Are you listening to me? Do you hear me out there?"

The cameraman looked to the side, right at the director who shrugged.

Gene stood up.

Good, thought Barron, very effective.

The cameraman had to react quickly, tilting the heavy camera up to keep it on Gene's face. Gene was sweating now, looking more and more confused. Barron saw the director look to the back, to someone at the back of the studio. He made a cutting sign with his hand, questioning.

Barron took a step toward the director. Just in case . . .

"You've got to listen," Gene stammered. "You hear me." Gene sat back on his stool. Worn out. Drained. Then, slowly, he looked up. "Listen to the voice of peace and healing . . . listen to—"

And here Barron had to laugh, hearing the name he invented . . .

"Listen to Jay."

The director shrugged. And Barron saw the red light blink off. And then, from across a sea of wires, someone was pointing at Jay.

Barron felt a funny rumbling in his stomach.

Do I have to do something now? he wondered . . .

But there was nothing.

Just the sound of hushed steps behind him . . . concerned steps.

He watched Jay open his eyes.

Jay looked right at the camera.

Big, black smoldering eyes. Black pearls sunk in a sea of milky white. Intelligent eyes. Jay opened his mouth.

Slowly. His white teeth gleamed under the lights.

And when Jay finally spoke even Barron felt blessed.

"You can go sulk in your bedroom, Johanna."

Whenever her mother called her Johanna it was bad news.

Johanna. Like she had suddenly become a stranger. It didn't feel good.

Driving to New York, her mother had only hinted at some of the new rules. There was going to be a whole new way of doing things.

This could be real bad, Jo realized.

But the worst past was what it might mean for her dad. Her mother had already said what she was going to do.

Driving with two hands locked tight on the steering wheel.

Her pretty face all scrunched-up and nasty-looking.

"I'm going to call my lawyer . . . get this on the court record. Since your father isn't able to watch you even for a couple of weeks. Christ! What is wrong with him?"

At first Jo said nothing. A good pout was usually the best defense when you did something really wrong. But Jo flashed on the fact that it wasn't going to work this time. Her mother had been scared . . . and angry.

We have a problem, she said to Jo.

As if she had some disease, something they have telethons about. Is your kid stubborn, willful? Does she do whatever she wants to do, no matter what the danger? Then call this 800 number and contribute.

Once Jo tried to explain—

(Not really knowing how she was going to pull off *that trick*.)

But her mother told her to be quiet. She had to just sit and listen to all the things that were going to be different.

Now, back at the apartment, the air conditioners jacked up to high, struggling to get the dead plastic smell out of the air, her mother was working, organizing her yellow pads, her tapes.

"Why do you have to work now?" Jo whined.

Her mother's fingers danced on the computer's keys. Jo looked up at the screen, watching the words magically appear.

"Because"—her mom kept on banging away—"if I don't get this done now I'll forget. It has to be fresh."

Jo nodded—an unseen gesture—and then backed away.

"Go watch some TV. In your room."

"Can I go down to the health club? Have a swim?"

Her mother stopped.

And turned, facing her.

Real mad.

"Absolutely not. You're on a short leash, Johanna. And I don't know for how long. Until I feel I can trust you. And that means no swimming in the pool unless I take you."

Jo nodded.

How horrible life suddenly turned.

(She thought then about the man chasing her. The dead dog. The hot sun and nice old guy who helped her. A bum, her mother called him. God, he saved me and Mom calls him a bum!)

She turned and walked out of the room, to her bedroom.

It was a small bedroom, done in a pale purple, with a small bed with captain's drawers underneath, and a white pine desk that she didn't like at all. That was the homework place. During summ she liked to forget about school, and the desk sitting there only reminded her.

In the corner there was a small color TV. Hooked up to cable.

She turned it on, knowing that there wouldn't be anything good on. No new shows, just dumb repeats of the same dumb sit-coms. More happy families spending all the time laughing and talking about dumb problems that aren't real.

She sat on the corner of her bed and pushed off her sneakers without untying them. She picked up the remote control and began zapping through the channels.

All the good-looking happy people on TV. She hated them. Then there was baseball. God, she thought. How can anyone watch baseball every day? It all looks the same. She came to wrestling, and she stopped for a moment. Hulk Hogan was on, screaming about someone called Macho Man. He was going to hurt Macho Man real bad. When he spoke he was spitting, spraying the bug-eyed announcer who was dressed in a tuxedo.

There was a girl standing next to Hulk Hogan. She had on an orange-red evening dress. Her titties seemed ready to pop out. Hulk Hogan kept calling her the "Beautiful Lady Elaine."

Jo didn't think she looked like a lady at all.

She zapped past *MASH*, then the weather channel.

See what's doing in Texas.

HBO had *The Abyss* on for the umpteenth time.

Now it was really downhill. The shopping channels. Just great if you were in the market for a combination toaster oven/answering machine. Zap. Baseball, this time from Chicago. God! The 700 Club. MTV had a rap song on.

That just reminded her of JJs Bump-o-Rama. Fat dudes dressed in black leather. She kept on going, just about to the end of the forty-two channels.

And then—

She saw a man. A black man.

It was as if he were looking at her, right at her.

But his voice—it was beautiful. Rich and deep.

She came closer to the screen. Listened to what he was saying.

He talked about pain. We all have our pain, he said, looking out of the screen.

Looking right at her.

We keep it secret. It's private.

But it won't go away. Not unless we share it.

She watched his eyes. They seemed to be able to see into her room. She squirmed on her bed.

It's like he can see me, she thought.

Her finger went to zap past the channel. It's just another religious show, one of those dopey things, she thought, where they talk about God and pray for you and beg Jesus to come into your life.

But her finger hesitated, resting on the rubber pad of the controller. And waited.

While she listened.

Just a bit more.

A religious show, she guessed.

And he didn't say anything about Jesus or God.

"Hello," Michael said, opening the door to the dark apartment. "Anybody home?"

But it was clear that the place was empty.

Funny, he thought. It was kind of late for Annie to have Jo out. He was annoyed at her for having her out so late. It wasn't too damn safe out there, no matter how street-smart Annie was.

He turned on the living-room light.

There was a note propped against the lamp.

He picked it up, letting his small carry-on bag slide onto the couch.

He read Annie's brief version of the day's events.

Jo running off . . . and Caryn's surprise return . . .

"Damn!" he said. And after the brief flash of anger, he was worried. His relationship with his ex, their arguments over Jo, were bad enough without this problem.

He hurried to the kitchen phone and dialed Caryn's number.

She picked up on the second ring.

"Hello," she said coldly, as if she had been waiting for his call.

"Caryn . . . it's Michael. Hey, I'm sorry—"

She cut him off quickly. "Save it, Michael. I'm calling my lawyer tomorrow. I'm not going to allow her to stay with you when you can't watch her."

"Great. Go give some more money to your husband-eating bull-dyke lawyer. That's just what Jo needs—"

"She sure as hell doesn't need her father leaving her alone, letting her—"

"I didn't leave her alone," Michael yelled. "I left her with Annie and—"

"Just 'cause she fucks you don't go dumping my daughter with—"

God, he thought. She thinks I fucked Annie. That's the problem with trust. Once you lose it, baby, it's gone forever.

"Hey—" he said quietly, struggling to get her calmed down. "Okay. I screwed up. But there was this problem in Woods Hole. The press will get it tomorrow. Everyone on the expedition di—"

"Spare me, Michael. I only give a damn about Jo. Do you know she was saved by a bum, do you know that? Some Coney Island alky saved your daughter."

Annie hadn't put that in her note.

Michael felt defeated, tired. There was no point in hashing this out now.

"Just do me a favor, Caryn. Just for tomorrow. Don't call your lawyer. I can't afford any more legal shit. And I don't see how you can. I'll call tomorrow, all right?"

There was a terrible pause.

She took a breath.

He heard her hit some keys on her computer. Modern prayer beads.

A big "no" was coming.

"Please," he said. "I'll call tomorrow."

She said, "All right."

And then she slammed down the phone.

At least it sounded like a slam. He was so tired, so mixed up in his head now, that he could imagine just about anything.

He took a breath.

And he picked up his small bag. He unzipped the top and slid out the three sealed vials with white, filmy chunks of the worm. The material looked limpid . . . still fresh. Good, he wanted Martin to spend the whole day looking at it tomorrow. He carried the vials into his small kitchen and put them in the fruit and vegetable drawer of the refrigerator, next to some dried bony-finger carrots.

He picked up a Coors light. And then he went back out to the living room.

He pulled the videocassette from the bag.

And with stray sirens echoing from the streets surrounding his apartment, he went over to the VCR and popped the tape in the machine.

Caryn's fingers stopped moving. The words stopped coming as her mind started thinking about Michael.

Part of her still wanted to nail him. She smiled at his fear of her lawyer. Pat was a very big lady, and a very good lawyer. And she *did* hate men. It brought a special fire to her courtroom style.

She could nail Michael's ass on this one.

But then there were other thoughts.

Why do this? God, Jo needs a father. Even if he's completely self-preoccupied. She loves him.

I can understand that.

Jo's so like him, she thought with dismay.

She'd have to scare him—just to make sure he watches her more closely. But maybe there was no need to haul his butt back to court.

She looked at her last word.

"Latest."

But the rest of the sentence wasn't in her head anymore. Instead, she thought of Jo.

Maybe it was time to talk with her.

She nodded to herself, knowing it was true.

She pushed away from her work station, the broad table covered with yellow pads, bits of paper with scrawled notes, and her microrecorder with her taped comments.

She had a lot to do.

But now she felt she should go check on Jo.

Jo was being *so quiet* back there . . .

Chapter Twenty

MAYBE Jo's asleep, Caryn thought.

And now she started to feel that maybe she had been too tough on her.

Fear will do that, she thought. If that's what this is really about. It wasn't just about Jo's dumb wandering off . . . getting into trouble. She knew herself better than that. There's something else.

Jo's so much like her father. Impulsive. Bull-headed. Proud.

Bright and naive at the same time.

Jo and Michael had a special thing and she was on the outside.

She walked quietly into her daughter's room. The TV was on, its flickering glow sending ghostly flashes spilling out into the hall.

"Jo," she whispered, near the doorway. "Jo, honey, what are you watching?"

She didn't like her watching TV in the dark. Bad for the eyes. Or something like that. She wouldn't nag her now, she'd already nagged her too much.

But—

She went inside Jo's room.

The purple walls gave off a shimmering fluorescent light.

"Jo . . ." she said.

Jo sat on the corner of the bed, her legs curled under her. She still had her clothes on. And she was sitting so close to the TV.

"Jo, it's really too late. I think you should—"

Caryn stopped. Jo wasn't just sitting there. She had her hand out, reaching out to the TV. Her fingers were touching the tube.

Then Caryn heard the man's voice. It was deep, beautiful. The voice was soothing, like the wise father everyone wished they had.

But none of us—surely not me, she knew—ever did.

She looked at his face.

There was nothing remarkable about it. A young black man in a T-shirt.

But his eyes.

It was uncanny. They seemed to notice that she was there. They looked over Jo. Up at her.

The eyes seemed to burn right through her. For a few moments she felt a strange longing, a sexual feeling. It embarrassed her, standing near her daughter. A warmth that made her bite her lip at its suddenness. She took a step back.

"Jo," she said. "Stop. Don't touch."

She tried listening to the man's words. He spoke about loneliness. Pain. His eyes were studying her. God, how do they do that, how can they make it seem like—?

She couldn't really understand him. She was still trying to deal with her sudden horniness.

She wished she could pick up her skirt.

And press herself.

Just. There.

Still looking at those eyes. And hearing him speak.

She licked her lips.

Then she heard something that scared her.

He was telling everyone—*telling her*—to listen tomorrow. That they *must* listen. For a special gift. A special message.

A message that will change their lives forever.

She saw Jo's fingertips reach up.

"Jo," she moaned. "Jo—"

The apartment was ice-cold. And yet—

And yet she had beads of sweat.

Jo's fingers touched the image's lips.

"Jo . . . no." Then, taking a step toward the TV. The voice looking at her, repeating, "Tomorrow night. Here. A special gift. For all of New York."

Caryn forced herself to walk toward the small color TV. Then, with a drunken lunge, she reached down and shut the set off.

Her daughter turned to her, screamed, "Mom!"

Caryn backed away, weak from the effort. Jo reached out to turn the set back on.

"Don't!" Caryn yelled back again. "Don't you dare touch that TV."

And then she just stood there, breathing. Still seeing the negative image of the face swimming in her retina, dancing in front of her eyes, fading, the colors reversed, slowly in the now-dark room.

* * *

Michael stopped the tape just as the volcanic scarp came into view.

It was a nice discovery. Nothing *that* abnormal for the deep Gulf. The camera was also picking up faint images of an ancient riverbed.

He checked the elapsed time counter in the corner. The tape might help him find out when the *Achilles* ran into trouble. He pressed the pause button and the tape rolled.

And a bacteria mat, a white and orange fluffy patch, came into view.

"Okay," Michael said to himself, taking a swig of his beer. "So they found life down there. Not—"

A tiny blotch of blackness appeared in the corner of the screen.

It was a fissure. No, not just a fissure, as he watched, it grew. It was a good-sized scarp, a genuine rift in the ocean floor. Very impressive.

And it was easy to guess what the *Achilles* team did next.

The screen faded to black.

The counter stopped. Then started again. Hours later.

They send the ROV down.

The one he saw on the deck of *Achilles*.

The one with a gigantic hole torn out of it.

He tilted his beer can back. It was empty. He stopped the tape and went to the kitchen. And when he opened the door, reaching down for his last Coors, he saw the fruit and vegetable bin, with its swirling script letters.

He took the beer. And he thought about what was in the bin. Inside the vials.

He was tempted to take one out and look at it.

Maybe after the show, boys and girls, he told himself.

He slammed the door and went back to the videotape . . .

"That's it," Barron said, clapping Gene on his shoulder. Gene looked up from his stool, a sick puppy, waiting for his master's approval.

"You did fine, Gene."

Barron was aware of everyone watching him.

Let them, he thought. Let them see whose show it is now.

It's so nice to have power again, he thought.

Barron saw the young director, the cute young director, looking at him, his face tight with concern. Serious.

I could do some fun things with you, Barron thought. Maybe

even have old Jay join in. Of course, he won't do much on his own except drool. Not without my instructions. But that might be fun too.

But then Barron looked around the studio.

There were a lot of concerned faces.

And he knew what he had to do.

"Tell them, Gene," he whispered. "Tell them we'll be back tomorrow. Same time . . . same channel." He leaned closer to Gene. The TV mystic looked like a lobotomy case. All wide eyes and stupid open mouth.

"Tell them!" Barron hissed.

And Gene stood up. And did what Barron ordered . . .

It was the camera on the ROV now. Michael sped past the area previously covered by the sled until the ROV got to the rift.

At first it looked small, but then the operator of the deep-sea robot started tilting and scanning from left to right. And the rift seemed to just get wider and wider.

Too wide.

It was not merely an unusual feature. It was completely abnormal.

If this is an ancient riverbed or an effluvial plain, it shouldn't be broken up by a rift, even by something small.

And this was getting deep.

The ROV tilted down, for a good look into the rift.

Lil Shit had great lights, real powerful suckers. HMI high-intensity lights that turned total blackness into day.

Only here, the light was gobbled up by the blackness below.

And Michael wondered what they could have been feeling in the *Achilles*'s control room.

They were discovering a brand-new world.

Michael reached out to make a note on a small pad.

"Check ONR. Mapping."

The Office of Naval Research would have the latest information on the Gulf floor, even before it came onto the computer maps. If anyone had seen this feature before, they would know.

He had turned his head away from the screen for a second.

And when he looked back, the screen was filled with animals.

"Shit," he said. "Now look at that."

A big albino crab scuttled away, just at the point the ROV seemed about to ram into it. A bacterial mat—the feeding ground of the crabs—covered the screen. Translucent shrimp scuttled by, big, fat bitter animals that tasted horrible no matter how much cocktail sauce you dipped them in. Something went funny when their cells exploded.

A herd of albino isopods—just like the dead Wally—scuttled to the side.

The camera jiggled.

Turbulence? Michael wondered. Some underwater current?

Or trouble on top? A storm, pulling the tether line tight, snapping the ROV around?

He wished he had the data disks.

The image steadied. And the ROV plowed on.

Sound. Did they record the ROV's engine noises onto the tape? He knew it was SOP to run the sound through the control room. It was an audible check on the ROV. There was no need to put the whirring sound on the tape.

Michael dug his TV remote control out of a crack in the couch, dragging up some crumbly Cape Cod popcorn that had escaped during a Mets game last week. He turned up the volume.

And there it was. The engine sound.

It was like he was *there*.

Inside the control room.

With all the poor bastards who didn't make it back. He listened for a second and then brought the sound down.

More crabs. One chewing on something pulpy, white. Hard to tell what it was.

Then—all of a sudden—the worms.

Not unexpected.

For all these things to be here, there had to be *Riftia* worms. But even for *Riftia*, these were big mothers. Twelve, maybe fifteen feet long, waving in the water. Disturbed by the motion of the ROV. Or maybe a current . . . from somewhere.

He took a sip of beer. Enjoying the way it bit at his tongue.

Strange animals. There were a dozen good explanations of how the worms lived. But none of them explained all the facts. How could you explain something that produced food from hydrogen sulfide, a goddam poison? How could you explain something that lived in a colony, but acted like a symbiotic parasite?

It will take fifty years to understand the rift creatures, Michael thought.

And he wished that he could be part of it.

The ROV plowed through the wheat field of worms.

He pressed fast forward, running the tape at two times normal speed.

He was losing interest. He had seen stuff like this before.

Then it was all different. The rift opened up, widened, and went even deeper.

Michael sat up.

The vent creatures were gone—without him ever seeing a single vent, a single smudgy smoker. A red light went on in the screen. The temperature—freezing cold a few minutes ago—started climbing. The numbers spun around.

It got hot. Real fast. He wished he had a tape of what everyone was saying in the *Achilles*'s control room.

Michael heard voices from out in the hall. A man, a woman, arguing. Drunken words.

The numbers spun around. And the ROV seemed to swivel left and right to get a look at this new rift. It seemed to hesitate—had someone gotten nervous? Maybe they thought about pulling the ROV out of there. It was an expensive piece of hardware . . .

Then the ROV turned. Pointed its camera at the side of the rift walls. (With the temperature getting over 300, and still climbing.)

He saw the worms. Or the eels. Or whatever the hell they were. Hundreds of them.

In small burrows, like tiny compartments—

Like a beehive. A stone honeycomb.

They seemed to snake out at the approach of the ROV.

The camera faced one head-on. It was nothing like the *Riftia*.

"Jeezus," Michael said. "They're going to try and grab one." As if he were watching the event happen. He leaned close to the screen. "Goddam, they're going to grab one."

He looked at the worm. No head. Just a fat, alabaster body, slithering in and out of the holes. The camera stopped by one burrow. Michael saw the arm reach out.

A fire engine raced by outside screaming, wailing by his apartment.

He held the VCR remote tightly. As if it gave him control.

He saw Lil Shit's manipulator arm reach out.

"God," he said. He watched the arm grab at the worm.

(It's definitely not a rift worm, he thought. It's different. It's moving, squirming around like a fat, bloodred night crawler on the end of a rusty hook.)

They were trying for another grab. The camera rocked. Had to be a storm. *Had to be*. He could check NOAA later. See what the Gulf had been doing. What else could it be? They must have wanted one bad, real bad. Bad enough to risk—

The pincer hands of the arm closed around the worm. Gotcha, Michael wanted to say.

But then the ROV shook like a rubber mouse being shaken by a catnip-crazed cat. The engine sound disappeared, replaced by a steady dull hiss. Then the screen went dark.

And that was it.

Michael pressed fast forward. The black screen stayed there, the temperature reading fell down to 0 as the instruments went off. Then the screen became fuzzy.

Blank tape.

He went a bit further, just to make sure there was nothing else.

That was it . . .

It started there.

And now I know what happened, Michael thought.

He stood up, already thinking about what he'd have to do. Call Cameron tomorrow. Yes, and—if necessary—go over his head. Call the Coast Guard. Speak to Barsky personally. Explain to him what happened . . . and what the possibilities might be.

Oh, shit, this wasn't good.

He *knew* what happened.

Whatever it was they found down there . . .

That was the same thing in Reilly. Only it was a lot smaller.

But that was impossible. Nothing that could live at that depth, at that fucking pressure, could live topside.

Nothing!

But it did, shit, and if it got out and spread through the ocean . . .

He walked to the window. It was late. He was exhausted. But he knew that sleep was impossible. He had to watch the tape. Two, maybe three more times. Decide what to do, who he'd call. There was plenty of work. He wished he hadn't had the two beers.

I'll make some coffee.

There were two other thoughts he had then.

Standing there, looking out at the street, over the nearby apartment building and out to the dark Atlantic dotted with ships waiting their turn to enter New York harbor.

If it can live *here*, at sea level, what kept the fucking worms down there?

What kept them down there?

And the other question.

For which he had no answer.

Nada.

What's going to stop it if it isn't dead?

What's going to stop it . . . *now that it's here . . .*

Chapter Twenty-one

MICHAEL put the three vials down in front of Martin.

Despite the coffee, despite watching the videotape over and over, he had fallen asleep, slumped over in his chair, caught completely unawares by his fatigue.

And by the time he got to the Aquarium, it was time to open for the day.

And Martin was already in the lab.

He looked up from his microscope when Michael entered. "Michael, you're back! You won't believe what I've found on—"

Michael put the three vials down in front of Martin. They were still sweaty from the cold of the refrigerator.

Martin looked at them. He picked one up.

"What are *these*?"

Michael watched Martin twist one of the vials in his hand, bringing his owl eyes close to the vial.

Not too close, Michael wanted to say.

"Find out what you can about them." He didn't want to tell Martin too much. Let him go in with no road map. Nothing. And see what he makes of them.

Martin looked up at him, squinting. "You're not going to tell me what they are . . . where they came from?"

Michael just patted his shoulder.

"Just take a look, Martin, and tell me what you see. Then I'll tell you everything."

Martin nodded. Then he looked up. "Michael, can I show you what I found? That thing on the giant isopod. It's remarkable—"

Michael put up his hand.

"Later. I've got a dozen calls to make." He shook his head, exhausted. "Show me later."

And Michael walked back to his office.

* * *

Barsky stood on the deck of the Coast Guard cutter. The Vineyard Sound was flat as a lake, reflecting the golden yellow sun.

It was going to be hot inside the heavy dry suit.

But that's not what bothered him.

No, he was diving alone,

Something he never liked to do.

Lots of things could happen. And if you're alone, there's no one to help you.

But they had only one dry suit in good working condition. The second suit had a leak in its double exhaust system. Not only could it let water back up into the helmet, but there was a chance of the regulator getting clogged.

They were waiting for parts. Like a fucking Buick languishing at Joe's tow.

He could have sent Dailey down. God knows he was eager enough.

But Barsky knew that this was his job.

And though his exec had given him the green light for the dive—the Sound was their responsibility—Barsky was still worried that he'd catch shit from Cameron. Woods Hole was important, and Cameron had a lot of clout.

The whole thing could end up with me getting screwed, he thought.

Dailey was at his feet checking the double seals of the boots.

"All set, Colonel. Ready for the gloves?"

Barsky nodded.

He felt like a gladiator girding himself for battle. The suit was designed for total protection from most toxic contaminants. All the connecting points, the gloves, the boots, the helmet, used a system of double seals. Nothing could get in. The suit itself was made out of vulcanized rubber. It was the best substance, synthetic or natural, for diving in toxic water.

And is that where I'm going? he wondered, lying awake last night.

Will there be anything toxic in the water?

Or just a fat, ribbony chunk of blown-up worm. Whatever was left of the thing from the bottom of the Gulf that ripped a hole in Reilly.

Damn, I wish I had some company.

Of course there was a radio. Since the air was fed into a sealed helmet, there was no problem with a mouthpiece. The radio was easy to use, and he knew that they'd keep in touch with him topside. At the first sign of trouble, they'd yank him out of there.

Dailey helped him slip the gloves on. Then he pulled the inner and outer snap rings shut. He smoothed them with his fingers, checking that there was no bump, no possible opening.

He always made real sure of that . . . ever since—

He shivered, letting himself remember another dive . . .

He had been checking on a midnight dump, some mob-financed haul of garbage.

The water was murky, bits and pieces of dead fish, rotted plant life floating, suspended in the brown, muddy water.

He and his partner couldn't see anything.

Then Barsky bumped into a canister.

A big metal barrel.

He kicked back, away from it. Looking at the can.

The top had opened.

The fucking top had opened, and there was this brownish-black sludge oozing out, mixing with the water.

He edged closer to the can.

There was nothing on the can to indicate what the hell was inside.

He took a plastic specimen bag, and using a plastic spatula, he scooped out a hamburger-sized chunk of the goop.

Barsky hadn't had a clue what it was. But it looked like the ugliest worst shit he'd ever seen.

What the hell could it be? he had kept asking everyone on the ship.

What's brown and black and looks disgusting?

He got a few comedians' answers on *that* one.

You come down here, he had called back.

You come down here and see how much you laugh, you dumb fucks.

Then, after he got the dollop in the bag, sealed tight, disgusted that he had to bring his gloved hands close to the junk, he asked to be pulled out.

He was hauled back to the ship, tethered like a puppet, yanked up with his prize.

Nobody came near him when he came on board.

He stayed to the rear—at the decontamination area—while they hosed him down with the first of many betadine scrubs. Effective against most chemical hazards, there was some shit that could still eat right through the heavy rubber suit. Nice things like chlordane, acrylontrile, and acetic anhydride.

The suit, the seals, could protect you from only so much.

Then, when the suit had been scrubbed four or five times, he checked every inch, looking for any sign of tears or decay. And down, by his legs, he found that one of the seals was loose. The boot was attached, but there had been a tiny hole. Some of the water had gotten in . . . touched his skin.

He imagined it trailing up his suit, sucked up by the capillary action, right to the family jewels.

He gagged. Then he undid the helmet, the snaps.

He wouldn't know what the hell was in the can until they got back to the lab.

Two hours later he found out what his surprise package was.

He took the call like someone getting a doctor's report. Petroleum by-products. Probably from some plastics manufacturing. Completely toxic sludge. Pure poison. Left there, the open canister could leach into the water for the next hundred years, dispensing enough material to give thousands of people all the cancer they'll ever need.

The next day he went in again. And supervised the removal of the can.

Making damn sure his suit was completely sealed.

And he always thought . . . we found this one. We got this can of deadly shit. But how many others are there that we don't have a fucking clue about . . . ?

Dailey held Barsky's helmet like an eager quarterback.

"All set?" the lieutenant said.

Barsky nodded. He never liked putting the helmet on. It was one thing to wear scuba gear. You felt the water, your face was still exposed. But the helmet sealed you off from the world. You felt nothing, except your own sweat. And everything you heard came through the small headphones.

It was so hot, so damn early in the morning . . .

"Okay, Jim, let's do it."

And Dailey helped him slide into the helmet. Like the gloves, it used a two-seal system. Only when one seal was snapped, then the other could be fastened.

Nice and tight, Barsky thought, running his gloved hand along the seal.

The air was already up and running.

Dailey reached for the hand-held microphone.

"Everything okay in there?"

Barsky nodded, then he remembered that he had to say something to make sure that the radio system was running.

"Okay. Hear you fine. How do I sound?"

"Clear as a bell, Colonel."

Barsky looked up. There was the *Achilles*, only about thirty feet away. Sometime this afternoon a small squad of Coast Guard investigators would go on the ship, searching every square inch for some idea of what happened.

They'll go to the rope locker, he thought.

A must on any tour.

And maybe they'll get some fucking idea about what happened.

Barsky had his.

Dailey was watching him, probably seeing that he was lost to his thoughts, just watching the research ship, thinking about the day before.

"You all right?"

"Sure," Barsky said, smiling behind the plate-glass window of the helmet. No point in that, he knew. Only his eyes could be seen.

And what did *they* say? he wondered. Were they big and bug-eyed with fear? Or the narrow slits of the cool-headed professional?

"Let's go," he said, and he started waddling toward the back of the ship.

The suit was heavy, cumbersome on land. But once in the water he knew he'd be able to move easily.

He stepped down to the small pallet at the back of the ship. It was close to the water. Dailey was feeding out his tether line and air tubes.

The water looked clear, still.

Barsky took some steps, to the edge of the pallet.

He could see Woods Hole in the distance.

Cameron didn't want him to do this.

Barsky had called the director this morning. To try and smooth things out. Didn't want some powerful schmuck getting on his case. Making trouble for him after it was all over.

I don't need that at all.

The switchboard put him through to Cameron's office.

There was no answer.

Then the main lab.

Still, no one answered.

Funny, the woman said.

Dr. Cameron usually showed up early, she said. With some of the other scientists.

Someone over there should be answering, she said.

She tried the lines again.

But still no one answered.

Maybe there's something wrong with the lines, she said cheerily. Could you try again later?

Sure, Barsky said. I'll try later. After my dive.

"All set here, Colonel."

Barsky didn't turn around—too much effort. He raised a hand and made a small salute.

He couldn't see his feet, the heavy boots. There was just the small oval view in front of him, like a small TV screen. He took another step and then bent over to see the pallet's edge.

The edge was inches away.

Unlike a wet suit dive, where you roll backward into the water, the heavy dry suit called for a different technique.

You just let yourself fall forward, into the water, arms close to your side.

Then, after you fell, the weight of the suit and your body slowly righted until you were falling straight down, feet first.

It was called the "deadman's launch."

"Here I go," Barsky said without any enthusiasm.

And he tilted forward, watching the shimmering water rushing toward his faceplate, smacking hard into his helmet, until he felt himself falling, plummeting into the water.

Chapter Twenty-two

JO woke up with the sheet all twisted around her ankles.

She kicked and pulled against it, thinking that she was still in her dream, still fighting against something—something holding her—when she heard the steady hum of the air conditioner. And below that noise, she heard other sounds. Cars and trucks outside, muffled by the closed windows. Her mother's thin blinds sent a mesh of sunlight across her body.

I had been fighting something, she thought.

But like cotton candy melting to nothing on her tongue, the dream faded so fast.

She pulled a spare pillow close. It was cool, comforting. She tried wriggling her feet free of the sheet but they were almost tied together. She felt like a mummy.

If I didn't wake up I'd be completely wrapped, she thought. She took a deep breath.

Then she heard her mother busy outside. The whirr of the coffee grinder—sounding so much like Dr. Watine's drill. Now you just let me know whether this hurts, he'd wheedle, looking at her through his filmy glasses.

Sure you can see okay? she wanted to ask. Can you see my mouth, you dumb dentist?

'Course, she couldn't ask *anything*. Her mouth was usually open and his thumb and the water-sucking tube were in it.

Been eating a lot of sweets? he asked ominously. And that's when she knew that he really enjoyed his work. He was just a sick freak who liked seeing kids writhe in pain.

The coffee grinder stopped.

She heard her mother walk into her room.

Saw her open the door, and then Jo heard the TV . . . some talk show, and the bright light of the kitchen.

"Rise and shine, sprout," her mother said.

Jo hugged the pillow tighter.

She loved her mother, she told herself. She really loved her. But there was something about staying here, in this tidy apartment with all the new furniture.

So neat and tidy.

Jo felt as if she didn't belong.

"You okay?" her mom said, taking a few steps closer to the bed.

(A bit of her dream, a tiny memory floated there in the room. Jo tried to focus on it. There was water. I was under the water. Fighting for the air. And I was all alone and—)

"Could I interest you in some oat bran waffles or oat bran bagels or even, if you're especially good, some honest to God oat bran . . . ?"

Jo smiled, knowing that it was expected of her.

"The bagel would be great."

"Good. You'll have to get up, Jo. I've got to run over to the magazine in a few minutes."

Jo let go of the pillow and sat up. Her mother walked to the blinds, twisting the rod, opening the slits, letting in great shafts of ugly sunlight. Her room was a mess, clothes on the floor, books and magazines piled on her desk, the chair, all over the place. She saw her mother make a disgusted face at the mess.

"I thought you had some days off," Jo said, trying to distract her. "I mean, since you came back early from Italy."

Her mother looked up from the mess, looking at Jo for the first time. "I do, I mean, I will take some days. But I have to drop off some stuff for fact checking. There's tons of stuff. It will be easier if I get the article started."

Jo nodded.

"You can come too, if you'd like."

Jo thought for a second, looking at her mother, trying to figure out whether she really wanted her along.

But she was all dressed. Jo could smell the faint aroma of her perfume. And Jo understood that her mother expected her to stay here.

"That's okay," Jo said. "I'll stay."

"All right. I shouldn't be too long. I'll be back by one . . . maybe two." She came closer to Jo, leaned down and rustled her hair.

The smell of the perfume was stronger.

That was the difference, Jo thought. When I'm with Dad I smell dried fish and salt. Here, it's perfume.

No wonder they're no longer together.

"Mom . . ." Jo said quietly.

"Yes?"

"If you're going to be gone for a while, I mean, there's not a lot to do."

Her mother stood back, getting ready for Jo's question.

"Uh-huh . . ."

"Do you think I could go to the pool—"

Her mother's face was covered in yellow-white sunlight. But it looked dark, hard . . .

Like a statue.

"Jo, I don't think—after yesterday—"

Jo knelt up in bed, pleading.

"It's just downstairs, Mom. All I have to do is go to the elevator. *That's it!* And there's a lifeguard . . . what can happen? I'll be bored crazy just staying here. Can't I go swimming?"

And then she waited.

"Please . . . ?"

Her mother shook her head. Then: "All right, missy. But just down to the club and back up. No side trips to the mall. Understand? And keep the door locked." She gave her head one final shake. And then turned back to the kitchen, saying she was going to fix Jo's bagel.

And Jo looked down at her feet.

She reached down at the knot, pulling at the tight, twisted sheet. She touched the sheet, pushed it.

And the movement, the act of pushing at the sheet, reminded her of something else from her vanished dream.

Under the water.

And *something* was holding me.

And I kept pushing, pushing at it, and it just wouldn't let go.

One foot finally popped free of the sheet, and then the other.

She slipped out of bed, ignoring the clothes on the floor, the scattered mess of the room. Maybe later she'd do something about it. Maybe not.

All she knew is that—for now—she just wanted to get out of the small room.

"Yes, I know," Michael said, yelling now into the phone. "But there has to be someone there." He looked at his watch. It was almost ten.

There was a knock on his door. And it creaked open.

It was Annie, looking in, sheepish. Embarrassed about Jo, he guessed. And though he had been mad at her, that didn't seem too important now.

Where the fuck is Cameron? he wondered.

The Woods Hole operator was trying all the exchanges.

And no one was answering.

What was it? A goddam holiday?

He gestured Annie to come into his cramped office. Then he made a sign to her to wait.

"Please try the Bigelow Lab," he said.

"Yes, sir," the operator said. "But no one's been answering there either. I've had a few calls and—"

"Just try it," Michael snapped. Christ . . .

She let him listen to the dull, repetitive drone of the ring for a long time before she came on the line again.

"What the hell's going on?" he asked. "Why won't anyone pick up?"

And then he heard the operator's voice. A small tremor, a tiny warble. She cleared her throat.

She's scared, he thought.

Goddam it, she's scared of something.

"I don't know," she said. Then, repeating it, "I don't know."

Michael shook his head and hung up.

He looked up at Annie who said quickly: "Michael . . . I'm sorry about what happened. I'm sorry about Jo."

He waved her away, still wondering . . . what's going on up at Woods Hole? Did crazy Cameron close the place? Maybe he should try Barsky again. Except it was too early. The diver couldn't be back yet.

He looked at Annie.

"It's okay. It wasn't your fault. Jo is—" He searched for the right word. Then he grinned. "She does what she wants to do. I should have warned you."

Annie made a sigh of relief. "I have a feeling that your—her mother will make some trouble about it."

Michael stood up, thinking he'd walk over and see how Martin was coming along. I want to hear what he's seen on his own, just looking at the samples, he thought. And then—then, I'll tell him how this thing, this worm, jumped out of Reilly's body, how it slithered over the side.

And maybe Martin will be able to explain how much trouble we're in.

Chapter Twenty-three

HE didn't fall long.

The water was shallow. The Long Island Sound sat on the edge of a continental shelf that led to Connecticut and New York. The area from the tip of Long Island all the way up to the Cape and beyond marked the boundary where the last glacier finally petered out, and dumped its rocky debris.

Barsky looked åround as he slid through the water, watching the tiny bits of sediment swirl past the glass plate of his helmet. He looked down, the headlamp on the helmet barely cutting through the murky water.

He landed unsteadily on the sandy bottom. One boot hit a bumpy rock. It sent him tilting backward, falling clumsily in the water.

He kicked his other leg back and got his balance.

"Okay, Colonel?" Dailey said, sounding too loud through the tinny speakers in the helmet.

"Just great. Could you check that the air and tether lines are clear?"

There was a pause while Barsky waited.

"Lines look good, sir."

Barsky looked around. Now came the hard part, searching for the worm. The lamp lit the water up, an eerie glow with tiny flecks that danced around him. But there wasn't much else to see. He wished he was wearing fins . . . he'd be able to cover more ground more quickly.

And get the hell out of here, he thought.

He checked his compass.

And started walking.

"Heading south-southwest," he said.

He looked around for a fish to come nosing about. They always did. Attracted by the light, the splash, the color underwater.

But he saw nothing.

He moved toward the *Achilles*.

In a few minutes he'd be under the spot.

If the worm was dead—if nothing came along and ate it—it should be sitting there.

That's what he wanted. The whole worm. Or as much as he could get. They'd send down a heavy latex specimen bag.

If the fucking thing was dead.

He looked up. He was in the shadow of the cutter behind him. Ahead, he saw a larger shadow.

"I think I see the *Achilles*," he said.

"That's it," Dailey answered. "Yeah, it's just ahead of you." There was another pause. "We'll wait until you get under it to see what you want to do."

"Right."

The research ship sent a muddy black shadow down to the bottom. Like a lighthouse, Barsky stiffly turned left and right, checking either side for the worm. It could be anywhere, he thought. If it didn't sink to the bottom, it could have drifted out to the ocean.

Or even in the other direction. Into the Sound.

Of course, some tiger shark could have come along and gobbled it up. God knows there was enough blood on the thing to pull in a lot of sharks.

And Barsky imagined a shark chewing at the fat, whitish ribbon.

He imagined the shark getting the thing it its mouth, the teeth chomping down. Before getting the surprise of its stupid life.

"See anything?" Dailey asked, startling him.

Barsky looked up. Now, he was directly under the *Achilles*, right under the research ship.

There should be fish here, he thought. There was algae on the ship's hull, and plankton all around. There were *always* fish near the big ships.

But there was nothing here.

In fact . . . Barsky thought, looking down at the bottom.

There was nothing.

No plants. No little shrimplike scuds darting in front of his light.

It was like a fucking dead aquarium.

He looked ahead.

Due south.

An underwater plateau.

It led right into the Long Island Sound, a giant shallow waterway filled with fish, leading right to New York.

He looked ahead.

At nothing.

"I'm going to walk around, under the ship a bit. Can you feed me enough line?"

Dailey didn't answer right away, as if he was busy doing something else. "Dailey, do you hear me? I said—"

"Okay, Colonel. We were just—" Dailey's voice clipped off. "We're all set. We can cruise behind you, feed the lines out. You don't see anything . . . ?"

"I see absolutely nothing, Lieutenant. There's absolutely nothing down here."

You understand, he wanted to say. *There's. Nothing.*

And Barsky flashed on those dried, paper-thin bodies in the rope locker.

The meat locker, he thought.

That's still ahead of me.

This afternoon.

Lucky me. I get to take everybody on board . . . get to see all that shit again.

He took a deep breath, the air smelly, stale.

"Stay with me," he said.

And he began his wide loop, walking like a moonman, around the abandoned research ship.

Barron was the first one up, the first one to walk through the thick rug, out to the glistening kitchen.

Stepping gingerly around all the sleeping bodies.

There was Jay, curled up on the floor, beside a fat black leather couch crowded with—what?

Two young women? Or two young men dressed remarkably like women? Did I sample them? Barron thought, smiling. Some dried goo cracked on his lips when he grinned.

His tongue tasted old and leathery.

I need juice, water, something, he thought. The back muscle of his tongue ached. A strange feeling, something he hadn't felt in a while.

It got a real workout last night.

He kept walking.

Jay snored loudly. A deep basso rumble.

(And what kind of bad dreams is he having? Barron wondered.)

He kept walking into the kitchen. The inch-high rug, purplish-black in the gloom, gave way to bright patterned linoleum. He saw the light switch but he shook his head.

He couldn't deal with that much light.

Not yet.

Barron looked around for something that would make coffee.

He saw a machine. With nozzles. A squat stainless steel device with an Italian name, Corigio.

No way I'm going to get that to work, he thought. No fucking way.

He pulled open the double door refrigerator.

The freezer was filled with steaks piled six high, and great tubs of Ben and Jerry's Ice Cream. And frozen yogurts. Packages of strawberries.

He opened the other door.

So much food. Dr. Gene Fasolt has done well for himself.

Yes, he grinned. Old Ramfar has been good to him.

He saw a gallon container of orange juice. Barron pulled it out and then searched the orderly cabinets until he found a drinking glass big enough for his terrible thirst.

He poured a glass, and then gulped it down, letting it run over his aching tongue. Then another glass.

He swished a gulp of it in his mouth. Then, as it picked up the taste, he spit it out into the sink.

His tongue still felt rough, scratchy.

Now he felt his bladder.

Full, heavy.

If he hadn't felt so shitty he could remember where the bathroom was. Now he had to take a piss.

He rubbed at his eyes. Rubbing flakes of sleep goo onto his knuckles.

And he padded out to the dark living room.

The elevator closed and Jo slid to the back, holding her Garfield bag tight. The fluffy tip of Super Mario's nose protruded from the top of the bag. And a half-read book, the latest installment in the Babysitter's Club, was pushed down on top of her Nintendo beach towel.

The elevator went down, soaring past four floors and then stopping—too abruptly she thought—at the twelfth floor.

The door opened and a man in a sleek gray suit stepped in. He pushed the button for the lobby.

Then he glanced back at her.

It felt weird, standing there in her orange and yellow swimsuit and flip-flops, looking at the glossy shine on the man's shoes.

She hoped he wouldn't say anything to her.

The elevator stopped again—only two more floors down. And an old lady—not much taller than she was—got on. She pulled a yapping fur ball behind her, a bowling ball-sized brown and black dog that kept scolding the old woman as she came into the elevator.

The man in the gray suit moved to the side.

The woman tried to pull the dog close.

The doors shut. Jo saw the woman check that her button was lit.

Funny, she and her mom had been here for a year. Ever since the divorce. And she hardly knew any adults. There were just bunches of gray-faced men who left early in the morning, just when Jo was picked up by the Barclay School minivan. She never saw them come home.

Probably because they always came home so late.

They're like vampires, she thought.

They're never here in the daytime.

And most of the women left too. Though some—with small babies that they fussed over—took the elevator down to the lobby. They took the strollers out, behind the building. To the small walkway that ran along the East River.

And Jo thought of that walkway. And the river.

She felt tiny pinpricks of gooseflesh pop up on her bare arms, her shoulders.

Silly.

She didn't like it back there.

The walkway was always littered, dirty. Even though Ray, the co-op's ace custodian, tried to get to it and sweep it every day.

It didn't help. There were broken bottles. Wrappers. Empty white McDonald's boxes splattered with ketchup, like drops of blood.

There was lots of garbage.

She didn't tell her mother that there were broken crack capsules there too.

She'd freak.

But as bad as the walkway was, as creepy as it looked, it was nothing—absolutely *nothing* compared to the river.

The way the water, filled with floating junk, just lapped against the wall, like it was licking it, no more than twenty feet from the building—it was something she didn't like thinking about.

She tried to forget that their building was right on the river.

Who'd want to be near *that*? she thought. It was totally disgustoid. Once, she swore she saw part of an animal floating there. A chunk of gray-black body. A rat, she guessed. Maybe something larger. A cat. A dog.

She imagined what might have happened to the rest of it.

And there was a filmy white scum that covered the black water, soup for all the bits of junk to float in.

Someday, she thought when they first moved there, yes, someday I'll look down here and see something *really* gross.

A turd floating near oil slicks. Or maybe—sure—a finger. A piece of a fat white arm, just bobbing around, knocking against the side of the wall.

The elevator opened.

The smell of chlorine.

The dog yapped, eager to get out and pee anywhere.

The old woman held him tight. As Jo walked out to the Riverview Health Club, the elevator whooshed closed behind her. And then there were just the echoes of her flip-flops padding to the reception desk.

His air line snagged.

"Give me a goddam break," he said, looking up behind him, to the cutter, to see what had happened.

But his two lines trailed off into the darkness.

He reached behind him and gave the two lines a gentle tug.

Then he heard Dailey. "It's okay, Colonel. We had some trouble getting the line to unspool smoothly." Dailey paused. Then: "You shouldn't have any more trouble."

"Great," Barsky said sarcastically. "I really appreciate that. It's no fucking picnic down here."

"I understand," Dailey said quietly.

Barsky had finished his loop under the *Achilles*. And now he knew that there was something very wrong down here.

Not only was there no sign of the worm, or whatever the hell it was—

There was no sign of anything.

It's—he thought, looking at the bare, sandy ground—as if something came and just sucked everything up.

Sucked up everything alive.

(He pictured the rope locker then. The dry bodies, like week-old rashers of bacon. Dried meat . . .)

"I want to head south," Barsky announced.

He heard some muffled talk from topside. They wanted to know why, he was sure. What was up? they wanted to know.

"Colonel, they'd like to know—"

Bingo.

Best to feed them some bullshit, Barsky guessed.

"I think I see some . . . debris in that direction. Just keep the cutter following me. Okay?"

Another pause while Barsky stood there—still in the *Achilles*'s shadow—waiting for an answer.

I don't have to do this, he thought.

I didn't find anything . . . so I didn't find anything.

No big fucking deal.

Except he wanted to see how *far* this went.

This underwater emptiness.

The dead aquarium look.

He waited.

"All right, sir. We're all set here. We should have no problem keeping close to you."

And Barsky nodded, muttering, "Good."

Too damn quiet for them to hear.

He walked out of the shadows of the *Achilles*, over the sand.

A living thing.

In an underwater graveyard.

Chapter Twenty-four

HE saw algae.

What used to be algae.

He stopped his grim march and bent over, taking care to keep his balance.

(Now there's nothing to be worried about here, he told himself. Nothing at all.)

Still, he took care.

He reached out with his chunky gloved hand and pulled at one of the reedy plants. The first living thing he'd seen since diving.

He tugged it, snapping it off the sandy bottom.

Barsky brought it close to his helmet.

No—scratch that.

It *wasn't* alive.

It was shriveled. Like a piece of paper that has floated so long in the water that it has begun to decompose, evaporate.

He looked up.

He saw the field of kelp. Some of it was bladder wrack. There should be puffy balloons on the end of the seaweed tendrils.

But there was nothing puffy, nothing balloonlike on this alage.

He pulled at the strand in his hand. It fell apart, gossamer, sere.

He took some more steps, cautious now.

"See anything?" Dailey's jarring voice interrupted.

"No. Just some—" He looked down at his hand, the tungsten lamp giving the desiccated seaweed a ghostly color.

"Seaweed," he said.

He kept walking, reaching over his shoulder now and then, to make sure that there was plenty of play left in his line.

Where are the fish? he wondered. And the crabs. The sea cucumbers.

The hundreds of living things that should be here.

(You're here, a voice whispered to him. You're here . . . you're alive.)

I should go up, he thought. He was cold in his suit. He had a headache. Too much fucking tension. Too much thinking. I'll give Dailey his shot. Let him come down—

Yeah. Enough of this shit, he thought. Enough—

When he saw something living.

A small thing, just ahead, catching the light. Only visible because it was moving, crawling over a rock.

Looking lost and forlorn.

And like the ancient mariner blessing some foul ocean eels because they were—praise God—alive, Barsky was happy.

He walked more quickly, hurrying.

Not noticing that there was lots of movement ahead.

In the gloom.

Shimmering, jerky, pulsating . . .

As soon as Jo dived into the cold water—always so cold, no matter what day of the week she went swimming—she knew it was a mistake.

Because Carrie Blau was there.

With nothing better to do than bug her.

Jo swam to the side of the pool, cutting across the lap lanes, while Carrie swam up to her.

"Hey, Jo-Jo. Don't say 'hi' or anything."

Jo pushed her hair off her face, away from her eyes. "Hi, Carrie," she sang.

"I thought you were gone all this week, you know, quality time with Daddy and all that. What happened?"

Jo took a breath and—crouched tight against the wall of the pool—then she pushed away, jetting out into the water.

Her head bobbed to the surface. Carrie called out, loud enough for the scattering of old farts and young mothers to hear.

(And the lifeguard. Eddie. Jo found herself looking at him whenever she came down here. He was like a living statue. He didn't say anything, barely did anything but crouch down and test the water for God-knows-what, before climbing up and taking his seat, his throne, by the pool. He was what people called a hunk. Not something that Jo was interested in. Or so she thought. But when Carrie yelled, she found herself quickly looking over at Eddie. To see if he heard, if he noticed how dumb and loud Carrie was acting.)

"My dad's plans changed," Jo lied.

Carrie swam out to her. She was a big girl, not fat, but older . . . more developed. Carrie had the beginnings of a real woman's body. When Jo looked at her she felt like she was getting a sneak preview of her fate.

That's *me* soon.

With bigger-than-life boobies. And a bottom that just won't quit.

The whole thing scared her.

That, and the once-a-month trick that God sent to teenage girls.

Thanks a lot, pal. That sure makes life interesting.

She looked over at Eddie again.

"Checking him out?" Carrie said slyly. The older girl, her blond curly hair staying off her face, licked her lip. "He's pretty fucking cool, if I do say so myself. Pretty fucking cool . . ." Carrie loved to use the infamous f-word. Just another way she was older, if not necessarily wiser.

"He's okay," Jo admitted, annoyed that her interest had been picked up.

"You check out his buns, Jo-Jo? We are talking *tight*." Carrie rolled her eyes. "I come down to swim even when I don't feel like it at all. Just to watch his ass . . ." She looked right at Jo. "I bet you do too."

Jo kicked back, backstroking to the other side. "Hardly," she yelled.

One of the old men was teeter-tottering into the pool, using the steps at the shallow end. It was cloudy outside, and probably hot too. But the enclosed pool was cool, and Jo could see the tall buildings that surrounded Riverview Co-ops.

Carrie kept following her.

"So you're back? To stay?"

Jo nodded.

"Great. Maybe we could do some stuff. You could come up to my place. Or I could go see what's in your refrigerator. Summer is wasting away, Jo-Jo."

"Yeah," Jo said. Carrie bugged her, but she was about her only friend in the building, the only girl near her age. And she could be funny sometimes, like when she talked dirty.

That could always be interesting. Carrie sure knew about lots of strange stuff.

Jo dove under the water. It was cold, almost icy.

Nothing bad in this water, she thought.

When she popped up, Carrie was sitting on the edge, watching her. "Hey . . . so let's go to the movies or something."

Jo nodded. Even though she knew her mother wouldn't let her go to the movies by herself.

"Yeah. That would be neat."

She saw Carrie squirming uncomfortably for a second.

As though she had sat down on some gravel that was sticking into her butt. The old man—wearing a bright yellow swim cap—was swimming toward them, his big, spotty arms cutting through the water, his face all scrunched up, like a prune or raisin. On every pair of strokes, he looked to the side, blew at the water streaming off his face, and then gulped more air.

Carrie said something, too quietly. Jo didn't hear it above the sound of the man's swimming, his blowing, his cutting through the water.

"Did you watch TV last night?"

The man kept coming. He had looked so frail stepping into the water, but now—slicing through the water like some eyeless walrus—all rough skin and bristle, he looked powerful.

He looked like he was going to swim right into her.

She started to swim close to the side, away from the man.

But then he seemed to tilt a bit, heading even more directly to her.

She kicked hard, but it just didn't seem to do anything. Harder, swimming full out, thinking maybe she should swim the other way.

Knowing . . .

I'm just moving closer to him.

Hesitating. Then moving toward the pool wall.

When the man seemed to grab at the water and shoot himself forward in a great lunge that sent his body—

(Big, heavy-looking, and glistening as if it was covered with some kind of oil.)

—Over her. His hand flapped down on her head, dunking her.

And when she popped up, he was looking at her.

A skull man, with his bathing cap. And his wet face and narrow eye slits, all red and blotchy from the chlorine.

"I'm sorry," she started to say. "I—"

But the skull man sniffed noisily. Some greenish goo dripped from his nose. She tried not to look, to stare.

And then the man kicked away.

She held on to the side of the pool.

Watching him swim away.

Hearing her heartbeat in her head. Then the splashes. Voices from the other end.

And Carrie. Talking.

"Ga-ad!" Carrie said. "You'd think the old fart owned the pool. Didn't even stay in his own lane."

Jo nodded.

Then she felt Carrie's big toe nudge her shoulder.

"So, did you watch the tube last night?"

"Yeah . . ." Jo said, then . . . "No. Not really."

"There was this really weird guy on last night." Carrie lowered her voice. Jo heard what Carrie said. A weird guy . . . TV . . . But it didn't mean anything to her. "I mean, this guy just sort of looked out of the TV like he could see you. He was—" She leaned down close to Jo, whispering in her ear. "He was this big black guy. A mean-looking dude. But the way he spoke . . . God, it made me feel horny, Jo-Jo. Real h-o-r-n-y."

Jo nodded. The old man had hit the other end and had swooped backward, coming back toward her.

"I think I'd better get out of the water," Jo said.

She reached around, clawing at the concrete ledge, pulling herself up.

(Hearing the old walrus, the skull man, slicing through the water.)

She got one leg up, and then the other.

The black man. I saw him too, Jo thought. For a while. Until Mom shut it off.

"Anyway, tonight he's on again. He's got this special message. A gift—"

Jo got her legs over. She sat on the ledge, pulling her knees close to her, now cold as the pool water beaded on her skin.

"—for the city. A gift! What do you think it could be, Jo-Jo? What do you think?"

Jo turned, smiled, and looked back at the swimmer.

"I don't know," she said. "I really don't know . . ."

Barron looked at the mirror. It was clean, shiny. No flecks of toothpaste . . . shaving lather . . . bits of expensive steak flossed out of Gene's mouth. None of that shit on this mirror.

Because it's cleaned every day.

The way mine used to be, Barron thought. And my beds were made, my meals prepared, my mountain house kept clean, immaculate, perfect.

There was a sound. A groan from the living room.

Someone with a bit of pain. Someone's body part, some orifice stretched just a wee bit too far.

Barron rubbed at his cheek. Heavy gray-black fuzz covered the skin.

He reached for the light switch and flicked it on.

Nothing happened.

Back and forth, but still nothing happened.

Oh, well, he thought. I'll have to shave in the shadow.

There was a gloomy square of light to his left, above the modern shower/bath stall. But a curtain blocked out most of the light.

No matter, he thought. He could see well enough.

He turned the water on, twisting the tapered, white handles. Class all the way, Barron thought. He looked around for old Gene's blade, opening the medicine chest, finding it resting in a special holder, looking all clean and new.

Barron took it.

Closed the chest.

The water was sending up a smoky steam, fogging the mirror. Barron scooped up water and splashed his face. He grabbed the soap and started to work up a lather. There was probably some smelly aerosol around, but he preferred working the bar of soap, working the lather into his beard.

And when he felt that his face was soapy enough, he picked up the blade and looked in the mirror.

He looked at the mirror.

Now isn't *that* funny, he thought.

There seems to be something wrong with the glass. An imperfection of some kind. There's a blotch, a dark spot on the mirror. Maybe it was just steaming up funny. Made it hard to see his face, see his beard . . . the soapy froth on his chin.

He moved to the side, hoping to catch a clear part of the mirror.

But no, the whole mirror was getting all dark . . . cloudy.

"Damn," he said.

Then, off to the left side, he saw a clear patch. Just enough, he thought, so he could see what the hell he was doing. Wouldn't want to cut my throat, he thought. Not when things were going so smoothly, so well . . .

He leaned to his left, tilting his chin up, his eyes squinting, looking down at the patch of mirror, watching the blade plow through his whiskers.

One great sweep up, and then another.

The clear patch seemed to grow smaller, surrounded by clouded-over mirror. He leaned closer. And then closer.

He heard another sound from outside.

Fresh moans. Small yelping sounds.

Someone was having fun again.

And we can have more fun tonight.

Can't we? he thought.

He looked up at the glass.

Can't we? he asked.

Then—he felt a breeze.

Though there was surely no way for a breeze to come in the room.

A cool breeze that made the water, the drying soap on his cheek, feel cool, cold. The small curtain above the shower rustled.

Barron realized he had asked a question.

His intestines coiled inside him, pulling tight, sleeping snakes getting close for protection . . . for heat.

Can't? We?

He slipped forward.

For a second, he looked down, onto the floor, as if it was wet, slippery.

Icy.

What the fuck is wrong down there? he thought. What the fuck—

Why am I slipping, like this? What the hell—

He slipped. Just a bit. The blade tumbled from his hand. He shot out a hand to catch himself, to stop his odd cantilever over the sink.

He had been so close to the mirror.

Now he was going to smack against it hard.

Smear the glass with soupy soap and hair goo on his face.

"Ahhgg—" he said, bracing himself for the slap of his head against the mirror.

(What the *fuck* is wrong with my feet? What the fu—)

But he didn't slap.

He felt his head hit the glass. And it felt like the tissue-thin plastic on a just-cleaned suit. So thin, it just tore away, tearing as his head pressed into it.

He made a sound. A cry for help.

But he heard nothing. There were no sounds here.

Sound didn't exist *here*.

He looked up, opening his eyes, after having them squeezed tight . . . from bracing himself.

He felt his hands resting on the basin, stopping at last, holding him.

He opened his eyes.

And as soon as he did he felt the snakes inside him pull tighter and tighter, until—God—they squeezed everything right out of him.

He looked up.

The sky was purple-black, dotted with sick-looking gray clouds that just hung in the sky. There were orange-red flashes. Lightning. Of some kind.

But there was no thunder, no crackling. No sound at all.

He was yammering. I know I'm yammering, he thought. My mouth is moving.

Of course, he tried to pull back.

Of course . . . *he tried.*

But it felt as if his head were in a stock.

Locked tight.

I'm not going anywhere.

Can't we . . . his mind repeated over and over again. Can't we have more fun?

Can't we?

He saw buildings. As black as the sky, except with a sheen that made them glow. And Barron knew that if he could hear anything, if ears were any *fucking good here at all*, wherever the hell here was, that he'd hear sounds coming from those buildings, great screaming waves of noise, pouring out of those buildings.

He knew that.

(And again he tried to—uh—just jerk his head back, get his head out of there. I don't really need a shave, heh-heh. No, I can get by just—)

Then he saw them start coming. Some from the tops of the buildings. Others from dark openings at the base of the buildings. And some came up from the ground, crawling out like earthworms in a heavy rain, deferring to those who came from the twisted spires of the building.

And some held things in their hands, like trophies, talismans.

Bits of gray-white that were the only light in this . . . this . . .

Hell.

(He still tried to talk, to yell for help. Even though he knew it would do no good. He knew his mouth was moving. Only now—only now, yes! He could taste it. His jaw was going up and down, chewing at his tongue, his lips, chew, chew, chew. The blood filling his mouth.)

They came.

Some low to the ground, slouched over, as dark as the ground, sliming along the ground with indeterminate limbs. Oh, is that an arm, he thought. A head there? Maybe a few legs just sort of dangling near the back, pushing at the soil, the dirt, whatever was that thick black sludge on the ground.

He felt something chewy and tasty in his mouth. A little treat. He bit at it, worked it like a piece of gum, eating it before realizing that he had just bitten off the tip of his tongue. And eaten it.

And the others.

Upright, he was glad to see. Oh, yes, they were walking upright. Blessed things. *They walked like us.* How wonderful. How different from us could they be, how strange could they really be? They walked! Just like us.

And they had eyes.

Or holes.

Dark holes with things inside them.

He tried to ignore the feathery whisker things that seemed to dangle from the holes. He thought of them as eyes and that thought made him feel better.

And for all the twisted black limbs, the melon heads with black sockets all over them like fingerholes in living bowling balls, all the long flat things that flopped toward him like hooked flounders . . .

For all this great diversity—

He saw only one thing that they had in common.

One.

He spat the blood out onto the black sludgy ground.

He looked down.

The ground moved. It *moved*. Something seemed to separate itself from the black ground.

A hole opened. A tongue. Something. Snaked out. Licked, dabbed at his bloody spittle. Hungrily.

There were other stirrings on the ground.

Not a sound.

Just more of them, squirming below him. The soil of this world. Living soil . . .

And more of them. Piled higher and higher. Layer after layer, all over this planet. This hell.

One thing.

That they all had in common.

They were hungry.

Oh, so hungry.

And now that he knew that one important fact.

They could let him go.

He jerked back. Into the bathroom.

The light was on. The water from the sink gushed over the edge onto the floor. The basin was dabbed with red, the swirling water was pink.

He dared to look up again at the mirror.

He couldn't see much.

It was so steamy, so shrouded with mist.

Except he saw his face, the red splotches. His open mouth. He heard the weird sounds, the horrible groaning, the babylike mumbles.

And for a second.

Looking at the mirror.

He thought he was looking right at one of those things.

Up close.

Right there.

But it was just his own blurry reflection . . .

FOUR

WURM

Chapter Twenty-five

SUDDENLY, there was life all around Barsky.

As though he was passing through the desert, coming to a wonderful oasis.

There were fish, sleek wide-mouth bass, schooling excitedly about, and great underwater fields of kelp and bladder wrack, swaying in the fierce currents that ran all the way into Long Island Sound.

And below him—just a few feet ahead—the floor moved: it was alive with all the skittering critters of a healthy sea floor.

He breathed a bit easier.

What *had* I been thinking? he thought, trying to recapture the strange ideas he had . . . only moments ago.

I had been thinking that whatever they brought up from the rifts had killed everything.

Was killing everything.

And unless it was found—

Unless *I* found it, it would just go on killing things.

Crazy idea.

There was one thing he didn't understand.

How could it all be happening so fast?

How could so much space be stripped of life?

It was impossible.

But now, seeing all these things, just ahead, moving about, he grinned.

And he felt his fear ebb.

A good feeling that.

I haven't been that scared in a long time, he thought.

Maybe never.

"Okay, Colonel?" Dailey's voice bleated at him.

"Yeah . . . fine. Lower your radio. You're burning my ears off."

"Yes, sir," Dailey said. "Er, we're not getting any sign of movement from you up here." Dailey paused. "Are you standing still?"

Barsky kept looking ahead. There seemed to be even more animals only a few meters away. Another school of fish . . . more bass, maybe blues. Yes, big bluefish, he saw, taking a step toward them, their iridescent scales catching the murky light.

Barsky laughed to himself.

It's as if there's an invisible wall, a barrier between me and them.

"No," he said to Dailey. "I've just been watching the show. There's lots of activity down here now, lots of life." He knew that there would be some relief on the cutter. "I'm ready to start moving again . . . though I don't think we're going to find anything . . ."

No. Whatever poisoned an area of the sea floor . . . near the *Achilles* . . . probably had died itself. Maybe chewed up by a wandering shark.

And when he thought that, Barsky looked over his shoulder. As if by thinking about it he could summon the shark. They weren't exactly common in these waters. But they were here. Just like the occasional Great White hooked off the rolling surf of Montauk.

They were here.

But behind him was just the watery wasteland. Nothing. He turned back.

He saw a couple of shiny beads of water on his helmet faceplate. They magnified and distorted things off to the side.

It's my sweat, he knew. I'm hot, sweating down here. These vulcanized suits were great if you were diving near any toxic shit. But they were unbelievably hot, sticky. The water was cold, but not cold enough. He had a little precipitation system going on inside his helmet.

No big deal, he thought. I'll just finish my look around and then go back up.

Case closed.

And some other fucker can take the afternoon crew onto the *Achilles*.

He walked slowly, crossing from the sandy, denuded area, into the lush gardenlike floor ahead.

And with every step, he saw more and more fish arrive. Absolutely uncanny, he thought.

(And again he looked over his shoulder.)

I swear . . . he thought . . . I swear I saw something.

Some movement, something waiting.

The school of bluefish made a sudden sharp turn, shimmering in the water.

He felt movement on his boot.

The boots were heavy. Rubber, like the rest of the toxic dive suit, but reinforced with thick soles and uppers—just in case you have to walk through some especially nasty shit.

He almost didn't feel the movement.

Just the tiniest sensation . . . right there . . . on his arch.

He bent over—always a tricky maneuver, if you didn't want to fall down. He looked at his right boot.

It was a sea star. What beachcombers called a starfish.

It was a wounded veteran, with four good arms and a fifth growing in nicely.

It was inching slowly up his arch, to his ankle.

"Where do you think you're going," Barsky said aloud.

"What's that, Colonel?" Dailey said.

"Nothing . . ." Barsky laughed. "Just talking to the fish."

The Portuguese fishermen along the Connecticut coast hated the sea stars. They ate the clams, prying them open with incredibly powerful arms, before injecting their stomachs into the clam's shell. Ready to eat its meat.

So the Portuguese cut the sea stars' arms off.

Ah, basta! And throw the hated chunks back into the water.

Where each arm turned into a brand-new sea star.

You don't survive 500 million years of evolution by being stupid.

Barsky reached down at the plucky animal crawling up his leg.

He watched—rather awkwardly—as his gloved hand reached down to pluck the starfish off.

"Sir, we have you standing still again. They're getting a bit—"

"Hold on," Barsky snapped. "Just wait a damn—"

He grabbed the sea star in a pincer, between his thumb and index finger. And he pulled.

It didn't move.

In fact, he felt it tighten its hold around his ankle.

"Shit. What the hell—"

He pulled harder. Sea stars were strong. But not *that* strong. Barsky had peeled them off the bottom of ships, tossing them into the air like ninja stars.

This one wasn't moving at all.

More beads of sweat appeared inside the faceplate. One bead ran into another, and then dripped down the inside of the faceplate, smearing the glass, blurring Barsky's peripheral vision.

Now it felt like the sea star was hurting his leg, hurting his fucking leg covered by the rubber suit. But that was impossible.

That was fucking impossible.

"Should we pull you up, Colonel? Everyone's real—"

Ridiculous. This is ridiculous. What the fuck could be the problem. What could be—

He gave one more gigantic tug, a tremendous pull with his full strength—

(He didn't see that the fish were so close now, swimming back and forth, cutting through the water, moving as if programmed, turning together, swimming, then turning again, their dull eyes looking straight ahead . . . except for when they passed by him . . .)

And it came off.

"God," Barsky said. "I—"

He felt pain at his ankle. Then the salt water licking at his wound. Shit, the suit is ripped. Damn, the suit's ripped! But that's crazy, that's fucking impossible.

Then he was tumbling backward, tipped over by the momentum of his yank, rolling backward.

He thought about the suit. That was okay. There obviously wasn't anything toxic down here. No problem there. Not with all these living things around.

He plopped back on the sand.

He still had the sea star in his hands.

Its hundreds of tiny suckers all quivering, reaching out, trying to get something to hold on to.

Barsky felt the water leaking into his suit.

"You'd better get me—" he started to say.

With the sea star held up in front of his face.

He saw the center of the animal. Where it had its stomach, that sick invention of nature that let it open the locked shells of bivalves and feast on their meat like a nimble-fingered Key West beach boy.

He saw something move.

Something was coming out.

Thin, white, snaking out of the center of the sea star.

What the fuck is that? he wondered. Now, what the hell—

Then he knew.

It was the kind of thing—you'd see it once, and you'd always know it. Like seeing a fox standing in the middle of a deserted country road. The pointy ears. The full, fluffy tail. The doglike snout. Without ever before seeing one, just seeing the shadow, the shape, you know it's a fox.

I know what this is, Barsky thought. I've seen it before.

On the *Achilles*.

"Colonel, what was that? You want us to get you up?"

Barsky thought of letting the sea star go. Tossing it away.

But he knew that would do no good.

He wasn't that stupid.

Maybe . . . he thought desperately, his fucking faceplate now a wet, smeary mess. Everything was so blurry. Maybe they could yank me up, real quick and—

"Get me the hell out of here!" he screamed. Then, "Hurry!"

And somewhere above him, he knew they were running around the cutter, getting the air and tether winches working together, ready to haul back their human catch.

He watched the worm snake out of the sea star.

Until it was dangling like a diseased pupa.

He tried to get away, stand up, before it fell out.

But it tumbled through the water. Just a few inches long.

A chunky red maggot with a pinkish-red tinge.

He saw the fish nearby. Waiting. Back and forth.

He knew then.

They all have it in them. All of them that are still alive. All of them that haven't been sucked dry.

He swung at it, flailing at the water, trying to bash the worm away, yelling, screaming at it, not caring that they were all listening above him—

"Get. The Fuck. Away. God D—"

But he only seemed to make it swirl down closer and closer.

A dark shadow passed over him.

Big, sleek, moving fast.

Oh, shit, no, he thought, looking around, knowing what that could be. Knowing *that* fucking shape.

He wasn't looking when the worm landed.

And ate through the thick rubber suit like it was tissue paper.

A hole seemed to appear, the rubber dissolving.

He felt the tether line go taut.

"Colonel, we're pulling you up now, we have—"

No, he wanted to say, as the pain, the bullet burrowing into his chest gave way to an odd moment of calm.

Don't.

The dark shadow soared over him again.

Waiting.

He saw his blood dripping out of the hole in his suit, mixing with water, as the worm corkscrewed deeper and deeper. Some of the animals . . . some crabs, a small lobster, popped out of rocky hiding places and scuttled toward him, even as he was lifted up, up, off the sea floor, leaving a reddish trail.

Don't, he thought.

But he couldn't say a word.

Chapter Twenty-six

JO heard her mother open the door, the reassuring click as she opened the three locks like a safecracker. Jo shut the TV off with her foot and went running out to her.

And one look at her mother's face showed that she was concerned about something, embarrassed—

It has to do with me, Jo knew.

"Hi," her mom said, letting her leather satchel slip to the floor. "Have a nice swim?"

She's trying to sound nice and casual, thought Jo. Before telling me something.

And she thought then of the old man, the skull swimmer, plodding blindly through the pool water. Over and over, back and forth. As if he had been doing it since he was born.

"Great! Carrie was there. H-how was your day? Did you—" Jo tried to remember what her mom had to do at the magazine. It was important to remember. Without Dad around, Mom had no one to talk with, to get excited with. Except Jo. So it was important to remember.

Except it was hard. The names, the articles, the assignments . . . everything that was so important to her mom just sort of blurred together.

"Did you get everything done?" Jo said, stepping back as her mom kicked her blue pumps off and walked into the kitchen. Jo stood at the entrance and watched her mom pour a tall glass of OJ.

"Not quite, sprout." She took a gulp. "I've still got to call Sygma—you know, the photo service—and get good shots of the Italian Parliament inside and out." She finished the glass. "Then I've got to write the darn thing."

Now Jo saw that her mom was looking right at her, and the moment had come.

"Jo, they asked me to cover something tonight. For the *In New York* section."

Jo nodded, knowing what was coming.

"It will just be a few hours. You could come. I mean, after yesterday—" Caryn hesitated. "But if you'd rather stay here. If you promise me you won't leave the apartment. I co—I mean, it will be okay, I could tell them to get someone else. It's not that important. I'll just—"

Her mother seemed to have decided what she was going to do.

I'm screwing her up, thought Jo. She worries about me and it messes up her work.

"No," Jo said quickly. "No, that's okay. I'll be fine."

Mom scrunched up her face. She looked cute when she did that, Jo thought. Not at all like a parent. More like another kid.

It was cute, but Jo didn't like it now.

Jo made herself smile. "I'll be fine, Mom. Really."

And she thought—God, what's wrong with me? Everyone always has someplace else they have to be, something else they have to do. And it's always a problem what they're going to do with me.

"Are you sure?" Caryn said.

Jo nodded. And her mother came to her and hugged her close. "You'll be good? Keep the door locked. You can even invite Carrie to come up and hang out with you. That would be fun, wouldn't it? Like a slumber party?" She pulled Jo away, holding her by the shoulders, looking right at her face. "You could watch TV together . . . or a tape?"

"Yeah, I'll be great." Then she asked a question. "Where are you going? What's the story?"

Her mother shook her head. "There's this weird religious broadcast, one of those goofy TV evangelists. He's going to make a gift to the city." She waved a hand through the air, too casually. "He's on that show you were watching last night." Caryn cleared her throat. "The one I shut off."

And Jo thought of the man's voice, the sweet, deep sound of it, warm and wonderful. How she felt lost when her mother shut the TV off.

And she thought she felt something from her mother last night . . . as she stood there, watching.

Now Jo said, not so sure she wanted her mother to have anything to do with that man. "It's a big story . . . an important one?"

"It's good to do these things when they ask me." Jo saw her

mother make a halfhearted grin. "Or after a while they stop asking."

Jo nodded. Then: "I think I'll call, Carrie," she said.

She wouldn't stop her mother. She never had before. But she didn't want to be alone.

Jo turned to leave the kitchen.

"Honey . . ." her mother called gently. Then, "Please . . . don't watch that show tonight. It's—it's—"

Jo nodded, and kept walking.

Martin sat in front of his microscope, quiet, phlegmatic. He had never come on to Annie . . . or, for that matter, Steven. As far as Michael knew, Martin had no life other than his work in the Aquarium's lab.

The only thing he and Michael ever talked about was his work. There were none of the dumb jokes he made with Annie or Steven.

Martin had nothing to do with any of the specimens on exhibit.

He did his research. Published his papers. Kept the Aquarium's name alive in the rarefied world of research.

Living in his own world.

Now Michael saw Martin stand up, his eyes wide with excitement, his thick glasses threatening to tumble off his nose.

"Michael, you have to come here and see this. I—"

But Michael had to do something before he saw what Martin had come up with.

He went to his desk, and called Woods Hole again. He let the phone ring ten, then fifteen times. He tried a second number—one of the individual labs.

"Michael—" Martin said, pacing by him. "Please, you have to see—"

Michael put up his hand.

Still no answer, not from any of the numbers.

This could get a lot of people laughing at me, Michael thought. He picked up the phone. Called Massachusetts Information. Asked for the number for the Falmouth Police.

Right on Route 495.

"What are you doing?" Martin asked, pushing his glasses back up. Annie came out of her office and stood near the lab table.

Michael shook his head, asking them to be quiet.

The phone rang once.

(Why do I feel so fucking cold? Michael wondered.)

It rang again. And again.

And nobody picked it up . . .

Chapter Twenty-seven

SERGEANT Rick Gallo, Falmouth Police, hung up the phone and slipped his feet off his desk.

I can't fucking believe it, he thought. There's no one else to send. Absolutely incredible. Usually he ended up sending his officers out to direct traffic, just to keep them busy. The weekends were hectic, with the living swarm, the crazed "New Yawkers," trying to bull their way onto the Cape.

But during the week it was dead.

But today there'd been—what? A big car accident, with some tiny Renault plowing into an eighteen-wheeler. Jee-sus! And a "domestic incident" that seemed to disappear by the time the officer showed up.

And there was one that scared him.

Even though he thought it would turn out to be nothing. Just a mistake.

A lost kid, on the bay-side beach of Falmouth—

Nobody said "Missing" kid. That was one kind of shit he didn't want here. No cute sandy-haired kids vanishing into some creep's van.

Gallo stood up.

Tommy Marlowe, his newest cop, hadn't called in about that one yet. Probably searching for the kid on the beach.

He'll turn up, Gallo thought. Yeah, sure.

But what about this?

He looked at his pad, at the notes he scribbled down while talking to this fellow. At first he thought the New York Aquarium director—he looked at the name on the pad, this . . . Michael Cross—just couldn't get a good connection.

But then Gallo tried.

Every single Woods Hole number he had.

And no one picked up.

Could just be a problem with the phone. Could be. In fact, he was tempted to just call New England Bell and let their lineman deal with the problem.

Just a problem in the lines, that's all.

But then Gallo realized that that wasn't exactly following procedure. No. If there's a report, it should be investigated.

He could wait until one of his officers called in or came back. Tell them to take a run down there.

But hell, they were all busy. Marlowe, out looking for the kid, wasn't even *answering* his radio phone. Probably walking the beach, poor bastard. Hot day, and the sand just sucking at the big, black cop shoes.

Hell, he thought. *I'll* have to do it. He grabbed his gray, big-brimmed hat from a hook behind the door. His two boys kidded him about the size of his hat. Extra big, he said, because of the brains.

Extra big, they laughed, 'cause you got such a fat—

He smiled. They never got to finish the sentence. He tore after them, grunting like a wild bull through the house, ready to grab them and toss them around the living room until his wife insisted that it stop, *this minute*. A husband and three sons. Poor girl, he thought, must drive her crazy.

Always complaining about putting the toilet seat down. Why doesn't anyone remember that I live here too? she'd say.

He walked out of his office. Told the clerk, a nice old lady who'd been doing the job since Gallo came to Falmouth. He told her he was taking a quick run down to Woods Hole.

It was just down the block, he thought.

"I'll be right back," he said.

And he walked out of the station, fixing his hat to keep the hot afternoon sun off his face.

"Michael . . ."

"Huh," Michael said, still standing by the phone.

What's going on? he wondered. What the hell is happening up there?

Martin reached out and pulled at his arm. "Michael!"

He turned and looked at Martin.

"Will you come and look now?" Martin said, angry.

What had he found out? Without seeing the tape . . . or the thing that popped out of Reilly . . . what the hell did Martin find out? He hasn't seen anything . . . doesn't know anything . . . yet.

And what exactly did I fucking *see*? What the hell do I *know*?

"Yeah, sure . . ." And he followed Martin to his worktable, a massive slate table filled with test tubes, an open spiral notebook, a dry coffee cup with a telltale stain—

And two microscopes.

"Sit down," Martin said, in charge.

This is his world, Michael thought. Of course, it doesn't help that I'm just standing here like a dazed idiot. I gotta snap out of it.

Martin looked at him.

"Where did you get this?"

"Can I tell you later?" Michael said, hearing how ragged and tired his voice sounded. "I'd like to hear what you think about it first . . ."

"Okay," Martin said, sitting back, scratching his head. He made a small laugh. "I don't know where to begin. When I first started looking at it I thought—well, it's some kind of worm. You know it has an outer body, no vertebrae, and something that looked like it could be a circulatory system, maybe organs inside. I mean, there wasn't a lot of it. I wasn't sure. But I thought, it's a worm . . ."

"A worm," Michael repeated.

"Yeah." Martin nodded. "But I was wrong. Completely wrong. You see, I looked at it under the opaque scope at fifty, then one hundred, then two hundred power. And that's when I saw something really weird."

I'm so tired, he thought. I'm too tired to be sitting here, listening to this. Thinking about Woods Hole. Thinking about—

Michael rubbed his eyes.

Martin waited to go on.

"There's two things here, Michael. There's the outside skin . . . pretty much normal tissue, not much unlike the deep-sea tube worms, the normal *Riftia*. That's when I guessed that this came from a hydrothermal vent."

Michael nodded.

"So then I expected to see a parasite, some colony that could process the inorganic material near the vents. There had to be chemoautotrophic bacteria—"

Right, Michael thought, grinning at how casually Martin rattled off the word that described something that could use the toxins to produce oxygen and carbon dioxide. It was a process that baffled marine biologists. But it was how the tube worms lived.

"And—?"

Martin took off his glasses, and rubbed them against his shirt. His eyes glowed, filled with excitement. This was a Martin Michael had never seen before. "Well, they're there, Michael. The bacteria . . . but with a difference . . . a *big* difference . . ."

Martin edged the microscope close to Michael.

"Look at this. Go ahead." After checking that it was in focus, Martin slid the microscope over to Michael.

It was set to 200x. Michael looked into the eyepiece. He saw the surface skin of the worm, the tears, the small ruptures where the sample had been cut. And for the first time he saw what was below that skin.

It looked like a coral, but not a coral you'd find diving off Aruba. This was primitive, a weird lattice, barbed, that seemed to be weaved together.

"Tell me what to look for," Michael said, feeling lost in the great well of the slide, a gigantic sea that filled his vision. "What am I seeing?"

"You see the colony. Look at how it's connected to the outer skin, the 'host animal.' "

Michael looked. The microscopic coral actually had barbed lines, hooklike things like bee stingers, or the serrated skin of a shark. The barbs hooked right into the outer skin.

"I see," Michael said. "Very nasty—"

Martin grabbed his arm. Squeezed it. "Now watch this."

Michael came up from the microscope, blinking his eyes. He didn't like looking at the thing. If anything, it looked worse this way than when it resembled a worm.

"What are you doing?" Michael asked.

Martin took a pipet and sucked up a few milliliters of water.

"Copepods," Martin said grimly, holding the filled pipet up to Michael's bloodshot eyes.

Michael nodded. He could see the balloon-shaped microorganisms diving up and down their small swimming tank, barely visible to the naked eye. Some dragged two ball-shaped objects from their back. Females with their egg cases.

He didn't have a clue what Martin was up to.

He looked over at the phone.

The Falmouth Police hadn't called back.

Then back at Martin . . . as he lowered the tip of the pipet to the well slide.

"Go ahead," Martin said, pausing. "Watch this." Then he

smiled, with a sick sort of grin that reminded Michael of Colin Clive in James Whale's *Frankenstein*.

Whatever was going to happen was going to be pretty over-the-top stuff.

"You won't fucking believe this . . ."

And Michael looked down, into the heart of the worm . . .

Gallo had passed the gate. There was no one there.

He had stopped long enough to check the guard kiosk, to see that a few of the phone lines were blinking. See, he thought, that's probably the problem. Phone trouble.

Then he continued into the main building, past the fence laced with rambler roses, most dried to a deep, almost purplish-red. He could see the Sound, the Woods Hole harbor. There were two large ships out there. Kind of unusual.

He wondered what they might be doing.

He saw the ferry coming back from Martha's Vineyard.

He drove past the Bradley House. He could check there later. Now he wanted to go to the main building, where the deep submergence lab was.

He pulled right in front, parking across some yellow stripes. When he got out, he hitched up his pants that were in a losing battle with what his wife called, "The Dunlop Disease." His stomach done-lapped over his belt.

When he got out of the car, he stood there a second.

He heard a vireo whistling in a tree. Its repetitive song . . . see me, here I am. See me, here I am. A gentle breeze rustled a nearby willow.

But that was all.

It was as if the place were closed down.

And for the first time he wondered whether something could have happened here. Maybe it wasn't just the phones . . .

He shook his head, and started up the steps. No. He remembered the blinking lights. That's all. Just phone trouble.

He walked into the main building.

There was a sign welcoming the visitor, a map of the buildings, a sign pointing to rest rooms. And the visitor's desk. There was usually someone here who sold tickets to the aquarium . . . explained what you could see. And two hallways, one left, one right, leading into the labs and offices.

There was no one here now.

"Okay," he said aloud. Then, calling, "Hello . . ." He paused. Louder, feeling foolish, "Anybody home?"

Gallo licked his lips. It sure was quiet.

His hand radio was in the car. He should get it, he thought. Another bit of basic procedure that he was ignoring. Too much time behind a desk, eating donuts, drinking coffee.

He was about to turn and walk out to his car.

Wanting to get out of the cool foyer. So quiet.

When he heard a sound.

From somewhere down the hall.

Not a big sound. Could have been a voice, he thought.

Gallo hitched his pants, up, pulling them as high as they would go, as if they would give him more time before they started tumbling to the floor.

He had been on his way out to his car.

But there! He heard the sound again. Damn! Voices, down the left hallway. He sniffed. Yeah, they're probably all running around trying to see what's wrong with the phones. Sure. That's what it is.

And he started down the left hall, following the sound of the voices.

Michael saw the worm, the milky-white skin, the twisted parasite colony inside. Then, a tidal wave splashed over it, swirling the water the fragment sat in. And dozens of copepods, called cyclops, were swimming around the thing.

What happened next was instantaneous.

The cyclops looked like balloon animals, wriggling around the curling coils of the worm's interior.

One second they were swimming, like hundreds of other microscopic pools Michael had seen.

Then it moved.

The whole worm piece—the tiny fragment that Michael thought was dead—seemed to move.

But actually it was just the interior moving, the parasite.

It moved quickly. Each copepod was swimming and then—faster than Michael could see—each minuscule creature was skewered by a barbed, pointed spear of the parasite.

It was sudden, violent.

The most incredible thing he'd ever seen.

"God . . . damn . . ." he muttered.

How could the colony respond to a dozen or more moving thin things, and catch each one, at the same damn instant?

It was incredible.

"I—I don't get this," Michael started to say.

Martin tapped his shoulder. "Keep watching, Michael. Keep watching."

The copepods were skewered on a barbed tip. They wriggled there a moment. Then they stopped their writhing. For a second Michael thought that they were being fed on, that the parasite colony was feeding on them.

That would have been strange enough.

But he watched the clear copepods change color, the reddish tinge of the parasite slowly filling them.

Then—in a matter of moments—they became indistinguishable from the parasite.

They had become just another piece added to the chain, part of the colony.

And then they were gone.

It was quiet in the well slide, inside the microscopic pool.

He pulled back.

Looked at Martin.

"Can you tell me what just happened?"

Martin nodded. "Sure. But tell me one thing first."

Michael nodded.

"Is this the *only* piece of this thing around? Has the fucking thing been quarantined? Because if it isn't, Michael, we're in big trouble."

"There's a videotape," Michael said. "You can watch it. You'll see where it came from." He looked back at the jars. "And this is just a few pieces of it." He looked up at Martin. "I thought they were dead."

Martin. Cool, unflappable, secretive. Now he looked like a scared rabbit. A kid who had done something real bad and was going to get the shit kicked out of him by his father.

And Michael told him: "But the rest of the thing got away . . ."

Chapter Twenty-eight

HE never wore a collar, not when on his ship, not when back at the Institute. He wasn't sure he even knew where it was . . .

When was the last time I said Mass in a church? wondered Father Louis Farrand. Not in a very long time.

Every day he said Mass, on the ship, right in the mess.

Besides, churches depressed him. When it all changed, the Catholic Church seemed as lost as the flock it intended to guide. Now the priest stood on the other side of the altar and faced the people, as if he were saying: It's just you and me, eh?

There's no wizard behind the curtain.

Farrand dug into his back pocket for the crumpled packet of tobacco and his pipe, still warm from his last smoke only minutes ago.

From the port side of his ship he could see the Gulf, slate-gray under some surprisingly heavy clouds. It was supposed to clear, but the air felt still, immobile. The calm . . . before the gale.

And the clouds looked fixed on the sky.

He tamped down the tobacco and then lit the bowl, puffing heavily to get a good fire going. The pipe gurgled—a sign that it needed a good cleaning.

But not now. All he wanted now was to just stand here and smoke.

How long have I been waiting? he wondered. How long has it been?

Four weeks, five? Well after the overhaul was completed and the ship was ready to take to sea again—I've been waiting.

And Farrand knew all too well what was coming.

They're going to ask me to come home.

They're going to ask me to retire . . .

He remembered his first call to the estimable Monsieur Langouche in Paris. Langouche was the new director of IFREMER—The Institut Français de Recherches Pour l'Exploitation des Mers.

It was early evening in Paris when he called.

What's going on, Farrand had asked. Why haven't my plans for another expedition been approved?

The director apologized . . . he explained that he was getting ready to go out to *un grand fête,* a dinner party. *Tant pis,* but he had to hurry. A benefit at the opera. *Tu connais, Père Farrand?* Monsieur Langouche, young and slick, was unabashed about using the less-formal word *tu.*

Oui, Farrand said. Yes, I understand.

Langouche must mingle with the moneyed, and wheedle their golden coffers away from them . . . while science sits and waits. This was the director's true role—more benefits, more nights at the opera.

And Farrand again told him about the worms.

Even now the idea made Farrand go cold with excitement. The idea was—*extraordinary.*

And Farrand tried to explain the idea. And why it was important that he return to the Gulf vents.

We must move quickly, Monsieur Directeur, he said. Others will eventually see the connection.

The possibilities . . .

We must be the first with proof . . . real proof . . .

And Langouche put him off. It was impossible at this time to give permission to take *Ariel* out, he said. Farrand must be patient. The board meets soon. Very soon.

There were many calls after that, always the same.

Until Farrand knew that they'd never give him permission to sail again.

So Farrand waited and smoked his pipe and watched the setting sun scorch the Gulf.

I feel, he thought . . . abused. The *Ariel* is *my* design—I turned the battered transport into a proper research vessel. And the submersible Cyana was constructed to *my* specifications.

In oceanography, there is Robert Ballard and his Jason.

And then there is me.

But Farrand knew he was being punished for not being a good enough salesman. You have to promote your projects . . . merchandise them.

The au courant word in oceanographic circles was "hype."

He watched a jet-black cormorant soar over the water in search of a shallow swimming school of fish. The bird seemed to pause in front of the gray backdrop of the sky, and then plunge down to the water.

And Farrand could imagine the line of dumb-eyed fish, swimming peacefully on the current that took them out to the ocean.

When all of a sudden there was a splash. A blur of phosphorus, and one of the fish feels the iron grip of talons closing around it.

And Farrand watched the bird emerge from the water with something wriggling in its beak.

The priest's pipe went out.

Merde, he thought. Knowing that now he'd have to clean it, digging up all the soggy tar that collects at the bottom of the bowl.

And—as he watched the cormorant—he envied it.

He envied its speed, its independence.

Its freedom.

A sharp breeze suddenly snapped off the water. The storm is coming, he thought. A big one, from the looks of things, and he decided to return to his cabin . . .

"Hello!" Gallo called out again, even as he took a few tentative steps down the left hall. He passed a pair of empty offices, saw more blinking phone lights.

Well damn, he thought, *someone's* talking somewhere, or the lines are broken, or—

He heard the voices, farther down. A laughing sound. A big laugh, he thought, ending in a sputtering cough.

The hall was shadowy, lit only by the light from the front of the building and a single window at the other end, overlooking the Sound.

From the map in the hall, Gallo knew that there were labs down there.

And people.

He hurried, walking quickly. Glad that the whole place hadn't turned into a ghost town.

Enough peculiar things had gone on for one day.

And he thought about that missing boy, the one who vanished on the beach. And he thought how much he hoped to God the boy showed up. He took things like that real hard.

You wear your heart on your sleeve, his wife said, not altogether kindly.

Gallo knew it was true. That's why he could never be a cop in Boston, or—God forbid—New York.

I couldn't handle it, he knew. No way in hell I could handle *that*.

I like it here. It's quiet, peaceful, nothing ever happens, nothing at—

He reached the lab.

There was a pair of metal doors. A metal plaque read Deep Submergence Lab One. One door was open, just a crack. The sounds escaped through that door.

He didn't hear any laughing now.

There were sounds though.

Talking.

No.

Not talking.

He put an ear to the crack.

Didn't want to just go blundering in.

He put his ear right up to the crack. Closer. Hearing sounds like—

Three, four voices. Making noises. Christ, weird noises that gave him the willies.

With one hand, he unbuckled the flap to his revolver. Feeling silly even as he did it.

What did they sound like?

And Gallo—a Roman Catholic from the day he was born—blushed.

They sounded like sex sounds. All kind of wet, and squishy and moans. There were moans.

What the heck? Was there some kind of orgy going on here?

Wouldn't that be a pisser? All those important scientists diddling each other. Damn!

He pressed closer against the crack.

Except—geez—it was all guys' voices.

Now that was something he didn't understand *at all!*

Another reason he'd make a bad city cop.

Squishy sounds. And sucking. And groaning. And—

The door opened. From the inside.

Suddenly.

And he nearly tumbled into the room.

He caught himself with one foot, kicking out to catch himself just in time.

He looked up.

And saw the boss of the whole place, Dr. Cameron, looking at him smiling.

Embarrassed by his eavesdropping, and what he thought he

might see, Gallo fixed Cameron with his eyes, looking right at him, acting very official.

"We got some calls about your phones," Gallo said. He cleared his throat, trying to just look in Cameron's eyes, no more than a few feet away—

(But catching then a bit of movement to the side. Other people, standing there. Moving, shaking, as Gallo talked.)

"No one answered so we felt we'd better come and—"

Cameron's expression hadn't changed. Still had a very pleasant smile on his face. Listening, concerned . . .

Even when Gallo's eyes trailed down, expecting to see the director standing there with his fly open, all hanging out—

He saw something that he thought was a joke.

It was a big white tube. Something wet-looking, shiny, stretching out of Cameron's middle. It was moving, God yes, back and forth, as if sucking. Like something being born, or crawling out of a cocoon. Except there was no cocoon here. It rippled.

"There were calls," Gallo said vacantly, following where this white tube, this balloon thing, led.

Knowing exactly where . . . even before he saw.

"From New York, and—"

There were other people there. Some standing close to Cameron. The tube ran right into one, and then on to another, and on to another, a daisy chain of bodies. And the very last in the line looked like it was a hundred years old, all dry and shriveled. It was crumpled in the corner, squatting on the floor, as this thing sucked at it.

And the horrible thing, this last person—man . . . woman . . . it was impossible to tell—had the same dopey-happy expression that Cameron did.

Gallo started to slide his gun out.

Knowing, thinking, I'm way over my head. Way over. And I don't even have a fucking radio. I don't have any way to get help.

Way over.

He saw the tube thing plop out of Cameron and land on the floor with a thud.

And Gallo saw the end, the tip of it. A deep red core, looking like a rusted Brillo pad, only wet and gloopy with bits and pieces of Cameron's entrails still sticking to it.

Red stuff spurted out onto the floor, the last wave brought by a ripple of the tube thing. The red glop—thick blood and bits of whitish meat—sat in the middle of the floor.

Gallo looked up at Cameron.

What do I do? he thought. What do I shoot?

The tube thing? Cameron? The others?

And he saw that Cameron's face didn't look happy anymore. He looked the way his littlest kid looked when he was told no. I won't buy you that toy. You can't have that thing you want, whatever the hell it is.

Cameron looked lost, deprived.

The tube thing moved.

It was all happening so fast and Gallo thought he was responding, thought he was doing *something*. Did it just seem like everything was going so slowly?

He brought his gun up.

The tube thing—unhurried, unconcerned—crawled close to the reddish glop. And then inside, the rusty Brillo pad moved over, scooping it up.

As though it couldn't bear to waste a bit.

Wouldn't waste a bit.

Gallo fired there, just at the end.

Even though it didn't look like a head, or anything at all that might have a brain.

He fired.

No one stopped him.

Cameron just stood there, looking sad, patient.

Gallo fired again.

Chunks of the tube, this gigantic maggot thing flew around the room.

Gallo stepped back.

Now it seemed aware of him.

Gallo heard it disconnect—he didn't watch it—from the others.

He heard the plop as it slid away from their bodies.

He kept looking at the part in front of him, firing, filling the lab with a heavy bluish smoke.

Someone was screaming now.

A new sound, real loud. Screaming, yelling, louder and louder. Cursing. Sonovabitch. Fuckin' sonovabitch!

It's me, Gallo thought, between pulls on the trigger.

He stepped out of the lab.

It took forever.

Because by the time he had one heavy cop foot outside the door, back in the quiet gloom lit only by the one window and the reflected glare off the Sound, it had him.

Right at his spine.

He heard the rip of his shirt and then felt the terrible tearing of his skin, his screaming turning to a higher pitch, begging, pleading before—

Before.

He stopped.

Turned.

And felt this wonderful feeling, this great warmth fill him.

And he knew he was smiling, a big, broad, shit-eating smile in his face as the worm dragged him back to the others, tugging him along as it crawled back to the others, burrowing back into their bodies. Nestling in them . . .

Bringing smiles back to everyone's face . . .

Chapter Twenty-nine

MICHAEL stopped the videotape just at the point the screen went to a sick-looking snow.

It was the second time he had shown it to Martin.

And Martin hadn't said a word. He just nodded, put up a hand . . . ruminating.

"So . . . ?"

"Michael . . . we're going to have to get help. I mean, right away."

That wasn't news to the Aquarium director. But he knew that before he started contacting people he needed as much information as he could get.

"All right," Michael said. "I'm ready to do that. But I need to know more. Tell me what you saw."

Martin took a breath. Then he began. "It's brand-new. Completely out of the books. I mean, did you see the way it moved? Nothing like it has been seen before. The tube worms are just a mild aberration compared to these. And they're definitely chemosynthesizers. No doubt about it. They'd have to be to live around the smokers."

"Go on."

"But they're not *just* chemosynthesizers. They don't just use an internal parasite to turn toxic H_2S into oxygen. They can use organic material too . . . but in a strange way. They take it and add it directly to its biosystem."

Michael nodded, and then rewound the tape to the last view of the worm just before it attacked the *Achilles*'s ROV. He froze the frame there.

Martin got up and walked over to the screen.

"Look!" he said, amazed, impressed. "Jeesus! They live in burrows. Like a community of prairie dogs. And do you know the most incredible thing? The thing went from an environment where the pressure is over two tons for every square inch, to a scant thirty-two pounds per square inch . . . without dying. That's what scares me."

"Is it going to live?" Michael asked.

"Live? Hell, Mike, the fucking thing should flourish. It's gone from an isolated, restricted environment, a chemically supported oasis in a freezing black abyss, to a wonderland of life forms. You saw what it did to the copepods. My guess is it could use anything organic. Anything . . . the bigger the better. But you know, I don't know why it would have to use organic material. That still confuses me. Why wouldn't it just find a nice waste treatment plant to curl up beside? It would be perfect . . ."

"Maybe it will. So the chunk that fell in the ocean . . . it will live?"

Martin laughed. Then he looked at Michael. "I know you've been calling Woods Hole, Cameron . . . I know what you've been worried about—"

"No," Michael tried to say, still trying to deny what he felt was happening . . . what he knew was happening—

"And you're right. Forget Woods Hole. The phones are dead for a reason. We're looking at the ultimate opportunist here. Hell, my guess is forget the Cape, the Sound."

"Shit."

Martin laughed again, sounding almost hysterical.

"Forget the whole East Coast."

Michael looked at the screen, at the frozen image of the worm lashing out at the ROV.

"So what kept it down there?" Michael said.

"Hmmm?"

Michael walked right up to Martin. He needed him alert, thinking, helping him—

(And he thought. I've got to call Caryn, Jo, make some plans. Try to explain. They should stay in the apartment. I've got to—)

He shook Martin's shoulder gently. "So what kept it down there, Martin? Talk to me!"

Martin looked away from the screen.

Again a laugh, inappropriate, weird . . . Martin's way of dealing with the situation. He rubbed his chin. "I thought you figured that one out for yourself. It's right there in the tape. Right there, on the screen. And we've got a chunk of the answer in the deep freeze here," he said, pointing to the coffin-shaped freezer they kept their dead specimens in. "I should have expected something like this . . . I mean, it makes so much sense now, now that I've seen this thing." He gestured at the screen.

"I don't get you," Michael said. "What are you talking about."

"*Bythnomus giganteous,*" Martin said.

And Michael watched him walk over to the freezer.

"Be good and—" Jo's mom looked over her shoulder, into the living room where Carrie was already blasting MTV. Her mother made a funny face, her review of the music.

Jo didn't know the song or the group.

But then, she didn't know a lot of the groups.

Her mom spoke quietly. "Make sure that Carrie keeps the volume down. We don't need the neighbors getting on our case with the co-op board. Okay?"

Jo nodded. Her mother touched her cheek.

"Are you sure you're okay?"

Jo forced a smile, as big a grin as she could manage. "I'll be great, Mom, really. Don't worry. Carrie is more than enough company."

The TV set's volume seemed to swell a bit more.

"You'll have to deal with *that* right away," Caryn said, indicating the TV.

Jo nodded.

"And there's microwave popcorn, and Coke . . . you just have a fun time. I'll call—"

"Don't worry, Mom. I'll be fine. What could happen?"

Her mother smiled, finally looking relieved.

"Right." She stood up straight. She wore makeup, and had heels on. Her hair was combed back, straight, lustrous, freshly washed. She looked beautiful.

Jo knew that she could never look like that.

"Super. Well, I'd better get going." She leaned down and gave Jo a quick, dry peck. "And remember to—"

"Lock all three locks."

Caryn laughed. "Good girl." And then, with a quick rustle of Jo's hair, she turned and left.

It was still early in the studio, but Barron was enjoying walking around. Why, tonight everyone seemed positively friendly.

Not at all like his entrance yesterday . . .

Oh, he still caught a few people staring at him as he walked by with Jay in tow. But the rest could see which way the wind was blowing, oh, yeah. This cable network, and all its new-age folderol, their connection to the blue-eyed Gene Fasolt, well . . . all of that depends on their being real nice to me.

The technicians—the guys who handled the coils of wire as though they were sleepy snakes—bobbed their heads as Paul Barron walked the set. A few of the assistant directors smiled, looking up from black ring binders that contained the secrets for putting together Gene's dog-and-pony show.

It all made perfect sense to Barron now.

Religion, dat ole-time religion, had fallen on hard times. Too many sex and money scandals—

But hey, I know the dangers of that trap, Barron thought. That, and nose candy. (And just thinking about a quick jolt of blow gave him a small rush. Life can be so good when all these people are throwing themselves at you, throwing their money, their tight, polished bodies. Take me, fuck me, and show me God.)

This new-age shit was a different wrinkle, a damned clever one. Old wine in new bottles. The emperor's new voodoo. It looked and smelled clean and nice. They had real signs, real messages from beyond. And channelers who spoke with the astral voices of old gods and spirits. Whole books were filled with the gobbledygook transcribed from Seth, Ramfar, and a host of other goofy astral mavens.

Boy, were they in for a surprise . . .

He heard some stumbling steps behind him.

"Eh?" he said, turning around, just in time to see Jay trip on some of the wires.

"Hey, watch out there—" one of the technicians said, just seeing his wires snap tight. Then, when he saw who it was who tripped, he stood back. Wiped his brow. Apologized . . .

"Oh, sorry, Jay. I—I have to get those things taped down. I—" The technician backed into the darkness, still mumbling.

Jay righted himself. He was "Jay" now, a power to be reckoned with. More powerful than Gene. Overnight.

And he was still wearing the same stinking outfit. Barron couldn't find any of Gene's clothes that fit him.

The same ripe outfit. Barron grinned.

Besides, it kind of suited Barron to have this seer, this ultimate bad-ass mystic mojo dressed as though he were about to sneak into your house and make off with your Sony Handicam and your luscious seventeen-year-old daughter.

That was pretty cool.

They reached the main studio area, the place where Jay would deliver his message to the city.

The newspapers were full of the story.

Full of the news about Jay, and the televised religious experience that "touched" a whole city. People who wouldn't be caught dead watching a TV evangelist zapped past Gene's channel . . . and got snagged. Some just watched out of curiosity. Then they heard the words. Felt those feelings.

People cried.

Others emptied their savings account and sent it to Gene's organization. Over-fucking-night. Federal Express showed up with duffel bags filled with checks.

(And I'll need to get a piece of *that*, Barron thought. If money still means anything when this is over. A big chunk of the money. And a hiding place . . . that's all I want. That's all—

I'm begging, he thought. And I'm not even sure they're listening.)

"Everything look okay, Mr. Barron?"

He turned. It was a young woman, armed with a binder. Smiling at him. She was generic, pleasant. Scrubbed and polished.

He looked at her. Smiled. She aroused in him only the most craven desires. To mess her up, to take her neatly cropped hair, her clothes, her cute, pert face, and make her over into his dream girl.

Perhaps later.

Barron looked at the set. It was different, the way he told them he wanted it after last night.

"Yes, it looks . . ." He scanned the brightly lit set. "Where is Jay's place? Where does Jay sit?"

The farm girl, this Ivory Girl, smiled. "Right there, Mr. Barron, in the center, where you told us you wanted it."

Barron nodded. "And where do I—?"

He caught her looking at Jay. Those who had watched—and felt—Jay's power seemed in awe of the black man today. Jay was a celebrity, even if it was to be short-lived.

The others, those who were busy getting the show out to the cable feed and missed Jay's show, couldn't understand what the hell he was doing here. Barron could see it in their eyes.

And even Barron looked into Jay's dull eyes, wondering . . . Where are you? What happened to the dude who sat down next to me in the bus?

Is that guy *ever* coming back?

"You're right there," the woman said, a bit nervously. She had obviously seen Jay's performance. She pointed to a pair of chairs near the back of the stage area. "Gene will sit next to you and—"

Barron nodded, held up a hand. I mustn't get too ambitious, he thought. This is Jay's night. Not mine.

I'm just his fucking trainer . . . his keeper.

He chewed at his fleshy lower lip. The tip of his tongue still bled, off and on. It wasn't a big chunk that was gone. Still, he was upset. My tongue . . .

Now he was nervous, thinking.

What happens to me afterward? What's in the plan?

I'll be rewarded for my service, won't I? Of course. I'll have to be.

(*Please*, he thought.)

He looked at the chair at the back of the stage.

Jay was just behind him.

He could smell him.

Reporters, TV news crews, were outside, waiting to get in.

The bright lights went off, and the set went dark. The technical rehearsal must have just ended.

I think I'll park you, Barron thought, turning around, looking at Jay.

And Jay walked over to the stool, in the center of the now-dark set.

He sat down.

Barron watched him.

Jay closed his eyes.

There, he thought. That's the boy. Now maybe I can stomach a bit of food . . . before show time . . .

"Shit," Carrie said, aiming the remote control at the TV set as if it was a magic ray gun.

Jo was beginning to think that maybe it wasn't such a hot idea having Carrie come stay with her.

"MTV has that stupid game show on now. Duh! Remote Control. What a bor-ing show. Can you believe all that shit with the popcorn bowls and easy chairs. And those nerdy questions about TV. If I wanted to watch dumb game shows, I'd watch Nickelodeon. And"—she flashed through a dozen channels at lightning speed—"there isn't anything else on."

"We could make some popcorn," Jo offered. "My mom said—"

Carrie—sitting on the floor—spun around. "Forget that, Jo-Jo. Do your parents have any"—she scrunched ahead, sliding on the rug, closer to Jo—"hot videos? You know, some cool adult stuff, if you know what I mean . . ."

For a second Jo didn't know what Carrie was talking about. But the other girl's wide grin made the light bulb flash.

"No. I don't think so. I mean"—Jo knew she was blushing—"my parents are divorced, so . . ."

Carrie scrunched a bit closer. And Jo was once again aware of how different the older girl was, how her body had already changed. It made Jo feel uncomfortable, almost as though she were with another adult.

A crazy adult.

"I don't think that my mom . . ."

Carrie stood up. "Yes, she would. My mom does. And she's divorced too. She has this one film where there are these two guys and—"

"I'm going to make some popcorn," Jo said, hoping it sounded casual. She felt how flush she was, trying to keep it from Carrie. I couldn't stand that, she thought. The kidding, the teasing . . .

But Carrie went on, getting up, following her.

"And these two guys, like they're really hunks, really good-looking. They take this woman's clothes off and—"

Jo made a lot of noise opening the cupboard, digging out a pouch of Orville Redenbacher's Microwave Popcorn, with Cheese Flavor. She opened the door—ready to nuke the bag. Still Carrie went on.

"First they lick her all over." Carrie laughed, a big, boomy sound. "I mean *all over*. Even places you wouldn't think anyone would want to lick. Then it's her turn and she—"

Jo punched the buttons and, inside the microwave, the bag started to swell, inflating with popped corn and hot air. She watched it.

Carrie kept talking. Jo thought about asking her to leave. A little of Carrie went a long way. This had been a bad idea.

And without any encouragement, Carrie went on a bit more about the movie—

"Anyway, Jo-Jo, it's one hot movie, let me tell you. I'll show it to you next time we're in my place and dear old Mom is working late."

The microwave beeped.

Carrie draped a hand on Jo's shoulder. "So, let's search your place. I bet there's a hidden video treasure here." Carrie made her eyes go clown-wide. "Maybe even some of your dad's left-over condoms we can blow up. Party balloons."

"Carrie . . ." Jo said.

Jo took out the popcorn.

She grabbed a big bowl. She opened the bag and poured the popcorn in. It never looked right, this microwave popcorn, not like real popcorn her mom always said. It always tasted kind of strange too. The cheese flavor helped some. But who thought that popcorn needed cheese?

"No way," Jo said strongly. Surprised at how strongly she said it.

I've gotten into enough trouble for one week, she thought.

Then for effect, she repeated . . . "No *fucking* way . . ."

"Hey, chill down, Jo-Jo. It was just an idea, that's all. A widdle idea." Carrie reached out and scarfed up a big handful of the popcorn, sending kernels tumbling to the floor. "No problem. 'Cause I've got lots of ideas." She chewed on the popcorn. Then, her grin blooming, bursting with the cheesy popcorn, she said, "Lots of ideas . . ."

Chapter Thirty

THE isopod was frozen into a bricklike shape, its antennae and legs locked into position.

"You saw these on the tape, right?" Martin asked, holding the dead animal up. Michael nodded. The albino isopod was a common-enough rift creature attracted by the odd food supply found near the hydrothermal vents.

"You saw lots of them," Martin said, putting the isopod down. "And not only that, Michael, there were things that—if I'm not wrong—have been labeled extinct for fifty or more million years."

"Such as?"

Martin rubbed his eyes.

And Michael thought . . . you think you're tired? You should feel the messages my body is sending. When I'm not thinking about the worm, and Cameron, and the thing multiplying all over the place, I've got only one thought.

Lying down.

Nice and flat.

Even a few minutes would be heaven.

I've got to get some coffee. Keep the caffeine coming, for as long as it takes.

"Like the limpet neomphalus. It's just a limpet, nothing extraordinary, a bit larger than your average limpet, with a more ornate shell. It's a grazing monovalve, like other limpets. But it's been considered extinct for over fifty million years. Except—it isn't. I saw a half dozen of them stuck to the side of those white bacterial mats, eating away, happy as"—Martin smiled—"clams."

"Like the coelacanth," Michael said, referring to the once-prehistoric fish caught off the coast of Africa.

"Yeah, like the coelacanth. But older, Mike. Much older. And there was another animal, the stalked barnacle. And man, that's even more important."

"Why?"

"The stalked barnacle was an incredibly crucial development in ocean life. Before the first barnacles, there had just been colony creatures, anemones, dozens of strange corallike animals. The stalked barnacle, starting as a free swimmer before settling down on a rock, was a brand-new life form . . . the first. And the only place I've ever seen one before was in the American Museum of Natural History." He paused. "But there are hundreds of them in your tape there."

They heard a cracking sound.

It came from the giant isopod. Thawing, splintering on the table before them. Another cracking sound.

Michael came close to it. Such a strange animal, a gigantic louse, as big as a dog. He remembered the question about it that they couldn't answer, the thing about *giganteous* that had everyone stumped.

What the hell does it eat . . . ?

Martin picked up a small dissecting scalpel. He lifted one of the animal's protective plates near its thorax.

It made a loud crunching sound.

It looked as though it would come to life.

"Remember that growth we found on it? The bacterial growth found on all the deep-sea isopods?"

Michael nodded. That seemed like years ago.

"When you were gone I looked at it. It was still alive. Even though the isopod was dead. As I suspected, it was a colony, and it responded, moved against my probe when I touched it. The weird thing was . . . it seemed to examine the probe, identify it . . . before it lost interest."

"And—"

Martin took a breath. "And the growth died, long after the isopod. Then I got curious. I should have checked with you, I mean, to get permission. But I went inside."

Martin reached out and turned the isopod over.

It has been dissected.

The internal organs had been removed.

Some had been replaced, pinned back into the frozen carapace.

But that's not what surprised Michael.

There were small tufts of the growth, the same as on the surface of the animal . . .

Michael reached out, and touched one.

It was frozen, crunchy.

"I found them all over . . . in every part of the animal. Every part, Michael. But they don't seem to interfere with the animal's functioning at all. That was incredible enough. I took some fluid from the isopod. I made a slide . . ."

Martin ran to the front of the small lab. He turned on the projection microscope, sending a blurry splash of color onto the lab wall.

"I've just got to focus . . . wait a sec . . . there—"

The image became clear. Greenish and brown blotches, the animals' "blood," all arranged in the familiar mosaic shape. And something else.

"What's that?" Michael said, walking up to the projection, cutting through the light, and then stepping to the side. He pointed at a series of reddish dots spread throughout the sample. Tiny, almost invisible.

"Single cells, Michael. Single-celled animals, inside the animals' circulatory system. They're identical to the cells that make up the colony."

"They killed it?"

Martin laughed.

"No. Don't you get it? God, look at it. What do they look like, *what do they fucking look like*?"

Michael rubbed his chin. Microbiology wasn't his forte. He never enjoyed hunkering down over a microscope or studying printouts from electron microscopes. But still there was something familiar here, something—

"I—I—"

Martin pointed them out. "Look at them, Michael. There's your answer, that's why those nasty motherfuckers, your worms, can't get out of the abyss. Look at those cells, filling the animal, probably inside every damn rift animal around the worm burrows, keeping them safe." He rubbed his eyes again, and looked straight at Michael. "They're like part of some ancient guard duty, something that's been forgotten by our genes after millions of years of safety."

"Wait a minute. You're not saying we once had these cells—"

"Not us. But go back, maybe thirty, fifty million years."

Martin took a bold marker and made big circles on the dots, right on the lab wall. "Don't you see what they look like?"

Then Michael saw it. Elementary stuff. Something he'd seen dozens of times in his Micro I course.

When looking at human blood. When he saw the way it

defended itself against attackers . . . against bacteria, and germs . . . any intruder that endangered its existence.

He spoke quietly. "They look like white blood cells."

And Martin slapped him on the back.

Caryn rubbed her bare arms. It had turned cool, much too cool for a midsummer's night. A breeze came whipping down 23rd Street, off the Hudson River.

She looked around at the growing crowd waiting outside the building that housed Unicorn Studios.

All the local news shows were represented and—God, she couldn't believe it—all three networks. NBC's Garrick Utley was standing behind an impromptu cordon that separated the battery of video cameras from the rest of the media.

The print reporters, the magazine and newspaper people, were forced to mingle with the growing crowd of loonies that filled the sidewalk.

Caryn very much doubted that anyone was going to get inside the building.

I can't believe this, she thought, looking around at the people. The crowd, orderly, expectant, cut across every chasm of New York society.

There were businessmen, generic types clutching sleek black attachés. And power secretaries dressed in skirts and the inevitable pair of Reeboks, ready for the fight to get back to Queens.

Then there were the flotsam and jetsam of New York . . . its most prevalent citizens. Young people wearing shoes without laces and filthy black shirts, half tucked in, half dangling out. And latino street kids, looking as if a rock star were going to come out of the building's heavy green door.

And more and more people came every minute.

"Damn," she muttered to herself. "I'm not going to see anything here."

"Don't be so sure about that . . ." someone said behind her.

She turned quickly, her street-smarts just there, ready to kick the prospective masher in the balls, if need be.

She laughed when she saw who it was.

"Winston," she said. "I thought you were some"—she lowered her voice—"religious pervert." It was Winston Neal, a feature editor at *Time*. He wrote New York–based stuff, some culture things. Loved the opera.

He even sang Otello for a small New Jersey amateur group.

"Didn't need any makeup." He laughed, rubbing his craggy black face.

He had asked her out. Twice. The first time she said no. Not because she wasn't attracted. She was. He was bright, intelligent, with eyes that made her feel very safe, very comfortable. She said no because it was too soon after Michael. No rebound romances for her. And she thought of Jo . . .

The second time he asked her out—to the opening night of Zeffirelli's new *Rigoletto* at The Met, she hesitated. But she still said no. I need a bit more time, she explained. She touched his hand. A strong, secure hand that was clean and warm to the touch.

The next time she knew she'd say yes.

Screw Michael.

Winston smiled, and looked around at the crowd. "Looks like a lot of folks got religion last night."

She nodded, then, "Did you see the show?"

He shook his head no, and then she told him about the few minutes she saw.

Leaving out the funny way it made her feel.

"Well, I hear he's a black man, this Jay, this channeler. I'm always glad to hear about some brother getting ahead in white society," he laughed.

More police arrived, their sirens on. Caryn looked past Winston to watch them close the street to traffic using police barricades. The people literally filled the street and there didn't seem to be any crowd control.

She looked back to Winston. "But aren't all these true believers going to miss this message, or whatever, that Jay has in store?"

Winston pointed to the left.

"They're putting a big monitor in that window there and I believe they'll have some heavy-duty speakers outside. So, the waiting masses will get the whole effect."

She smiled. "Great. I could use some help from above."

Winston smiled back. "You look cold," he said.

She rubbed her arms. "It is cold, isn't it? I mean, what was it this morning, eighty-five, ninety? Now, it feels like it's fifty."

The reporter nodded. "Yeah, does feel a bit nippy. How about some coffee?"

Caryn looked around. "If we leave here, we'll lose our place. Look how far back the crowd goes."

Winston reached out and gave her a big bear hug, pulled her close. "No. You stay here. I can barrel my way through the crowd, flash my all-powerful Time, Inc. badge. Cream and sugar?"

"Black," she said, then smiling, recalling a dumb joke about coffee and black men . . .

Winston smiled back—a look of recognition? she wondered "Black it is. And can I force a donut on you?"

"No need to force at all."

"Be back in five minutes."

Caryn nodded, watched him leave. And then she turned. The sun was down. The river had lost its golden glow and now it just looked cool, dark, oily as a tug pulled a heavy barge—probably loaded with garbage, she imagined—out, past the Twin Towers, past Lady Liberty, under the mammoth Verrazano Narrows Bridge, to the sudden expanse of the Atlantic.

She rubbed at her gooseflesh.

Chapter Thirty-one

ALL of Michael's calls to Cape Cod brought the same result. There was still no answer at Woods Hole.

(I expected that, Michael told himself, rubbing his fingers. How long did it take for the *Achilles*'s crew to be sucked dry?)

But now there was no answer from the Falmouth Police.

For fun, he tried another Falmouth number. A motor inn on 495.

It rang ten, eleven times. Finally he hung up.

New England Bell gave him the number for the state police on the western part of the Cape.

He let that one ring a long time too.

"Jesus," he said to himself.

Then he and Martin started dividing their calls. The Massachusetts governor's office, the New York governor's office, then the mayors of Boston, New York, Hartford . . . And each call brought the same, not unreasonable request.

Send your information to this office. Please. And the proper authority will look into it. Someone will get back to you.

"No, you don't understand," Michael screamed to some switchboard operator—he saw that it was past quitting time. "You can't fucking *wait* until tomorrow morning, you see by tomorrow morning everyone might be gone, you—"

They hung up.

He called the ONR, the Office of Naval Research. He got an answering machine. He left a message, knowing how whacked out, how crazy it must sound. I should just come out and tell them the whole thing, he thought. There's something in the water, moving through every living thing, taking them over, spreading like the goddam plague.

Then Martin calmed him down.

Because he had a plan.

In fact, Michael suspected that Martin had been thinking about this idea he had for a long time, just keeping it to himself, afraid to say anything until he had really thought it out.

Don't worry, Michael wanted to say to him. Anything you've come up with isn't going to sound any weirder than what I've been thinking.

Martin grabbed Michael's arm as he was about to make another, probably useless call.

The idea was simple, Martin explained, taking a breath . . . trying to calm himself. We came from the ocean. All land animals evolved from first animals in the ocean. We evolved, and discarded things that don't have any relevance to our survival.

Michael listened, trying to anticipate where Martin was going.

Martin mentioned that old bit of trivia, how we're 70 percent water, that we carry our own saline ocean around with us. Except it's not just trivia. It's true. But tens of millions of years of natural selection has changed that ocean, changed just what we carry inside our veins.

(And here Martin squeezed Michael's wrist, as if he needed to convince him that his next statement just *had* to be accepted. Because they didn't have any time to prove it.)

These worms are an alien form of life . . . but they may be as old as anything on the planet. They're alien because they *lost* the planet. They're chemosynthesizers, and that's not how life developed on this planet. They lost, just like the first anechoic bacteria that didn't use oxygen. *Because there was no oxygen* when the planet made its chemical soup. The chemosynthesizers lost. When life was just beginning . . . when the other life, the animals beginning to make food from light and water and oxygen, began developing . . .

They lost.

But not completely.

In places where the planet stayed a violent chemical factory, remained the toxic, strange planet it was from its birth, the chemosynthesizers continued.

Kept in check, imprisoned by other creatures that were immune to any infestation. Protected by the colony of helpful cells that could destroy the bacterial parasite of the worm.

Michael listened. It made sense. And he wondered what odd battles raged between the two life forms, the two codes of existence. He thought of the periodic mass extinctions . . . of almost an entire planet killed. Yet life, a life based on sun, and oxygen, and soil, returned each time.

He felt dizzy then. He grabbed the back of a chair. Where am I? he wondered. Where the fuck am I? And what the hell is happening?

The Aquarium had closed without his noticing it, Stephen and Annie were in the other offices, making calls. They had the hardest time accepting what was going on.

There wasn't time to show them what the worm could do.

The sun was nearly down, as Coney Island gave itself to the night.

He heard Annie's voice, then Stephen's . . . talking on the phone.

And Michael and Martin were alone. With their crazy ideas. (And Michael pictured all of Cape Cod, God, maybe all of Massachusetts, having the same fun experience that the crew of the *Achilles* had.)

Martin went on talking . . .

"If we get animals from the rifts," he said, his eyes looking away, focused on some distant abyss in his mind . . . "the ones like the isopods that carry the odd cells, the colony of bacteria that *know* the worm, can recognize it, destroy it, we *might* be able to stop it."

Michael nodded, listening, trying to think things through.

Because if we don't, what would stop them from touching everyone . . . everything? Traveling through the worldwide water cycle, until everyone had it in them, feeding, growing stronger—

(And then Michael sat down, troubled by something, something that still wasn't clear. Feeling as if there was *something else* going on here.)

But he knew Martin was right.

If they took the small chunks of the worm he had brought back, chopped them into a thousand tiny pieces, pushed them through the lab's grinding insinkerator, and flushed them out to some fucking water treatment plant—

They would still live, thrive. Each tiny little piece . . .

It had to be stopped at the most basic level.

At the level of a single-celled microorganism.

The rest Michael could fill in. "Right," he sighed. "We have to get samples," he said. "Rift creatures, with living colonies, with these 'defender' cells in their blood."

"They'll all have it, Mike. It's the only way they could live there."

Michael looked out the lab window. He saw Surf Avenue,

already filled with souped-up heaps rocketing up and down the tacky strip, cruising for God-knows-what.

Martin said, "But I don't have a clue how we're going to do that . . . I . . ."

Michael turned. "I do." He grinned. A crazy grin, he knew, born of equal parts panic and desperation. "All we have to do is find a submersible. Easy, right? And then just convince whoever has it to let us use it. No problem," he laughed.

But Martin didn't lose his serious tone. "But wait . . . wait a minute. There's *Alvin*—"

Alvin was the Woods Hole sub. "That's in the Pacific working the East Pacific Rise."

"Then how about the commercial divers?"

Now that was an idea. He knew a company that had just the right vehicle. Northern Marine Inc. Michael went to his desk, dug out his directory, and called the Toronto-based diving company. They supplied state-of-the-art diving technology to the commercial mining interests.

The phone rang four, five times.

Martin watched him.

This is getting crazy, Michael thought. Phone calls are getting to be pretty spooky things to make. Then someone picked up.

"Hello," a voice said.

"Hi," Michael said, trying to keep the frantic sound out of his voice. "Er, I'm Dr. Michael Cross, the director of the New York Aquarium—"

"Sorry," the person interrupted, "but hey, we're all closed up here. I was just clearing my desk . . . can you call back—"

"No! Now just wait a minute." He was losing it, shit . . . losing his grip. He tried to calm down. "No, please, don't hang up. There's something bad happening here, I mean, it happened—"

He decided that he wouldn't tell the guy the real story. That was too damn risky.

"We have a toxic spill here, off our shore. And—"

"Hey, shouldn't your Coast Guard be on that?"

"Yes, but—they're all tied up. We need a submersible. Something with powerful manipulator arms. Something like the Ocean Rover."

Michael remembered reading about the Ocean Rover, how it was the most advanced submersible available for deep-ocean work, good maneuverability, a fast propulsion system and—

"Sorry, mate, but we have just two Ocean Rovers. One is in the shop with a busted navigation system. That one won't be ready for a week or two."

"And the other?"

I'll need a ship, Michael thought. God. Something to get me out to the Gulf, and Jesus! Was this even possible?

"It's crawling the bottom of Crater Lake, and coming up with some very weird stuff too. Dr. Pennington is running that expedition for the University of Colorado. If you want his num—"

"No," Michael said dully. That won't do any fucking good at all. He heard a muffler-less car roar past the Aquarium.

"I'm sorry," the man said. "What got dumped? Something bad?"

"Uh-huh."

There had to be something else, he thought.

"Wait a second," the guy said as if sensing Michael's desperation. "Hey, I know about another sub stateside. And it's on the East Coast. I don't know if it's operational or what but—"

"What is it?"

"It's a French number, modeled on *Alvin*. They bought some parts from us last week. I don't know if they're still there. But—anyway, it's worth a shot. The ship is called *Ariel*, from the French Oceanographic Institute."

"Do you have a phone number?"

There was static on the line. The man's voice drifted in, then out, garbled, then covered by static.

"Damn," Michael muttered, then louder, "I can't hear you. *I can't hear you.*"

The man spoke again, barely audible. But this time Michael could understand him.

"No. Sorry. But it's just docked right on the Gulf, a port called Flamingo. It's on the western side of the Everglades National Park. In some big boat yard. But . . ." More static. ". . . might be . . ."

The line went dead.

He tried calling again. Got a recorded message.

Michael listened to the dull voice.

". . . please try your call later . . ."

"Here you go," Winston said, elbowing his way past the last few people between Caryn and him.

She took the coffee—feeling that it was already lukewarm. The donut looked tempting, oozing a dark red jelly.

"Dinner's on me." Winston grinned.

"I'll take a rain check on a real dinner," she said. She took a slug of the black coffee through the special sipping lip. The lip felt scaly, almost lizardlike against her lips. She left a brownish-orange smear on the plastic lip.

"It's getting positively lethal around here. I'm not too sure the cops have everything under control."

Winston looked around, his face registering concern. But he turned back to her and said, "Nah, they're fine. The street's closed off, and they're not letting anyone else even come near the building."

Caryn nodded, and bit into her jelly donut.

Then the big monitor in the ground-level window flickered on with a display of rainbow bars. A goofy "ooh" sound ran through the audience.

"Getting near show time," Winston said.

"How much money do you have?" Michael asked Martin.

Martin fished his wallet out of his jeans. From its thin and compact appearance, Michael knew it wasn't stuffed with hundred-dollar bills.

Martin opened it with the disappointed expression of a prospector who always came up empty. "Twenty dollars"—he started to dig through his pocket, rattling some coins—"and—"

Michael plucked the twenty out of Martin's wallet. "This will help. And I've got enough plastic to get me down there. If the damn ship is still there."

"You could call the dock. They'd—"

"Yeah, maybe. But if the ship is moored, just hanging in the Gulf, waiting for a part or something, the dock people wouldn't know that. No, I can catch the last plane . . . and get to Miami just after midnight. How long to the Everglades?"

"Two hours. Maybe more."

Michael nodded.

"You keep at it with the phones. Get to some people who will listen. Just keep trying. God, they got to keep people off the beaches and—"

"Even rivers, Michael. *Any* body of water that hooks up to the ocean."

"Right. Call the NSF, and the Office of Naval Research. See if you can get the Environmental Office to do something. Just tell them, they don't got a lot of time. Ask them to try and get through to Cape Cod. That could get things happening."

Michael froze.

Caryn always said it.

He never did spend too much time thinking about his family, worrying about them.

"Jo and Caryn. I don't—"

"Call them," Martin ordered, his face also concerned. "Tell them to stay inside their apartment. Until you get back."

"Maybe I should get them here," he thought, looking at Martin.

He thought of the city, surrounded by water. Manhattan Island.

Fun City. Especially during a mass extinction.

Michael went to the phone, an instrument that was becoming more and more useless.

"What if this doesn't work, Martin? What if there's *nothing* that can be done? What the hell then?"

His ex-wife's line rang once.

Martin rubbed his chin.

"What then?"

Another ring.

Come on, Michael thought. Where the hell could you be, where the hell—

The ringing stopped. And he heard a loud noise from the TV . . . and then Jo saying, "Hello?"

Jo had drifted into the living room. Carrie finally stopped her endless prowling of the cable TV's dozens of channels.

And Jo heard a song that made her pay attention.

The video was in black and white. Old people, shuffling along, looking as though they were waiting for an overdue bus off the planet. Homeless people curled up in the street, cardboard boxes pulled over them. A woman tugging at her dirty folds of clothing.

Jo came closer.

Then the singer was there. A balding guy with glasses.

He spun around. Jumped into the air. Looked at the camera.

"Reach out, you've got to learn to live again . . . Reach out for the healing hands . . ."

It was wonderful, the tremendous rhythms . . . then a choir, while the man spun around . . . "There's a light where the darkness ends . . . reach out, reach out . . . for the healing hands . . ."

Black children's faces in a hospital, some in bandages, some scarred, dark purple blotches marring their faces. And then these thin men, with short hair, so young but looking old, like trees that have lost their leaves.

And the music was exciting, beautiful, and—

Carrie groaned and zapped past MTV.

Jo yelled, surprising herself, actually yelled at her.

"Put that back, Carrie Blau. Right now."

"God! You like Elton John? What a sappy song, and look at him," Carrie laughed cruelly. "He's practically bald!"

Jo walked to her and snatched the remote back from her and then listened again, catching just the last part of the song. It was close on the singer now, Elton John. He lifted his hands from the piano, held them out to the audience, pleading, begging, "You've got to wade to the water . . . you've got to learn to live again. Touch me now, and let me see again . . ."

Jo started bouncing standing there, as the images started flying for the screen. People hurt, hungry people, hurt people, and the words . . . making Jo feel so wonderful.

Then it was over.

"Yu-uck. God, I hope that they play some Bon Jovi now. That was *really* lame."

Jo ignored her, cherishing the last few minutes of the special glow made by the song.

"Any more eats, Jo-Jo?" Carrie said, waving the empty popcorn bowl at her.

Jo nodded. "There's some pretzels," she said. And she went to the kitchen, looking at the clock. I hope Mom gets home soon, she thought. She felt at sea, floating, waiting for someone to pick her up. I'm fine, she thought. I'm okay. But why do I feel like I need . . . something?

Some heavy metal blared from the TV. She heard Carrie say, "All right!"

And the phone rang.

"Jo . . . Jo? Hi, honey. Is your mom there?"

The music was too loud. Her father would hear it, would wonder what's going on.

She knew that she couldn't tell him she was alone. It would just become one more thing for her mom and dad to fight about. She was always in the middle. The reason for their battles.

"Hi, Dad. She's in the shower now," Jo lied.

There was a pause. There was something strange about this call. He never called at night. Hardly ever wanted to talk to Mom.

"I need to talk with her, honey. But . . . But I may not be here."

Carrie stormed out to the kitchen and made a chomping eating motion with her hand. Jo nodded, and pointed to a nearby cabinet. Carrie opened it and took down a half-eaten bag of Slim Jim Pretzels.

I hope they're stale, Jo thought.

"Is someone else there with you?" her father asked.

"Er, yes. Carrie. My friend in the building . . . Carrie, you know," Jo said with difficulty. Carrie walked out with her prize, giving Jo's hair a rustle as she walked out.

"That's good. Tell your mom. Tell her—"

What's he trying to say? Jo wondered. What's he having such a bad time saying?

"Tell her I'll call . . . later . . . and—"

Jo chewed her lip. Would her mother be back in time?

"Tell her—I mean, ask her please not to leave the apartment. Either of you. Ask her that. And I'll call back—" She imagined him looking at his watch. "In an hour. Maybe sooner. Will you tell her?"

"Yes, Dad."

"Good, pumpkin." Another pause. "I love you, Jo. You know that, don't you?"

"Uh-huh," Jo said. And she knew she should say it back. And I love you too, Dad.

But she didn't say it.

"I'll tell her."

Her father said good-bye.

And Jo said good-bye.

And in the living room Carrie had left MTV. There was no music coming from the living room. There was no sound at all.

She had moved to another station. Jo looked at the clock. Nearly eight. She heard the endless rumble of the FDR Drive, so close to their building. She usually never noticed the sound. Now, in the sudden silence, it was all she heard.

She walked into the living room, expecting to see Carrie zapping through the channels.

But the older girl sat there, watching the screen filled with color bars, a test pattern of some kind.

"Carrie . . ." Jo said.

But the girl shushed her.

"Quiet, Jo. It's time for that show. That guy from last night." Carried waved at her to sit down and listen. "This might be real cool . . ."

And though Jo wanted to go into her room, to lie down in her unmade bed and get lost in the trouble of the Babysitter's Club, she instead plopped down in the easy chair . . . and watched the colors begin to fade.

Chapter Thirty-two

"I'LL call you from the airport. Wait," Michael said, digging out his wallet. "I've got to make sure I have my phone card. Yeah, okay. I'd better go."

"Michael . . . I have to tell you. I can't promise that I'm right. About any of this stuff. I mean, it seems to make sense—"

He felt Martin's hand on his shoulder. It occurred to him that Martin's personal life was totally unknown to him. At times he speculated that he was gay, and then felt guilty for even giving a shit about that. What the hell does that matter?

But things were different these days. Being out of the closet wasn't such a cool thing to do.

In these days of the new plague.

But he suspected that Martin wasn't much of anything. He seemed to live for his work, understanding ocean life at its most basic, molecular level.

I never even had a meal, sitting down to break bread with him.

And what does that say about me? Michael wondered.

"Don't worry. It's a good idea, a logical idea. We'll know more if I can get some samples back."

"If there's time."

"Right." Michael nodded. If there's time . . .

"Martin, are you staying here?"

The scientist nodded, looking around the lab. "Yeah. There's a cot. I thought . . . that until this was over, it might be—"

"Fine," said Michael. He had to get going. If he hit any traffic taking the Belt Parkway to Kennedy Airport he'd miss the shuttle. "Keep calling . . . you have the list of numbers. And start in the morning—first thing. We've got to get the Coast Guard Office of Marine Environment and Systems helping. They've got the hardware."

"Not the Environmental Department?"

"Yeah, them too. But the Coast Guard can move fast. Once they're convinced . . ."

"And what do you think will convince them?"

Wasn't that obvious? Michael thought. By morning everyone will know that something happened on the Cape.

Maybe was already happening inland.

"There's one thing I want you to promise me."

Martin nodded. "Yes."

"Don't screw with the samples, the bits of worm. They're still alive. Don't risk anything stupid. Just wait . . . until I get back."

Martin nodded and said, "No problem . . ."

"Okay then. Good-bye, pal."

And Michael walked out of the lab, out to the hot summer air, filled with the smell of salt and car exhaust.

Farrand was falling asleep with the Bible in his lap.

Though tied securely to the dock, *Ariel* was rocking back and forth. Farrand wanted to stay awake, but the motion and exhaustion made his eyes droop. And then he'd blink awake looking at the blurry page in front of him.

He was reading Genesis.

A fairy tale.

The great creation myth . . . How *strange*. Once he thought that he knew this book as well as his own hands. Or so he used to think. But he studied the notes, the codex to the third chapter.

Temptation and Fall.

The serpent promises everlasting life. There will be no pain, no suffering . . .

No death.

But man, woman . . . all of nature must taste knowledge.

Knowledge.

And yes, here there were so *many* footnotes on the different meanings, the different translations, in Hebrew, and Greek, and Latin. All the changes, the shades of meaning to that one word, translated into English . . . the word "knowledge."

The Greeks gave it the most chilling interpretation.

To know, from "conos." And then its other meaning, a more simple, more direct meaning.

To become one with.

And then there was that other odd word.

Serpent.

Usually a talking snake in children's picture books.

The Gutenberg Bible introduced *that* interpretation of the Greek word. In German it became "*Schlange* . . ."

The serpent.

But there was another choice for the Greek. Something that conjured up a darker creature, born of dead flesh and rotting things, without any integrity as an animal. Something that could live in two pieces . . . just as easily as one . . . or even a thousand.

For the other choice, the German word was "*Wurm.*"

Farrand's eyes blinked again and fell shut.

And once again, he fell into his nightmare.

He's in Cyana, the submersible.

And he hears sounds. Little beeps that indicate the depth. A buzzing noise tells him the status of the air feed. There are colored dials for outside pressure readings, inside pressure, depth . . .

Deeper, deeper . . .

Until the shimmering blue gives way to the deepest black.

And here, in his dream—though it was strictly forbidden—he shuts off the sub's exterior lights . . . at least the ones that could be shut off.

So that it was just this darkness, the deep infinite blackness, and his body encased in a titanium globe . . . drifting so peacefully.

Until it enters that other world.

Then he sees them. Tiny translucent shrimp attracted to Cyana's lights, now confused, swarming around the submersible, covering its window and held by the tiny instrument lights. They'd cover the port, three and four shrimp thick, the way they'd swarm around the life-giving bacterial gardens below.

He sees an eel, and a giant needle-nosed eurybathic fish suddenly rears close to the sub and then darts away. A small school of phosphorescent boas, looking prehistoric and fiercely predatory, glide by . . .

But then something seems wrong with the sub.

He's knocked to the side of the submersible.

Then again! He is rocked from one side to another.

He turns on the lights of Cyana. Now he's scared by the blackness, and the hundreds of eerie phosphorescent lights glowing out there, in the void.

But the lights don't come on.

He flicks the switch back and forth. In the darkness he grabs for the radio. The few instrument lights that were on slowly go out.

The radio is dead.

And he can feel himself moving. The rocking stops. In the darkness he stares out at the galaxy of lights, the milky way of weird phosphorescent animals.

And he thinks: I'm just like them now.

Trapped in the darkness.

Just the wall of the sub keeps me from being with them.

There is no more rocking. The tungsten lamps flicker back to life.

What caused it? he wonders. But such questions don't last long in a dream.

Now he feels better.

Now he doesn't feel scared, being here, so close to all this wonderful life, this ancient life . . . He leans closer to the bubble-shaped window of the Cyana.

He is still falling.

Surrounded by the blackness and the small glowing lights. And he knows . . . I'm going too deep, too far down—

The rocking begins again.

And somehow he can see, as if the sea floor itself was giving off a dull glow.

He sees his tube worms, snaking their way out of burrows.

And how far down do those burrows go, how deep is the land of the worms? he wonders. And where do those burrows lead? Do all those worms meet in one big chamber somewhere, all part of one big—

More rocking.

He feels a fine mist spraying him. A pressure leak.

He tastes salt.

And though the submersible should simply go straight down, a dead weight now—

It starts gliding . . . *toward the burrows.*

Closer, and closer, until—my God—he sees something at the end of each animal.

Blurry shapes at first, then clearer.

Farrand presses his face against the sub's bubble.

(Inside his cabin, on the *Ariel*, he moans now, louder and louder, louder than the creaking of the ship pulling on its lines.)

Faces. At the ends of the worms. He sees eyes, human eyes, and mouths, opening and calling. Begging for help. For release. But Farrand hears nothing.

And the Cyana glides right to the burrows.

This is hell, he thinks. It's where souls are trapped, condemned to scream for help, silently, in the deep. Farrand throws his hands against the window of the sub—and bangs against it—

Hell . . .

Until he wakes up . . . and the Bible slides to the floor of his cabin.

Gene Fasolt grabbed Barron's wrist.

Barron glared at him. It was almost time to begin. And Gene looked mad, stark raving crazy. He's just about slobbering, Barron thought. This won't do. Not with the camera just there, focused on Jay, but catching Gene and me in the background, reassuring everyone that this was still Dr. Gene's ministry.

"I'll be okay," Gene bleated. "Won't I? I'll be all right, won't I? *Tell me!*"

Barron tried to free himself from Gene's clawlike grasp. He saw that all of the good doctor's cool was gone. God, he's about to slip to his knees and beg me for help.

Barron looked around, to see what the crew was making of this.

But they were tending to their own business. Checking the lights, slowly dollying the heavy cameras into position.

They were all focused on Jay.

The prophet, some were calling him.

Jay's eyes were closed, as though he was in peaceful meditation.

When actually he was like a radio shut off. There's nothing going on there, Barron knew. Absolutely nothing.

"Calm down," Barron said gently. But when that did nothing to remove Gene's wild-eyed stare, Barron hissed, nastily, threatening . . . *"Calm down!"*

Gene repeated his query. "Please, Mr. Barron. I'll—I'll be fine, won't I? After this is over—"

Barron nodded, enjoying the spectacle. It did, however, raise Barron's own fears to the surface. They told me that I would be able to remain, he thought. That I could continue to help them.

They had told me that, hadn't they?

Even when he knew, *knew* that the planet was to become their garden, their feast, their banquet and playground.

They let him know that he would remain.

A trusted friend.

For as long as the planet could support his existence.

(And Barron had been tempted—tempted to ask. Might some others remain? For my own pleasure. As a possible . . . reward? But such a thought might upset them. Maybe they decided that he should simply be added to the harvest, the living storehouse.)

He knew Gene's fate.

They will take you.

The worms first. Controlling you, controlling everything. Then they will come, the others who lost the planet. The dark ones, the nonliving things that lived in a way that only madmen might have guessed. Gene will just be one more, another human maggot, to be nibbled among so many billions.

"You'll be fine, Gene," Barron said, turning warm, looking right into the terrified man's eyes. "Perfectly fine. You *know* their power," he said, gesturing at Jay. "They will reward you for your part in their return."

Gene seemed to relax. He licked at his dry lips.

Barron noticed a young man looking over, concerned.

It was time to begin.

The man took a step toward the set.

"Turn and smile at that man, Gene. Let him know everything is okay."

Gene nodded, still looking at Barron, still holding on to his wrists, as if afraid to break the contact. Then he turned and nodded at the man, smiling.

As someone said aloud, waving his fingers at Jay . . . "Five."

Open your eyes, Barron thought.

"Four. Three."

Barron felt Jay looking up, awakening. He felt everyone in the studio looking at him, this seer.

"Two."

Jay straightened in his seat.

"One."

The man who had been counting pointed at Jay. The camera's red light, a beady eye, came on.

And Jay spoke . . .

The people squealed, actually squealed when Jay's face came on the screen.

A short man pushed against Caryn, jabbing her kidneys with a bony elbow.

"Will you please watch what you're—" she started to say, but the man weaseled his way past her too quickly, hurrying closer to the window, to the big monitor.

"Do you believe this?" Winston said. He looked around at the crowd. "Everyone here's excited about *that* guy?" he said incredulously.

This channeler, this Jay, was the antithesis of Winston. She sensed the reporter's embarrassment. "There's one born every—" he said, laughing, grinning—

While Jay spoke.

The speakers were big, two of them towering above the crowd. When Jay spoke it was as if he were a giant, his voice booming over the crowded street.

She listened.

And she remembered the way it made her feel last night. The warm feeling, the guilty, almost embarrassingly sweet intimacy of that sound. As though the voice could penetrate her skull, and stir up her most secret desires and fantasies.

The voice knew her.

Knew what she wanted . . . what she liked.

She felt Winston's hand slip from her shoulder.

She heard the words too. He welcomed his friends, and his brown eyes scanned to the left and right. It was just a TV screen, but he seemed to search for each person in the crowd.

Caryn felt him finally look at her.

More words, about this wonderful moment, this special moment.

(And there was this delicious tingle. God, she thought, I'm getting wet. She was tempted to touch herself, to bump against Winston. She looked at Winston next to her . . . wondering what effect it was having on him.)

Jay kept speaking . . . about mankind's years struggling against pain, fighting to live in peace and harmony. And now peace was coming, peace and happiness and every wonderful thing that anyone could want.

(She saw the cameramen from the news stations—who had been scanning the crowd. They stopped, moved away from their cameras, to better see the monitor. Everyone watched Jay. *Had* to watch and listen.)

Jay spoke.

Now, the agents from the past, the ones who have watched over mankind, were ready to encircle the planet in welcoming arms. To give them the gift of understanding, to let them know their *true* heritage.

Wonderful words. But none of them mattered.

She pressed close, wanting to get as close as she could to the screen. She pushed hard against the unyielding backs of the massed crowd.

The sound was enough.

The voice filled her entire body.

People were calling from the crowd, calling out to the TV image.

She joined them, mumbling at first, but then louder, yelling out his name. Louder, crying.

Then he smiled.

The crowd laughed. How wonderful! He made everyone laugh. They relaxed. Jay smiled. He's ready to tell us something even more beautiful, more—

The person in front of her stumbled backward, pushing into her. Caryn fell to the ground. She landed hard, her hands flying out to break her fall. No one tried to help her up. She couldn't hear Jay so well. It was muffled, diluted. She howled, angry now.

She tried to elbow herself up. A woman stepped on her hand, driving a spiked heel into her hand.

Caryn yelled, the sudden pain intrusive.

It brought her out of it just a bit.

There was a tiny window of distance—

Enough to see the forest of legs, moving closer, surrounding her, ready to stomp over her.

With blood running from her palm—no matter that, she thought. It's only blood.

She grabbed at a man's leg, grabbed it, and pulled herself up. The leg kicked back, trying to shake her off. But she latched another hand on and was sitting on the ground. Then she dug her leg under her, a knee, gasping, standing up.

In time to see—

People crying. Bodies pressed against the glass. And had some others fallen? Were they still there? The cameras were gone. Knocked to the ground?

But like a special radio signal being broadcast only to her, she was up where she could hear clearly again.

The voice echoed, rolled across the canyon of buildings.

"Come out onto the streets," he said, speaking to everyone watching inside their homes, their apartments. He ordered. "Come . . . and look at this wonderful gift—"

Caryn knew where to look. Everyone knew where to look.

There was no question about that.

She turned, looking east, standing on her toes, peering through the cracks of the human wall, the mob—

Looking at the murky dark ribbon of the river . . .

Chapter Thirty-three

MICHAEL punched in his phone card number, a twenty-plus digit monster that had—so far—resisted memorization. He was in the Eastern Terminal, home to the Trump Shuttle. And it was the witching hour at the airport. Bleary-eyed business commuters staggered in from the Chicago flight. And tribes of chattering people from countries where McDonald's is unknown were having noisy, hysterical reunions. Limo drivers, half in the bag, slouched against the wall holding crumpled signs with names on them, flashing the people coming out while dripping cigarette ashes on their regulation shabby black suits.

He had ten minutes before his flight.

He got a busy signal.

"Damn," he said. He slapped down the phone. And waited a few seconds. He dialed again.

And again it was busy.

Come on, he thought. Who the fuck are you talking to? Get off the phone!

He hung up.

He watched a young woman pass through the departure gates, crisp and professional in a pale blue blouse and a matching short skirt. He felt an unexpected yearning. It's been a while, he thought. A while . . . for what they call a "social life."

Like the one that put a capper on his marriage.

He waited, watching, until the woman disappeared into the tunnel leading to the planes. He dialed again. His ticket was in his shirt pocket, and the plane was boarding.

This time the busy signal sounded even louder, more obnoxious.

And he slammed the phone down.

Damn. I'll call her from Florida, he thought.

He didn't think anything was wrong.

* * *

The crowd moved slowly, almost religiously, moving away from the monitor.

Caryn still heard Jay's voice urging them to *look*.

The river was black, reflecting only the pinprick lights of the apartments that lined the Jersey side, facing Manhattan. Then there seemed to be some bubbling, a foamy glow that appeared on the surface.

The crowd started moving quickly.

And Caryn felt like this was the most wonderful thing that had ever happened to her.

A vision. Being shared with all these people. Idly, she saw Winston ahead, pushing ahead, rushing to the front, forgetting her. But that didn't matter at all. Nothing did, nothing but to keep moving, and looking at the water.

Everyone was moving faster, pushing at her from the rear.

She slipped off the curb, onto the street, nearly falling.

It was hard to walk this fast and keep looking ahead . . .

The foamy glow on the water, like bubbles in some dark bathtub, changed. Now there was real light. The crowd gasped, the people, calling out to this moonglow, yelling, running . . .

Everyone was running. And Caryn had to run too. She *had* to move as fast as she could just to stay away from the hundreds, the thousands behind her.

The river became full of light. A soft, cool phosphorescence that filled the surface as though some gigantic field of light covered the river like a blanket.

She moaned at the beauty.

Someone fell against her. But she moved forward and the person tumbled to the ground. She heard the splat of the person's head smacking the street. Then—someone else—screaming.

A distracted thought occurred to her.

People are walking over other people . . .

Like a—like a—

A picture formed itself hazily in her mind. Just for a moment.

Like cattle, churning up the dry dirt, running madly away from men on horses.

But then the water rippled. The light became brighter.

She crossed Tenth Avenue. There was an old pier straight ahead, down this block, under the highway. Already people were filling the rusted pier and its skeletal building. She wiped at her eyes. Crying. Thinking. *There'll be no room for me. I won't get to be there.*

Another block and everyone was running full out. Out-of-shape people were gasping, choking, trying to breathe. Caryn pumped with her arms like a jogger, passing people now, trying to cut through this incredible swarm.

She saw Winston ahead. She wished she were there. With him. Closer to the front.

At the intersection cars were stopped. Some drivers just beeped, a constant honking at the human tide. Others had gotten out of their cars and were looking at the water, seeing the river.

It's alive, she thought.

Living waters, she thought.

I want to be next to the living waters.

She ran to the dank cavern under the West Side Highway. Garbage and thick piles of encrusted black soot and dirt seemed to cover the ground. A truck reared nastily in front of the crowd, stopping it.

It was dark here . . . hard to see the ground.

The tide behind her pressed closer, packing itself more densely.

She chewed at her lip.

Looked ahead.

The lights, the pale glowing things seemed to be everywhere in the water, now popping up and down, eagerly. Up and down, like puppy dogs. She hated the ones who were close, right near the water's edge and—

(She saw a young girl. Six years old, maybe seven. With dark hispanic eyes, glowing. Running by herself. And a few unwelcome thoughts entered Caryn's mind. Where's her mommy? Who's watching that little girl? And—and—what's she doing here so—)

The crowd pushed forward, running even though there was no place to run to, slamming against her, bodies knocking. Her foot fell into a pothole, twisted, a sudden sharp pain from miles away. A dim message of something wrong.

Then her leg didn't feel right and she fell, smacking into the blackish street.

The legs kept coming at her.

Jo was breathing hard.

She thought of the song. The words that became imprinted on her mind. Healing Hands.

She watched this man on the TV. He was asking her to leave the apartment. It felt like an order. A command. She heard the steady bleeping of the phone, off the hook. She watched Carrie stand up.

No, she said to herself.

(And she felt alone then. Alone in this building, in this world, in the whole terribly black universe. Alone . . .)

She started breathing harder.

"No," she whispered.

The man's voice was everywhere, calling to her. Promising an end to her loneliness, to bring her warmth and love and happiness.

Jo screamed, and pushed a stack of books off the coffee table, sending them flying at the screen.

No, she thought. Covering her ears. No!

She ran out to the kitchen, coughing, doubled up. I'm going to be sick, she thought. I'm going to throw up.

She hacked at the ground, spitting onto the gleaming linoleum.

While outside, she heard Carrie moving.

She expected that the girl would come out . . . ask her what's wrong.

But when Jo stopped hacking, spitting at the floor, she looked to the side. The man's face was still there, still smiling. Offering her help. If only she'd look—

And Carrie was at the window. Her arms extended against the glass, palms flat. Carrie stood there. And Jo saw her move against the glass, her body rippling.

"Carrie . . ." Jo coughed, straightening up. A step into the living room. Then Jo froze. No. The TV was there. And—the window.

She stayed in the kitchen. Calling her. "Carrie . . . please come away . . ."

Carrie was making noises, strange noises, her mouth, her lips muffled against the glass.

"Carrie!" Jo screamed. "Stop. Please stop what you're doing, please stop!"

Carrie turned.

And Jo felt afraid. She's going to do something to me. She's gone crazy and—

But Carrie smiled, then ran to the door. One by one she undid the locks on the apartment door.

"Carrie, don't. We're supposed to—"

One. Then more clicks, and the second dead bolt was clear. Jo staggered closer to the girl, still scared, still feeling sick. "Carrie," she begged. "Please don't leave. Please don't!"

The last lock opened with a noisy click. And then Carrie flung the door open.

(And Jo heard screams from down the hall, coming from other people. Yells and whoops.)

Jo walked to the door. People rushed by, without looking at her. An old man who lived next door and never smiled. A young woman who wore so much makeup it made Jo laugh just to look at her. They went screaming by her door.

They looked crazy. Mad.

And Carrie was with them.

Jo reached out for the door. Scared to touch it, and she slammed it shut.

Then she started crying . . .

Chapter Thirty-four

MARTIN sat at his lab table, yawning, rubbing his eyes. The only light was a small fluorescent bulb in the corner of the room. He had the radio on. Sibelius's Second Symphony, cold, icy music, majestic even through the small portable radio's speaker.

When the music stopped.

An announcer interrupted. He sounded confused.

Something's wrong with the station's CD, Martin thought. It's skipping. They do that sometimes. They get their digital information all jammed up and they just skip, or spit out synthetic gibberish.

But it wasn't that. The announcer said that there were reports of a riot near the rivers surrounding Manhattan. He cleared his throat. There was an eerie silence for a few seconds. The sound of papers being shuffled.

The police were saying that no one should go outside, he said. He sounded confused, embarrassed.

They recommended locking your doors.

Another pause. And then—as an afterthought—the music came back on.

And Martin made a decision.

The fall, the nasty wrench to her ankle—was it broken? Caryn wondered—made her snap out of it.

Just a bit.

Just enough to see what was happening to the others.

They were only twenty feet ahead of her, piled like crazed rats against the edge of the pier. People were screaming, hollering. She heard babies crying. Then—a sound that made her sick—a splash. But different, as though people were falling off the pier and landing onto something floating on top of the river. As though they were plopping onto rafts.

What am I doing? she wondered. What the hell am I doing? And what are all these people doing? And—

A sudden wave of screaming washed over her. But it wasn't the sound of terror. It was joy, excitement, sounds you'd hear at a carnival.

Then, with the screaming swelling, randomly punctuated by the plopping of bodies into the water, she saw what was happening.

(The throbbing in her ankle began to subside. The pain started to fade. And she felt the old presence of the warmth, the beauty, like the sticky-sweet taste of cotton candy left on your lips, to be licked at while you lay in bed after a day at the circus.)

The white things were out of the water. Glowing even more brightly. Were they leaping out? She couldn't see. They seemed to just slither up the side of the pier, up the rotted pilings, then through the feet of the crowd, before they reared up—

And how big were they? She never saw an end to one.

But no. They could just snap! Like that. And come apart. One became two. Two, four. And again, and again.

She saw people embracing these things, Christ! Reaching out, like blind people grabbing at food, water, a lover. Unaware that there was anything strange here, anything peculiar.

(The pain was almost gone. She slid her ankle out of the pothole. There was blood. She could feel the wetness, saw it streaking across the thick patina of black-encrusted soot. It didn't matter. Everything was beginning to feel . . . better.)

Some people just opened their mouths. Like going to the dentist. And the worm slid inside, smoothly, sleekly.

Other people seemed to rebel at the last minute, snapping out of their frenzy, and the worm simply chewed a hole into them, sending blood and flecks of skin flying onto anyone nearby. And then they'd be okay. They stood there a moment.

Then they turned, and walked away.

Back toward the city.

They were fine.

A few people suddenly started to run away, to break out of the pack of ratlike people lined at the dock.

Oh, I forgot something. Back at my apartment.

They didn't get far.

A few steps.

When something quickly curled around their feet and pulled them in.

There. Got that one. And this one. And that one and—

It reminded her of something. Something she saw. A painting.

It came into her head, all golden yellow, and sunlit, even in the dark blackness under the highway.

(The rattle of the cars continued overhead, on the West Side Highway. A steady dull drone, unconcerned with what was going on below.)

A painting. All these peasant women, dressed in coarse brown dresses and starched white bonnets, brilliant white headpieces, pulled tight. And they walked through the cornfield, cutting corn, dropping the ears into great sacks that trailed behind them.

The Harvest.

That was the name of the painting.

And she felt a wave of warmth wash over her, clean and sensual. She imagined what a warm tropical breeze under a bright blue sky might feel like.

It made her want to stay there.

To just *wait* for them.

(They're coming, she could see. Working their way through the others. Now only a few feet away. Sensing her, starting to slide toward her.)

No.

She groaned, pulling away from that breeze, from that warmth. She tried to stand up.

Now the pain slammed into her ankle and traveled like electricity up her leg, past her torso, right into her brain. A jolt that made brilliant fireworks appear in her eyes.

The pain was unbearable.

Her eyes teared.

She turned. Some people were still screaming behind her. But there were fewer of them now.

And she took a step away, back off the street, hobbling like a cripple, into the heart of the city.

The captain, Larsson, looked at Farrand and shook his head. The Swedish captain's English was poor, his French nonexistent. But he was experienced and ran the *Ariel* as though it was his private yacht.

There never were any mistakes with Larsson.

His first mate, a grizzled old Portuguese who spoke a half-dozen languages, brought them steaming mugs of predawn coffee.

It was still horribly dark out.

"Thank you," Farrand said, nodding to the barrel-chested sailor.

The captain was restless, Farrand knew. The wind storm

seemed to have eased up a bit, but there were thick cloud blocking the early morning glow in the east. A grayish gloom hung over everything.

Larsson shook his head and sipped the scalding black coffee

There was a time, Farrand knew, when the captain of the *Ari* answered only to me. Now, there were committees and budget and approval to be sought.

More scratching at his head. The captain took another sip c coffee. He ruminated long on things, speaking only when hi thoughts were absolutely clear.

Must drive his poor wife crazy.

But then, how often did she see him?

The salty wind only made Farrand think of his small cabin, wit its two rows of wooden bookshelves, a small desk and chair, an his rumpled bed.

Perhaps I should return there, he thought . . .

"I'll let you get on with—" Farrand started to say.

But there was a noise from outside, a muffled cry. Then mor voices. The man on watch called to someone, yelling at them Then another voice, the first mate.

Larsson's eyebrows went up.

"Hmm," Farrand said. "What do you suppose?"

The voices grew louder. Angry sounds.

Until finally there was a knock on the bridge door.

Larsson opened it.

The first mate held someone by the wrist, dragging them int the bridge.

"This man ran up the gangplank, Captain . . . onto the deck We tried to make him go down, but he demanded to see Fathe Farrand."

"Eh?" the priest said, taking a step closer to the entrance. Th chunky first mate now had the man's shoulders locked by hi meaty hands.

It's still almost night, he thought. Who could this be?

"Then let him in," Farrand said.

The crewman stepped aside and the mate steered the intrude into the now-crowded bridge.

The man had dark hair, an intelligent face.

The intruder was breathing hard. But not from exertion. It wa in his eyes. Bright, flashing.

Scared eyes.

"So, you wanted to see me. Well, here I am. Now what is it yo want?" Farrand said.

The man took a big breath. Tried to pull closer—but he was restrained by the first mate.

"My name is Michael Cross, Father."

That meant nothing to Farrand. But he knows who I am, Farrand thought. This is . . . interesting.

The man tried to take a step, and again the mate squeezed Michael's shoulder, pinning him to his place. "I'm the director of the New York Aquarium."

Ah, yes. Of course . . . Farrand thought. I know that name. Dr. Michael Cross. But why is he here? What is he—

Farrand looked up at the first mate, signaling him to let the man go.

Now Michael took his step closer.

He looked as if he might cry, or collapse—Farrand saw the captain studying the man as if he were dangerous, crazy—

A lunatic.

"I need your help . . ." the crazy man said quietly.

That was it.

Barron saw Jay slump over.

The studio was nearly empty. Just a few camera people, a pair of producers working the board behind the glass booths.

Everyone else was gone.

Everyone else was outside.

To be with everyone else. To run to the river.

And Jay slumped over.

"Is th-that it?" Gene stammered, grabbing Barron's arm as he slid off his stool. "Is—is it all over?"

Barron shook the man's arm off, repelled by his begging, his wheedling.

And already Barron was wondering. How will it happen? How will they start the next stage.

And he waited for the message that would tell him what he was to do . . . what his role was to be—

"Please, Barron, you have to tell me what—"

The cameraman hadn't moved. Barron took another step.

He saw the man's head.

It was impaled against the eyepiece. As if he had banged his head against the eyepiece over and over, again and again, breaking through the bone, right into his eye sockets, until he couldn't bang anymore. Barron looked down. Saw the puddle of red around the camera's base.

The cameraman had to stay, Barron thought. They *made* him stay.

Guess he couldn't handle the disappointment.

But there was something wrong about that, wrong, a mistake. As if they couldn't control him as easily as they wanted to, as though the message got fucked up, and he killed himself.

They make mistakes . . .

And that thought made him shiver. That didn't fit into the plan at all. Not at all.

Jay moved.

He just slipped a few more inches. His slouch worsening. He collapsed into himself, doubled over, ready to—

He tumbled to the floor.

The black man landed hard against the shiny floor.

He's off camera, Barron thought, grinning. No more show.

"Barron, Mr. Barron, what now? I mean, I helped and—"

Barron was about to turn and say something to poor Gene Fasolt, to tell him, get the fuck away from me, you charlatan, you money-grubbing scumbag. Your scam days are over. Go out and join the party.

It's party time in Fun City.

Get out and boogie.

But he saw Gene freeze. He was looking down. Down to where Jay was, curled up, like a sleeping drunk.

Then Jay rolled over. He groaned. The sound a cat might make when it gets caught under the tire of a car, as it rolls over the animal's pinned body in slow motion. Jay let out a long, prolonged groan that shattered the silence of the studio.

He lay flat on his back, arms out, legs spread, and now with eyes wide open. His jaw moved up and down, marionettelike—but soundless now. Soon Barron saw a churning foamy bubble form in Jay's mouth.

"What's happening?" Gene bleated. But he didn't move. He had to watch.

So did Barron, staring at Jay.

Something was happening *inside* Jay.

Their channeler.

They heard a tearing sound. Like a long strip of paper being slowly and cleanly torn in half, the tip nearly as loud as Jay's groan.

"What's happening?" Gene shrieked.

Gene had grabbed Barron's wrist, twisting it, pulling at it.

Barron wanted him to let go, but he was too busy watching, wondering—

What are they doing?

What the hell are they doing?

Then another tearing sound. This time, Jay's shirt and his pants, ripping cleanly down the middle, making a neat symmetrical cut from his neck down to his crotch. The two halves pulled apart, as though repelled.

And Barron saw what the first cut had been.

Jay was split open. Like the cracked underbelly of a broiler lobster.

Gene was crying, pulling at Barron.

Barron thought of running away. I don't want to see this, he thought. I could go—

Where?

There was nowhere to go.

Nowhere in New York.

Nowhere on the whole fucking planet.

He knew that.

The opening, this valley in Jay, widened, exposing a lot of red meat, and muscle, tissue and organs. The rib cage came apart like a bear trap opening. He saw organs. Was that the heart, that pinkish thing, pulsating, pumping up and down? And there were other bits in there.

Don't know what they are, thought Barron.

I'm no doctor.

Then wider, as the organs moved to the side, sliding left and right, over the exposed bones.

As if something was digging at them, pushing them away . . .

From below.

A funny giggle escaped Barron's mouth.

Did I make that noise?

Gene was wringing his arm, waving it up and down, jabbering.

Wider still, until there was this good-sized pit right there, in the floor, in front of them. Inside Jay's body . . .

A hole. He smelled blood, a rich metallic smell, overpowering. And now another smell, bile, old food sitting somewhere in there and—

Then a breeze. A gust that escaped the hole. Some nightmarish wind that farted out of the hole and—

The stench blotted out any other smell. There was no blood smell, no old food rotting in Jay's gut, just this *smell*, beyond description, wet, moist, touching his cheeks, filling his mouth, his gullet, stronger now.

Gene let go of him.

He was too busy hacking at the ground, clutching his stomach, to hold on. A thought occurred to Barron. He looked at Gene. Was he just throwing up or—

Then the breeze seemed to lessen. Something seemed to be blocking it. Tiny bubbles began surfacing at the bottom of this hole, this rift in the center of Jay. More bubbles and a bigger one, a popping sound, and then—

Something came out.

Like a hand.

It had fingers. A few twisted things at the end of a fleshy knob. Reaching out. Yes, a hand! It grabbed at the sides of the valley, at the sides of Jay.

Can I leave? Barron wondered. Can I back away?

Then another, reaching out more quickly, more assuredly, like a mountain climber finishing the last leg of a treacherous climb, almost there.

The fingers, the twisted things, grabbed into the bones, the pulsating organs, and pulled up, and up, and—

More bubbles, and great popping sounds.

Something big and squarish quickly popped out.

It had a head. A recognizable head. True, it was shaped more like a blocky chunk of clay, covered with the slimy blood and stringy bits of Jay's flesh. But it *had* to be a head.

It made a sound.

A roar. Filled with the smell, the alien stench of another world.

The head turned.

Looked up.

The cameraman was missing it, thought Barron. The camera isn't fucking aimed right . . .

The head looked up.

There were eyes. There, and there, and there, and—

Dark jelly things. Maybe they were eyes . . . Maybe they weren't.

And now a hole. From nowhere. A gigantic hole in the middle of the head.

Barron looked around. He saw the whole studio moving, rocking, shaking—

No. It was him. *He* was shaking, standing there, thinking—

I'm here to greet them. I'm the welcoming party, I'm—

But he fell to the ground.

Close to Jay.

Then he saw Gene fall. They were close enough to be lovers.

He tried to get back up. And though he could tilt his head up and get a look, a good look at his body and this thing crawling out of Jay, he couldn't get his fucking back off the floor.

We had a deal, Barron thought.

I helped you.

The black eye things seemed to pass over him.

Barron felt a charley horse. Then worse.

We had a fucking deal . . . !

He heard a tearing sound. Right next to him. It was Gene now. And again there was that sound, another cat, another car, all in slow, slow motion.

Then it was his turn . . . and Barron screamed as the first tear started at his throat and slowly trailed down . . .

Chapter Thirty-five

I'M making progress, she thought. She could cry for joy.

I'm getting *away,* Caryn thought.

Each step she took sent this razor-sharp prick of pain streaming up her left leg, step after step. She was crying, hysterical, saying to herself, over and over when she had to slam down her bad foot, all bruised, the blood flowing fresh—

They're behind me . . .

So many of them.

Feeding. That's why they're doing. They're feeding. And there are plenty of people to feed on, hundreds, thousands piled like sausages.

They won't bother with me.

She dared look ahead, through the misty glare of her teary eyes. She saw cars. An empty bus, people crossing the street, all of them unaware of what was happening. But they represented normalcy, and safety.

There would be police ahead, and if not, there were places to hide, and—

There was Jo.

At last she thought of her girl.

How could she have forgotten her? How could she have gone for *so long* without thinking about her?

What had that TV show done to her?

Had she left the apartment . . . had she gone down to the river . . . ?

Tenth Avenue was ahead.

The light changed from red to green. More steps. She heard her labored breathing, her grunts of pain. Green to red. A lone car passed the intersection. One car . . . where were the rest, where was the mad traffic of New York?

Even the sounds were gone, the constant roar of cars and horns and people.

It was quiet.

Jo.

If she's in the apartment, she's okay. If she just stayed there, she's fine. I can get to her and—

And she thought about how she'd get there. The subway—

(She pictured the subway. The long wait for a train that might not come. Being trapped on the platform while people and *those things* drifted down, still hungry. She thought of running, into the black tunnel, the dark black hole that ran under the city.)

No. Even if the trains were running she wouldn't dare go down there. Maybe she could find a cab . . . if she could find one, if she could get one to stop. Now she looked at the intersection looking for a yellow cab with the light on. She saw another car. But no cab.

I might have to walk there. Twenty, maybe thirty blocks.

She groaned at the thought. I can't do it, I can't make it.

Her foot was numb from the pain. Now her calf and her knee felt like they were going to snap apart. They wobbled sickly with each step.

Oh, God, she thought. Please don't let my legs stop working. Let me—

She hadn't been paying attention.

She had been thinking. Trying to plan. She hadn't been paying attention. To her foot, to the sidewalk. Too many things to think about . . .

Her left foot, the hurt foot that she had to just drag now, got caught in some crack on the sidewalk. *She hadn't been paying attention*. And now she was going to fall down again.

She fell, gasping, crying.

Her elbow hit hard, cutting away the skin right to the bone.

"Ah-ohhh," she moaned. But it was just more pain. She tried to tell herself that it didn't matter, that nothing matters, because she was one of the lucky ones, *she* had gotten away, *she'd* make it out—

A lucky one!

When lying down, resting on her scraped elbows, she turned and looked behind her, back to where she just came from . . .

The people were marching briskly toward her.

A parade of people. A few with the telltale signs of the violence done to them by the worms, the bloody flaps of skin around the throat, the softball-sized holes in their chests.

Otherwise, they didn't appear hurt, or harmed.

And they were *so close*, just down the block a bit, moving quickly, some crossing the street, beginning to head uptown.

"No," Caryn said, then screamed, "No!" And she clawed to her feet, kicking at the pavement, a human crab scuttling forward, and then up.

Now she couldn't feel the lower part of her hurt leg, couldn't tell what it was doing. So she skipped forward, dragging it along, a dead weight now, just using it for balance, breathing hard, thankful that she ran and worked out and could do *this*, she could just keep pushing, no matter how hard it was, no matter how much pain it caused her.

No pain, she thought, no gain. And again, no pain . . . and I got plenty of pain. Plenty.

She was almost at Tenth Avenue. The light changed from red. To green. No cars moved through the intersection. It was quiet enough that she heard the clicking of the traffic light as the automated signals made the light change. She heard that and—

And steps.

Just behind her.

She didn't turn around, couldn't turn around. It would cost her a few precious seconds, a few more steps away from them.

If only I reach the corner, she thought. If I get there, I'll be okay.

She imagined the wide avenue to be a river, a great black river that would keep them away as she swam across it to safety.

I've got to get to Jo. I've got to get to my girl.

Please. She begged.

Please.

She was almost at the corner, gasping, skipping madly, but barely getting her feet above the sidewalk, moving only a few feet.

The light clicked.

There were steps.

And there—just behind her—another sound, close and liquid, right near her ear.

Touching her. Hurting her.

No pain, no—

As she tried to skip off the curb onto the deserted street.

One TV station went off completely. Not even a test pattern. Another began showing *I Love Lucy* shows. Lucy didn't seem concerned with what was going on in New York. The Public TV station, based in Newark, was on the air, live, trying to explain what was happening.

They had helicopter pictures of the river, the water foaming, churning, alive with them . . .

Alive with them! Martin thought. Then the camera picked up jiggling pictures of the worms and the people together.

When the reporter came back on camera she looked shaken, scared. She mumbled something. She fiddled with papers. Fuck this, Martin imagined her thinking. I want to get the hell out of here.

Martin had his list of numbers to call. They'll listen now, he thought. Now they'll know just what the hell I'm talking about. They'll listen now . . .

But first there was something he wanted to do.

Something he *had* to do.

We have to be sure, he thought—*I* have to be sure. If my idea doesn't work, if it's all wrong, then Michael's wasting his time, and every hour is too damn precious to waste.

(How far had they gone in one day? How long before they were everywhere?)

The plan—this test—had been in his mind even when Michael was leaving, even when he was giving him assurances that he wouldn't do anything, nothing except sit and wait and call.

He looked at the three jars with the worm samples.

He watched them carefully. He saw how they moved—just a bit—when he turned a jar around.

It's alive. Just waiting for a good opportunity.

He got up and went to the rack of test tubes under the fluorescent light.

The microorganisms from the isopod had been culturing for over twenty-four hours.

Martin hadn't quite told Michael the truth.

True, the colonies from the isopod were dead.

But the individual organisms, some of the individual cells, were still alive. He separated the cells in a centrifuge, and then thermoclaved the ones that appeared alive. He put them in a petri dish to culture them.

And when he saw signs of growth . . . of some kind . . . he transferred them to the test tubes, until he had a lot of them.

Thriving.

He brought the test-tube rack back to the phone, back to the jars with the worm samples.

He laughed. The TV reporter was talking, but Martin had the

sound down. He didn't want to be distracted while doing this. A tricky business, he thought. Very tricky.

He opened the drawer and brought out the hypodermic. It had a long needle that looked much too blunt. It was the same sucker they used on the sharks, the dolphins, all the big animals. It wasn't designed for humans. It would hurt.

And my needle technique isn't that great, he thought. He wished Annie were here. She did most of the jabbing.

But she's out there somewhere. She said she'd try to get back.

(He heard screams, yells, all around the building. He ignored them. They were like the sound of summer crickets, cicadas buzzing noisily in the tall grass. The yells, the screaming . . . he couldn't pay attention to them now.)

He picked up the needle in one hand. And then he picked up a test tube in the other. He inserted the long needle into the tube and sucked up the solution filled with thousands of the cells . . . the cells that he hoped protected the giant isopod . . . and the other animals.

He removed the needle and a bit of liquid dribbled onto the floor.

He stuck out his arm. I should try to get it in a vein, he reasoned. It will get through my system that much faster.

He made a fist over and over, watching his greenish-blue veins move under his skin.

He saw a clear vein, right at the crook of his elbow. A bluish river close to the surface.

Maybe the fucking needle is too big? he worried. Maybe it will rip the vein wide open. Shit, what will I do then? Try to get to some emergency room.

(And he could well imagine the mayhem there, the people coming in with their funny wounds, bits and pieces of their insides trailing behind them . . . just take a look at this, Doc, I just can't get to sleep . . .)

He pushed the tip of the needle against the skin.

And then, a bit of pressure, until he felt pain.

Just got to do it.

But—at the moment he was about to press home—there was a banging outside, something being thrown against the building's western wall, the side that faced Surf Avenue. Banging, and yells, and his hand moved—

The needle jabbed into clear skin, well away from the vein.

He hadn't pushed the plunger.

He pulled it out watching the blood trickle out of the wound, the tip of the needle red now.

"Shit . . ." he whispered.

Martin rubbed the bloody spot against his shirt, smearing it, and then stuck his arm out again, flexing his hand. A droplet of sweat fell off his nose.

He saw the vein pulse a bit. He brought the needle down, straightened the angle—

(It's too big, he thought, the needle's too fuckin' big and—)

He pushed down.

And he waited.

He looked down. No blood was coming out.

He remembered something he once saw in a hospital show. With his thumb and forefinger of his right hand he pulled *back* on the plunger, sucking a small bit of his blood into the needle. It swirled around, mixing with the solution.

"Here goes," he said. And he was surprised at how thin and frail his voice sounded.

As though he were gone, disappearing.

He pushed down on the plunger, shooting the liquid into his vein. Now there was pain as though the liquid was rushing in too fast, stretching the walls of the vein. He slowed down, just easing down on the plunger with his thumb. There, he thought. The pain stopped. He kept pushing.

This stuff will hit my brain in about fifteen seconds.

Then I'll know whether or not it kills me.

He counted inside his head while he finished pushing the needle down. One. Two. Three.

The hypo was empty.

Nine. Ten. Eleven.

He took the needle out, tossed it down onto the table, and grabbed a tissue. Blood started trickling out of the vein.

Twelve. Thirteen.

He stuck the tissue right over the pinprick and then closed up his arm, locking the tissue tight against his arm.

Fourteen.

He took a breath.

Fifteen.

He felt nothing. He smiled.

No time to pause for self-congratulation.

Now, he thought, comes the hard part.

He reached out with his right hand and grabbed one of the jars with a worm sample, the jar with the biggest sample.

Might as well do the biggest fucking test possible, he thought grimly . . .

Michael rushed through the story the first time, fingering the evidence, the tape, sitting in Farrand's cramped cabin.

What does the tape really show? he thought, even as he spoke disjointedly—about the *Achilles*, the rope locker, Reilly.

He heard the sound of the crew, clambering around in the morning blackness. Metallic echoes rumbled from above and below.

And this priest, this world-famous oceanographer, gave no sign that he believed Michael's story at all.

Instead he held up a hand, a brown, rough hand, weathered and aged like the ship's rope. Farrand held up a hand and asked him to stop, to start again, from the beginning, only more *slowly* this time. Michael suggested that the priest look at the videotape, the information from the *Achilles*'s data logger—

But Farrand said, "No. Just *tell* me. But this time leave nothing out. No detail, eh?" The old scientist managed a smile, an expression that sent a net of wrinkles spreading across his face.

And Michael started in once again.

And this time he saw Farrand look away, as if he was embarrassed. As if Michael's words were bothersome, painful—

He doesn't believe me, Michael thought.

He's going to throw my ass off the ship and—

Then there was a knock on the door. Farrand muttered absently for the person to come in. The captain entered with some papers in his hand.

He's going to order him to throw my ass off the ship, Michael thought.

"Yes, Captain?" Farrand said.

"Father, we are getting radio reports. Something happened—"

Michael looked up.

"—in New York. There's an emergency, a catastrophe . . . something . . . it's not clear what—"

Michael stood up. He looked at Farrand.

Farrand made another smile. Sad and resigned, thought Michael. "Perhaps you are already too late, eh, Dr. Cross? Perhaps"—Farrand stood up, and twisted his hands together angrily, his face gone hard and angry—"perhaps it is already too late."

Michael felt a sick chill running over him. New York. That was impossible . . . that was *too* far away, *much too far*. He thought of the city, and about the pile of twisted, drained corpses in the hold of the *Achilles*. He thought of Reilly.

The whole city . . .

And he thought of Jo.

Caryn.

I can't stay here, he thought.

And he said that: "I can't stay here. I have my wife. My daughter. I can't—"

He couldn't breathe in the tiny room. He was sweating. The ship was rocking, swaying.

He started for the door, making the captain back away.

Jo. Caryn. New York. I can get them away. Somewhere. *I can get them the hell away.* And then I'll call people, the authorities, the government, and tell them what they have to do, tell them—

It's their fucking problem.

Just let there be time.

Please . . .

He started out the door, mumbling, "I'm sorry, but—"

Farrand grabbed him, a strong pincer lock on his wrist. Michael pulled against the man's gnarled, strong fingers.

"I have to go!" Michael said, hearing the hysterical tone in his voice. He was having trouble thinking, remembering why he was here, just what the hell he was doing . . . *here*. He just thought of Jo, and those things. His Jo . . .

But Farrand held him tight.

"No," the priest said quietly. "No. You *must* stay here. You must take me down to this rift." Farrand stepped closer to him. "You must do what you came here to do, Michael. Or there'll be no reason for you to go back for anyone . . . none at all . . ."

Michael's mouth fell open. He was going to say something. But—for that brief moment—there was a bit of light.

And he knew that Farrand was right. That this had to be done. That nothing else mattered.

He repeated that to himself.

Nothing else matters.

It moves too fast, grows too fast.

And he understood something else. That Farrand knew something about this. The priest wasn't surprised. Not at all. Michael could see that in his eyes.

And that made him even more afraid . . .

Martin gingerly unscrewed the lid. His hands were shaking.

The lid came off too easily. Martin wished that it had been more difficult, that it would take more effort.

The goddam thing seemed almost eager to be out.

He put the lid down.

The piece of worm sat at the bottom of the jar, jellylike, resting in a few inches of briny water.

He stared at it for what seemed like forever, unable to do the next thing, the necessary thing.

Despite being injected with fifteen ccs of the microorganisms from the isopod, he felt no different.

If I'm wrong, he thought, taking a dry lick at his lips, well, then I'll become like all the rest.

(And he could see them on his silent TV, the helicopter hovering, coming not too close but using the camera to get nice tight shots of crowds of people stumbling through the streets of New York . . . Looking for the uninitiated.)

I'll become *one of them.*

If this fucking thing doesn't work.

He tilted the jar to a slight angle. The thing slid a bit, moving against the side of the glass jar. It moved—because of Martin's action. But then it seemed to ripple. Just a bit, barely noticeable.

As if I had awakened it, he thought.

He took a breath.

Here goes. Like when he was a kid, and had to dive into the canal that ran by his family's sun-bleached house in Long Island. The water was always so oily, so black, covered by the iridescent trails of the fishing boats that traveled the narrow canal. When he dived in, he felt the slimy stalks of algae and small crabs that didn't know the difference between a little boy's toes and the gloppy chunks of bait fish discarded after the day's catch.

Here goes . . .

He stuck out his arm—the left arm for no other reason than it seemed like a good place to start, the same place he had injected himself.

He tilted the jar slowly.

No quick alley-oop dump here. Nice and slow, breathing heavily, noisily, making small sounds, feeling as if he were about to cry out, scream out. Stop this—please stop what you're doing—

To yourself.

He tilted it a bit more. The white slimy worm chunk rolled over itself—too quickly, nearly tumbling out onto his arm.

"Oh, sweet Jesus," he said. Not an idle curse this time. But a prayer. This time, a prayer. If there's a God there, he thought. If you're listening.

It was right at the lip of the jar—just there. He gave it another tilt. And the worm chunk slid out, making a small sucking sound as it disengaged from the glass and plopped onto his arm.

It landed on his arm, right near the hole made by the oversized hypo. It draped itself over his arm, sitting like an overcooked fried egg.

And Martin thought: It's not alive. It's dead. It's just going to sit there. And I won't be able to tell a goddam thing because—

But he detected some movement. Seemingly below the surface. A barely visible ripple that traveled under the whitish surface, and then back again. It was stirring, moving.

Martin looked up at the TV.

The copter was low to the ground, getting a shot of crowds of people coming onto the streets. It looked like New Year's Eve. Or VE day. Except no one was smiling. No happy sailors kissing their best girl.

He looked at his arm.

More rippling, quite visible now.

There was a flash from the TV. The screen went to snow. The picture had vanished.

No more remotes from the copter.

Then there was the reporter. Looking upset, sweaty, confused.

Lost a copter, huh, thought Martin. Lost a—

He felt the movement.

The thing, the stupid-looking chunk, feeling his arm, as if sensing what it was, becoming more active, excited—

Then Martin got to see something really incredible. Up close.

The white outer covering, the dumb host to the bacterial colony inside, pulled away, like lips baring teeth. And now the worm's inner core had unobstructed access to his arm.

He heard a clicking noise. Tiny, but clear and rhythmic.

Martin felt himself gag. He grabbed at the edge of his lab table to steady himself. I'm going to black out, he thought. I'm going to fucking black out. I can't let that—

With a sudden savagery it ripped into his arm.

A tiny spray of blood flew into the air. Tiny specks hit his forehead.

He cried, a quiet sound of a baby. The pain was terrible.

But he forced himself to watch it, watch the long reddish string inside the worm bore its way inside the tender white meat of his forearm, cutting right into the vein—

He knew what it was doing, grabbing his own blood cells, and muscle tissue, building them onto itself at an incredible rate, making itself larger, stronger, even as it worked its way inside his body.

And what does it do then? Martin wondered. Head right for the spinal cord? Tap right into the cerebellum? Right into the brain's control center, the same kidney-shaped control box that responds so crazily to cocaine?

Telling the brain that this, *this* is what you live for.

He watched it start to disappear, squeezing into his arm, pushing the skin away even as he screamed at it, grabbing the table hard, begging not to black out, forcing himself—even as he yelled—to keep watching the worm.

Nothing happened to the worm. It just went on drilling away.

I was wrong, I was goddamn wrong!

It was halfway in.

And then it stopped.

It froze there. Martin felt no new cutting, no new burrowing.

Then, it started to back out.

It fucking started to back out.

Fast, then faster, like a mouse that just spied the biggest fucking cat in the world.

Martin—through his screams, his tears—laughed. And now it fairly scuttled out, using its slimy rippling to get the hell out of his arm.

It popped out, making a noisy sucking sound against his arm.

He was bleeding all over the place.

God, maybe I'm going to die, he thought, but he kept looking at the worm.

Its insides were shaking, quivering, stricken with strange tremors that looked like they would shake it to pieces. He looked at it, closely. The tips of the core were covered with bits of his blood . . . and something else, a whitish fuzz, like mold on bread. And the fuzz seemed to spread, a thick hoarfrost that traveled the length of the core, coating it, covering it. He watched the tremors subside.

Until the thing was still.

The table was splattered with his blood.

But Martin hopped off the stool, he yelled, a primitive yelp of triumph. It's dead, he thought. Dead!

He thanked God.

And then he wrapped a thick towel around his arm, and pulled it tight. The blood soaked through, reddening the blue towel. But gradually the spread of the red blotch slowed, then stopped.

We can stop the fucker, he thought.

If there's enough time.
We can stop the fucker . . .

Jo checked the three locks again, including the dead bolt that could only be opened from the inside.
Mom will come back. Jo had absolute faith that her mom would show up.
Despite all the screaming, the yelling that echoed from the halls . . .
Mom will come back.
Jo could hear noises from outside too.
Not that she was going to go to the window and look.
No way that she'd do that.
Go ahead, a tiny voice in her mind suggested. Take a look. Go ahead. See what's happening down there.
You like interesting things.
Go . . . look.
Down at the river.
But—leaning against the locked door, shaking—she knew she wouldn't do that.
I can hear them, she thought. I can hear the sounds down there. The crazy splashing noises, the cries. The weird voices of grown-ups and kids, calling up to the building.
Carrie is with them.
I'm not going to look, she told herself.
She moved away from the door and over to the fat easy chair near the bookshelf, near the stereo.
She sat down. And picked up the headphones. She turned on the receiver, watching its red and green lights flash on eagerly. Jo heard a voice, a tiny voice through the headphones that she hadn't put on. She quickly reached out and changed the setting from tuner to tape. I don't want to hear anyone talking.
She had seen it on TV. She had heard the reporters, shuffling papers in front of them, telling people to stay inside . . . not to worry . . . that—
She had only one thought.
Mom is out there.
But she'll come back, Jo told herself. She'll come back and I'll wait here until it's all over.
She put the headphones on. Her nose felt pinched, tight. Her eyes were heavy, worn out. It's from the crying, all the crying and rubbing at my eyes, my nose.

At least I'm not crying anymore, she thought. At least I've stopped crying.

She picked up a tape, not caring what it was.

She put it in the machine and pressed play.

It was something classical.

Strings, then quiet horns. Soothing.

She brought her legs up tight against her. She reached up and pressed the headphones tight against her ears, trying to keep all the other sounds away.

And she waited.

Waited for Mom to come home . . .

FIVE

GILGAMESH

Chapter Thirty-six

THE *Ariel* steamed out of Flamingo harbor. Michael stood close to Farrand. A few dark birds swooped over the ship—cormorants, Michael guessed—scouting the ship, eager for garbage. The Flamingo Hotel—land's end for the Everglades' tourists—was right on the edge of the bay. The Georgian-style building was dark except for a few lights on the lower floors. No fishermen were about. It was still too early even for them.

So they sailed out of Flamingo Bay unobserved, unnoticed, as though sneaking away in the night to do some terrible deed.

Farrand had been asking him more about what the worm looked like, how it acted, when the captain came out of the bridge of the sleek, modern ship.

"More reports, Father. Reports describing New York as a disaster site."

Michael looked at Farrand. He grabbed at the railing.

Farrand nodded to Larsson.

"Just make all the speed that you can."

Michael shifted on his feet, about to say something. But Farrand extended a hand, touched his shoulder. Knowing what he was thinking. "They'll be fine. If they stay inside . . . they'll be all right."

Sure, Michael thought. Not really believing him. But knowing . . . I'm here . . . I have to do this.

The ship took a hard course to the starboard, then cutting back to port. The bay seemed dotted with hundreds of tiny islands, and hidden shoals that had to make navigating the big ship very difficult. But Farrand seemed unconcerned with the big ship's zigzagging. Michael saw buoys, and lights out there. He heard the dull ringing sound of bells. There were poles, channel markings, standing awkwardly in the water. And Farrand wasn't worried.

That was some comfort.

And once they were in open sea, in the Gulf, Michael imagined that the *Ariel* could cruise at forty knots or even faster, depending upon the weather. Small tropical storms could pop up quickly, and the *Ariel*, like all research vessels, was probably sluggish in rough seas.

"Let me show you Cyana . . . the sub," Farrand said, patting Michael's shoulder,

Michael nodded.

Farrand led him down the steps to the side, off the main deck, and then down to a walkway leading back to the rear of the ship. A giant U-shaped winch stuck out of the back of the ship. And sitting close to it, on the rear deck, was Cyana.

"It's not all that much different from *Alvin*," Farrand said. "You have, of course, dived in *Alvin*?"

Michael shook his head. "I've got no submersible experience whatsoever."

"Good." Farrand laughed. "Then I won't have to unteach you anything, eh?"

Michael couldn't laugh, couldn't smile. He walked up to the sub.

It was shaped like a bath toy, more like the Beatles' Yellow Submarine than something real.

Farrand patted the sides. "Titanium alloy . . . good for any depth we're likely to find in the Gulf. It can handle pressure of over two and one-half tons per square inch." He walked to the back of the sub and pointed to an array of small propellers encircled with metal bands.

"There are two lateral thrusters, one vertical thruster, and," Farrand said, pointing to the top of the sub, "a main thruster. We can move quite adequately with any combination of two."

The ship cut hard to starboard again, rocking Michael a bit on his feet. He suddenly remembered being seasick . . . a long time ago. When his father took him blue fishing. And Michael lost his lunch of a peanut butter and jelly sandwich and Twinkies.

Can't happen now. I've got nothing in my stomach.

Farrand touched a globe-shaped part of the sub, with a viewing port. "This is the crew compartment. The port is made of two-inch acrylic. And in case of an emergency, the compartment can disengage from the main sub for a safe return to the surface. The entire compartment is kept, of course, at atmospheric pressure."

Michael saw two large arms on what he imagined to be the front of the sub. They looked strong, menacing. Surrounding the arms, on the top and sides of the sub, were lights, each one pointing in a different direction.

The *Ariel* was passing out of the bay, and he heard the ship pick up speed, the rumble under his feet swelling. Then, with the speed, there was a breeze, blowing in from the Gulf.

Farrand had grabbed something on the sub, clicked it open.

"Eh, *bien,* it's open. Here, come—look inside. I want you to see this now. Before we start our dive."

Michael moved beside Farrand and peered in.

The compartment looked incredibly tiny. Barely enough room for one person, let alone two.

Farrand pointed to a bank of controls to one side.

"There, those are the switches for the ballast tanks. Water is taken on to dive and then—whoosh—compressed air is used to empty the ballast tanks to get us up again. I'll take care of them, but over here," he said, craning around, "that is the control for the main thruster. That will determine how fast we go. Its operation is very simple . . . you just move that stick forward, or back, and the thruster moves us forward or back." Michael slowly flashed on the idea that he was to work the propeller. "Don't worry. It's very easy. I'll use the other thrusters to keep us on a good trim."

The air inside the compartment was dank. Michael saw a bottle near the back, behind one of the tiny seats in front of the viewport.

"Someone's garbage?" he asked.

Farrand laughed again. "No, it's—what do the Woods Hole people call it? A yes, a *HERE*—a human element range extender."

Michael gave him a confused look.

Farrand grinned a bit more.

And then the use of the bottle—in a ship with no toilet—became clear.

"Oh," Michael said.

The rumble of the *Ariel* increased its rhythm, the pitch of the engine, the whine rising.

"And now, let us look again at your charts from the *Achilles* while my crew readies the sub."

And Farrand led him back to the bridge.

The cassette ended. There was silence. And the heaviness of the headphones pressing against her ears, resting on her head.

And she heard the sounds again. From the outside.

Jo slipped the headphones off.

There weren't as many sounds now. The halls outside the apartment seemed quiet. Except—except—

There! she thought. That was something. Echoing from below, maybe traveling up the stairway or elevator. *That* was somebody. Yelling. Screaming.

She imagined the word. Though it was just a tiny noise, a small squeak. She imagined what the word was.

Help.

And even outside, out there, beyond the glass of the window that she wouldn't look out of, the sounds were dying down. But there were still lots of voices. Moaning, crying, gibberish that she couldn't understand. It was muffled by the glass, by the ten flights of the apartment building.

She grabbed at the tapes.

Again, she opened a plastic case up, and put the new tape in.

Maybe I should look at the TV, she thought. Maybe I should look at the news. Maybe it's all over and, and—

But no. She was afraid of what she'd see.

Or what she wouldn't see.

She shut the door to the cassette recorder and pressed play.

It was Mozart.

She knew that. She watched a movie about him with her mom. Mozart giggled all the time wearing this dopey wig. And the women were dressed so that their boobs were ready to jump out of their dresses.

She loved that movie. She loved the music.

But now it was just noise.

She made the volume as loud as she could stand and then pressed the headphones tight against her head . . .

The calm water of the bay gave way to the choppy water of the Gulf. Now the squat ship rocked a bit.

And Michael had to touch the wall of the ship to get his balance from time to time as Farrand's crew connected the Cyana to the great winch.

Farrand was up on the bridge, going over his plans with the captain. It was, he had explained, like flying. You filed a plan with the R/V's captain. Cyana would not be tethered to the ship—that was impossible. But the captain was to keep the R/V following on the surface, monitoring the submersible's depth, its position, and the water temperature.

The radio, Farrand said reassuringly, would always be on.

They'd always be able to hear the voice of the surface.

The crew—no longer looking sleepy—crawled on top of the submersible, checking that the claw hooks of the winch were lined up properly. Then one of the crew gave a signal. The claws closed on the sub. Then opened. Then closed again.

And they left it that way.

It was still dark, but Michael thought that he saw some light in the east, the first teasing warning of dawn. Or maybe it was just the effect of the clouds overhead, spreading the moonlight through the sky.

He heard steps, and people talking. He turned to see Farrand walking toward him, speaking in French to the man who had hooked up the submersible.

The captain was behind him.

Farrand looked up.

"We're all set, Michael. I think it's time we got inside."

Michael nodded.

Never thought I was claustrophobic, he thought. But there wasn't one thing he'd rather do less than crawl inside the bubble of the sub.

Farrand gave him a smile. Reading my mind again? Michael wondered.

The winch moved. Michael turned, startled by the sound of the engine. Larsson signaled a crewman on the winch's controls, his hands on a trio of long sticks that were above them, on the upper deck.

The Cyana rose a few feet in the air. And then stopped.

"Eh, *bien,* Michael, let's get in. We're nearing 86 degrees 57 minutes west. We'll be over the entrance to the rift soon." Farrand's face turned grim, determined. "We have to get going."

"Yes," Michael said, and he followed the priest to the sub's entrance.

Farrand popped open the hatch and disappeared unceremoniously into the sub.

Michael felt the crew watching him. He felt the breeze, laced with salt and the balmy tropical air. The ship had a steady roll now, rocking back and forth, and Michael wondered whether they were all old hands at this kind of thing, launching the sub in choppy water.

Michael took a breath—his last gasp of unprocessed air—and crawled inside.

Inside, it was dark, lit only by the colorful instrument lights. Farrand's face had an eerie, multicolored pallor.

The priest was fidgeting with something behind him, twisting in his small seat, his arms and elbows moving around awkwardly. It was difficult for Michael to find his place.

Then Farrand stopped whatever he was doing and looked at Michael. "The hatch?" he said.

"Oh," Michael said. He pulled it shut.

"And throw that lever down," Farrand said, pointing to a barlike handle similar to the latch on an airplane's door.

Farrand threw a switch. Michael heard a faint hiss.

"We are all set here, Captain," Farrand said. "You can get us into position whenever you're ready."

"Yes . . ."

Michael heard the voice clearly, a bright metallic sound, strident in the tiny compartment. He heard the whoosh of the air, a steady hiss coming from somewhere behind him.

"You've never done this?" Farrand said. "Well, you are in for a thrill, Michael. A real—"

Michael heard the winch motor start again, a dull sound now. And then the submersible moved. He felt the sub being lifted. He could see the deck through the porthole, and then the water. He leaned forward, pressing his nose against the thick acrylic glass. They were up in the air, and then moving out, away, over the water, until water was all he could see.

"The captain is back on the bridge," Farrand said, as if explaining the procedure. "And he will tell us when we can be lowered and then—"

On cue, Larsson's voice came out of the air.

"Father, we have reached 86 degrees 57 minutes west, and we're moving down to latitude 25 degrees 13 minutes north. It should be in a few minutes . . ."

"Good, Captain . . ." Farrand said. He turned to Michael. "Once we're down, Michael, throw that switch there," he said, pointing to a black switch to Michael's left. "That starts the main thruster. Move the stick a few inches forward . . . until I get the sub properly balanced for the dive. If I ask you to pull back, do so very gently . . . don't—"

"Twenty-five, twenty . . ." Johnson said.

"Nice and easy, eh? We don't want to be flipped upside down. That can be very uncomfortable."

Michael took a breath, the air tasting as bad as he thought it would.

"Twenty-five, eighteen . . . All engines slow . . ."

Farrand looked at the part of the viewport right in front of Michael. He saw something . . . a smear . . . and he leaned forward and wiped at it with the cuff of his shirt.

"Try to keep moisture off the viewport. They fog easily. And—"

"Twenty-five, thirteen . . . All engines stop. Ready to be lowered?"

"Ready . . ." Farrand said. They waited—in silence—for the ship to stop. Still there was that side-to-side movement. The sea seemed rougher, Michael thought.

No. It was rougher.

And again he heard the terrible winch sound.

The Cyana was going down.

More groaning and he felt the sub hit something, and now it was being slapped noisily by the water. The ship rolled hard, as if off balance. And Michael was thrown against Farrand, and then against the side of the sub.

"Don't worry," Farrand said. "This will stop once we're underwater. It will be calm . . ."

Another rock, and Michael banged his head against the viewport.

"Are you all right?"

Michael rubbed his head.

But then the rocking ebbed, replaced by a more gentle movement, to and fro.

Michael looked ahead.

He hadn't even noticed that the viewport was underwater. It was greenish-gray, tinged with colors reflected back from the cabin.

"Ready to release, Father."

"Fine, Captain. We are ready."

Farrand turned to Michael. "In a moment . . . Michael . . . the switch," the priest said quietly.

Michael nodded. He reached out, moving his hand close to the switch. Ready.

This isn't happening, he thought. This is a dream. A crazy strange dream. I'm not in the middle of the Gulf of Mexico about to dive—what? 3000, 3500 meters? It's not happening.

"Release, if you would, Captain."

Another sound. A click, a sliding noise of metal scraping against metal, and the sub was free, rocking back and forth, bobbing. A tiny crescent of cloudy sky appeared in the viewport and then disappeared as the sub bobbed up and down.

"Taking in ballast," Farrand muttered to himself. "Good. Now, Michael, the main propeller."

The sub bobbled around again, rocking left and right, free of the ship. Michael's hand, poised for grabbing the switch, reached out and missed.

"Now . . ." Farrand repeated gently.

Michael whipped a bit forward. And then he threw the switch.

He heard a whirring sound from behind them.

"Good, now—gently—move the stick a few inches forward."

The whirring noise grew louder. The rocking began to subside.

Michael breathed. He hadn't realized that he'd been holding his breath. We're okay. He looked over at Farrand, adjusting what he assumed were the ballast controls.

"We have you diving," Larsson said through the speaker.

"Good . . . that is precisely what we are doing," Farrand answered.

He turned to Michael. "A bit more speed. The currents are strong and we need to go as straight down as . . . possible."

Michael inched the stick ahead. Farrand turned around, checking other dials, looking at other switches.

"Well," he said, turning around, looking at Michael, "we are off. And—for a bit—we can relax."

Michael tried to smile. Relaxing didn't seem like a viable option at the moment. The viewport was black. They could have as easily been in outer space.

His hand was locked on the propeller stick.

"Oh, you can let go of that now. We are"—Farrand looked at the depth gauge—"diving quite well now, already past five hundred meters . . ."

Michael released the stick. His hand was imprinted with the ribbed impression of the stick.

"Now, let's see what's out there this morning . . ." Farrand said. He leaned forward and flicked on some switches.

The Cyana's brilliant lights came on, and the viewport was filled with the picture of the water as they plunged down.

There was nothing to see, nothing except a steady swirl of specks falling in front of them.

"Marine snow," Farrand said. "Bits of fish, and plants, the steady fall of organic material, raining on the bottom. It feeds much of the life in the abyssal plains."

"Everything except the thermal vent creatures," Michael said.

Farrand grunted. "Yes . . ."

The snow—the bits and specks—made the water outside look like one of those Christmas scenes inside a plastic hemisphere. It looked like the bits of Styrofoam snow suspended in the water.

Michael kept watching.

There was nothing else outside except for the snow.
And then—all of a sudden—there were lots of things . . .

She woke up.
Just like when her alarm screamed in her ear and she had to crawl out of her warm bed, get onto the cold floor, and get ready for school.
Except there had been no alarm.
She had been dreaming.
Or maybe it wasn't a dream.
Carrie was talking to her, laughing. About boys, and tight buns. Then Carrie was gone. The apartment was empty.
She blinked. Rubbed her eyes. This is no dream, she realized. I'm awake.
What woke her up? she thought.
She felt the headphones on her head.
The silence.
She took the headphones off.
It was quiet.
So quiet . . .
She heard her heart beating.
Maybe it didn't happen. Maybe I imagined the whole thing and—
Jo turned and looked at the door. All locked up tight. Nobody was getting in. Nobody—
Except.
God! Her mother still wasn't back.
(And she remembered how those screams sounded. The mixture of words and yelps.)
Had her mother come back and tried to get in? Maybe Jo hadn't heard her. God, maybe her mom had tried to open the door but was stopped by the dead bolt. Maybe she banged on the door but Mozart was blasting away and didn't let me hear her.
Maybe, she thought, *she's still out there.*
Jo walked to the door.
Slowly.
As if it would suddenly fly open. Surprise! We were only fooling. We're all still here. Ready to party.
She kept walking to the door. Chilled now by her sleep. Her bare feet made soft padding sounds on the floor.
She reached the door. Touched it.
"Mom," she said. A whisper. Then louder. "Mom." Again,

even louder yelling. "Mommy! Mommy, are you there? Can you hear me! Mom-meeee!"

She waited, crying again, mad that she was crying again.

And here she thought she was all out of tears.

Maybe Mom had been there . . .

She reached up and undid the dead bolt.

"Mom . . ." she whispered.

She turned around.

And she saw the phone off the hook. Saw the pillow on top of it. And she heard a voice now.

Very faint.

Please hang up and try your call again. If you need assistance, dial your operator. Please hang up—

I didn't call anyone, Jo thought.

She walked to the phone and took off the pillow.

"I didn't call anyone," she said, hanging the phone up.

(Was that a sound from the hall? Some noise? The elevator?)

She turned around.

Just as the phone rang.

The others were dead, Barron saw. Gene, and Jay. Their lifeless heads lay next to the oozing pits like lifeless melons, like pumpkin heads gone to rot weeks after Halloween.

But I'm okay, he thought.

I'm here.

Yeah.

They're letting me see, letting me stick around.

Sure. That's my reward.

There were four of them, the pit things, in the studio now. Are they the ones who spoke to me? he wondered. Or were there still others to come . . . ?

Their skin shimmered, and glowed, unlike anything he had ever seen. It seemed to move on their bodies, like the orange stripes that swirled around Jupiter. A living skin, moving over them.

And some kind of offal, an alien dropping collected into globules on their backsides and rolled off, like gigantic drops of sweat.

They didn't seem to breathe.

That made sense, he thought. Sure.

Barron saw one of them look down at him.

With those eyes, those filmy black things that looked more like holes.

Then it looked away.

I'm still here, he thought giddily.

Barron tried not to look down at his own body, at the pit that was now his midsection.

Best not to think about that, he thought. Best not to concentrate on the negative.

He could feel another one crawling out. It was apparently pretty difficult, this crawling through the hole, coming from wherever they came from.

It took time . . . effort.

Barron tried to move his hands. He could see them. They were there, still attached to his arms.

But nothing happened. He concentrated on moving them, but there was nothing. He knew better than to try to move his legs. They were below the pit. He grinned. No way they're still working.

No way.

The creatures walked around.

Their feet were clawlike, a more refined version of the *Tyrannosaurus rex*. But they were built on a human scale. In fact, their bodies seemed to be a sick version of a human's body.

Barron wondered whether they had mouths. He couldn't see any opening *like a mouth*.

The doors to the studio opened.

Barron tried to tilt his head to see what was coming in.

The six o'clock news team, maybe. Yeah, they want to do some interviews.

"Tell us, Mr. Barron, how does it feel to be the first—"

He had only the smallest muscles left below his head. He could only tilt forward just the slightest bit.

But he saw people come into the studio. Lots of them, filling the room—a regular party—

(Taking care—he was glad to see—not to step on his body, or anywhere near the pit.)

They gathered around him, and the others, and stood there, silently. He saw that they had been hurt, that they all had big bloody spots. Here, a hole in a chest ruining a good suit. There, a yawning slit right above the gold chain.

Until each person in the crowded room, all these men and women, began to writhe, dancing in front of him, spastic, corkscrewing around until—

Oops, out of the wounds, out of the holes in their bodies, these white things came slithering out.

And what the *hell* are they? Barron wondered.

Each person had one.

And the things from the pit stepped into the crowd. And they grabbed people, two, three at a time, holding them steady with their claw feet, and their claw hands, and—

Dark holes opened in their heads.

Big dark holes.

And like snakes with gigantic detachable jaws swallowing some confused gazelles, they stuffed the people into these holes, worms and all.

Worms and all . . . marveled Barron.

(I'm here, he reminded himself. They're letting me see, letting me watch. I'm okay!)

And now he knew that, yes, they had mouths.

The biggest fucking mouths he'd ever seen . . .

Chapter Thirty-seven

THEY filled the viewport, hundreds, thousand of flitting creatures looking like wingless hummingbirds.

Michael jumped away from the screen, as if they were about to crawl their way in.

Farrand laughed.

"You know what they are?"

"Yes," Michael said. He watched them jockey for position, a moving swarm. "Red shrimp." Their eyes, bloated, pink-white globules, pressed against the acrylic viewport.

"It's the light," Farrand said, tapping the viewport. "They go absolutely crazy for the light. They won't stay for long, though. Another few minutes and it will be too deep for them."

As Farrand predicted, the small shrimp with their feathery swimming motion were suddenly swept away, as if an undersea gas jockey came by and cleaned the windshield. They were gone, and again there was nothing.

Farrand leaned forward and flicked the lights off.

It was completely black.

But no, Michael saw, not completely. Out there, in the murky darkness, he saw something. Like faint stars, thousands of light-years away. Some of the stars moved, sudden spasms that sent a thin arc of light shooting in front of the sub.

"Five hundred meters to the bottom," Larsson said.

Michael looked over to see Farrand check the depth gauge. Then he turned back to the viewport. And a face was there.

"Wha—" he said, startled.

It had long curved teeth, rapierlike, and a jaw that was devilish. The hungry-looking fish followed the submersible on its dive, and then cut away quickly.

"What was that—?"

"*Chauliodus sloanei*. A remarkable animal. Remarkable. It

opens its gill chambers and throat, actually disengages them, in order to swallow prey larger than its own body."

More strange fish swam by. A school of lantern fish, all dangling their bioluminescent lures in front of their mouths.

Nice . . .

"They see our cabin lights," Farrand whispered. "So they think we're some new fish." He paused. "It's beautiful down here, no? So black, lit only by the animals. It's another world . . . another universe . . ."

"Three hundred meters," Larsson announced.

"Best to pull back a bit on the main thruster, Michael."

Michael reached over and inched the stick backward. He felt the propeller slow.

A giant eel zigzagged across the viewport, ultra-thin with a needle-sharp snout.

"It's amazing . . . this is the only way you can see these animals alive," Michael said.

"Yes . . . it's wonderful."

"One hundred fifty meters."

Farrand put the lights back on, and the stars outside disappeared. "Sorry," he said, "we're getting close to the bottom." Then Farrand adjusted the controls, and Michael felt the submersible's plummet being slowed.

Still, there was no bottom, no rock formations in sight.

"One hundred meters . . . ninety meters . . . eighty meters."

"Ease up a bit more," Farrand said, tapping Michael who had his eyes glued to the viewport.

Then—as if they were landing blind on the moon—he saw the bottom appear. Flat, sandy, barely discernible from the murky water.

Farrand quickly leveled off the submersible.

Michael saw a cluster of clams. They were giant, immense, their dull gaping mouths open, sucking at the ice-cold salt water. They had a reddish tinge near the edge, where their meat was most exposed. Michael knew the color came from hemoglobin, used to produce chemical energy from bacteria-mediated oxygen. It was a strange process. What made it even stranger was what it meant for human evolutionary history. We came from the sea, and the clams were more living proof of our common genetic heritage.

Very odd, he thought, looking at the clams work the water.

Then he spotted crabs scuttling away, alarmed by the movement, the vibrations of the submersible.

"Look," Farrand said, "over there." He pointed to the far right, to a spot on the sea bottom just catching some light.

An enormous creature that looked like a giant plant, or an internal organ turned inside-out, was snaking across the sand, crawling like a hyperactive snail.

It was hard to judge its size.

But it looked to be about the size of a person.

"A giant sea cucumber," Farrand said. "No one knew they moved—like that—until I brought back the film."

The cucumber, one of the most primitive sea animals, lurched out of sight.

There were stone pillars ahead and giant rock formations with eyeholes cut into them. "See that," Farrand said, pointing to one. "That used to be a cliff when a river flowed here. The water dug right through that rock, cut that hole . . . This area is called the Mississippi Cone. The effluvial runoff travels thousands of miles, off the continental shelf, even down to here. Even down to here," he repeated quietly.

Farrand used the thrusters to navigate through the pillars.

This was like being in the Grand Canyon, Michael thought, but only submerged—in total blackness—underwater.

Then Michael saw the first smoker, the first tower of volcanic stone pouring out superheated hydrogen sulfide.

It was an amazing sight, a forty-foot stone tower, pumping out a smoky chemical sludge into the water. He was excited. He grabbed Farrand and pointed to it.

And he thought of the tape, the slow prowl of the *Achilles*'s ROV that ended in a snowy TV picture.

What if we don't get back up? he thought.

"You should be at the beginning of the rift," Larsson said. The sudden intrusion of the captain's voice made Michael jump.

"Steady, Dr. Cross," Farrand said quietly.

The submersible skirted the smoker. It was hot—the outside water reading was climbing well past freezing then up, over 100 degrees. Michael knew it was 350 degrees, maybe even hotter, near the smoker itself.

Then they flew over the bacterial mat, a long carpet of white, then orange, hiding a host of rift creatures. They came to a smooth dip in the floor. The sub, following the dip, arched downward.

And it suddenly glided over a rolling field of worms, long white tube worms with reddish tops, waving in the backwash of the sub's propellers.

Farrand tapped his hand.

"Slower," he said, gesturing to the stick to Michael's right. "Slow it down . . ."

Jo picked up the phone.

I had forgotten about it, she thought. How stupid. How really dumb of me! It's probably my mom. Sure. Telling me not to worry. That everything's okay.

"Mom," she said, pulling the phone to her ear.

The line was bad. Full of static. She heard a voice, a man's voice.

"Jo, Jo? This is Martin, from the Aquarium."

She chewed her lip. It's not my mom. She had trouble listening to Martin's words, trouble concentrating.

(She heard a sound outside again. Yes, that was *definitely* something. The elevator. Someone opening the door, checking if it was all clear, like a dumb game of hide and seek.)

"Jo, please put your mother on, I—"

"She's not here," Jo said dully.

(*More sounds!* Someone in the hall. Walking outside, and something being dragged. She thought of putting the phone down, and running to the door, throwing the dead bolt on again.

But then Mom wouldn't be able to get in. No, she couldn't do that.)

"Jo, listen to me. Do you know where your mom is? Have you seen her, did she go someplace?"

(The steps stopped. Just outside. If they *were* steps, if she wasn't just imagining it.)

"She went out to cover a story," Jo said. "She said she'd be back. But it's late and I—"

She felt them coming again, the tears, she felt her eyes going all full and puffy. She sniffed, and the air burned her nose.

I don't want to cry, she thought.

"I don't know where she is . . ."

"Are your doors locked?"

Jo nodded, then remembered that she was on the phone. "Yes."

"Are you okay?"

"I'm okay."

One ear listened to Martin's questions—so many questions! Why does he need to know so much?

Her other ear was cocked, aimed at the door to the apartment, listening, hearing nothing outside now.

"All right, now listen to me, Jo. Are you listening? Keep the door locked. Stay inside, right where you are, and—and—don't let anyone in."

Jo heard that. "My mom will be home soon. I'll let her in."

Martin said nothing. There was just the static.

"Jo, don't let *anyone* in. Your mom is probably someplace else. She'll be a lot happier knowing you're safe. Don't open the door."

"Yes," Jo said, not really paying attention.

"Your dad is doing something important. But he'll come and get you. You just wait and you'll be fine."

"Yes."

"I'll call again in a half hour."

"Okay," she said.

"Sit tight," Martin said.

Another sound. Steps. Just outside. And a shuffling, dragging.

Jo let the beige phone fall back onto its cradle.

Barron was getting sprayed. All this blood and other stuff was just squirting all over, dripping onto his face, running down his cheeks, dripping off his nose.

He had to make a great honking sound to clear his nose to breathe.

Do I need to breathe? he wondered. Is that something that's still important to do?

The people, the worm people, were being thrown into the pits now, stuffed into the body holes as if it were part of some demented clown act. Let's see how many we can get inside this itty-bitty hole in the ground.

But it goes someplace, Barron knew. Sure, that was easy to figure out. The pits went someplace, just like a door.

Funny thing—they weren't using *his* hole. A few more of the things crawled out, dripping great chunks of stuff right near his head, bits of blackish glop that rolled off their backs. A few plopped near his mouth.

(Which he kept shut.)

His nose was beyond reacting.

There were enough bizarre, sick smells in the room so that if he had a stomach—which, he could see, he quite clearly didn't have—he would just keep retching over and over and over.

See, he thought. There are advantages to being this way. Real advantages.

I'm special.

Then he saw some of them come over to him, stand there, and look down.

He worried. Maybe they changed their minds. But they stood there while he felt this tiny digging, just there, just from inside his body, from inside the pit. Small, almost feathery movements, not like before.

He craned forward, blinking away the drying spatters of blood that threatened to block his eyes. He tried to look down and see what was happening.

He saw two small claw hands reach out, pulling at the whitish exposed slats of his ribs, tugging to get out, to be born.

Thoughtlessly he let his mouth open. And—from one of the things standing near him—something rolled off its back, picking up size and speed like a runaway snowball. It fell into his mouth. And sat there. He tried to spit it out but it was gummy, sticky, and fastened itself to his teeth.

Better than Krazy Glue.

And now was added the sensation of taste. His tongue touched it, burning, and then it recoiled, filled with this terrible aftertaste, a sick rotten flavor that wouldn't go away.

He kept his tongue as flat against the bottom of his mouth as he could. But this thing just kept slowly dripping onto his tongue.

He made a sound, a muffled groan.

Little hands. He saw little hands, then a black-red head, but so small. Two, no, three of them, crawling out of the hole, and then up to his face, leaning forward as if they smelled the wedge stuck in his mouth.

They were babies, small.

(What the fuck is going on here? he thought. *What the fuck is going on now?*)

One small claw hand touched the chunk in his mouth, then trailed away to the softness of his cheek.

The other claw came closer.

And closer.

(No, Barron thought. I know what's happening here. No way. Hey, no way, I did what I was—)

Then—all together—openings appeared in their faces, mouths, black pits that Barron could see real well.

They leaned close to his face. The holes opened.

He knew what was happening.

Baby food.

That's what I am.

Baby food . . .

(He prayed that they wouldn't let him feel it, that it would just happen.)

He blinked.

They were on him, covering his face, scaling it like a boulder tossed on a hillside.

But he felt everything.

Everything.

Until there was nothing left to feel.

The Cyana just floated, drifting, its momentum making it glide over the tube worms. Farrand was keeping it at a constant depth.

Michael saw the scientist's face. Tight, the small cracks and lines catching the colored lights of the instrument.

"What's the matter? Is there—"

Farrand held up his hand. He pressed against the compartment viewport, looking left then right, grunting. Michael watched the worms. It looked like an alien wheat field. Small animals played in the field. Up ahead—if they were in the right location—they'd come to the great underwater valley, and then the yawning crevasse of the rift.

And they should find hundreds of the isopods, just inside the narrow cleft in the sea floor.

Waiting there . . .

The submersible tilted a bit to one side. There was movement down here, Michael thought. He wouldn't have expected deep currents perhaps, or maybe—

"You see that," Farrand said, gesturing to the worms outside, the great stand of *Riftia pogonophosa Jones*. "All that movement, it's—"

"Just a current," Michael offered, "normal water turbidity."

Farrand shook his head.

"Father," Larsson interrupted.

"Yes," Farrand said, not taking his attention away from the viewport. The sub rocked again and Farrand fiddled with the smaller thrusters working to keep the sub gliding steady.

"There's a call for Dr. Cross, on the radiophone. From a Martin Langelaan."

"Pipe it in," Farrand snapped.

Then, amazingly, Michael heard Martin's voice—so clear he could be in the ship above them.

"Michael, I got through to Jo. She's fine. Locked up in her apartment. Told her you'd come and get her."

"And I will. How's her mother?"

There was no sound for a second and Michael thought that the line had gone dead.

And Martin told him that Jo was alone.

He grabbed the edge of his small seat.

Thinking: Jo's alone. And Caryn is still outside.

"Did you tell her to keep the door locked? No matter what."

"Yes, and—"

"Call her again. Tell her not to let anyone in, goddammit. Not even her mother."

"Right. Michael, I also got the Coast Guard Marine Environment Office working with us, and the U.S. Navy. The governors of the coastal states have declared the highest level emergency. National Guard soldiers are coming here to protect the lab. They know what you're doing," Martin said. "They're not too sure why, but they understand that they have to help us."

"*Call Jo,*" Michael said. There was a pause.

Martin didn't say anything. Then: "Michael . . . it works."

What does he mean, Michael wondered. It works? What the hell does he mean by that? *What works?*

Then he knew.

"You stupid bastard."

"*It works, Michael!* We can stop them, Jesus, we can stop them. If you get enough material, we can start breeding colonies, cover the drinking water, the oceans, the lakes. Hell, we can shoot it right into people. But—"

There was a sudden burst of static, as if a bolt of lightning slashed across the sky.

"Martin . . . .are you still there? Can you hear me . . . .?"

Farrand tapped Martin's arm. "Give us a bit of power. Quickly . . . now."

Michael nodded, and moved the stick forward with his left hand.

"Martin, Jesus, can you—"

". . . ill here."

"Have a copter pick me up from the ship. Do you hear me? And have a plane ready to fly to New York. Someplace secure . . ."

"There's a base they're using"—more static—"on their list of places to quarantine."

"And, Martin, they should have a copter waiting in New York. You got that?"

"Yes, I—"

Another burst of static.

Then, "—bye, Michael. God—"

The speaker went quiet. And Michael was lost, thinking: Where the hell is Caryn?

"Michael." Farrand tapped his shoulder hard. "I need your help. Pay attention now. Please."

Michael looked outside. They were at the edge of the worm field. A black smoker was to the side, the thermal life source for the deep-sea community.

"What's wrong?"

Farrand looked at him. His eyes were hooded by heavy eyelids. The man was tired . . .

Perhaps scared.

"The water"—he gestured outside—"it's much too rough. I thought it was our own backwash . . . that's why I stopped moving. But something is stirring things up here—"

"A current?"

"No. Not this deep. Not—like that."

Michael took a breath. What was Farrand saying? Was there something wrong here? Something he should be worried about?

"This is an unstable area. It connects with the fault line that runs through the tip of Mexico out into the Pacific. But there's been no major movement since 1929, when the Gulf floor was wracked with earthquakes."

Oh, shit, Michael thought. Isn't that good news? Undersea earthquakes.

"Is that what's happening now?"

Farrand shook his head. "No. This is probably just some open volcanic gash somewhere, a hot seep making the water move around. It could have been going on for months. It might go on for months more before disappearing . . . but—"

"But what—?"

They had left the worm field, and now the sunken valley and the rift floor were directly ahead. It looked like a funnel, ever narrowing, and they were going straight into it.

It was like watching the tape, the *Achilles* tape that he watched over and over.

Only this time, I'm here. Lucky me. *I'm here*.

"It will make it harder getting down there. We have to be very careful." Farrand leaned forward. "Thirty-two hundred meters. Very deep . . . The pressure makes any bang, any scrape, all the more dangerous. I will tell Larsson not to interrupt us. Not unless it is something very important. You understand?"

Michael nodded.

And as Farrand called up to the *Ariel*, Michael watched as they glided right into the mouth of the rift . . .

* * *

Jo stood there.

She twitched her big toe. A habit. When she was nervous. Or upset.

Like when she used to hear them fighting, her mother yelling at Dad.

She heard another woman's name. Someone else. A stranger, not part of their family. Another name . . .

And Jo understood what they were fighting about.

Someone was on the other side of the door.

The dead bolt was open.

She stood there.

She saw the door handle twitch left, then right.

A grunt. Someone tried to push open.

Then—oh, yes!—the sound of a key going into one lock. She watched the knob inside turn. Then—a pause that lasted an eternity—and another key, into the door lock.

Jo smiled.

Her lips moved, as if to say a word. To say, Mom.

You're home. Mommy, you're—

But Jo just stood there.

Next to the phone. Martin's words still ringing in her ears.

Words that she hadn't really listened to.

What had he said? What did he mean?

Now the knob turned again.

And the door opened . . .

Chapter Thirty-eight

THE door opened.

And her mother was there.

Jo stood there, watching the door swing open wide, banging against the wall.

Her mother didn't look up.

(She's not looking up, Jo thought. Why isn't she looking up?)

"Mom?" Jo said, hardly believing that it was her, that she wasn't all alone anymore.

Now I'll be fine, she thought. Now everything will be okay. We can get out of here and—

"Mom!" she said now, louder, the joy filling her, erupting, blinding her to the fact that—

(Something's wrong with my mom's foot.)

Jo started to run to her. Actually galloped three giant steps toward the door, still wondering: Why won't she look up?)

Caryn took a step. A dull shuffle really, pawing at the foyer carpet like a hurt cat she once had three years ago. Its back legs just didn't work anymore, and it had to try to balance on them, and then claw at the carpet with its front legs.

This was like that. Her mom moved like that.

Jo stopped running, "Mom," she said. Looking down at Caryn's left foot. It was twisted at a bad angle, and it was covered in thick crusty blood.

It had to hurt real bad.

Caryn slid forward, grabbing at the wall for balance.

And then she looked up at Jo.

She looked up, right at Jo. Jo stared at her, waiting to see that wonderful glow, that great spark that said we *know* each other. And it's okay now, everything is okay. Even though I'm hurt, we're going to be fine, sprout. No problem.

Mommy's here and everything is—

Jo looked at those eyes.

And she whispered one word, to herself. Quiet.

(But it seemed to echo inside her head, clanging like some dull, horrid bell. One word.)

"No . . ."

Another step, another terrible lurch. And Jo backed up a few feet.

The eyes were empty. No, worse than that. They seemed to open wider when they spied Jo, wider, and Jo felt the eyes looking right at her.

Don't say anything, Jo begged. But she saw her mother's lips moving . . .

(You're not my mother, she thought. You're not my mother!)

"Jo," the voice said. It was a rough and scratchy voice. Her tongue snaked out, all dry, white and crusty. Then a raspy breath, in and out, and Jo imagined the throat all dried up, clogged with bits of dry phlegm. "Jo," the voice barked, "help . . . me . . ."

And now she wondered—

Stepping backward.

Bumping into the couch, nearly falling into it. Yelping, because she almost fell down and Mom was so close.

Now, she wondered . . . *Maybe she is okay.* Maybe she just got hurt. Maybe I'm just scared. Sure, after last night, that would make sense. I'm just scared. I'm—

Jo brought her hand up, gesturing at the person coming toward her. Begging it to give some sign that she was okay.

Mom seemed to understand. She hopped forward a bit more, then her face broke into a grin.

She spoke again. A dry, scratchy noise. "Jo, come here. Help me get to the couch, honey. Please, help me, I—"

Jo started crying. It's my mommy. *She's okay!* She's been hurt. Why can't I see that? What is wrong with me? Why am I being *so stupid?*

"Jo . . . please . . . honey."

Step. Drag. Step. Drag.

Jo walked to her.

The rift was narrowing quickly. It was half a kilometer wide, and narrowing quickly.

Michael guessed that they should have been protected from the currents that swirled across the great undersea Mississippi Plain. But the submersible was rocking, back and forth, rhythmically.

Farrand was jerking the controls left and right trying to keep the Cyana level.

The dark floor of the rift was filled with deep-sea bottom dwellers, the albino crabs, and diaphanous squid that hid in the ruffles of the bacterial mats.

And there, just ahead, Michael saw dozens of the isopods, whole families of them. Munching at small red shrimp that dared swim too close. Grabbing at lantern fish.

He saw the growth on their backs, in different spots, but all of them had it. All of them . . .

The benevolent parasite who could stop the worm.

"You'd better get as many as you can." Farrand looked over and smiled uneasily. "It's getting very rough down here. Too rough. I don't know how long we'll be able to stay."

"I never—" Michael started to say, gesturing at the controls for the pair of manipulator arms.

"I can't let go of these thrusters to demonstrate. So, Michael, I hope you are a quick learner. You turn on the hydraulic system down there."

Michael saw a button below the stick-shift controls.

"Okay."

"Now push forward to extend the arm. And you open the claw—"

The submersible lurched to the left, flying at an angle toward the ground. Michael looked out the viewport and saw the floor rushing toward the sub. Only a meter or so away, the movement stopped. When the Cyana rested steady, Farrand spoke.

"Squeeze the controls to open the claw. Then when you let go—very slowly—they'll close. But don't let go completely. They'll crush the isopods."

"Got it," Michael said.

"Only now," Farrand said, looking ahead, "we're too far away from them, eh?" The isopods had scurried deeper into the rift.

Farrand angled the sub over to the center of the rift. He eased the submersible forward, until the Cyana was sandwiched between the walls of the rift, only a few meters space on either side.

Michael remembered the *Achilles*, remembered what it looked like when they sent the ROV into the rift.

They're not far away, he thought. The burrows, the strange worms. Just ahead. A big black opening in the sea floor, lined with the burrows and those snaky animals, jutting in and out, waiting . . .

The isopods were scurrying away, toward the burrows, scared by the submersible.

"Quickly," Farrand hissed, moving closer to them, even as the isopods moved deeper into the rift. The walls were closer. They had only a meter on each side, while below them there was a tremendous slope leading down.

Michael moved one manipulator arm out, concentrating on a fat isopod near the back of the pack. It was a true giant, two meters long, and covered with the bacterial colony like a fuzzy beard.

Michael encircled it with the claws but he was too late in closing them and the isopod scuttled right through.

"Damn," Michael said. Then, remembering Farrand's missing collar, he apologized, "Sorry."

But Farrand said, not too kindly Michael thought, "Quickly, try it again."

This time Michael had a better feel for the controls. As soon as he had another isopod encircled, he eased up quickly, feeling the right amount of pressure. It didn't matter too much whether the isopod died. But it would be better if they got them alive. Their entire system had to be filled with the bacteria.

He gently eased the handle.

The isopod was caught.

He pulled back on the manipulator arm and deposited the animal inside the large specimen container on the side of the passenger bubble. There were two such containers, and he hoped they would hold about a dozen of the animals.

Is that enough? he wondered. Will that give us a chance?

The nest of isopods scurried deeper into the rift, closer to the burrows.

Farrand had to follow.

The priest was growing exasperated. It was all taking too long.

They don't seem afraid of what is ahead, Michael thought. Whatever lives in the burrows doesn't seem to worry them . . .

Michael started grabbing isopods quickly, killing a few, but getting most intact and alive into the containers.

The submersible rocked back and forth again.

Michael was growing used to it. Farrand said nothing, totally preoccupied with keeping the sub level.

When he heard a roar. An underwater rumble.

Dull, muffled, as though it came from miles away.

Michael looked up at the viewport, then over at Farrand.

"What is it?" he asked. "What's happening?"

Farrand put a hand up, quieting him as he listened to the rolling rumble, like underwater thunder.

"God in heaven," Farrand said. "No . . ." he whispered. Then, "The main thruster, Michael. Now, get it—"

Michael let go of the manipulator arms, and reached out for the main thruster.

But he never even got to touch it before the submersible flipped upside down.

Soldiers were on the way. Fort Hamilton regulars.

They should be here, Martin thought, standing in the lab, two metal cases beside him, feeling like a businessman who had missed his train.

Where the hell were they? It was all arranged. The Coast Guard lab in Staten Island was being readied. Martin picked up the phone and started dialing the number.

He didn't hear so many sounds outside anymore.

Only the occasional scream. Then someone banging against the wall of the lab.

As if they know I'm in here, he thought. As if they fucking know . . .

He dialed the first three numbers of the base, looking at the yellow pad next to the phone, filled with numbers. Then he stopped.

I might be out of here any minute, he thought.

He wanted to tell Jo to sit tight again, not to worry. That they'd get her out.

Sure they would.

But he didn't believe that.

The whole city was gone.

The whole fucking city.

And they were going to get Jo out?

Not a fucking chance.

He dialed the apartment number.

The phone rang.

She knew who she was.

That never left.

I'm Caryn Cross.

And she had some dim memory of what had happened to her. Very dim.

Not an unpleasant memory. Not at all.

I'm better now, she thought. I wasn't feeling so good, but now, well now I'm just fine.

Except she knew that she wanted something from this apartment, from her daughter, standing there so close.

Come to me, she thought. It was so hard to move. So hard. All those streets, feeling so hungry, so empty. Everyone who was still . . . free . . . was too fast for her. And when she passed one building and something dark and gray scurried in between some garbage cans, she had a not-unwelcome thought.

Maybe I could catch that.

She might have a chance.

But then she thought of Jo, waiting. And—terrible thought, beautiful thought—she would be easy. Jo would be easy . . .

So she lumbered on. Block after block, until her left foot became a dull bloody load she dragged behind her, like some ancient Indian deathsled.

Now she waited for her daughter to run to her, to embrace her. She knew she would. And then this pain, this hunger would be gone.

And that would be good.

"Mommy," she heard her say.

And then the girl ran to her, her arms out, open, and—

The phone rang.

Jo stopped.

It was loud, breaking the eerie hush of noises, her own whimpering, her mother's raspy breathing.

The phone was right there, on the small table at the end of the couch.

It rang again. Loud, insistent. Her mother shook her head, tried to smile.

(Sad. She looks *so sad.*)

Jo reached out.

Picked up the phone.

"Jo, are you still okay? You still have the doors locked and—"

Martin heard her say that her mom was back, that Mom was here, and wasn't that great? Now everything will be fine and—

"Jo," Martin yelled.

He heard the sounds of a helicopter. Above the Aquarium. The sound got lower, louder.

He looked down at his feet to make sure the cases were there.

"Jo," he moaned, knowing already that it was too late. Too

fucking late. "Look at her. Are you sure your mom's all right, are you—?"

Then there was static.

And nothing else.

No dial tone. No excited girl's voice.

Nothing.

And Martin put the phone down, the dead phone. And he waited for the knock on the lab door.

Static.

And just the sound of Martin's last words.

(Her mother had slid closer while Jo was on the phone. She *saw* that.)

Jo was smiling, then she let her smile melt.

She moved to the side. And away. Just a bit. Just so she could see . . .

Look at her, Martin said. She already knew her eyes were dead. She already knew that. Now she looked at the rest of her mother's body.

She kept moving to the side, backing into the kitchen. Her mother turned, slowly, with difficulty. She spoke. "Jo . . ." she croaked. "Jo."

A voice from a million miles away.

Jo kept moving. She saw flaps hanging off her mother's back. Bits of stuff just hanging off, like ripped flaps of clothing. Except it wasn't her dress. No, it was bits of skin, and bone, and—

Something was back there.

It popped out.

Impatient.

Couldn't wait.

Got tired of waiting.

Too hungry.

"Oh, Mommy," Jo moaned.

"What is it?" Michael said. He finally had a hand on the main thruster.

Farrand grunted, trying to right the submersible, steady it.

"It's a quake, a shifting in the sea floor. I—"

Another great shock wave hit them, sending a cloud of sand in front of their viewports, eerie in the bright tungsten lights. Michael saw crazed creatures swirling about too, crabs, shrimp kicking, trying to control their movement.

The submersible rotated to the left, leveling, and then Michael felt something shove it hard. The sub banged against the rock. Then it bounced away.

He looked over his shoulder, expecting to see water seeping in. And that would be the end, he thought. Over two tons of pressure on every inch. It would pop at the first crack.

The Cyana was tilted down now, moving into the narrowing rift, getting wedged between the walls. Michael heard the sound of metal, twisting, a wrenching noise.

"The arms," Farrand said, looking at the control board. "The arms are gone."

All right, Michael thought. That's okay. We have enough of the isopods. If we can just get out of here. If we can just get the fuck up with the ones we have—

Then—in answer to his plea—he heard the submersible scrape against rock. On one side. Then the other.

And it stopped moving.

"More on your thruster, Michael! As much as you can!" Farrand yelled.

Michael pressed hard. He heard the complaining whine of the engine.

But it was clear that they weren't moving.

They were stuck.

Farrand tapped his arm, telling him to ease up.

"Save the battery," Farrand said with a gentle smile. "We're not going anywhere."

And slowly the sandy swirl in front of the viewport began to clear . . .

It crawled out of this hole in her mother's back, as if impatient with her mom's slow-moving body.

And Jo felt that it knew where she was.

"No," she screamed, moving through the kitchen, stepping backward, past the shiny countertop, out to the dining area—

(Where they never ate too many meals together. They just never had any time.)

Now it flopped to the floor.

Big, pulsating. Like a boa constrictor she once saw in the zoo.

It jerked forward, nearly reaching her in one great arch.

While it dragged Caryn behind.

Like some kid being pulled into the dentist's office.

Jo yelled. She saw this red stuff in the center of the worm. It moved, pulsated, sending a wet spray onto the shiny linoleum floor.

She looked right, for some place to run.

There was the other side of the living room.

And the sliding glass door to the small patio.

Their minipatio, her mother had called it.

She ran.

And she heard it flopping after her, smacking against the chairs in the dining room, hitting the wall—or was that just her mother's body banging against the wall?

She grabbed the glass door.

Maybe it will keep it out.

Maybe it—

The door didn't open.

It's locked.

Oh, God, no—she prayed. It's locked. She fiddled with the latch. It was stuck.

More banging. Right behind her.

She thought—

Where will it bore a hole into me?

Jo thought about turning around, to see where it was. But then the lock clicked open. She grunted and slid the heavy door open. She stepped out onto the patio, and pulled, harder, faster, please—

She begged.

Sliding it behind her.

It shut.

For a second all she heard was the sound of the city. Strangely silent.

No cars, no cabs honking their horns. It was still dark out.

It had to be morning soon, she thought. It's been night . . . forever.

There were two iron chairs on the patio, and a small iron table with a glass top. All painted white. Heavy. So they wouldn't blow off in a thunderstorm, her mom said.

It was quiet. She didn't look at the patio door.

Then the glass behind her shattered into a thousand pieces.

She screamed.

The glass sprayed over her back. She felt tiny chards cut into her neck, the base of her scalp, through her shirt.

But the big chunks fell at her feet.

She spun around, moving against the table, pushing it to the side. She was near the barrier that separated their patio from the one next door.

The worm was there.

Looking at her.

Except it had no eyes, no face. Nothing like that. Still, it just seemed to be looking at her.

Her mother's body dragged behind it, out over the broken glass. Slowing it down. Jo watched the worm trying to screw itself out of the body. She screamed out. Over and over, her voice going hoarse.

"Go away! Go . . . away . . . go . . . away!"

It was caught on something.

A bit of bone.

It wanted out. And she knew where it wanted to go.

She smelled it. It smelled like the stench in the train station, in the black-wet corners of the station. A disgusting smell that always made her hurry up, hurry up the steps, to the light and air above, holding on to her mom's hand.

The worm dropped down on her.

Jo moved back, the few inches to the thick plastic divider. The worm hit the ground hard, held in check by Caryn's body.

It rose again.

Next time it gets me, Jo thought. Next time it—

She reached down for a chair.

The worm came at her.

The chair was heavy, all metal, but she held it up, right in front of her. The worm hit the chair, pushing Jo hard against the divider separating the patios. It started grinding its body right into the metal legs, the mesh of the seat, *oozing* through it to get to her.

Jo screamed and yelled at it. It was right there, almost touching her hands.

"Go . . . away . . . go . . . away!"

She lifted the chair higher. So hard, too heavy. I can't do it, she thought. It's too hard!

And then she threw the chair to the side. Off the patio.

The heavy chair tumbled away pulling the worm with it, its own body followed it.

Then it snapped taut.

Held by her mother's body.

Rooted to the patio by her mother's body.

"No . . ." she said. "No . . ."

She walked over to her mother. Crying now, coughing, gagging at the smell and the way her beautiful mother looked.

The worm was holding on to the body. Holding on. Rippling. Moving back.

Jo kicked at the body.

(It's just a body, she thought. *Just a body*. Mom is dead. Mom is dead. *Mom is dead!*)

"Let it go!" she screamed.

The worm was inching back, still enmeshed in the chair.

Jo kicked the body again.

Her mother's eyes opened, looked at her.

They were really her eyes this time. Jo moaned, wept.

Then they closed.

And the worm suddenly went streaming out of her mother's body, flying away, like a runaway clothesline whipping over the railing down to the parking lot below.

Jo stood there, breathing fast, gasping.

She looked at her mother's body.

It was quiet again.

There was no movement.

No breathing. Nothing.

She's dead, Jo thought.

Jo looked up.

But I'm not.

And I have to get out of here, she thought. I have to get away.

Because I'm . . . not . . . dead . . .

Chapter Thirty-nine

MICHAEL watched Farrand shut off the outside lights, and then turn off all the switches inside the cabin until they were sitting in nearly total darkness. There was no sound from the radio. That was obviously gone. There was just the pale greenish light from a small bulb right over their heads.

It was the battery indicator.

When that went dark, there'd be no power.

Farrand sat back. And Michael waited for him to say something.

But he didn't.

Michael had to ask, "What—?"

"Shhh. Quiet," Farrand said.

This is like being buried with someone, he thought. We're sitting here as quietly as if we're in the confessional together.

Bless me, Father, for I have—

Then Farrand broke his silence.

"There. I think that's it. Do you hear anything?"

"No," Michael said. Now he figured out that Farrand had been listening for more rumbles.

"Then maybe it's done. I certainly hope so. On the other hand—"

Farrand flicked on two switches. The depth gauge and—right next to it—the outside water temperature.

"Thirty-six hundred meters. We couldn't go much deeper. The submersible couldn't take it. How deep *is* this rift?"

Michael shook his head, then said, "I don't know."

"Very hot here too. I didn't see any smokers, but it's very hot. They have to be near. Very—"

Farrand turned off the two switches and flashed on the lights.

Their trap was illuminated, but muddied by the sandy swirl of particles dancing in front of the viewport.

"If only I could see better," the priest said.

"Are tremors common down here?"

Farrand laughed. "Common? Hardly. The last major tremors were in 1929. They sent tidal waves rushing toward the Gulf Coast . . . destroyed the Louisiana coastline. This was bad for us. But I can't imagine that it did much on the surface." He flicked the lights off.

And they sat in the darkness again.

Michael didn't think he could handle much more waiting.

"So what are we going to do?"

"Do? You mean besides sit here and wait. A good question, Michael. There are a few—" Farrand threw another switch, and the sub's sonar went on, giving a rough outline of the surrounding sea floor. "There are . . . a few options." He turned to Michael, his face catching the green light in an eerie way. "Tell me, do you know the epic of Gilgamesh?"

"Gilgamesh." The name was familiar to Michael. Familiar . . . but it meant nothing. "No, I don't—"

"An anonymous story . . . from two thousand years before Christ. Maybe earlier. At least, that's when it was written down. It's an odd tale, a parable about the transitory nature of human existence and the importance of friendship. Gilgamesh was a king and he goes down to the bottom of the sea in search of immortality. A noble quest . . . to search for immortality. He fights and defeats monsters. But the real monster he has to fight is his own animal instinct-driven nature. From that springs civilization."

Michael half listened. He kept watch at the viewport, as the water slowly cleared.

"That's what we'll find, you know? Immortality. We'll either get out of here and—if you're right, if we're both not crazy—save civilization."

Michael took a breath. How much air? he wondered. How much air do we have? He was afraid to ask.

"Or we'll stay here. We won't save anyone. And that will be a kind of immortality too, won't it?"

"You said options . . ." Michael reminded him . . . wondering: Is this old man going crazy?

"Options. Yes." Farrand flicked the lights on. The sediment and sand had cleared a bit, and Michael saw farther into the black yawning mouth of the rift.

Farrand tapped the window, startling Michael.

"There. I see some cloudy deposits. Hydrothermal seeps of some kind."

Michael leaned forward. An albino crab scuttled over the twisted stump of one of the manipulator arms. And Michael wondered how the isopods were faring in their specimen containers.

"How far away . . ." Farrand said, putting his face right up to the glass, "how far away do you think those animals are, those worms on the tape?"

Michael licked his lips. "Not far. I guess—"

Farrand looked at him. "I've seen them before, you know. I saw the worms before I ever dived."

"What do you mean?" Michael said.

"In Oman. Giant fossils . . . unlike anything I've ever uncovered. But when I saw them alive—" Farrand turned away. "It was an amazing moment."

A mad thought hit Michael: Farrand wants to go deeper into the rift.

God, he'd like to go down to the burrows.

"The fossils were sixty-five million years old . . . perhaps more. And I heard of rumors of a similar find by the Soviets in the Antarctic. But there were no monographs, no papers . . ."

"Sixty-five million . . . ?" Michael asked. It was incredible.

"And I had an idea, Michael. A crazy old priest's idea. You see there, Michael, out there, with those isopods and crabs and bacterial colonies, *there* is the real battle between light and darkness."

The priest's eyes wandered around the small cabin, as if summoning these thoughts from some hidden place. "Ours is a planet of *life*. It uses minerals and light to *live*. But we know it wasn't always this way. There was something else . . . things like the first acheoic bacteria that bred in the primal organic soup, things that lived without oxygen, without light." Farrand shook his head. "There were two types of existence, one we called life and the other . . . was something different."

"And what would you call that?"

Farrand laughed. "There's a name for it in the book of Genesis. The Bible"—he laughed sadly again—"had a name for it." Farrand looked outside.

Then, he said quietly, "It's called evil, Michael. Darkness warring against the light. A simple idea, no? And it's not just these creatures, these worm creatures in their burrows, imprisoned here.

It's much more than that." Farrand looked up, as if he could look through the sub, up to the surface and beyond.

"More?"

Farrand nodded. "It's the reason behind the mass extinctions that have plagued life on earth. It's the source of the great battles that have left a whole planet dead, and species rendered extinct *overnight!* Yet . . . new species always emerged to continue the fight. Microscopic life forms, single cells genetically shaped to save the planet."

He rubbed his chin. "That's what this is about, Michael. Not just here. But I guess the battle goes on in all of God's universe." Farrand looked over at him. "Except this time we might lose . . ."

"You said we have options."

"Yes," Farrand sighed. "Options." The priest tapped the side wall of the crew compartment. "This compartment can be released. I explained that to you. And—if we're not wedged in too badly, if we're not hopelessly trapped in the rift, well, we might stand a chance of getting to the surface."

"Then we should do it."

"But if we disengage, we have"—he leaned close to one of the gauges—"twenty minutes of air. More than enough to keep us alive as we float to the surface. But if we stay stuck, then we're cut off from the main tanks of the submersible. You understand that? If we stay, the submersible could free up later if there's more shifting of the sea floor . . . But if we disengage and don't get away, we'd be dead already."

Michael nodded. Gilgamesh, he thought. The human species as just one more transitory life form. This was like an ancient riddle. The lady or the tiger. Either way, we might lose.

"So, what do you think, Michael?"

One image, one idea made that question easy.

He thought of Jo.

"Release the compartment."

Farrand smiled. "That's what I would say. I don't think the Cyana has any chance of getting free. But the compartment . . . perhaps . . ."

Farrand turned on the lights again.

(And some movement near the viewport caught Michael's eye. There was something out there, lurking in the darkness, watching them.)

Farrand started one of the thrusters.

"It takes a few minutes to close off the hydraulic tubes leading to the main tanks. Then, the three main latches are sprung. If we are lucky . . ." Farrand looked out the viewport, as if he had just seen something too. "No . . ." he said quietly, "if God is with us, we will go up."

A red light went on. Then there was a beeping noise.

"She is ready," Farrand said. He flipped up three large latches—two behind them, and one in front. He pushed a button. There was a whoosh, and the sound of the compressed air moving in the compartment.

They didn't move.

"Is that it?" Michael asked. "Did you just do it?"

"I'm afraid so . . ."

They sat there in the silence, separated from the main body of the sub, still locked in the jaws of the rift.

Jo put the note on the kitchen table.

As if she were leaving some cute message for Mom.

Gone swimming. Back to chow down later.

This wasn't a cute note. In fact, she could hardly read it . . . even though it was the third note she tried to write. Something was *wrong* with her handwriting. It was all wriggly and all over the place.

It said: *I can't stay here. I've gone to reach my dad—Jo.*

She folded the note so it made a triangle and she could sit it in the center of the table.

There was a breeze blowing through the smashed patio door.

(Something happened out there. Jo didn't think about what happened. Just that there was this hole, and now the wind blew in.)

She grabbed a salt shaker, a little ceramic penguin in a black top hat. She used his feet to hold the bottom of the note in place.

Then—giving herself one last chance to think: Is this what I should do? Won't I really be safer here?

(And knowing that she couldn't stay. They'd come. More and more of them. Until they got her.)

She ran out of the apartment.

She looked at the elevator.

Did it work?

She touched a button. It lit up.

In the silent building.

(So quiet it was the scariest place she'd ever been . . .)

She heard the whirr of the elevator.

Jo waited.
Counted.
1.2.3.4.5.6.7.8.9.10.
An idea occurred to her.
The slow-moving elevator was closer.
What if someone was in the elevator? Or something?
What if she got in and it stopped on a floor and someone got on?
Closer. Just a floor or two below her.
She looked down the hallway.
Quieter still. Some apartment doors were open. But there was no noise.
She saw the emergency exit sign. The stairs leading down.
The elevator was nearly there.
She turned and ran down the hallway.

She went down each zigzagging flight of stairs halfway. Then she stopped, and listened. Even here she could hear the elevator, rumbling back down again. Maybe it might have been safe.
At least here I can run, she thought.
And when she was sure that each flight of stairs was empty, that there was no one by a door, she stepped down, so quietly, past the doorway to the floor, and on down to the next turn in the stairs. More listening.
And on and on.
After five floors, she heard something.
Her heart felt like it was going to explode.
She thought she'd cry out. She couldn't handle the terrible suspense.
I'm here, she wanted to yell. I'm here. You can get me. Just don't hurt me. Don't do to me what you did to my—my–
(Her mom had opened her eyes. And she had been there again, Jo thought. For just a few seconds. She helped me, let the thing slide out and—)
More sounds.
Jo slid up another step, quietly, hoping she wouldn't be seen.
Then there was a squeal, and a flash of brown ran across the floor.
Only a mouse, she thought. She nearly laughed.
But she wondered. It could be inside a mouse too, couldn't it?
Couldn't it?
The mouse disappeared.
She started down again, losing count of how many floors she passed.

She heard the elevator again.

Someone's using the elevator, she thought.

Maybe they're even going to my floor.

Then Jo reached a floor and there were no more stairs. She panicked. How am I going to go down now? she thought. There are no more stairs, I'll have to go out in the hallway, get in the elevator, and—

Then she realized that she was at the bottom floor.

The hallway outside, just past the big green metal door, led to the entrance hall to the co-op. With its phony marble floor, and a chandelier, and dozens of tiny mailboxes.

She went to the door. Pressed her head against it, listening.

No sounds.

Everyone's gone.

(Where did everyone go?)

She opened the door.

Michael got up from his seat and tried to rock the compartment, trying to free it. It didn't budge.

"Save your energy," Farrand said. "And your breath."

Michael looked at the clock. How long had they been disconnected? Five minutes. Ten? How long before it didn't matter if they got freed.

He heard Farrand muttering in French.

"Wh-what are you doing?" he asked, thinking that the old man had started to come unglued.

Farrand muttered a few more words. Then, a bit louder, he said, "I'm praying, Michael." He covered Michael's hand with his own. "Why don't you join me?"

Jo opened the door, the door to the city.

The streetlights were on. Somehow she didn't expect that. The parking lot was full of cars. She even saw a barge out in the East River.

But ahead, on the ramp of the FDR Drive, she heard no cars moving. Not even one.

She started walking away from the building, away from the river.

The parking lot was behind her.

(It might still be there, she thought. The body. Maybe it could fall like that and live. In fact, the more she thought about it, the more she was sure of it.)

She looked over her shoulder.

It was quiet.

Now, as she walked, her sneakers making a soft padding noise on the sidewalk, she thought she heard other sounds. Voices, far away, calling out. Then disappearing. Swallowed by the city.

Riverview Apartments was right at First Avenue. She reached the corner. Deserted, a stray bit of newspaper flying around, then landing, then whipping around again.

It's nearly morning, she thought.

I have to get to Brooklyn. That's where I'm going.

My mother is dead. But my father has to be alive.

But now that she was out here that seemed impossible.

Across the block was the The Original Ray's Pizza place she and her mom used to have dinner at. And a liquor store. A magazine shop that she wasn't allowed to go into.

It had a gigantic LOTTO sign in the window. There were always these skinny skeleton men inside, standing around, with hollow eyes, all of them needing a shave.

There was the subway entrance.

Right near the magazine store.

It was a stupid thought.

She knew that right away. Stupid. The subway. Right, like that's *really* going to be running, like there are still trains that go places.

But then she thought that maybe it could be true. Maybe the subway *was* safe, under the ground. Maybe that's where all the people were, the ones that were still left. That's where they went. They used the trains and—

She crossed the street.

Chapter Forty

THE old man muttered.

Praying.

Michael put his face against the thick acrylic window. He kept looking for whatever was moving around out there, farther into the rift.

He caught just a glimpse of a blackish shape moving against an even darker background, blocking the few luminescent creatures that dotted the night of the deep sea.

The old man muttered.

And Michael heard a rumbling.

Another tremor, rolling toward them like a summer storm from the mountains.

This time we'll be crushed, Michael thought.

The tremor roared closer. Farrand prayed louder, his words audible, intelligible to Michael.

The compartment started shaking, vibrating, the single green light going blurry. There was the sound of metal scraping against rock, screeching.

We're going to be crushed.

And then the scraping stopped.

Michael felt movement.

Farrand reached out and threw the lights on.

The swirl of debris and sediment flew past them.

It flew down.

We're going up, thought Michael.

We're going up! He just hoped that the specimen containers were still attached.

Farrand whispered the first words.

"Praise God . . ."

The IRT station looked perfectly normal.

Except there was no one there. No one to sell tokens. No one waiting.

The lights were on. One bulb made a spitting noise. It flickered on and off.

Jo climbed over the turnstile. She had seen people do that, waiting until no one was watching.

There was no one to see her do it now.

She walked to the edge of the platform.

She looked to her left. Two green lights—just like traffic lights—glowed in the darkness.

Jo turned and looked right.

Sometimes, she thought, a train came screaming out of the black tunnel, whipping past the platform—especially if it was an express—ready to suck people right along with it.

She kept looking. She didn't see anything or hear anything.

She walked down the platform. Past the advertisements in Spanish for Breck Shampoo. Past beer ads with graffiti on them, and plastic benches all chewed up as if hungry animals had sat in them.

She walked down to the end of the platform, at the mouth of the tunnel, for another look.

To make sure that there were no trains.

(Then what will I do? she wondered.)

She went to the edge.

She heard a splashing noise.

She backed up a few feet.

More splashing, then something else. Steps. From inside the tunnel.

She backed up some more.

Turning, hurrying now.

She turned around—just a glance toward the tunnel—and saw people running out, tripping over the slats of the track, stumbling, then scrambling onto the platform.

She ran back to the turnstile, looking over her shoulder every few steps.

(Thinking: I shouldn't have come in here. Why did I come in here?)

One person was up. Running after her.

Maybe it's someone trying to get away. Someone like me, she thought.

But that was just some stupid hope.

There's just you. You're the only one left.

And they want you . . .

She ran to the turnstile, and climbed over—having some

difficulty. Her laces got caught on one of the spokes of the turnstile.

She grunted, tugged at them.

She looked down the platform. There were two of them now running toward her.

One had—

(She tugged. She pulled.)

One had something attached to his chest, something furry, moving, squealing. Big and gray.

He was holding it there.

(She let the sneaker slide off, leaping from the turnstile—)

No. Not holding it. The rat was just there, just stuck to this man, *part of him*—

She ran up the stairs, pumping, her bare foot feeling the metal grid of the steps, the bits of glass, the half-smoked cigarettes, up to the street.

The bubble rose. Farrand tried the radio but it was still dead. The antenna must be broken, Michael figured.

The lights were on, and they flew past a crazed procession of animals, shrimp and deep-sea fish, with their alienlike jaws, gave way to a heard of fat slow-moving groupers nonplussed by the quake below.

A buzzer sounded.

"What's that—?" Michael asked dully.

"Compressed air warning. One minute left."

"One minute. Is that enough—?"

Farrand didn't answer.

The buzzer droned on. There were other fish, past a ray, swooping close to them. Then a small tiger shark nosing about with hungry interest. Then nothing, just the marine snow until—

Michael leaned closer to the viewport.

(Thinking: I've been counting. I've been counting one minute.)

The buzzer started going on and off, repetitively. Michael guessed what it meant.

We're just breathing the air that's in here.

That's all we have.

It made him gulp.

And he was right beside Farrand, both of them looking out of the viewport for one thing . . .

Looking for the black to give way to a purple, a royal blue, until—

The air felt stale.

Michael tried to breathe shallow. He couldn't hear Farrand breathe at all.

The water wasn't black anymore. It was definitely lighter.

"We're going to do it," Michael said. "We're—"

"Easy," Farrand cautioned.

Still they flew up. The air turned foul. They both had to suck the air in many more times.

Then there was something above them. Michael could see it. A bit of light.

The compartment broke the surface, and he heard the blessed noise of the waves lapping against the side of the compartment.

Farrand quickly had the hatch open, and fresh air and a spray of water rushed into the cabin. It was rough out there.

"How will Larsson find us?" Michael said. "Can he track—?"

Michael's question was drowned out. He heard the other sound. A helicopter, above them, blotting out the stars and the faint bluish glow in the east.

"Go. Get up," Farrand said. And Michael scuttled to the open hatch.

He sat in the hovering helicopter, wrapped in a scratchy, rough blanket that felt wonderful. The pilot and copilot had hooked the two specimen containers and were bringing them up, close to the helicopter.

"Sir," the pilot said, talking to Michael. He acted as if he did this kind of thing every day. "We'll have you at the South Miami Naval Airport in thirty minutes. They will fly you immediately to the Coast Guard Environmental Station in Staten Island, with your samples. It's a safe and secure area."

A secure area. What did that mean? Michael wondered. Chain-link fences with 200 volts of electricity running through them? Squads of Navy SEALs armed with flamethrowers? Just what the hell was a *secure area*?

But he just nodded. And he sipped the hot coffee they poured for him from a silver thermos. He turned to Farrand. "You'll come too?"

"Of course . . ." Farrand said, as if the question wasn't even worth asking.

The copilot stopped the winch and told the pilot that the containers from the sub were secure. The pilot picked up his radio and spoke to the captain of *Ariel*. Then he turned back to them. "We're all ready," he said. He started moving the copter up, away from the rough sea. The main rotor made a din that blotted out all of Michael's thoughts.

All his thoughts. Except one.

"Tell them—" he said. But then Michael realized that he'd have to yell to be heard. "Call them . . . and tell them to have a helicopter . . . waiting for me at Staten Island. Tell them that! Do you hear me?"

The pilot nodded.

He spoke into his radio.

Then Michael pulled the blanket tight.

Jo ran down deserted blocks, dream blocks, empty—just like they would be in a dream.

Whenever she heard noises, she just ran faster. When she saw a light come on, she'd turn down a corner, away from the light. Her left foot hurt now. Every step she took rubbed the skin raw.

She didn't know what she was doing.

Maybe I should go back to the apartment? I could lock the door. And just wait for help.

No. She knew that help might never come. But *they'd* come for her. They'll come for everybody.

They have to, she told herself. As if she were looking at one of the sharks in her dad's Aquarium tear up a whole tuna.

It's just their nature.

That's all.

They're not really bad.

(Yes they are . . . yes they are . . . *yes they are!*)

She was on Broadway. A few blocks ago she had passed Worth Street, where her dentist had his office. He was a skinny scarecrow man who smiled all the time while he stuck pokey metal things in her mouth.

There you go, he said. This won't hurt a bit.

Liar, liar, hope your shorts go on fire!

There was a big street ahead. Filled with stores.

She ran a bit. Then someone opened a door across the street. Gianella's Bakery. A little fat man came out and looked at the ground.

She hurried, glancing at him—

The man looked outside the bakery as if something was supposed to be there. He looked up at Jo. Raised a hand, about to say something.

(He's not one of them, she thought. I could go to him, get help—)

She shook her head.

No one can help you, she told herself. You have to get away, get off the island. Like she read in that book, *Escape from Warsaw* . . . the Jewish family had to hide and run and hide . . .

I have a chance if I'm alone, she thought.

Only . . .

She chewed her lip.

Only I wish I had my sneaker back. Because this is starting to hurt real bad.

She reached the block, Nassau Street. Of course. Nassau Street. Lot of shops. Lots of traffic.

But there were no cars now.

Nassau Street.

She ran into the middle of the street. She heard the clicking of the traffic lights. The buzzing and zapping of neon lights from the stores. No cars anywhere.

She looked left.

And there it was.

The Brooklyn Bridge.

Five blocks away. Maybe a bit more. She could just see one of the stone towers. The roadway seemed to curve away, away from Manhattan, out over the water.

There were lights on the cables, and below, more lights, car lights, on the roadway.

None of them were moving.

She stood there—just a second—in the middle of the road.

The bakery man called to her.

" 'Ey, kid. Whatsa goin' on?"

She waved him away. He'll have to help himself.

The cars on the bridge were all stopped. Sure. Too many of them. They couldn't move. Jammed up. Sure, that made perfect sense. Perfect. But she could walk over, to Brooklyn, and then, and then—

(Maybe there were trains running, or there were police, stopping the things coming from New York, or maybe—)

"Where'sa my goddam bread?" the bakery man said to the empty night air.

Jo nodded to herself. And she ran down the block, right in the middle.

Away from the dark storefront, the alleyways, the quiet apartment buildings.

* * *

She ran up the walkway, climbing, puffing hard. She stepped on some glass. She felt only a little pain. But then—as she kept on going, up the walkway of the old bridge—she saw that she was leaving little dime-sized red blotches.

Some of the cars had open doors, the interior lights pale, the headlights fading. Others looked dead, no lights, nothing. They were jumbled together, immovable, like an impossible sliding number puzzle.

It took forever to reach the first stone towers, watching the cable climb up.

She and her mom had walked across the bridge once. And her mom had told her things. About the day the bridge opened, over a hundred years ago. Not that she had been there, her mom had laughed. There were all these great sailboats, and cannons firing. There were no cars then.

And she told her how men died sinking the great stone towers deep underwater, how they got a strange disease because of the pressure.

It had a funny name.

(She passed under one of the stone towers, climbing up the arch of the bridge. There were trucks up here too, their cab doors open, and even a bus, deserted but still lit by brilliant lights inside.)

They died in the caissons. Deep under the mud of the East River. And some of the men—this was really true, Mom said—were left buried in the caissons, right inside the mud and the stone.

Her hand reached out and grabbed the metal railing. It was cool. Cool, like it was under the water, under the mud, with the hundred-year-old skeletons, looking up.

She slowed down a bit, trying to catch her breath. The wind made one of the giant cables move—just a bit—back and forth, like some giant elephant's trunk.

She used to love the bridge. But now it seemed scary. Alive.

What did it do to all these people?

(She had a thought: All these cars—the people, they must have gotten out when they couldn't get over in their cars. They must have gotten out and walked right across the bridge, where she was going.

And what did they find? she wondered.)

The subway tracks were to her right. No train came by. Though if one did, she'd expect it to be filled with skeleton people, looking out, reading newspapers, traveling to Brooklyn.

Why didn't my dad come and get me? she thought.

Why did he leave me?

She kept climbing. The cable started streaming down from the tower, snaking toward the middle of the suspension.

Right over the middle of the river.

That's why it's so safe here, she knew. Because I'm so *high* above the water. They *can't* get up here.

(She thought of the rule. It made sense and now she hoped they followed it.)

Higher, and she saw a tinge of orange at the horizon.

Morning.

The dime-sized dabs of blood on the ground were growing. Getting larger with each step, she saw. They were more the size of quarters now.

She neared the center of the bridge and she could see over to the other side, to Brooklyn. She could see the rest of the endless line of cars that didn't move, see the yellow building that shouted "Awake!" and "Watchtower." And another with big block letters. BONDS CLOTHES. And all the low buildings leading to the ocean, to the Aquarium.

I'll just keep walking and hiding and—

Her eyes followed the trail of cars leading down to the other side of the bridge.

And she saw people.

Lots of them.

They were near some accident, a bunch of cars all crashed together. She saw the broken and twisted metal catching the lights of the bridge. There were people there, around the smashed cars, in the smashed cars and—

(She grabbed the railing.)

They were all *connected*. Trapped by the accident, and connected by a giant white tube running from person to person, spreading out for the accident. It couldn't move.

She was sure of that.

It just grew, snatching the people who came by, adding them to its chain.

There was no way she'd get past it.

She turned.

I'll go another way. There's other bridges. The Manhattan Bridge, and—

She turned.

To see people coming over the bridge from the Manhattan side.

Two, three.

(Not from the subway, no, please, not the ones from the

subway. She stood there, studying them, watching them turn blurry, 'cause, 'cause—)

She rubbed away her tears.

Maybe they didn't see her yet.

Run and hide and run and—

She looked up. At the lattice of wires, at the fat cable stretching down to touch the middle of the bridge. She saw the girders.

The early morning wind blew her hair, dried the tears into salty splotches.

She stepped over the railing, and walked to the cable. She touched it, and then grabbed at one of the thin metal wires that ran alongside it.

Chapter Forty-one

THE plane landed on the small Coast Guard strip just as the sun broke the horizon. Michael watched bleary-eyed as a clean golden wave of light spread over the late summer lawns and beaches of the island, this forgotten New York borough. Farrand, completely exhausted, was next to him, sleeping uneasily, making sounds, waking up.

The plane touched down. He saw people waiting for him, waiting for what the plane carried. Coast Guard officers, and some other Army people. A couple of cars.

But no helicopter.

He grabbed the arm of his seat. The small jet came down quickly and hard, without the nice gentle bump of a commercial flight.

No helicopter, he thought.

The engines screamed out, trying to brake. Michael held tight.

"Michael . . ." Farrand said. "I should have stayed awake with you. I—"

Michael got the seat belt off before the plane stopped. He stood up. And walked to the hatch of the small jet.

A soldier who hadn't said anything during the two-hour flight, letting Michael look out the window and think, stood up.

"Sir, you'd better sit down—"

Michael didn't move. He just waited by the door until Farrand came beside him.

The plane turned around, over to the party waiting on the airstrip. The six portholes were filled with the morning light.

He saw Martin.

Tired, looking half dead, his shirttail out.

That was stupid what he did, Michael thought. Experimenting on himself. Stupid. But incredibly brave.

If anyone helped, it was Martin.

The plane stopped. The soldier said, "Excuse me," and opened the door hatch. Michael edged close to the opening and saw the stairs being wheeled into place.

As soon as the stairs knocked against the plane, he ran down the stairs.

Martin ran up to him.

"Michael, we're all ready here. We've set the lab up—"

"Where's the helicopter?"

An officer, wearing a crisp peaked hat and a jacket filled with colorful decorations, walked up to him. "Dr. Cross, I'm Major Richard Hawthorne. We have the base under quarantine. I can explain everything." He looked at Farrand, not knowing who he was. "The status of the city, the East Coast beaches, the precautions for the waterways. But I think you should get some rest, then help in the lab and—"

Hawthorne was used to giving orders.

Michael walked up to the man.

He smelled his cologne.

The major had crisp blue eyes, eyes that weren't dead with fatigue, or terrified with fear. Eyes that were still calm, cool . . . in control.

"I said . . . I want a fucking helicopter. My daughter is in the city. Do you hear what I'm saying? I said I want a helicopter. She's still there and I'm going to get her the hell out."

"Dr. Cross, I understand what you must be feeling." The major looked away to the other officers, looking for support. "It's a terrible situation. A national disaster. We're fighting time. But the city has been lost. I can show you what Central Park looks like, the millions of people, but not people anymore. The bodies . . . We have photographs. You have to—"

Michael grabbed the officer's coat.

"If I don't get a helicopter, you don't touch one of those fucking things I brought from the Gulf."

"I'm afraid that we already—"

Michael turned.

"Perhaps he's right," Farrand whispered to him.

A small wagon, like a golf cart, had sidled up to the rear of the plane. The specimen containers, covered with heavy plastic tarps, were being off-loaded.

"Hey," Michael screamed, taking a step toward them. "Don't even fucking think about touching them—"

Now Hawthorne reached out and held Michael.

"We have to get on with it . . . we can hold them back for so long . . . keeping the bridges . . . the tunnels closed. The ones in the ocean may move farther south and—"

Michael turned to him, begging, and without wanting it, knowing that it would mean that he lost, that it was all over, he started crying.

"Please," he said. "My baby is there. She said she'd wait." He looked to Martin for support. Martin nodded. "She said that she'd keep the door locked. Do you know what I'm saying. She's a good girl. She's . . ." Farrand stood beside him, the old man holding his arm, helping him. "I just need . . . a helicopter and a pilot. You have what you need . . . I did what I had to . . ."

The major backed away.

He took a breath.

One of the officers had a radio. It crackled and he took it from his side, speaking quietly into it.

I'm going crazy, Michael knew. I can't have gotten this far. Not this far, only to have it end like this.

The officer with the radio whispered something to Hawthorne. The major listened, nodded, and looked shaken by the news.

The cart with the specimens pulled away from the plane.

Michael's hand reached out to the air. A pathetic begging gesture he knew . . .

I'd go to my knees.

"Please," he said.

Hawthorne looked at him. Then, with a resigned sigh, a disapproving sound, the officer nodded, and said: "Okay . . ."

She fell asleep. Perched there, way above the roadway, lying on a flat girder.

It had big metal bumps that bit into her back. And if she turned a few inches to either side, she could roll off, onto the fat cable, then down to the road or, even worse, the subway tracks.

Still . . .

When the sun hit her face, a soothing, overwhelming warmth, she let her eyes close. *Had* to let them close.

And even though she knew they were coming for her, that she should keep watch, she fell asleep.

Hoping that she'd never ever wake up again.

Chapter Forty-two

MICHAEL walked into the apartment.

He wasn't alone. There were two soldiers on the roof, with the copter, and two right beside him, holding snub-nosed rifles that they assured him shot a directed, powerful blast of fire.

Not that they had any need of it.

The building, the streets, were deserted.

(Unlike the park, unlike uptown, where millions were moving, still feeding . . .)

He walked into the apartment, ignoring the almost-funny posturing of the two soldiers, whipping around, tough guys ready to torch anyone.

Michael insisted on going in first.

He wouldn't give them a chance of being spooked, and shooting Jo.

Even though he knew she wasn't here.

The door was wide open.

Martin had told her to keep it locked. Locked, goddam it. Jesus, Jo, why can't you ever do what the hell we tell you to? Why the hell won't you ever listen?

One of the soldiers pointed to the patio. Michael looked up. He had only been here three times. It was Caryn's apartment. A forbidden land for him. It had nothing of his life in it. Nothing, except Jo.

He walked to the patio.

He saw the shattered glass.

He looked down. He saw Caryn.

"Oh, Christ," he said. He started to lean down, to touch it.

"Sir, I don't think you should . . ."

Michael froze.

Right.

Don't want to get like them, now do I?

Don't want to become one of them, do we?

(Or do I really give a shit anymore . . .)

But one of the soldiers gave the body a rough kick, sending Caryn rolling against the railing, exposing the big, empty hole in her back.

Michael turned away.

"Are you okay, sir?" one of the soldiers asked from a million miles away.

Michael was looking back into the kitchen.

A big empty hole. She's free at least, God—she's free.

But what of Jo?

He saw the dining-area table, a nice piece of Swedish wood. And he saw something on it.

He walked back into the apartment.

And over to the table. It was a penguin. A salt shaker. He bought it at the Aquarium the day he got the job. So they'd all remember that day. Caryn laughed at it—they were still a family then. She laughed at it, saying it was so tacky. Yeah, he said. That's what makes it so wonderful.

The penguin had a top hat with holes. And a happy smile.

It was on the table, knocked down.

Michael felt the wind gusting through the broken door.

One of the soldiers tapped him.

"Ready to go?" he said gently.

Michael nodded.

He felt the breeze on his back, strong from the East River.

He fingered the pathetic penguin.

In the center of the table.

Michael took a step away. Just a step, and then he stopped, bumping one of the soldiers.

He turned around, and looked down to the floor.

The breeze, the penguin . . .

A small folded piece of paper was flush against one of the table's legs, fluttering as the wind pressed, holding it there.

And Michael—feeling nothing now, certainly nothing like hope—crouched down and picked it up.

Jo woke up.

The metal had grown hot. Her body was stiff. But that's not what woke her up.

There were noises, coming from below.

And she turned and looked down, wishing that it all could have happened while she slept.

Thinking that—now I'll have to feel everything.

Feel them touch me, and cut into me, and then make me go with them . . .

Wherever they are going.

They have pale faces, sunken eyes. They are hungry.

There's not many like me left, she guessed.

She sniffed at the air and she saw the worms in them, moving in and out, excited . . .

She watched them, looking up at the girder. They saw her. They climbed clumsily, grabbing the fat cable and falling backward onto the ground.

She looked up at the web of girders and cable, and she thought about climbing higher, all the way to the top of the bridge.

But she knew she couldn't do that.

I'm as high as I can go.

I can stay here. Or I can go down.

Now another one, a woman dressed in a tattered dress with one sagging breast flopping out, grabbed at the strand of wires that traveled with the cable.

Her worm was smaller, near her midsection. It squirmed into her, hiding, while she slid her fat belly onto the cable.

Then she was on, grunting, puffing. Only ten feet away from Jo. The others followed her now, using the smaller metal wire, until they were there.

Looking up at her.

Jo backed away, she bumped against a girder that cut up, crossing above her. It was nothing that she could climb.

She could crouch, maybe get into the crack, the cavelike crack where the two girders meet. But there was no point in doing that.

None at all.

Now the woman reached up for the girder, the same one Jo was on.

And it was hard for her. She got up, kicked at the air, and then slid down a few feet on the cable, knocking one of the others down.

Then she was up again. Jo watched the woman's fingers claw at the greenish metal, dig at the bumps.

I can step on her hand, Jo thought.

I can step on her. Like stepping on an ant or a spider.

But she might grab my ankle—quickly, fast—and then pull me down.

Jo looked over her shoulder. The East River looked beautiful. Calm, a deep, deep blue. Just a few whitecaps dotting the water.

If I was nearer the water, close to it, she thought . . . if it was possible, I might jump into it.

That would be better. But the subway tracks were below her.

She turned back and the woman was up, her big behind moving like a snake, her legs kicking at the metal.

The woman stood up. Now the worm was out, a foot or more, so close to Jo. Waving at her.

I have no more tears, Jo thought.

And there's no one to scream to.

The woman reached out for her.

Jo backed up a bit more and her head banged against the girder that crossed over her.

She closed her eyes.

I don't want to watch this. I don't want to see what they do to me. Nothing they can do can make me watch.

And when she opened her eyes, the woman was filled with the sun, covered with light, glowing—

The morning sunlight on her, Jo thought.

No.

She was on fire.

And there was this noise above her.

The worm tried to squirm out of the burning woman. One foot, two feet, reaching down for the girder, only steps away from Jo. The burning woman—her hair and her skin crackling and popping, the smell making Jo gag—tottered backward.

Still the worm stretched out, almost down to the girder. Not easy to do. But it was almost there, almost ready to caress the metal.

The woman fell to her knees.

Like she's praying, Jo thought.

The worm sucked onto the girder.

Why is she on fire?

The worm was out.

It moved fast. So fast. Jo tensed. Waited. And closed her eyes.

Something grabbed her around her stomach, tight. It's there now, she thought. It has me.

She opened her eyes.

And she knew it wasn't the worm . . .

It's not the worm—she could see that—and—

Then Jo was lifted away. Flying into the air. Miraculous. Like an angel from a children's book of Bible stories.

She turned.

(The bridge was down there, below her. It's *down there*, she saw as she flew through the air.)

She heard the sound now. Why didn't she hear it before?

Why didn't I hear that?

An arm held her . . . held her tight against a body. She turned.

And she saw her father.

Daddy, she thought she said. Oh, Daddy . . .

But she said nothing.

But she heard him, shouting into her ear as they were pulled into the belly of the helicopter.

"It's okay Jo . . . you're okay now, honey . . ."

She nodded. And said, again, *Daddy*.

But she made no sound.

There were just her dry lips moving soundlessly, over and over, trying to say the same word.

"Daddy . . .

Epilogue

"C'MON, sprout, burn it in. Let's see you really throw the ball."

Michael watched Jo scrunch up her face. She squinted as if she were deciphering an inscrutable message from the catcher before letting go with an admirable fastball.

The ball thwacked hard into Michael's glove, delivering a respectful sting to the palm of his hand.

"Atta girl. Here's a pop fly—going, going—"

He tossed the ball hard, into the blue sky, already bright with the clarity and cool ocean breezes of fall. The ball arched away, and Jo had to run back, bringing her glove up.

The ball ricocheted off her glove and dribbled behind her.

And he watched her run across the field to the ball.

There's healing going on, he thought.

Slowly.

She still wouldn't sleep by herself, and the entire base was familiar with the sound of her screaming at night. It didn't help that they were still living here, on the base, surrounded by a fence and—

He looked behind him. Yes, there was the guard walking patrol, armed with what they called a Hot Tommy—a state-of-the-art flamethrower.

But things were quiet here.

Hawthorne had suggested that he and Jo might want to move, out to the Midwest while the quarantine and seeding went on.

But after everything that had happened, it made Michael feel safer to stay here. Behind the fence. With the guards.

For now.

Jo lobbed the ball back and—not paying attention—it slipped by him.

Much of the work fell on Martin and Farrand. The breeding of the bacterial colonies went quickly. At the right temperature and in a saline mixture, each cell split thirty-two times a minute. After the first twenty-four-hour period, there was a truck filled with canisters of the friendly bacteria.

He tossed the ball back to Jo, hard. She smoothly turned her glove and made a backhand catch.

"Sleek, sprout, very sleek."

She grinned, looking almost as if she were happy.

She always was a good actress.

The city was the first target. A squadron of heavy-duty copters flew in the bacteria. The reservoirs were hit, all the water surrounding the city. Martin discovered that—in large enough quantities—the bacteria could be absorbed directly through the skin. They rained the mixture down directly on the madhouse crowds, especially the millions crowded into Central Park—

(As if they were waiting for something, one of the pilots said. Now what the hell could they have been waiting for?)

Then the 101st Airborne, out of Fort Hamilton, began a bizarre search and destroy mission. Any of the Contaminated—as they came to be called—who didn't absorb the bacteria were torched. Most of them were dead anyway, just kept "alive" by the worms. So, they were burned to a crisp. Michael heard some pilots talking about napalm. And Michael saw the great blackish-gray clouds rising from the streets.

A cloud of human flesh.

Some of the worms crawled out of people, wriggling to get away from the poison bacteria. Funny, here was a creature that could process toxins for food, and this primitive bacteria could destroy it. Sometimes the people lived. But not often. Usually their bodies were so torn apart by the worm's residency that they had no chance to survive with the parasite gone.

And the worms had to be destroyed quickly or they'd scuttle away.

"Dad," Jo called. "Are *you* paying attention?"

He smiled. "Sorry. Started daydreaming . . ."

They both did a lot of that. The one thing they talked about once, only once, was Caryn. Jo had heaved, fallen against him, started beating his chest.

"*I want her back*," she had screamed.

Shh, he had whispered, burying his face in her hair.

She'd have to talk about it again.

Someday. Not now.

She burned another pitch in, an impish smile on her face, enjoying her power, her ability.

Farrand had looked at some of the bodies they brought in. And he had some ideas on how the worm worked. From the damage to the spinal cord, the entry holes sliced up into the cerebral cortex. The worm integrated itself into the nervous system of the host, right into the brain. The worm tapped into the walnut-sized control center in what was called Broca's area, in the cerebral cortex.

As far as Farrand and the doctors could tell, the worm zeroed in on the same area as cocaine . . . only with total, absolute control.

A large transport circled the base. Michael looked up. The transports came every hour, picking up canisters of the bacteria. His own work mostly involved planning the protection of the uncontaminated waterways. The lakes, the rivers, even ponds. Anything liquid. The bacteria were introduced into the food chain, and then monitored, to make sure that they continued to thrive in everything, from the smallest spring peeper to a deer lapping at the river's edge.

The military's resources were divided between supporting that work, and keeping order in the country. Most of the cities were under martial law. Looting had gotten out of control in many of the coastal cities.

It was speculated that it would be five years before everything was back to something approaching normal.

There were now precautions for people to take, drawn up by Michael and the other scientists working at this base, and the other bases that were scattered around the world.

Only water that has been treated can be drunk.

That was the most important rule. There was a process to be followed in introducing the bacteria and allowing it to develop for twenty-four hours before touching the water. Some coastal areas and rivers, most importantly the area from Northern Massachusetts down to Virginia Beach, were off limits. Fences had gone up, and the National Guard and local militia were organized to patrol them. The ocean and the tidal estuaries were too big to expect a quick turnaround.

There was a new law.

Anyone who violated any quarantined areas would be shot on sight.

A barbaric law, the type of law they might have imposed during the plague. But it was essential.

Eventually things might get back to normal.

The ball came flying back. He looked at Jo, her hair long, blowing into the wind, the fence and blue sky a strange backdrop.

Everything might get back to normal.

(*He had a fear . . .*)

Except for Jo.

He threw the ball, the dull, repetitive catch soothing, offering a small salvation.

And then he heard someone call his name. "Dr. Cross . . . Dr. Cross!" He turned. A soldier was running over to him.

Michael stood there, lowered his glove.

"Major Hawthorne would like to see you."

Michael smiled, nodded. In the days after the first bacteria drops, he had gained a cautious respect for Hawthorne.

"Okay," he said. He turned to Jo in the outfield. "Be right back!" he shouted. And—after taking one step with his glove still on—he let it fall onto the lush grass.

Jo felt the sun on her back. She saw the fence. She always kept looking at the fence. And she watched her dad walk away.

She tossed the ball into the air, catching it once. Then on her next try, losing it in the sun.

She didn't like being here alone.

He says it's all over, she thought. And maybe, yeah, maybe Dad believes that. It's a war, he told her. And we're winning, he told her. It will take a while, but we're—

She threw the ball up and caught it.

—winning.

And maybe he was right.

But then why are we here behind the fence? And why are there guards?

The air was cool. Summer had just ended.

Would they still be here in winter?

She looked around for someone, anyone to be here, outside, where she could see them. But she was alone.

She licked her lips.

She saw her father's glove, sitting out in the grass, abandoned.

She looked around. No, she told herself. You're not going to get scared. There's nothing to get scared about. There's nothing . . .

She looked over at the Quonset hut where they slept. She felt frozen here, the wind playing with her, whipping around her body.

And she made a crying sound, another one of those tiny cries just came out of her, a small cry that she couldn't stop . . .

* * *

"Michael . . ." Hawthorne said, pointing to a seat. Michael sat down. Now, weeks later, Hawthorne looked exhausted too, his eyes sunken, surrounded by red blotches that looked like permanent marks on his face. Though this was just one of the stations now fighting the contamination, the infestation, they had been the first. And Michael very much doubted that Hawthorne had seen more than a few hours sleep since it began.

"One of our squads finally reached that TV studio," Hawthorne said, rubbing his cheek. "There were some bodies . . ."

Michael shifted in his seat.

"Bodies?" There were people in the studio when that crazy show was broadcast. He had seen the tape. But he assumed that they had all moved on, like the rest of Manhattan . . . to the north, to the park.

The show was the one thing that no one understood. A few scientists said it was just a coincidence. Others—the more flaky scientists—speculated that Gene Fasolt, and this Jay, were prophets, predicting a new-age Armageddon.

Michael, always the pragmatic agnostic, rejected that completely.

Still, it was odd.

Hawthorne rubbed his chin. His lips moved, as if he was trying to find the right words to explain. "Three bodies, on the floor." He reached down for an envelope. "They took pictures." He opened the envelope.

Bodies? Michael wondered. What's the big deal about bodies. The city was filled with bodies. There were bodies everywhere. Bulldozers were making gigantic piles, steam shovels digging giant pits, from all the bodies. The city had become a giant charnel house.

"I don't—" he started to say.

"These are different bodies. Something new. Here, take a look."

Hawthorne removed the stack of photos and handed Michael the first one.

It was a man with a beard, glasses. He recognized him from the videotape of the show. It was Gene Fasolt. His face was untouched. But below his neck, his body was exploded, peeled back, the skin popped open.

Hawthorne handed him the next photo.

Closer on the same body.

He had no insides, just a red, soupy mess, a miniswamp made

up of blood and organs. He looked like he had been put through a meat-grinder.

"Jeesus," Michael said.

"Here are the other two," Hawthorne said. He passed Michael two more pictures, a black man—Jay, the supposed prophet—and someone else, someone who looked real bad. This guy had no skin left on his face. There were small jagged holes at the top of the skull, as if something had smashed into his skull to get at the brain underneath.

"Did this guy still have—?" Michael started to ask, hefting the photo.

Hawthorne anticipated his question. "No brain matter left. It was gone."

Michael looked at the photo again. The worst thing about it was the eye sockets. Empty, of course, but the head was tilted up, the neck craning, and the black, empty eyeholes were straining, looking down at its own exploded body.

"Nasty," Michael said. "And you haven't seen any others like this?"

Hawthorne shook his head.

The major turned away, looked out his window. Michael watched him. He could see just the foamy tip of the ocean, just above a sand dune. "Then they saw something else," Hawthorne said. "Something they almost missed. They had"—Hawthorne turned around—"walked all around there, stepping near the bodies, onto all the red goo. Another few minutes and it would have been too late."

"Too late? For what?"

"One soldier saw something on the ground. He told his captain and he made everyone step back. They got up on chairs, looked around all the bodies. Then they took these shots."

He handed Michael three more photos.

For a second Michael didn't see anything. Just the weird bodies from farther away, surrounded by red pools. And, as he kept rifling through the three photos, he noticed something else.

The soldiers' footprints. The waffle stamps moving erratically around the bodies.

And—

His breath caught in his throat.

Other footprints. Most of them muddied by the soldiers. But yes, he thought, going from photo to photo, clear enough now. Footprints, big footprints, twice as large as the soldiers. Triangular, birdlike, with the clear impression of two clawlike prongs in the front, and a larger bump in the back.

They came from the open pits of the bodies. And walked away, across the studio floor, growing fainter.

And near the photo of the man with no face there were more, smaller ones, dancing around the face, overlapping, until at least three pairs walked away.

Walked away. Out of the studio . . .

Michael put the photos down. Hawthorne finally sat, facing him.

"Michael . . . do you have any idea what they are, I mean, any idea at all? What could have made them. Any—?"

He looked at the photo.

They came from the bodies. And—

They walked away.

"Anything you might have seen, on the *Achilles*. Jeezus, Michael, any idea what the hell—?"

Hawthorne let his voice rise, desperate.

Afraid.

Michael looked up at him. Shook his head.

And he slowly handed the photos back to him.

He got up to leave, thinking:

Maybe it was time to get out of here.

Far away.

As far away as he and Jo could get . . .

Michael ran outside. The air, the blue sky, the breeze from the water, wasn't sweet anymore. He saw his glove sitting on the field.

But he didn't see Jo.

A guard, just to his left, was finishing his loop. He turned.

"Hey," Michael yelled. Then, screaming, "Hey! Did you see—"

The guard stopped.

Michael heard a voice.

"Dad?"

Michael turned. And Jo came out of the Quonset hut.

She ran over to him.

"Daddy, what's wrong?"

"I—I didn't see you."

"Just had to go to the bathroom," she said. Michael heard her forced casualness. She tilted her head, studying him. "Are *you* okay?" He saw the red lines in her eyes. They're always there, he thought with a terrible pang. Always.

"Yeah." He smiled. "I'm fine, sprout. Let's get back to baseball."

Jo smiled back, catching his lie he guessed, but letting it pass. There'll be time for truth later.

And she ran away, to their make-believe outfield.